THE SAFETY NET

Heinrich Böll is the first German to win the Nobel Prize for literature since Thomas Mann in 1929. Born in Cologne, Germany, in 1917, Böll was reared in a liberal Catholic, pacifist family. Drafted into the Wehrmacht, he served on the Russian and French fronts and was wounded four times before he found himself in an American prisoner-of-war camp. After the war he enrolled in the University of Cologne but dropped out to write about his shattering experiences as a soldier. His first novel, *The Train Was on Time*, was published in 1949, and he went on to become one of the most prolific and important of the postwar German writers. His best-known novels include *Billiards at Half-Past Nine*, *The Clown*, and *Group Portrait with Lady*. He is also famous as a writer of short stories. Böll is past president of the International P.E.N. and is a leading defender of the intellectual freedom of writers throughout the world. He and his wife divide their time between Cologne and a farmhouse in the Eifel mountains.

The Safety Net

HEINRICH BÖLL

Translated from the German by

Leila Vennewitz

PENGUIN BOOKS

Penguin Books Ltd, Harmondsworth, Middlesex, England
Penguin Books, 625 Madison Avenue, New York, New York 10022, U.S.A.
Penguin Books Australia Ltd, Ringwood, Victoria, Australia
Penguin Books Canada Limited, 2801 John Street,
Markham, Ontario, Canada L3R 1B4
Penguin Books (N.Z.) Ltd, 182–190 Wairau Road,
Auckland 10, New Zealand

Originally published in the Federal Republic of Germany
under the title *Fürsorgliche Belagerung* by
Verlag Kiepenheuer & Witsch, Köln, 1979
First published in the United States of America by
Alfred A. Knopf, Inc., 1982
First published in Canada by
Random House of Canada Limited 1982
Published in Penguin Books 1983

LIBRARY OF CONGRESS CATALOGING IN PUBLICATION DATA
Böll, Heinrich, 1917–
The safety net.
Translation of: Fürsorgliche Belagerung.
Originally published: New York: Knopf, 1982.
I. Title.
[PT2603.O394F8513 1983] 833′.912 82-16485
ISBN 0 14 00.6468 0

Printed in the United States of America by
R. R. Donnelley & Sons Company, Harrisonburg, Virginia
Set in Janson

Characters, situations, actions, problems, and conflicts in this novel are the free inventions of the author. If at any point they should coincide even approximately with so-called reality, the author is—as always—innocent.

My husband William has contributed unending patience and knowledge to this translation, and for this I warmly thank him.

LEILA VENNEWITZ

List of Characters

The Family

T O L M, Fritz, president of the Association; a newspaper owner
    Käthe, née Schmitz, his wife
    Sabine, their daughter, married to Erwin Fischer
    Herbert, their son, one of the "alternate society"
    Rolf, their second son, a former political activist; lives with
        Katharina Schröter; father of Holger I (with Veronica) and
        of Holger II (with Katharina)
    Holger I, son of Rolf and Veronica
    Holger II, son of Rolf and Katharina
F I S C H E R, Sabine, née Tolm
    Erwin, her husband
    Kit, their daughter
F I S C H E R, Mr. and Mrs., Erwin's parents
S C H R Ö T E R, Katharina, lives with Rolf, mother of Holger II
S C H R Ö T E R, Mr. and Mrs., Katharina's parents

The Newspaper People

A M P L A N G E R senior, representative of Bleibl
A M P L A N G E R junior, his son; secretary of the Association
B L Ö R L, elderly printer on Tolm's newspaper

B L U M E
B O B E R I N G } small newspaper owners
K Ü S T E R
T H Ö N I S, editor-in-chief of Tolm's newspaper
P L I E F G E R
P L O T T E T I } objects of attempted assassinations

ZATGER, Birgit, Tolm's secretary
ZUMMERLING senior, a publisher
ZUMMERLING junior, his son

The Industrialists and Delegates

BLEIBL, married to (1) Hilde, (2) Margret, (3) Elisabeth, (4) Edelgard née Köhler;
  Martin and Robert, his sons with Hilde
GROLZER
KOLZHEIM } employees of Bleibl
HERBTHOLER
KLIEHM, one of Zummerling's men
KORTSCHEDE, a friend of Fritz Tolm's; lover of Peter Schlumm;
  Verena, his daughter
POTTSIEKER

"They"

BEVERLOH, Heinrich ("Bev"), an underground activist; lover of
  Veronica Zelger
  "Old Beverloh," his father
TOLM, Herbert, son of Fritz and Käthe
ZELGER, Veronica, former wife of Rolf Tolm; mother of Holger I

The Police

HENDLER, Hubert, security guard; Sabine Fischer's lover
  Helga, his wife
  Bernhard, their son
  Heinz, Hubert's brother
  Monika (Monka), Helga's sister
HOLZPUKE, officer in charge of security for the Tolm family
  Dollmer, Holzpuke's boss
  Stabski, Dollmer's boss
KÜBLER
LÜHLER

Rohner
Zurmack
Kiernter, Dr., psychologist

Friends and Neighbors

The Beeretzes, farmers
The Blömers, architect and lawyer
The Groebels, friends of the young Fischers
The Hermeses, neighbors of the Hendlers
The Klobers, friends of the young Fischers
The Hermannses, farmers
Breuer, Erna, née Hermes, lover of Peter Schubler
     Mr. Breuer, her husband
Grebnitzer, Dr., the Tolms' family doctor
Halster, Jupp, farmer who murdered his wife
Kohlschröder, Pastor
     Gerta, his housekeeper and companion
Tolm, Count Holger, former owner of the Tolm manor house
Tolmshoven, Countess Gerlind, sister of Count Holger; childhood girlfriend of Fritz Tolm
Roickler, Pastor
     Anna Plauck, his lover
Schmergen, Heinrich, farmer's son; friend of Rolf and Katharina
Schubler, Peter, lover of Erna Breuer

Others

Bangors, a U.S. Army officer
     Mary, his wife
Blum, Maria, nursemaid to Kit Fischer
Blurtmehl, Alois, manservant to Fritz Tolm
Klensch, Eva, lover of Blurtmehl
Kulgreve, secretary to Fritz Tolm
Schlumm, Peter (Horst), lover of Kortschede
Zelger, Dr. and Mrs., parents of Veronica
Zurmeyen, Karl, lover of Monka

The Safety Net

I

Shortly before the conference came to an end, before the balloting, during the final, crucial session, the fear had suddenly left him. It had been replaced by curiosity. By the time he faced the inevitable interviews he was cheerful, surprised at the ease with which he trotted out the phrases: growth, expansion, conciliation, tariff autonomy, correlation of interests, looking back, looking ahead, the common ground of the early days—which allowed the sprinkling of a few discreet autobiographical details, his role in the development of a democratic press—the advantages and dangers of bigness, the invaluable role of both work force and unions, struggling not in confrontation but shoulder to shoulder. Much of what he said had actually sounded quite convincing even to his own ears, although Rolf's trenchant analyses and Kortschede's gloomy predictions were beginning to acquire more and more credibility in spite of the fundamentally different premises on which they were based. He had enjoyed weaving in allusions to history, even to art, cathedrals and Menzel, Bismarck and Van Gogh, whose social (or perhaps even incipient socialist) energy and missionary zeal had found their outlet in art; Bismarck and Van Gogh as contemporaries: brief, thoughtful observations on this theme added color to the purely economic statements expected of him. He had been able to recapture a seemingly off-the-cuff elegance which, more than forty years earlier, had proved so useful in Truckler's seminar and which he had later been able to exploit at numerous editorial conferences but until now had never been able to bring off in public.

What he was saying, ad-libbing, came out almost automatically, prefabricated, allowing him to think of other things, to determine at what point his fear had suddenly left him: most likely at the moment when he realized the inevitability of being elected. This would hoist him into a position where his fear should have been intensified, and—so his thoughts ran while he gave yet another interview—instinct had told him that the better course was to have no fear at all rather than more. No fear at all, merely curiosity; the fear that had weighed on him for months, the fear for his life, for Käthe's life, for Sabine's and Kit's lives, was gone. Of course they would get him, probably even kill him, and there remained only the suspense of wondering: who, and how? And what he felt for Sabine had been transformed from fear into concern. He had reason to be concerned about the child.

During these last few months his fear had been directed almost entirely toward technical matters, security measures. Concern had been supplanted; now it was no longer fear *of* something but fear *for:* for Sabine, and for Herbert, for Käthe's follies, least of all— and this surprised him—for Rolf. Sabine's extreme religious devotion had always troubled him, he had felt envious too, and that fellow Fischer, his son-in-law, whose boyishness had fooled them all—but not him, even Käthe admitted that, not him—was not the right partner for her. The craftiness with which he was using Sabine and their child for his own purposes must surely have opened the eyes of all of them. As for Käthe, a trustee should simply have been appointed to look after her money: she gave to all and sundry while denying herself nothing, and someday— soon, he feared—she would come a fearful cropper.

All this was going through his mind while they were holding microphones to his mouth like hand grenades, while the glaring spotlights were trained on him. Amplanger had coordinated and timed the interviews with great precision, made sure there was mineral water and coffee on hand, kept eau de cologne in readi- ness—all this moved through his mind on double tracks, and even awkward questions concerning his family failed to disconcert him. While "on the rear track of his thoughts" he continued to mull

over the worries lying behind his technical fear, in the foreground
he was wondering whether it was possible to speak of "concerned
cheerfulness," as they questioned him without regard for his
feelings about Rolf, Veronica, Holger, and even Heinrich Beverloh (didn't they know yet that he now had a second grandson
called Holger?). He displayed sincere and deep distress over
Veronica's chosen path, would not be lured into dissociating himself from Rolf (although they all tried more or less to put the
words into his mouth), did not deny Rolf's offenses, stressed the
fact that his son had paid the penalty, also admitted his serious,
his deep concern for Holger (the older, they obviously still knew
nothing about Holger the younger).

This double-track function, which might also have been called
media-induced schizophrenia, was beginning to amuse him: it
was possible to reel off answers even to awkward questions while
thinking about Sabine, who had obviously been shocked—probably by Kohlschröder, how else?—and was now pursuing her
Madonna cult more fervently, more intensely, than ever. What
he found difficult, while seeming to ad-lib into the microphones
in a staccato laced with discreet little throat clearings, was to
abandon the dream he had been cherishing for so long: Kit as a
girl or a young woman in the manor house, in the park, in the
corridors, feeding the ducks, in the orangery—and he couldn't
bring himself to cut this film once and for all—this dream, this
game which, according to Kortschede's devastating prediction,
would now never be played; never would Kit—even as a ten-
year-old—wander through the manor house, live here, never.

In the background the conference was breaking up, people were
having their last drinks, chauffeurs were carrying suitcases out
into the courtyard, board members were sipping the cold remains
of their coffee, applauding when, in their view, he happened to
have successfully concluded a major interview. Between two
interviews, his predecessor Pliefger insisted on rushing up to him.

With his usual condescension (steel condescending toward publishing, nothing personal, merely a matter of different branches of industry) and an expression of such surprise that it was almost insulting (as if they really had taken him for a senile half-wit), he said, pumping his hand up and down: "First class, my dear Tolm, positively outstanding, we have every reason to congratulate ourselves on your election." And Kliehm, the Zummerling supporter, displayed such astonishment at Tolm's eloquence that it really came very close to being an insult.

Was there actually something like envy in Bleibl's expression? Surprise, certainly, at the ease with which he discharged these duties, at the unexpected cheerfulness when Bleibl must have expected dejection, nervousness, and inarticulateness, after having succeeded in "hoisting" him—that's how he had openly phrased it himself—to exactly where he wanted him: to the most endangered place, the most dangerous position, which no one expected to suit him, a role that no one expected him to play so well—he, the rapidly aging, ideologically somewhat insecure Fritz Tolm, the "swaying reed," the weakling, the pushover, the extemporizer among the board members, "somehow" obscurely linked through his family with "them"—as open to attack as he was vulnerable.

No doubt about it: Bleibl was surprised, probably wondering whether it had been wise after all to nominate him, to toss his name into the meeting, which, after three hours of debate, was now totally exhausted—after the rejection of so many who would not have refused: Tolm, of all people.

More cars drove up, more suitcases were carried out, chauffeurs hurried back and forth, security officials took up new positions, TV and radio crews packed up, dishes rattled, bottles were stacked in crates; and at that moment, when the media had had their fill, it occurred to him that during the whole press conference he had never been quite that relaxed, almost lighthearted, quite that casual in his statements, the two tracks had never run so smoothly side by side, they had collided—but now he had to have a cigarette; voluptuously, hungrily, for a few moments he felt young, as in his old student days after a particularly boring seminar, or as a young officer after a successful withdrawal, when he had reached for a cigarette. And promptly a young puppy of a photographer who was still hanging around had snapped him: just as he was taking the crumpled package out of his pocket, fishing out a cigarette, lighting up with his own hands without anybody rushing over to offer him a light. And he foresaw— that much he did understand about journalism, that much he *had* learned, although it was generally held against him that, while being "in the trade and controlling it, he neither was of the trade nor knew anything about it"—he foresaw that these pictures would eventually make the front page: the white-haired, dignified new president, known for his charm and courtesy, this seemingly easygoing old gentleman who lacked some of the ingredients of a truly stable and serious-minded character, hair slightly tousled, clothes correct yet with a dash of casualness, relaxed despite his extreme jeopardy, standing there with a cigarette between his lips, not entirely consistent with his dignity, not at all with his new status, holding the crumpled package, the scruffy matchbox, the conqueror—whereas in fact he had been conquered by Bleibl.

Now Bleibl had him where he had always wanted him: right at the top, where there was to be no more rest, no pause, no relaxation, no private life for him, where he was to be hounded to death, protected to death, exposed to the utmost risk, yet he had just discovered the double-track function, just in these last two hours rediscovered his private life: his children and grandchildren and Käthe, no longer afraid of speeches to be made, of press conferences to be conducted, of interviews to be granted. There was much more stored up in him than even he would ever have expected: thoughts as yet unuttered, insights he could draw upon, prefabricated formulations lying in readiness. They could ask him whatever they liked, the aggressive journalists; and the fawning ones, those who were both fawning and aggressive; and even if he wasn't a member of the trade and had never been really part of it, journalists were people he knew something about, and he had always preferred the aggressive ones to the fawning ones. After all, he had been boss of the newspaper, his "little paper," for the past thirty-two years, and he had seen them come and seen them go, had seen them rise and fall, had got along reasonably well with them, although he had never quite grasped what journalism was all about, no matter how often they had dinned into him at conferences that *jour* means day. And to chat away pleasantly into microphones for one *day*, for one *day*, on his front consciousness-track, faced by cameras and sharpened pencils, for the *day*: that's what he had learned in those moments when the fear for his own life had so suddenly vanished.

So once again, as always, Kortschede had also been mentioned as a candidate, Kortschede who hadn't shown up this time; and once again there had been some pretty direct allusions to his "leanings" which made him unfit for this office, "totally unfit, though there can be no doubt about his capabilities."

Inevitable that Bleibl should now come up to him, while Amplanger stayed in the background; Bleibl, who really did have a coarse face, a regular "mug," actually, and coarse manners too; old now yet still with the lusty youthfulness of the man who, while never a woman's ideal he-man, nevertheless had many affairs. Strange, for the first time in thirty-five years to see Bleibl verging on embarrassment, surprise at any rate, giving an appreciative nod; but then the arrow from a quite unexpected quarter: "So the Fischers are expecting? And I had to see it in the sports section of one newspaper and the social column of the other—you never told us, even Käthe, when I mentioned it, was surprised." Bleibl was watching closely, discovering instantly, of course, that he knew nothing about it either. Sabine pregnant? No one had told him, and there was some mystery about it, some whispering going on, none of the reporters seemed to have known, no one had asked him: "How do you feel about the new grandchild expected in the Fischer family?" He sensed that behind this remark, behind this question of Bleibl's lurked something he didn't know about. "Congratulations, on both counts: your performance here, which was brilliant—I see I shall have to read the literary section more often to keep up with you in future—and on your grandchild: in four months' time, I understand. Take care."

It was all over sooner than expected, Käthe was not yet back from Sabine's. When there were meetings or conferences, she always withdrew, presiding only briefly as the lady of the house over afternoon tea or coffee, offering homemade cookies and little cakes, she happened to have a weakness for petits fours, which she produced herself in her own delightful kitchen—and she did all this so nicely, so graciously, that it didn't seem like a mere duty, and she chatted with the men, looked after the secretaries, who appeared genuinely to like her and asked for recipes and advice. "No, really—what fantastic things you always make!" When wives were admitted to the male sanctuary for a few hours, she would ask them upstairs for tea, a chat, a drink, sometimes even showed them her wardrobe to the accompaniment of "Ah's" and "Oh's," talked about children, grandchildren, travel plans, entertained without discrimination even the men's girlfriends, referring to these openly to her husband as mistresses, doing this so nicely, inspiring immediate confidence, even reassuring these girlfriends—former stewardesses, secretaries, or salesgirls—when they seemed a bit out of their depth in these unaccustomed surroundings. Maintained her dignity and wouldn't tolerate any snide remarks if someone tried to malign Rolf or Katharina, Veronica or Holger I; defended Herbert, who was decried as a visionary, would not rise to vicious remarks about their seven-year-old grandson, whose present whereabouts were unknown. "Your son's current girlfriend, Katharina—she's a Communist, isn't she?" And she would reply: "Yes, I believe she is, but I'd rather you asked her personally—I greatly dislike defining other people's politics." Comments on the extramarital affairs of her son-in-law Erwin also did not seem to upset her. Hints about Sabine's life—she remained completely unruffled, while security guards in the corridor, on the balcony, and in the rambling storerooms were watching over her.

He missed Käthe now. If Sabine was to have her child in four months, she must soon be in her sixth month—and had said nothing to anyone. One thing was safe to assume when it came to Bleibl's pointed remarks—whether he was talking about Rolf, Katharina, Herbert, or Holger I: he always got his facts straight. If he said "in four months," then it was four months, even if Sabine herself might not be that sure. Such things all came from Zummerling sources, and they had their ear not only to the pulse of the times but also to the abdomens of prominent women; they knew better than the lady herself when a period was missed, they were abdomen researchers of a special kind, no doubt they questioned housemaids and pharmacists, rummaged through garbage cans, snooped around in medical files, perhaps even monitored phone calls, all for the benefit of the public. Surely Käthe would have told him if she had known, and he couldn't fathom why Sabine hadn't told them. If Bleibl had read it in the sports page, it must have something to do with riding; he didn't want to give way immediately to his urge to rush to the phone and call. He was longing to go upstairs to Käthe and have tea with her. He was sure she would refrain from facetious remarks about his election, if—something he would probably never find out—she felt like being facetious at all. She would hear it on the radio, of course, or see it on TV at Sabine's, and she would be more likely to feel alarmed than facetious since she knew that Bleibl was out not only to make him deeply afraid but to destroy him.

At last the clatter in the conference room had stopped, all the media people had left, and he could sit down for a moment without being photographed; he felt fatigue settling over his face like a cobweb, actually felt the creases spreading, exhaustion after the amusing and tiring game of his double-track function, but he mustn't smoke another cigarette just yet. He hated these confrontations with Grebnitzer, his doctor, and no doubt Amplanger would report: three during the session, one after lunch, a fourth one after the interviews. Amplanger had been re-elected secretary by acclamation, without lengthy discussion, and although he was from his own stable—hadn't he won his spurs on the paper at his father's side, built up a career in it and on it?—he was never quite sure whether Amplanger wasn't really a Bleibl or even a Zummerling man. Pleasant, well educated, skillful, he rarely revealed his streak of ruthlessness, and then most clearly when he smiled: he had never seen a harder smile, you could almost hear his teeth grinding. All the Amplangers smiled, his wife, his four children, and malicious wags claimed that soon his dog, his cat, and his parakeets would start smiling too. Amplanger's smile was notorious and feared—as the head of personnel on the paper he had been feared; there were still a few people left from the paper's early days with whom he could talk on familiar terms, and they had told him there was a saying: "When Amplanger smiles, you've had it."

Now presumably Amplanger was tired too, too tired to smile?

He seemed almost human as he sat down beside him, looking out over the park, seemed even a bit rumpled about his white shirt collar as if he had been perspiring, his hair slightly untidy—he seemed almost a "real human being" as he said: "Have another cigarette, sir, I won't tell." But he shook his head and merely asked: "What's all this about my daughter and the newspaper report about her being pregnant?" "It seems your daughter Sabine has withdrawn from training for the championship, and this has led to some speculation, I'll have it thoroughly checked out—I was surprised myself by Mr. Bleibl's news. But now—if I may say so—you ought to lie down a bit. This has been a wild day, I'm worn out too, and as soon as I can be sure you're upstairs in your own domain, I'll be on my way. Fantastic, if you'll allow me to say so, the way you coped with the media, simply fantastic."

"Must I start work tomorrow—I mean, go to the office?"

"No, not till the day after, we'll have a little ceremony then, a sort of reception for the whole staff—you know most of the department heads, of course. No, not tomorrow."

"I'll sit here for a while, you might as well go home—give my regards to your wife and family."

"I'm sure I needn't spell it out to you that all the security measures taken so far for Mr. Pliefger will now be transferred to you. If you wish, Mr. Holzpuke will give you the details—he'd like to do it himself, though of course I'd be glad to, only I don't want to tread on his toes. So if I may assume that under these circumstances you will be able to reach your apartment without my help, which you might possibly find bothersome, I'll say goodbye."

"Thank you, goodbye—see you the day after tomorrow."

What he really wanted was to go off right then, walk, across the courtyard, the bridge over the moat, along the avenue into the village, slowly from house to house, as far as the church. There he would have sat down, maybe even said a prayer, later knocked at Kohlschröder's door, invited himself for coffee and a chat, about the world, not about God, about whom he was less inclined to speak with Kohlschröder than with anyone, probably because he was a priest. He would have stopped in front of his parents' house, that one-and-a-half-story "cot" recently refaced with asbestos shingles where the teacher was still living, a young fellow with a car and a wife in jeans: the teacher had added a garage and turned the vegetable garden into a lawn, a thick close-cropped lawn on which the bright plastic toys of his two children could be seen lying around. So far he had refrained—and he intended to go on refraining—from asking if he might be allowed to see the house again from the inside: the two sloping attic rooms, downstairs the living room, kitchen, and tool shed, in the basement the laundry room and storeroom; probably it had all been modernized, and he wondered where they would have put in a bathroom, whether upstairs or down. He would have recalled his parents and his brother Hans—all dead, his parents buried here, his brother far, far away, if there had been anything left to bury. Direct hit. Rocket launcher. Some time or other he must pay another visit to the graves, as Käthe often did—then she would drive to Neu-Iffenhoven to visit her parents' transplanted graves on her way home, taking along flowers, buying copper candle holders, commissioning gravestones from young sculptors of which he had seen only the designs: roses-and-crucifix symbolism, in marble, almost identical, with only slight variations, for both sets of parents, but he didn't like going to cemeteries, never had, or to funerals, which some people seemed positively to enjoy.

He would have recalled the milk soup, whose flavor he had never encountered again, neither in war nor in peace; and even Käthe, who made superb soups, had never been able to reproduce that flavor, even after he had explained a hundred times what went into the soup: dollops of beaten egg white, that very discreet flavor of vanilla sugar—she always put in too much—and above all a certain, apparently inimitable creaminess which with Käthe always turned out too thick or too thin. Well, of course, he didn't know the recipe, he could only remember the taste—and that was the very thing that couldn't be recaptured, any more than the smell one had been conscious of on a particular evening somewhere—like the smell of autumn leaves rising from the courtyard in Dresden as he lay with Käthe in the room they had rented for the night.

His most vivid memory was of Saturdays: after confession the bath, in a galvanized washtub in the laundry room, after the bath the soup, bread and margarine, on lucky days cocoa, and not even the memory of confession had diluted the memory of the

flavor of the soup. And he would have stopped in front of the
Pütz house, the Kelz house, and would have wondered, although
he knew he would never do it, whether he should go in and say
hello to Anna Pütz (whose present name he knew to be Kommertz) or Bertha Kelz (whose present name he didn't know);
simply go in, say hello, and look into the faces of those old women,
who would no doubt have been shy because he now lived in a
manor house and was such an influential person. He would have
searched in their faces for the girls with whom, more than fifty
years ago, he had been so violently in love that it had made him
ill: Bertha when he was thirteen, Anna when he was fourteen,
one blond, the other dark—girls' eyes, breasts, legs, hair—he had
followed them, sneaked after them, tried to kiss them, made a
pass at their breasts and tried to stroke their legs, neither of them
had been offended, they just found him a nuisance, probably went
through the same thing with other boys, were perhaps used to it,
but not yet curious enough to seduce him, as Gerlind Tolmshoven
later did—and he had never known how to answer the strange
question put to him in the confessional: "Alone or with others?"
Pastor Nuppertz seemed to take one or the other for granted
with a boy of his age. Was it "with others" when he sneaked up
on girls and tried to grab them or merely—and sometimes they
allowed that and they would both be amazed in a beautiful, poetic
kind of way—wanted to look into their eyes: long and deep, while
keeping—as he solemnly promised—his hands to himself. Was that
"with others," to look in a girl's eyes and search for What? and find
What? And Nuppertz's insufferable question as to whether during
his bath on Saturdays he "fiddled around" with himself, and that
it would be better to have the bath water not too hot and to
wear swim trunks—that actually gave him ideas he had never
had before.

He had never got over that and had stopped going to confession, so the memory of subsequent Saturdays was unsullied
—and he shuddered at the thought that the other day his dear
child Sabine had actually come over here to have Kohlschröder—

of all people!—hear her confession! Just his bath and the milk soup, Mother's flushed face over the stove, Hans pushing his cocoa toward him—he would usually leave then and, somewhere else, get something better than cocoa!—Father, who fortunately was away, with bike and rucksack looking for cheap land, he had a pathological craving for property, to own pieces of this earth, even if only the swampy meadows, now useless, of bankrupt farmers. Father, who wanted to own land and was not gentle of spirit—a strict, a hated teacher, also a vegetarian—would ride around with bike and rucksack, collecting land, craving earth, collecting acres and square feet, eventually acquiring a few acres of useless soil, rummaging in his papers, collecting land-registry extracts, deeds, all notarized; consumption, death (and those few acres of land around Iffenhoven, Blückhoven, and Hetzigrath had certainly made life a bit easier for his mother after the war: she had exchanged land for food, converting acre after acre into milk, butter, and potatoes—later, when the bulldozing started in that area, the farmers got a hundred times what they had paid for it).

The village children, including Anna Pütz and Bertha Kelz, sighed with relief when his father died, especially the boys, who, now grandfathers, still tell their grandchildren about that dreadful teacher Mr. Tolm, of whom nobody even knew whether he was "at least a Catholic," a "real" Catholic—granted he went to church and kept order, but he had never been seen in the confessional or at the Communion bench, not even in the neighboring villages where he spent some of his Sundays, with bike and rucksack, tempting the farmers with a bit of cash, offering a down payment over a glass of beer, preliminary deals sealed after mass with a handshake, among witnesses, ridiculed because he never drank, at most a glass of water or a mug of milk, a tall, bony, skinny fellow, joyless and friendless. His mother, to be sure, had not been without joy: her children and garden, her kitchen and church, she had been active in the Mothers' Union, had gone on pilgrimages, never been flustered, and had even succeeded—rarely, oh so rarely—in conjuring a smile onto Father's face when she reminded him of their youth in Blückhoven, of her parents, of his, who had lived there on top of the brown coal.

He really must go and inspect the graves again, Käthe's floral arrangements, the crucifix-and-roses marble symbolism, the lighted candle in its copper housing. No doubt he would have visited the church and, in spite of all his reluctance, looked in on Kohl-schröder, that was a man one could at least talk to about architecture and painting, and about music too; and he might even have gone to the Kommertz house, where the Schröters lived, the present parents-in-law, so to speak, of Rolf, Katharina's parents. Although to this day, fifty years later, he still felt embarrassed at having sometimes done with Peter Kommertz and Konrad Wergen what he called "alone with others," the two of them having enlightened him when he asked what old Nuppertz could have meant by "fiddling"—and he had preferred to wait for dreams and then very soon, while commuting to school, he had met Gerlind. Later he coached her in mathematics, right here in the manor house; what with her being a countess, he hadn't dared make a pass at her legs or breasts, but he had looked deep, deep into her eyes too, and she into his, and one day she had "made short work of it," saying in her flippant way: "Let's take pity on ourselves," adding: "No complexes, Fritz dear—you're not the first, and you probably won't be the last, and I know that for you I am the first." That girl, regarded as a "brazen hussy," had turned gentle, silent, and even breathless, and that wild rapture in her face, that happiness which might almost be called bliss—he would never forget that, never, nor her smile at his joy. In triumph, not in remorse, he had gone back once more to the confessional to get rid of that "with others," to take final leave of confession, maybe of the Church that was trying to force him every week to confess remorsefully to something which an hour later he would do again without remorse. Never forgotten, Nuppertz's blatant, more than indiscreet, blustering, the barefaced question spat out at him: "With whom?!" which had nothing to do with the secret of the confessional, and besides: he must have known, the whole village knew, and they all knew too that there would be a row, and there was. The usual, the inevitable, happened: strict boarding school for Gerlind, and to everyone's surprise no banning from the manor house for him. There was even a rumor that the old countess might have not only foreseen it but desired it: the fact that she liked him, encouraged him, was too obvious, and now he coached Gerlind's brother Holger, also in math. It felt good to be able to give his mother something from time to time, to be able to buy the odd thing for himself. Moreover, there were such things as bicycles, and not even the nuns in Cologne could keep the school hermetically sealed. Gerlind insisted on her right, "guaranteed by ecclesiastical law and theology," to seek out a father confessor other than the priest attached to the school. And not only were there bicycles, there were also parks, apartments belonging to the parents of Gerlind's friends: in particular, one near the South Station on the Moselstrasse, where when the windows were open they could hear the trains, and Gerlind always laughed when he insisted on looking into her eyes. He knew, she knew: what he found there was not what he had sought in Bertha's and Anna's eyes, and yet it was good: end of the confessional and milk soup.

He could, after all, have gloated when he sometimes sat in church, looking at the unchanged neo-Gothic confessional; gloated over the fact that they, Nuppertz's successors—well, if not all, at least a great many of them—had been caught in the sex trap that for centuries they had been setting for others. Where did they confess that "with others," not to mention that "alone"? Where indeed, and how, and with what penances? What was going on in their well-kept, spacious homes, in those fashionably furnished rooms which Rolf so bitingly and so mercilessly took to pieces? With their women and housekeepers and distant cousins and God knows what, and never a thought of explaining why matters were so arranged that male virility, joy, desire, and even lust were at their peak when you couldn't—weren't allowed to—didn't have enough money to—get married, and were driven to whores or "loose women," of which Gerlind was one, and forced to that joyless "alone" that he had never liked. Where, then, were the "others," if a Gerlind didn't happen along, a stroke of luck, of happiness—why on earth didn't they make saints of the Gerlinds? Again and again, ever since he had entered the confessional after the last time with Gerlind, still that sense of gloating (although much restrained) when he invited himself for coffee at Kohlschröder's—that mixture of triumph, disgust, and sorrow as it became increasingly obvious that Kohlschröder was shacked up with this Gerta, his housekeeper, with all that that entailed both physically and psychically. It was common knowledge, wasn't it, never denied, it was plain to see, not merely to be sensed, when he brushed her dyed red hair with his hand in passing, or when she poured him his coffee, the way their hands met when she gave him a light—there was more intimacy and naturalness in that than if they had been caught in bed together; an understanding in look and gesture, a familiarity that was as embarrassing as it was touching, the buxom, blooming forty-year-old in the denim skirt and floppy blouse, which she allowed to reveal quite a bit—nothing was left of the magic of romantic love, it was all more indecent, whorelike. It never ceased to be a shock to him. It wouldn't have been so bad if it had been open, if they hadn't kept on inveighing against the moral turpitude of others and defending their lousy celibacy, and thundering about the immorality of youth and the world—Kohlschröder, anyway. This carefully cultivated disintegration, this tastefully, stylishly guarded chaos, pained him, and damn it, what did they do not to have children, surely they had to do something which they forbade others to do? Damn it, who confessed what to whom, and who absolved whom from what? After all, he had never, not for a second, intended to become a priest, had never taken any vow of chastity and never lusted after another man's wife; not even Edith had been married. This carefully cultivated decay, this chaos, in the very shadow of the church, but with all that there was one thing she was good at, making coffee, Gerta was, a person it was a real pleasure to look at, gentle, with a pleasant voice, dyed red hair—yet there was something bawdy about her that he resented precisely because she wasn't living in a bawdy house. Sometimes he dropped in anyway, uninvited, and he no longer felt any desire to gloat, all that was left was sorrow and disgust; after all, at one time something had been there that meant a lot to many people—to Sabine and Käthe a great deal, even to him, even today, much more than could be dreamed of by those who were so gracefully skimming along a course on which they had allowed millions, if not billions, to lose their footing "alone or with others." Chaos on all sides, disintegration behind carefully rouged, stylish façades.

He couldn't discuss that with Käthe. She was naïve and credulous in a way that he had no wish to destroy. And anyway there was nothing to be proved. Herbert always just laughed, for him the Church was no subject for discussion, whereas for Rolf it was. Rolf was fully aware that it had molded him, one way or another, as well as Katharina and Sabine—he was more worried about her than about Käthe in this respect, how often he had wished for a lover for Sabine, a nice, uncomplicated fellow, even, if need be, a member of the Riding Club. He was pretty sure that she hadn't found happiness with Erwin Fischer, or "with others" for that matter. He would never have mentioned this, never been able to prove it or discuss it with anyone, and yet: Sabine had deserved someone who really loved her, not that snooty bastard whom, when he was alone with Käthe, he called "that human repellent."

Käthe had planned to be back from Sabine's around six. It was only just four-thirty; the cars were all gone, goodbyes all said. There would have been time simply to walk to the village. But that wasn't possible anymore, he could no longer just walk off like that, not even at his own risk. Bleibl had put it well in the overt sarcasm of his congratulatory address: "Now you will belong even less to yourself, and even less to your family." And supposing he took a chance—surely they wouldn't actually re-

strain him, or would they? He couldn't saddle the tireless young
guards with that; although it would have been his fault, they
would have to take the blame, they would bear the responsibility,
swallow the disgrace. Moreover, he had promised Holzpuke
faithfully not to indulge in escapades or tolerate any on Käthe's
part, in fact to inform him if Käthe had any in mind. There had
been a few occasions when she had succeeded in going beyond
the park, through the strip of forest, and walking to Hetzigrath,
and from there going by taxi, unescorted, into town. She had
soon been tracked down—there were only her two old friends,
whose addresses were known, of course, and only the two cafés,
Getzloser's and Kaint's, or Zwirner's shoe store or Holdkamp's
and Breslitzer's dress shops, or the four churches she loved—she
had soon been picked up, once even in the taxi on her way into
town (by this time Holzpuke presumably had a system going with
all the taxi companies), but still it was annoying, a nuisance, a
waste of effort, and by now she had acknowledged herself to be
"converted" and had "come to terms with Tolmshoven Prison."

He did not doubt for a moment that all the measures, no matter how crazy and extreme they might seem, were justified. He
wanted to be cooperative, indeed had to be; as it was, he sometimes worried about the mental stamina of the men, and his mind
was not entirely set at ease by Holzpuke's assurance that they
were under the constant psychological observation of an outstanding specialist, a certain Dr. Kiernter. He knew only too well
that there were many things he had never told his doctor, never
told Grebnitzer. He had never yet mentioned the deadly boredom in the vast offices of his "little paper." And to walk into the
village *with* an escort, he wouldn't want to do that. What would
young Hendler think, for instance, if he went into the village
church and sat down, then looked in on the priest? Everyone—
certainly Holzpuke—knew that the priest was carrying on with
Gerta and that, since Veronica had recently had the eccentric
idea of phoning Käthe there—of all places—he had been drawn,
perhaps unwittingly, into the entire safety net. The possible

thoughts of the security guards killed all spontaneity in him. Holzpuke had introduced them to him: Hendler, Zurmack, Lüh- ler, "a good team, a magnificently balanced group, which has proved its excellence in protecting your daughter, your son-in- law, and your granddaughter." Needless to say, he had contacted Sabine by phone, although he knew the line must be bugged, and she had nothing but praise for all three, especially for that young Hendler, whom she described as "a very serious, considerate, and courteous person."

His mind was always turning to Sabine, who was now more and more often asking for Käthe, calling her up, inviting her over, or coming over herself. Probably due to that idiot Fischer, who couldn't resist letting the weekly illustrateds in on his erotic and sexual escapades.

It wasn't only the security measures that deterred him from simply walking to the village: it was also his legs, which no longer behaved as well as they used to, and he couldn't have said which deterred him more: his legs or that inescapable surveillance. His cheerfulness, that new sense of relief after the disappearance of his fear, had not yet communicated itself to his legs, they remained heavy, stiff, cold down to his feet. On Käthe's arm he might have managed, alone he couldn't risk suddenly giving way, perhaps having to support himself on that young Hendler, whose vigilance would thus be impaired, nor did he want to ask Blurtmehl to accompany him. What would Blurtmehl, what would any of them think, if he suddenly stopped outside the Pütz house or the Kelz house? Whatever they thought or imagined, it would stifle his memory, and he would never recapture the two girls' faces; or if he sat down in the empty church, staring at the confessional, the neo-Gothic windows, thinking in sorrow and disgust of what he had never yet been able to come to terms with: that disgusting drivel of Nuppertz's that had stifled all, all poetry, all beauty, even the sad enjoyment of the "alone." The very idea of what they might think killed his memory, killed the memory of those two girls—once so nice, so sensible—of the blustering, indiscreet

Nuppertz, of the "with others." Probably it was better not to return to the places of memory. It wasn't the men, the guards, but what they might think that pursued him, thoughts they probably never even had.

He took the stairs rather than the elevator in order to avoid yet another encounter with the faces of possible stragglers: Pottsieker and Herbtholer, and all those others he hadn't been able to get away from during the four days of isolation: Bleibl, who might still be in the building; friends, enemies, waiters. Always that tension in the elevator; forced smile, awkwardness with cigar or cigarette ash (Kulgreve never remembered to have ashtrays installed in the elevator—he would have to mention that to Amplanger, who would see that it was done), and those brief ironic remarks about Tolmshoven, manor house and meeting place that they called his "castle of nostalgia"; some of them couldn't resist dubbing him "Friedrich von Tolm zu Tolm," whereas he was plain Fritz Tolm and happened to have been born in the village named after the manor and the local aristocracy. Yet everyone, including Bleibl, had been forced to admit that the purchase of the manor had turned out to be ideal. The remodeling and modernization had been worthwhile, even financially; two airports within thirty minutes' drive, another within forty, and, in an emergency, landing permission could even be obtained from the British military airfield only twenty minutes away. It had been an excellent idea to get away from the hotels rented by the day or the week. After vain attempts to persuade the Association to make the purchase, he had eventually bought it himself, from Holger Count Tolm, the last of the name, who for many years now had been disporting himself with women and gambling somewhere in southern Spain, trying without success to be accepted by the international playboy set: the very image of an embarrassing type of decay which, in its unashamedness, was still more to his liking than the decay of the clergy behind carefully preserved façades. In Holger's case, not even hair and teeth had held out. He had even become a bit lachrymose, dotty—Holger, with whom he could never be angry, much less resent, ever since his childhood, his youth, when Holger had covered up for his love affair with Gerlind, provided alibis, helped arrange trysts; Holger, driven by the war into an unsuccessful career in the air force and to drink, whose sole talent was that of golden boy of the officers' mess, their *maître de plaisir,* hanging around staff head-quarters, arranging dinners, obtaining caviar, champagne, and women, eventually making it to the rank of major and ending up wobblier in the knees than he would care to admit to himself. Even if Holger was becoming tiresome, that youthful credit would never be exhausted, in spite of his gradually becoming a genuine embarrassment, totally debauched as he described himself, by this time hardly respected by any of the cliques. Tolm, while creeping up the stairs, was still thinking of the nice boy with whom he used to cycle to Cologne, ostensibly to visit museums and churches or to buy additions to his electric railway, or simply "for no particular reason," while Gerlind was waiting for him somewhere—usually in the Moselstrasse apartment—laughing and, as one would say today, "topless."

He couldn't help smiling now: it was true that he had paid too much for Tolmshoven, for Holger's sake and also for Gerlind's, who had turned up out of the blue: to his surprise quite sedate, already in her early sixties, married to a commoner, a lawyer by the name of Fottger who was on the staff of the Foreign Office; plumpish too, Gerlind, smiling, even blushing—something she never used to do—and saying: "We can really use the money, seeing that our children have to go to university while we traipse around the world, and I'm so glad you're getting the place—and sometimes, you know, I feel I should have held on to you, should have tried—it was lovely with you, you were such a child." Fortunately he didn't try any tricks, which wouldn't have done her much good in any case—no hand touching, no sighing, no eyelid fluttering, nothing—when they had gone on from the conveyancing office to Café Getzloser, where Fottger, who was apparently a Social Democrat, defended Germany's *Ostpolitik.*

She had never been actually pretty: attractive, yes—pretty, never, and her flighty ways had obviously long since left her. He was also thinking of the old countess, who had always gone out of her way to help him. She had stubbornly insisted that he study for a degree, and she had been exceptionally charming to Käthe.

Now he was back at Tolmshoven as lord of the manor and had offered it to the Association as a permanent conference site. Telex, telephones, elevator, an excellent, hundred-percent reliable staff; sauna, the popular, spacious card room, where they could play poker or stronger stuff if they felt like it; and, on balance, Kulgreve had been a good choice (though he never remembered ashtrays for the elevator), alert, keen, discreet. A deciding though unforeseen factor was that Tolmshoven had turned out to be ideal for security purposes: the wide moat, the easily scanned French garden (let them call it his "seventeenth-hand Versailles"! Let them laugh at him as they sat there in their ostentatious villas weighed down with copper and slate!). Easy to survey and easy to guard, all the way to the edge of the forest. Even as an investment the manor had proved worthwhile; with its up-to-date kitchen and other facilities it could easily be sold as a luxury hotel, if, if—and here he had been thinking of the children, who had never liked Tolmshoven, had been thinking of the grandchildren —if . . . if it hadn't been for Kortschede's grim prognosis that frustrated all his plans, all his speculations; the manor might even be said to have considerable art-historical and museum value, an original structure from the twelfth century, additions and alterations from almost every subsequent century, an architectural anthology if you like—and nothing would remain, nothing, nothing. . . . Already the coal mines were coming closer, the power stations making their own weather on the horizon. "Leveling and digging," Bleibl called it, and quiet old Kortschede had confirmed it. "They've already decided what can't yet have been decided. You'll see, they're all in cahoots—the union and the Association, state and Church"—he always gave an odd little giggle when he mentioned the Church, as if he were speaking

about a comical, rather selfish old maid in some old ladies' home—
"it's all decided, Fritz, and it'll happen in your lifetime—not a
thing will remain, not one stone upon another—just don't be too
surprised; nothing is more dangerous than when unions and the
Association are in agreement. Energy. Jobs."

Four flights, eleven steps each, and he knew every one of them,
knew every uneven spot, even the smallest, every nuance, where
the rod holding the stair carpet had come loose and he had to
take care not to stumble. He had vigorously, with "almost unreasonable vehemence," as the architects put it, resisted having
the staircase straightened, the carpet replaced, and they were
right: unreasonable and sentimental, and they could have no
inkling of the latter, couldn't know how often, as a boy, he had
gone up, crept up, the stairs to reach Gerlind's room, now occupied by Bleibl.

He was tired, feeling his age, sometimes in his thighs, sometimes all the way down to his feet; now he felt a new fear: having
to move, move away—where to, where to? In the whole village
not a wall would be left standing, not a patch of lawn preserved, not a boxwood in the cemetery, and he wondered whether
they would take the neo-Gothic confessional along to Neu-
Tolmshoven, whether Kohlschröder would take along his Gerta,
to an even more fashionable apartment where Chagall would hang
beside Warhol, and everything would be moved, the old girls,
old women, Anna and Bertha, the farmers and the cemetery, as
had happened at Eickelhof and Iffenhoven. The family had never
forgiven him for that, nor had Rolf, least of all Käthe, yet they
should have known that he was as helpless as he was powerless,
not a fighter, never had been, known that the money attracted
him too, his growing wealth, the unforgettable poverty of his
childhood—perhaps his father's craving for land! And damn it
all, why did there have to be so much brown coal in the ground
right *here*, where they had been born, raised, and spent their
lives?

He still refused to be persuaded by Grebnitzer to use a cane, and he wondered which was more ridiculous: to cling to the banister or to use a cane, or to ask for assistance from Blurtmehl, who would, needless to say, have been ready at any time to give him a helping hand. Eventually he would have no choice but cane or elevator, perhaps both, and then one day the wheelchair, where Bleibl would have liked to see him right now. A president in a wheelchair: white-haired, benevolent, cultured—what a feast for the media! He could already hear those obvious, facile comments comparing him with Roosevelt, his liberal leanings in economics with the New Deal. Allegories, clichés, lay ready, waiting to be used, whole series of corny stupidities: what a scoop for the media if they—who? how?—were to catch him in a wheelchair, preferably with cameras at the ready: himself, covered with blood, tipping out of the wheelchair, the wheelchair bouncing down the stairs, the inevitable comparison with the movie *Potemkin*. Stairs, perambulators; stairs, wheelchair—and no doubt the cameraman would swear and say: "For God's sake, why does the staircase have only eleven steps—this take's too short!"—and perhaps, in order to extend the take, he would send the bloodstained wheelchair careening down still more stairs.

He flinched when Blurtmehl opened the door for him at the very moment he touched the handle outside; he thought: that's how it'll be, it'll be someone I know, someone I trust, someone who has passed every security test. For God's sake, had Blurtmehl learned to see through wood? Or had he received a message from somewhere: "Now he's standing at the door, touching the handle"? That wasn't unlikely; after all, they were standing up here in the corridor—at least one of them was—with their transceivers, though hidden in recesses, chests, doorways, or behind jutting old walls. Blurtmehl carried one too, and someone might have signaled his arrival out of sheer kindness, as a favor. The worst of it was that he now stumbled into the room through the open door, falling forward, so that Blurtmehl had to catch him: an embarrassing, totally superfluous demonstration of his physical helplessness that would be attributed to his state of health, not to the sheer technical fact that the door had suddenly given way. Surely he was still able to turn a door handle and enter a room without assistance!

These and other attentions and courtesies had long been accepted by him as indications of his increasingly rigorous imprisonment, in which everything, every courteous gesture, was transformed into both surveillance and threat. Fresh in the minds of all of them was the shock caused by Kortschede's suddenly yelling and racing around the conference table like a madman when a waiter, unbidden, offered him a light for his cigarette: the silent approach of the waiter, the soft click that could easily have been taken for a muffled shot, had robbed Kortschede of the last of his composure, the silent courtesy had deprived him of all self-control —he yelled and yelled, raced around the table to the door, which was locked, back again, beside himself, no one could stop him, until Amplanger finally caught him in outstretched arms, but he had torn himself away (which later prompted Bleibl, who was always hinting at Kortschede's homosexual proclivities, to remark cynically: "Like Joseph with Potiphar's wife"), leaving his jacket behind in Amplanger's arms, and there had been no alternative but to seize him with the aid of the police officers, who knew the right holds and applied them vigorously. It looked brutal but must have been necessary, they held on to him, clapping his mouth shut, until at last Grebnitzer arrived to give him a tranquilizing injection. Then, sobbing and gasping, he had subsided, collapsed, and had to be taken to his room, watched over by a nurse, until his family arrived to take care of him.

Blurtmehl led him to the armchair by the window, seemed somewhat embarrassed, brought some mineral water, added a shot of

whiskey, and said: "Your wife will be back around six, in an hour
—she asked me to tell you. I'll have some tea and toast ready then.
Meanwhile I'll get your bath ready." It had been an effort to
persuade Blurtmehl to drop the "Madam" or "the mistress." He
didn't care for such language, Käthe even less, yet in the beginning
it had been as if, by forbidding Blurtmehl to use such forms of
address, one were robbing him of some inherent right. Finally
they had succeeded by making a joke of it. Every time he used
either one, every time it "slipped out," as he put it, Blurtmehl had
to forfeit a cigarette and put it into the attractive malachite box,
the gift of some Soviet character.

The other day, at the sanatorium in Trollscheid, where he was
visiting Kortschede and they were having a cup of tea on the
roofed terrace in the rain, Kortschede had confessed to his homosexual proclivities. The intensity of these had surprised him, especially Kortschede's dependence on a man called Horst that
Kortschede himself described as pathological. Horst was regarded
as a dangerous criminal and had to be kept under constant surveillance, even at night when he was in bed with Kortschede. Horst
was the key figure in a case of blackmail and robbery that had
ended in murder—and the microphones were lying in wait for
spilled details, or better still a confession. "I have had to consent
to this in order for him to be permitted to visit me—and you may
not believe this: the boy loves me—and I am betraying him—
but now you can imagine the state my nerves are in—sometimes
I want to scream when a door is banged somewhere in the building, when you—forgive me—put down your cup with a click. . . ."

He, Kortschede, gave Tolmshoven four, at most five, more
years, and of course he hadn't told Käthe this; why worry her now,
why? Hard to imagine that there would be nothing left, nothing:
only dredges and a gigantic hole, conveyor belts and pumps, and
the wind that forms in such cavities, and yet another cloud-
forming power station; the manor sold at a high profit, this ancient
pile received long ago by some Tolm as a reward for success in

battle—for or against Spain, no one seemed to know exactly, and the countess of those days, who had been for or against the Spaniards, had been forced to marry him. They would bulldoze it all, church and manor, the Kelz house, the Pütz house, the Kommertz house, and the nice little arbor at the end of the vicarage garden where in summer one could sit and drink a glass of wine—pond and bridge, ducks and owls—where would the owl fly to?

"It's all decided, Tolm, decided before anything's been discussed, before they allow the local enthusiasts to start shouting, it's settled, before it could have been settled—billions of tons lie there, and nothing, nothing will stop them from extracting them—and farther off, beyond Hetzigrath, not a house, not a tree will remain standing, not a snail keep its house, not a mole its run, and they will advance right up to the Dutch border and one day they'll talk the Dutch into it also, if any coal happens to be there too. . . . There's not a thing you can do about it, Tolm, nothing, my dear Fritz, and if you want to continue investing in Tolmshoven you should know that of course you'll be compensated at a profit, but as for all the work, the annoyance, the upheaval involved in any remodeling, you should spare yourself that. Believe me: the plans are ready, the calculations already under way—I assure you."

In the rain, over tea on the terrace in Trollscheid, and Kortschede could no longer live without his Horst, without tranquilizers. And added with a smile: "And you know of course, or at least you have a hunch, that the paper will fall into Zummerling's lap—and into mine—just as Tolmshoven will fall prey to the dredges. You should really have paid more attention to economic trends, you should have read the financial pages more than the literary section—and here's some advice for you: never start anything against a Fischer—you know that the Resistance photos Zummerling has of him are unbeatable. God-fearing textile industry versus liberal newspaper . . . you couldn't win, not with

your family background, with Rolf, Veronica, and Katharina . . .
watch out! Take care."

Since the incident with Kortschede, the last vestiges of irony
had vanished from their comments on security surveillance; only
Bleibl occasionally permitted himself a passing shot. Their relations with the guards had changed too, since Kortschede's fit their
friendly but sometimes patronizing manner was no longer possible, and since the affair of Pliefger's birthday cake joking wasn't
possible either—there was work for Kiernter the psychologist,
there were long conferences with Holzpuke (in charge of security), who asked for forbearance, after all the guards were only
doing their duty, and as for themselves, surely they wanted to safe-
guard their lives, so they must accept apparent pedantries—such
as a guard inspecting the toilet before one of them used it, or
"lady visitors" being closely scrutinized—and, please, escapades
such as those occasionally indulged in by Käthe should be avoided.
Yet they should have realized that there was no such thing as
security, either internal or external; he knew that all these measures had to be yet would prevent nothing.

Still, it was both pleasant and reassuring to look out over moat and
terrace onto the park, to imagine that one day it might be possible again to have a party there with all the children and grandchildren: outdoors, on a summer evening with paper lanterns and
little lights, with modest fireworks for the grandchildren, ice
cream, a barbecue, and cocktails—whatever they wanted; and
bitter to know that, for the time being and perhaps forever, it
was out of the question, considering that one of his sons was himself regarded as a security risk and that his son-in-law refused
"to sit at the same table with someone who after November
'seventy-four had named another of his children Holger," for
who could forget that it had been in November 1974 that Holger
Meins, one of the hardest of the hard-core terrorists, had died in
prison during a hunger strike? . . . Another four or five years, so

he might as well suppress the fear of moving, although he knew that it would continue to nag him, to gnaw away at him: "not a snail keep its house, not a mole its run . . ."

And doubtless "they" would see to it that there were no more carefree parties, among them his former daughter-in-law, who, as was hardly a matter of guesswork anymore, had now joined "them"—and that other one, the young man who had studied banking at his expense and been his frequent guest at Eickelhof.

Fortunately Blurtmehl had, over the years, learned to attune himself to his moods and was probably still embarrassed over his uncalled-for opening of the door: he had left the room before being asked to leave him alone for a while, and had even moved the malachite box close enough so that he need only stretch out his arm, although Grebnitzer had given Blurtmehl strict instructions never to move cigarettes within his reach. But he preferred to take out his crumpled package, which must still contain one cigarette, and there it was, squashed, almost broken in two, but it was still possible to smooth and straighten it out, and it drew when he lit it. He carefully examined the package, discovered one more, a broken one—and it still went against the grain to throw away the package with the two halves, that was more deeply entrenched than the memory of hunger. The memory of being deprived of tobacco lay as deep as the memory of the confessional and Gerlind's "Let's take pity on ourselves," as deep as the smell of autumn leaves in Dresden; that memory of humiliating interrogations, almost cross-examinations, when some upstart of an officer puffed out the aroma of a Virginia cigarette into the air and tossed the cigarette, hardly begun, over his shoulder, how hard it had been for him then to decline the proffered cigarette, but he knew: it was meant to seduce him into confessing something he had never done. No, he really hadn't had any idea that his godfather Friedrich, whom he scarcely knew, who occasionally turned up for his birthday with a gift, he really hadn't had any idea that Friedrich had left him the *Bevenicher Tagblatt*, and no one, no one in his family had taken part in any Aryanization. In January 1945 he had been involved in some withdrawal movements along the Bavarian-Czech border, no more and no less; yes, his dissertation had been on "The Rhenish Farmhouse in the Nineteenth Century," but here in camp, while being interrogated, he had heard for the first time that he was the owner of the *Bevenicher Tagblatt*. Those cigarettes, those stubs, those hardly smoked Virginians they threw away—only with Käthe could he speak about that, with no one else, least of all with Bleibl, although he had first met him in the internment camp.

Now Bleibl really had been a Nazi (textiles, had his fingers in that, through his family), and had always, "at every stage of his life" as he put it, "had the best of everything," in war and peace, in camps and tents, in hovels and palaces, always "the best of everything." In camp he had invariably, with unfailing instinct, sniffed out the most corrupt among the officers and proposed deals to him in which he, Bleibl, could act as go-between. Land occupied by destroyed and undestroyed buildings, vacant lots too, and how many dollars had to be offered to this person or that. He carried around the entire land-registry records of the District of Doberach in his head, knew—since he had been one of them himself—where the worst Nazis had lived; knew how their families, or even they themselves as they sat trembling in their cellar hideouts, could be persuaded with good old dollars to sell their houses or properties in a sort of "counter-Aryanization," as he called it—through middlemen, of course—and with those dollars they could then clear out, God knows where to, and Bleibl killed two birds with one stone: provided the Nazis with dollars and the means to escape, and the corrupt officer with property, and naturally he could expect a commission from both, in dollars of course, which he could use to acquire this or that property for himself, through middlemen of course, for obviously a Nazi of Bleibl's stamp couldn't acquire real estate while still in the internment camp. There were some wild rumors: that Bleibl, together with a small U.S. Army patrol, was "cleaning up" in the vaults of destroyed banks—safes and cash deposits; they simply—so the rumor went—drove up in armored scout cars, cleaned up and cleaned out—"positively shoveled out money and valuables"—in the chaos of the ruined city. Later Bleibl had free access to the commandant's barracks, could telephone, was allowed out, was taken along, presumably also to the brothels—and there the rest of them were, almost weeping at the sight, even from a distance, of a woman, any woman—and he tormented them with a recital of his numerous "erections," brought along whole cartons of cigarettes and let them all have a sniff, drove them crazy—advanced from a textile whiz to a real estate genius. It was not difficult to imagine him "cleaning up" in bank vaults. And before long he was appointed—what was it called? probably "Textile Administrator" for an entire region.

No, Bleibl knew his weakness only too well, and to this day would grin when he lit up anyway, mouthing meaningfully: "Virginia, O Virginia!"; Bleibl enjoyed protection, right at the top, way in the rear, maybe even on both sides of the ocean, he couldn't be got at. They all knew of his weakness, of course, but didn't know where it originated—only Käthe, he had told her all about it, yet even she didn't know that it was the same with cigarettes as with the milk soup: that taste, that smell, that Virginia aroma—he never found it again, never found it, kept looking for it, probably smoked to find it again, and never did.

Already twilight beyond the forest, the tops of the old trees gray in the rose-red light, those ancient, magnificent trees toward which the owl would soon be flying. The trees were dearer to him than the manor, he sometimes wondered whether he hadn't bought the whole thing for the sake of the trees, also as compensation for the trees lost at Eickelhof. The owl glided without a sound, perhaps the same one that at Eickelhof had flown every evening from the turret to the edge of the forest, he and Käthe had watched it together. Käthe was afraid when the owl took off from the turret and flew away, she would cling to him and whisper: "We must leave this place, we must leave"—twenty years before they really had to leave. It also made Käthe nervous when the screech owls started calling; and still, before thunderstorms, when crows and starlings suddenly flew up and flapped away, she would cling to him.

Tranquil, the view over the park, no sound of elevator or departing cars, or of Bleibl's reverberating laughter that drowned out even elevator noises, those triumphal chest tones with which he blared out that he had finally succeeded in having "one of our oldest members, one of our best," elected, in a situation where he had been quite unable, at any price, to refuse the candidacy; there were all the prefabricated clichés he had used himself during the interviews: "In the hour of greatest danger. At a moment when each one of us is expected to prove himself. Steadfastness . . ." So of course they had to elect him, the weakest, the most vulnerable, rendered even more conspicuous by family connections with those "others"—elect him, at a moment when everyone knew that family connections meant increased threat; and he still, neither in private conversation nor secretly, much less publicly, did not dissociate himself from Rolf. That was the question to which his public reply was feared most by his enemies and friends and least by himself, his stereotype answer, identical on video and audio tape: "He is my son, he broke the law, paid the penalty, and since then has lived within the law," and was tempted to wax biblical and say: "He is my beloved Son, in whom I am well pleased." He was not even afraid of being asked about Veronica: "She was my daughter-in-law, is suspected of serious crimes, and has disappeared. My grandson, of whom she was given custody after the divorce, which took place before the alleged crime, has disappeared with her. He bears our name, the name of his father, my son." No, he didn't think "bad egg" was the right term, he sometimes thought they might be the true immigrants from the distant stars, satellite dwellers for whom no yardsticks, no words, had yet been found. Insane? That was too earthbound a description. Yes, he had also known Beverloh, who had been his guest, frequently, he had found him a nice fellow. Nice? Yes. The terms "nice" and "niceness" said nothing, nothing whatever, about what a person was capable of. It was just that one shouldn't trust nice people too much. After all, criminal behavior was nothing new either, and there was nothing new about murder since the days of Abel.

They'd get him all right. Who? How? No, the fear didn't return, it had been completely thrust aside by curiosity, and behind that in turn hovered the pressing fear of being driven out of Tolmshoven. It wasn't even inconceivable that Bleibl had assigned him the role of decoy bird, released to be shot down, tired, old, so worn out that the role of victim was just about all he was good for: shot down in his wheelchair on the top step. *Potemkin*. And himself shot down, the kindly, cultured, white-haired, nice old man; no business tycoon. Invested with the martyr's crown. He didn't wish for this crown, he wanted to drink his tea and watch the birds in flight: the wide, elegant, arrogant wingbeats of the great predators, the short-winged flutter of insect eaters, among whom the swallows were his favorites. Käthe knitting or playing the piano—albeit inexpertly—in the background; three grandchildren, of whom two were called Holger, one of them aged seven, somewhere down there in Iraq or Lebanon, the other aged three, twenty kilometers from Tolmshoven, in Hubreichen, a lively youngster who might or might not bear his name.

To this day he had never found out whether Rolf was just living with Katharina or was married to her, and he didn't like to ask Holzpuke of security about it or ask him to find out for him. Käthe could do that, she could do something he daren't risk: ask Rolf or Katharina outright, and he knew the answer: "If you are actually interested in something so totally irrelevant, if you find something so trivial of even the slightest importance, we will do you the favor of hereby declaring: we are (or are not) married. Kindly delete what is not applicable!" It was possible that such a question might become important to them for tactical reasons—temporarily, of course—for the sake of some papers or other, but beyond that it was of no real interest, was not even worth mentioning. It was fairly certain that they weren't married, because Katharina was probably receiving some kind of support; but the question of marriage *per se* was of no interest, didn't exist. Technically, yes, and hence politically, but on no other level. It was exactly the same with Church and religion. They existed, of course, there was no doubt about that, but it was enough for him to say "like potatoes, which grow too, of course," for him to be lectured: potatoes had a genuine, an important, basic reason for existence, as well as a function, an important one: as food. Church and religion didn't; they were present, no doubt about that—but for them there was no inherent problem. It wasn't worth talking about, and the fact that Pastor Roickler in Hubreichen was being so nice to them—had offered them a roof, taken them into his own house, defended them against incipient animosity, had placed his enormous vicarage garden at their disposal in return for an absurdly low payment-in-kind of potatoes, eggs, and apples—his being so nice was attributed by them not to his religion, let alone to his Church, but to the very fact that, despite Church and religion, he had remained or become a human being, and they emphasized that they would have found it more typical if he *hadn't* been nice. They even admitted that they were grateful to him, considered him "truly nice and human," but of course there were also nice and human capitalists, even nice Communists, nice Liberals, and they themselves were, in a way, nice too.

How all this could have come about remained a mystery to him, since only ten years ago all of them, the whole lot—Rolf and Katharina and Veronica and even that fellow Beverloh—had been truly religious, almost devout, only that "alone or with others," that even in those days had ceased to torment them as much as him. He would have understood if they had raged at the churches and had viciously and polemically analyzed religion to the point of excess, to the point of cruelly wounding feelings that were still so very much alive in Käthe and Sabine and to some extent in his own memory too—but for them not even the memory was painful, and so, as far as he was concerned, they too were "satellite children," from another star, from another world. Yet he didn't feel alien to the tea he drank with them, the bread he ate with them, the apples they put in his car for him: after all, they were his children, and tea, bread, soup, and apples were of this world.

What frightened him was that unearthly alien quality in their thoughts and deeds. It wasn't coldness—it was a state of being alien, out of which, of course, a shot could suddenly be fired or a grenade thrown, yet they too had become the objects of his curiosity rather than of his fear: his own son, growing tomatoes, caring for apple trees, keeping chickens, planting potatoes and Chinese cabbage, all in that lovely old walled vicarage garden in Hubreichen. Living comfortably—there was no other word for it—in the adjoining shack, quite pretty now that they had painted it and put geraniums in the window boxes; fetching milk each evening in a red enamel pitcher from farmer Hermes, spending the odd evening at one of the two village pubs, drinking beer, with Holger along, who was given lemonade: the purest of pure idylls in which no trace of bitterness was discernible. They had long since given up trying to explain their—yes, "their"—brand of socialism to the farmers and laborers, had given up reacting to taunts from drunken oafs, or discussing rural politics, strikes, and highway construction, or rising to the snotty, snot-nosed spoutings of motorcyclists: they would smile, drink their beer, discuss the weather—and yet behind all that (where?), behind that idyllic façade, which was not even contrived—whitewashed house, green shutters, and red geraniums—behind all that there must be something capable of generating the horror: an eerie calm. Certainly, a waiting for something—for what? Katharina had no job yet, but a few women in the village had placed their children in her care; she took them for walks through the woods, across the fields, told them stories, taught them gym and dancing in wet weather, sang songs with them—accepted money for it, of course, and when he thought of Rolf's and Katharina's calm, that eerie calm, fear was followed not only by curiosity but also by envy. They were under surveillance but not under guard, and he sometimes wondered which he would have preferred, given the fact that, ever since Veronica had started her telephoning, Käthe, Sabine, and himself were all under surveillance as well as under guard. Rolf was making out quite well, seemed even to know something about engines, was consulted when a tractor or a Honda acted up; he also looked after the priest's car, and that nice priest would ask them over, for coffee, for a drink, while scrupulously avoiding the subject of religion.

Scarcely imaginable that those two, Rolf and Katharina, had been attending Kohlschröder's church as recently as twelve, maybe even ten years ago: nice young people carrying prayer books at a time when Kohlschröder was lashing out against moral decay even more stridently than today. They felt not the slightest pang that Kohlschröder himself should have meanwhile succumbed to moral decay. They found it entirely logical that he should sleep with Gerta, logical for quite different reasons from those of the farmers, who blamed it on "nature." They found nothing embarrassing—for them it wasn't a matter of good taste—when girls who wanted something from Kohlschröder (the vicarage hall for a meeting or a movie or a debate) went to see him and unconcernedly allowed him "a glimpse or two," as it were "showing their wares," sometimes even in Gerta's presence. Rolf and Katharina didn't find this at all disgusting, or even "natural," but inherent in the system. In their eyes it corresponded to the human product of the system, which was in no way "natural"; they saw in it a quite specific form of suppression, as well as an indication of decay and rot, and almost rejoiced that decay should now have become manifest in such phenomena. They even prophesied something similar for their nice Pastor Roickler, except that he would never remain in office, would never practice that bourgeois lechery but would go away—he, too, a victim of the system, would have a hard time of it. They could tell just by watching him with women and girls: sad, troubled, self-conscious, laconic; of course they liked him and would have liked to help him, find him a nice girl or a young woman with whom he could have decamped. Nor did they feel that Kohlschröder had become "humanized": for them he was the classic personification of the absolute inhumanity of the system. This inhumanity manifested itself in the fact that a human being was legally denied something—in a legal system that exercised its own jurisdiction, and that in a democratic (ha-ha) state! He had made a commitment to celibacy, after all, but then through the back door he was allowed a Gerta, allowed those strange little games with the girls, it was tolerated, he was humiliated doubly, triply, because at any given moment two kinds of law could be mobilized against him: ecclesiastical and, if necessary, secular, for if there was any truth in what the girls "showed" him, it could at any time have been ruled "indecent behavior with minors," which would most certainly happen if any leftist teacher asked a schoolgirl to show him her tits.

And yet there remained a reticence, there remained the consolation offered by this reticence of theirs: in Sabine's or Käthe's presence, Kohlschröder was never discussed, nor was Roickler, to whom they were terribly nice: Rolf looked after his car, remodeled his house, the vicarage—twelve rooms, of which eight were always left empty, something they called "corruption by vacant space in view of the rental situation." It must drive a sensitive person—and Roickler, in contrast to Kohlschröder, was that—crazy to have eight rooms empty if he made even the most casual inquiries about the rents being paid all around him; those empty, fully furnished rooms, one of them known as "the bishop's room," where during the past sixteen years a bishop had once changed his clothes, not even slept; those empty rooms that Roickler was not allowed to rent, that he was not even allowed to offer rent-free to anyone—they spoke of them as "extortion by standardized ritual expressed in totally senseless extravagance." Roickler would have much rather given them a few rooms, but he wasn't allowed to, he was only allowed to give them that three-and-a-half-room shack, only a fifth of the square footage standing empty in the vicarage. "A nihilism," said Rolf, "that no nihilist can afford."

Well, they got along fine with Roickler, were, in their eerily calm way, nice to him, amazingly logical and down-to-earth with surprising elements of warmth. And yet all that might be no more than camouflage. Perhaps they had resolved to spend three or four years in Hubreichen and build up a good reputation in a whitewashed shack with green shutters and geraniums in the window boxes. Rolf was already being consulted about growing vegetables, Katharina about handling children (they were certainly thorough, methodical, hard-working!)—yet someday they might launch an attack from within that invisible space, that reservoir of calm—no, he would never dissociate himself from them, but he wouldn't guarantee for them either.

Was it possible that Rolf, that Katharina, would be this "Who"? Why not? Rolf more likely than Katharina, she did have a certain warmth, a "Communist warmth" as he called it, but only to himself (never would he mention that, never, not even on one of those double tracks), a warmth that he remembered in the Communists of his young days, in his fellow student Helga Zimmerlein, for instance, who had died in the penitentiary, or in old Löhr in the village, the only Thälmann voter, who got along so well with children that he had acquired the reputation of a Pied Piper—it had existed, that Communist warmth which had driven him as a student into Red taverns.

No, Rolf more likely than Katharina—his eyes held such an inscrutable dimension, shadowed by a strange melancholy, a dimension that remained opaque, grew even more shrouded when he played with his little son Holger, held him on his knees or tipped out the bag of building blocks and began to build a house with him on the floor—then he would hold the child close or look at him with such remote, cool tenderness and melancholy. There was always something eerie about that tender, shrouded gaze, even when he looked at Katharina, in fleeting tenderness, touching her shoulder in passing, or her hand when he gave her a light or took a cup from her, that was worlds removed from the suggestiveness with which Kohlschröder imbued such gestures. It lay as deep as the mute utterances of a desperate man who knows what is in store for him—what?

Of course it had been fatal for him to have studied banking with that fellow Beverloh, but that happened to have been his dearest wish. Later he had even worked in one of Bleibl's branch offices, quietly efficient—until he started throwing rocks, overturning cars and setting fire to them, at which time he had met Veronica. He never spoke about his oldest son, or about Veronica or Beverloh, just went on conscientiously studying financial and stock-exchange reports, and had such a quiet, dry, uncanny way of whispering over a cup of tea or coffee or a mug of milk: "Today I came across one hundred and eleven dead between the lines of the financial supplement, but it may have been only ninety-nine or perhaps a hundred and twenty."

It sounded cold, precise, pitiless, like a casualty report after an attack or a retreat. Even Rolf hadn't succeeded in explaining "economic processes," as Kortschede called them, to him, he had never even properly grasped the economic processes involved in and around his paper, he had fought shy of them. Whether from laziness or indifference—he argued with himself about that. He had been dissuaded from taking an interest first by the older Amplanger, later by the younger: "Just leave that to us."

Luckily Blurtmehl had a sense of humor, manifested in succinct, brief comments made while dressing him, driving him, serving him, bathing and massaging him—it was the humor of an expert masseur who knew how to avoid sensitive spots, how far he could go, knew too that he had hit the right nerve when he casually said, for example: "May I be permitted the observation that Director-General Bleibl has never gone through such bad times as you—and never will?" Blurtmehl discovered barely detectable damage suffered as a child, a young man, during the war, after the war, as a prisoner of war, forgotten illnesses of bowels and stomach, traces of typhoid and malaria, the scars of minute injuries, spoke of them as "lying deep, deeper than the skin, going far deeper than the skin . . . no, no, sir, you're not thick-skinned!" —here, of course, he was again alluding to Bleibl. Blurtmehl even spoke of the "burden of responsibility placed upon your shoulders which others should be bearing," and no doubt was referring to the heart of the problem that made his limbs feel so leaden: that he was fed up with the paper, was bored to death when occasionally seated at his vast desk where there was nothing, nothing left, for him to decide—he had let his paper slip through his fingers, had allowed it to be taken away from him, stood only nominally for it, while Amplanger senior had long been representing Bleibl's interests. He was no longer himself, he was merely the image of himself: irreplaceable as an image; had allowed himself to be deceived by an ever-increasing income, by a proliferating fortune—there must be something very mysterious in Blurtmehl's hands for him to arrive at such insights under those hands, whereas Grebnitzer, even during long sessions of questioning, never penetrated to the heart of the problem. After all, there was nothing organic to discover, he had never had a heart attack, even his blood count was excellent—and yet there was that lead, that chill, in his limbs. Sometimes he actually feared a total paralysis when seated there at his desk, powerless "at the power center, at the very heart of capitalism," while his fortune proliferated and he was anxiously concerned not to let a single cigarette "go to waste."

And now this new office, in which he could decide even less, assuming that he was capable of arriving at any decisions at all.

They had made it pretty clear to him, not only Bleibl but Pottsieker and Kliehm too, and most of all Amplanger: he played his
part well. By mentioning the literary section, Bleibl had alluded
quite plainly, brutally, to his occasional contributions to the paper,
when he happened to write about Hieronymus Bosch or Salvador
Dali. In him the Association had finally acquired a "literary section," something for "the ladies."

Blurtmehl knocked, heard the feeble "Come in!," entered,
and announced: "Your bath is ready." He was quite obviously
ill at ease, would certainly never again open the door in such a
way as to make it look as if his boss were stumbling headlong
into the room, never again. He was embarrassed after this his
first faux pas in seven years, but probably Holzpuke had personally assumed command of him, had given him the order over
the transceiver: "Dr. Tolm, our president, is very exhausted, he
is struggling up the stairs with his last ounce of strength, now
he is entering the corridor, now he is reaching for the door
handle—now!" and he had almost fallen into Blurtmehl's arms.
It was with just such precision that assassinations were planned,
and the Who began to take shape in the question: would it be
Blurtmehl? Why not? He smiled at Blurtmehl, rose slowly to
his feet. Of course he knew Blurtmehl's past history, knew his
personal habits down to the last detail, knew about his girlfriend
as well as *her* history and *her* personal habits, but no one could
know his thoughts. Who could assess and predict the suscepti-
bility of this sensitive, emotional man? No doubt he had enough
knowledge of anatomy to apply a throttling grip in the bathtub
that would leave no trace and make his death appear the result of
his notorious frailty. The holding open of the door had made
him suspicious since till then Blurtmehl had taken scrupulous
care to let him do certain things for himself: open doors, light cigarettes, and certain unavoidable manipulations on the toilet. After
all, he had known Kortschede, too, for over twenty years: that
man of fine limbs and fine mind who ruled with quiet ceremony

over banks and newsprint, steel and real estate, and yet permitted the whisperings of his beloved Horst to be monitored.

"All right, I'm coming," he said. Smiling, he thought: No, not today, certainly not today.

II

In the end she had allowed Miss Blum to go off with Kit for the milk after all, though she knew she didn't need it anymore and wouldn't be taking it with her. Kit insisted on this ritual, also on carrying the milk pitcher, which, of course, was empty and would only be full on the return trip, when the four kilos would get too heavy for her. She loved the cows, the smell of the stable, and for Miss Blum it was a welcome excuse for a chat with the Beeretzes, who were about her age, sixtyish, and somehow related, and there was always plenty to talk about, from the past, present, and future: Blorr in ten or twenty years, if bungalows and roads went on being built at this rate. They were still trying to guess who among the thirty-four eligible voters might have actually voted for the Socialist Party: seven people, and it always boiled down to the newcomers who had rented the old vicarage and fixed it up, a nice couple but a bit of a mystery, they seemed Liberal but almost certainly didn't vote Liberal: the Blömers, he was an architect, she was an attorney, with grown-up children, four cars, and her brother, who didn't seem to do anything much, just worked a bit on the house and in the garden, smoked a pipe— seven exactly if you counted the children of voting age. The main thing was that there was plenty to talk about, and fetching the milk would take at least half an hour, or even longer, she hoped: she wanted some time to herself before Mama, before Käthe, arrived, wanted to say goodbye to Blorr, and found herself thinking about the milk: would Erwin be drinking it, would Miss Blum use it to make a dessert for him, or let it stand and thicken?—

those last two of the many liters of milk they had fetched from the Beeretz farm: every day for five years, two a day, it must run into thousands.

She was too strung up to figure it out; besides, the fear had returned, rising this time from below, seeming to rise from her feet, heating her calves, blocking bladder and kidneys, creeping over her breast like a heavy, hot cloud, into her head; at other times it moved down from above, beginning in her head, sinking down, and Grebnitzer, whom Father still swore by, was still inclined to think that this was all due to her pregnancy. Of course the fear had to do with the pregnancy, yet these were not pregnancy symptoms; this was no longer the daily, familiar fear that they would kidnap Kit, and herself as well, or herself, or Erwin, or that they would simply do away with all three of them (she imagined someone drawing a line through their pictures and writing underneath: "Done"); it was no longer that intangible yet very real fear, it was quite different—palpable, tangible— and she couldn't talk to anybody about it. There was no room inside her for two fears of such dimensions, so the tangible fear had supplanted the intangible one: for the past three months, ever since she had known positively that she was pregnant, and not by Erwin. In the four months before that Erwin had not once had contact with her in any way that could have caused the pregnancy.

Sometimes, yes, she did think of suicide: take some stuff or other, and it would all be over. What held her back was not the sinfulness, as such, in which she had been taught so emphatically to believe; but the thought of Kit, of Hubert, of her parents and brothers, even of Katharina and the nephews, and last of all—least of all, she realized—it was the thought of Erwin Fischer, her husband. Leaving him was easy enough, and now she had made up her mind and hadn't discussed it with anybody, had sent off Miss Blum and Kit with the milk pitcher as if nothing had changed. Everything, everything had changed. This time Kübler had gone along with them for protection; like all those before him, even Hubert, he would refuse to come into the house for a drink, he would stay in the courtyard, watchful, aloof, keeping a sharp eye on both entrances to the courtyard, while Rohner was indoors guarding her, keeping a watching eye on the weak points of the bungalow: the terrace, where she was now standing looking down on Blorr, and the rear garage door leading into the garden. What they all feared most was dusk, and now, in late fall, the milk had to be fetched earlier, and, although she hoped Miss Blum would take her time, she mustn't stay out until dusk. That would lead to more trouble with Holzpuke; not that he became angry exactly, but he didn't hide his annoyance when they failed to follow advice or instructions, and was always stressing—quite rightly, as she knew from Hubert—the nervous tension of his men, who would be held responsible if . . . After all, the affair of Pliefger's birthday cake had been extremely serious, and as for Father—he was already dreaming of flying saucers descending on him and Käthe, now he was even scared of birds since that business with the duck and since old Kortschede had gone completely around the bend at the click of a lighter. And there had been that terrible business with Plotteti's cigarette package.

Her fear was for Hubert, not for herself; she would be able to handle Erwin and the whole clique, the scandal and the howls of the Zummerling gang; she looked forward to the baby that was kicking away in such lively fashion inside her, she was afraid only for its father: Hubert, with whom for the past six weeks she hadn't been able to exchange a single word. Since he had been made a bodyguard at Father and Käthe's, she sometimes caught a glimpse of him, saw his silhouette in the corridor upstairs in the manor, couldn't speak to him, couldn't write to him, couldn't phone him. Because of Veronica, of course, she was being not only guarded but kept under constant surveillance, and fortunately neither Rolf nor Father nor Käthe had let on that she too had at one time been friendly with Beverloh. He had been Father's protégé, after all, as well as Rolf's friend, and Veronica had at one time been Rolf's wife.

Fear also for Helga, Hubert's wife, whom she had never met, of whom she knew only that she was blond, was called Helga, and was a very nice person, and then there was a dear little boy called Bernhard, who would soon be receiving his First Communion; she knew the address but couldn't go there, of course. Kübler and Rohner, the new guards, never let her out of their sight, and she couldn't very well—while escorted and observed by Kübler or Rohner—go to Hubert's home, stand outside the house, and wait for Helga and Bernhard to come out. Divorce was out of the question for Hubert, and Erwin in his pride and vanity still believed that she was three months pregnant by him, whereas the sixth month had just begun.

He had been away for four months, traveling to Singapore, Panama, Djakarta, and Hong Kong, carrying on complex negotiations for the Beehive. He had had to establish whole production chains, find agencies, install mechanical equipment, hire representatives—and after successfully concluding this campaign he had come home jubilant. She must speak to Erwin, too, before he ran into Grebnitzer, who would congratulate him on the baby due in four months but which Erwin didn't expect for six: a healthy child from a healthy mother, a healthy father. "Those hot flushes your wife suffers from sometimes are quite natural, perfectly normal," and Erwin had already generously declared: "Even if it's another girl, we'll celebrate!" Of course he would let the press in on it, and the illustrated weeklies. "New blood in the Beehive! New blood in the Fisherman's Shack," as their smart bungalow was called. "A blessed event expected by one of our hopeful horsewomen: Sabine Fischer of the Tolm clan—one of our most endangered women!" Now the lid would be put on all that, no champagne, no paper lanterns, while somewhere— where?—she would give birth to the child of a policeman. Where? Not here in Blorr, probably not at Tolmshoven, perhaps at Rolf's, if he could spare her a room. She supposed she could have discussed it with Katharina, maybe with Rolf too, but first she had to speak to Hubert, she couldn't very well let others into the secret over his head, and over Helga's and Bernhard's heads, before they suspected anything, she mustn't start rumors, and there was one more thing that was as serious for Hubert as for Holzpuke: dereliction of duty.

If only Hubert were not so serious—yet she liked him serious the way he was, longed for him, pined for him, and wouldn't have minded the scandal, would simply have gone up to him, put her arms around him and kissed him, if it hadn't been for Helga and Bernhard: no, she couldn't do that, she didn't want to hurt that woman she'd never met, who had never done her any harm and certainly never would, and perhaps she would simply have gone to see her, talked to her—but not over Hubert's head.

It was a good thing that Mama, that Käthe, was coming and that she could drive back with her and stay at Tolmshoven; there she was close to him and surely would find a chance to speak to him.

Long before Erwin went off to put his "production chain," or whatever it was called, "on a firm footing," his efforts to make love to her hadn't amounted to much. He still asked anxiously, or even impatiently: "Did you remember to take it?" although he knew she took it reluctantly, was afraid of the stuff, had religious scruples too, but she took it, and he waited for her nod in answer to his question before making love to her. But she couldn't get in the mood, managed to less and less often, was overtaken by something that, if not precisely dislike or hatred, didn't enhance the mood: pity for this seasoned athlete, known as an outstanding horseman, dancer, tennis player, yachtsman, and, more recently, also as surf rider and balloonist, and who still couldn't bring it off (even in her thoughts she suppressed the vulgar phrases she knew from the weeklies, from wild parties, from the porn scenes scattered about the gutter press, and from her former neighbor Erna Breuer)—pity for the man who had so much trouble reaching a climax; sometimes he never got there at all, blaming her for it. Since then, she had been less ready to believe his whispered confessions when he came back from places like London or Bangkok. "Well, you can probably imagine what a lonely man is sometimes capable of, so far from his sweet little wife. . . ." She couldn't really believe him, in any case found it disgusting, whether it was true or a lie, the "sweet little wife" bit made her feel sick, and she wondered whether he knew what a lonely woman might be capable of, yet she wasn't even thinking of what her neighbor Erna Breuer openly defined by a vulgar word. These days the word was no longer avoided even at parties, there were women there, from so-called respectable circles, who spoke about their tits and described their husbands as lovers. Sometimes they accompanied them to foreign parts, to Asia, where Western restraint in lovemaking was disregarded.

No, she had never been able to bring herself to denounce her upbringing, to nourish resentment at the nuns, she was only shocked, deeply hurt, almost mortally wounded, since she had gone to Kohlschröder for relief. Kohlschröder had insisted on her giving all the details, until a dark suspicion rose in her: she was horrified at the way he quizzed her, also about what she had been up to with Hubert, hm? At that point she had stood up and run away: never again, never again anything like confession. Never again, then rather chat with Erna Breuer, and at the Fischers', Erwin's parents, where one sometimes met such amusing, modish, flippant clerics, they would certainly have laughed if she had confessed to them: "I have committed adultery"—characters who could be expected at any time to indulge in a clerical striptease, they bragged about their no-risk love affairs, sometimes brought along their women. Chaos, disintegration, all around—and the fear, not for one's life, not on account of the scandal, fear for Helga, and for Hubert, for whom it was as serious as it was for her, couldn't be anything but serious, and who had apparently had more luck at confession than she had.

Fear, too, of losing her neighbors, the growing resentment in

Blorr, which, because of her, had become a "den of cops." Ever since that business of Pliefger's birthday cake, the controls had been stepped up. As a result, the love affair of her neighbor Erna Breuer with one of her husband's drivers had been burst wide open; a nice, pleasant woman, pretty too, not exactly young, probably in her middle or late thirties, with whom one could have a chat across the fence about flowers and cleaning and recipes, who could be asked over for coffee, who, before the controls were stepped up, used occasionally to look after Kit, pass across a head of lettuce or a cauliflower, a perfectly ordinary woman who suffered a bit melodramatically from her childlessness, deploring her "barren womb"—"It's not my husband, you see, he has children from his first marriage, it's me"; a nice woman, that Erna Breuer, grew up in Hubreichen, daughter of Hermes, the farmer from whom Rolf got his milk, a dark, now rather buxom beauty, who also complained that "My old man never takes me dancing," so they had been invited a few times, when there was a party in the garden with dancing, beside the swimming pool, with paper lanterns and fruit punch, champagne and general jollification, and Erwin had swung Erna Breuer around, and the flushed, breathless Erna Breuer had been ecstatic, and her husband, not exactly young either, probably in his early fifties, was also ecstatic, beaming at the sight of his Erna having a real good fling. A wonderful evening, their other neighbors had been invited too, Klober, owner of the cartage company, with wife and daughter, a seventeen-year-old who went in for the "topless" fashion; and Helmsfeld, the paper's editor, who held forth learnedly, somewhat too learnedly for most of the guests, on terrorism. Even the Blums had come, and the Beeretzes had sent their oldest son, who danced with her quite often. Erna Breuer had been happy that evening, and with a tolerant smile her husband had overlooked the fact that she allowed herself to be kissed in a quiet corner by Helmsfeld, who, after the others had left, stayed on for coffee and praised—a bit too patronizingly, she felt—Mrs. Breuer's "vulgar eroticism."

But then Zurmack and Lühler had been struck by the rather too frequent presence, usually between ten and twelve in the morning, of a gray Mercedes outside the Breuer house. A boyish-looking man in his late twenties would get out, dressed not quite as might have been expected of a normal visitor to the Breuers': a little too casually, not in jeans but in corduroys, his hair slightly longer than was by now accepted as smart by the weeklies and by the police; not exactly unkempt, this fellow, but: he wasn't your average, accepted "long-hair" and, as Zurmack put it, showed a "suspicious nonchalance," had a way of moving his shoulders and legs known to Zurmack only from demonstrations and riots in the films shown to the police for the study of "certain types." He didn't look like a hippie, or a disco type, such things are hard to describe, it was just that his movements were something more than youthful and casual: Zurmack had seen something "political" in them.

This visitor came at least twice a week, and it was easy to tell from the license plate that it was one of Breuer's business cars, that this young man ran all kinds of errands for Breuer, to banks, customers, government offices, other firms (Breuer owned a watch and jewelry business, which, as it turned out, was on the verge of bankruptcy, he had overextended himself in building his new house, and anyway the watch business was in a serious slump). Discreet, very discreet inquiries had naturally been made about this young man: his name was Peter Schubler, he had dropped out of the study of sociology, had taken part in demonstrations, had once been photographed throwing tomatoes. It so happened that the Breuer house was very near the "Fisherman's Shack"—sometimes the women waved to each other from kitchen to kitchen, and from the Breuers' terrace there was an unimpeded view of the Fischers' swimming pool. That was reason enough to wonder whether Schubler wasn't actually spying out the land, and the next time the gray Mercedes stopped outside the Breuer house Zurmack followed him five minutes later, rang, waited politely, waited, rang—and then there were angry, raised voices, till, finally, after the third ring, Schubler opened the door, dressed "not quite correctly," as it was tactfully reported, and Erna Breuer appeared in her housecoat, made a scene—in fact, it was exactly what used to be called a "compromising situation." This person, she said, cool as you please, was her lover, and there was nothing illegal about that. She must insist that her husband be told nothing about it. But lover—that might also be merely a camouflage. Those types were capable of anything, and to play the lover of such a pretty woman was a role none of them would have found too difficult.

Of course it got out, Breuer didn't think it was at all nice, it really was going much too far, he split up with Erna—a routine, painful scandal with terrible consequences and with hatred for the Fischers, for "If we hadn't been living in a place that was always swarming with cops, it would never have got out." Then other neighbors were made jittery too by "all this everlasting fuss over security." Who does like it, anyway, always having the police all over the place with their transceivers and cameras on the street? Blorr, this hamlet with its twelve farmhouses and four bungalows, the old chapel and the old vicarage, was so tiny anyway that it was easy enough to observe everything that was going on; and "Who," said Helmsfeld, "doesn't have his secrets, or some friend whose way of moving can be read as political rather than a matter of style?" He himself, for instance, had a girlfriend, Erika Pöhler, aged about thirty, and she had been, if not exactly interrogated, certainly questioned a few times because she so often drove to Blorr, in the type of car known as a "student's car," and although Erika was leftist and a sociologist, she had no hankering—either theoretical or even vaguely practical —after any form of violence.

Klober, the cartage-company owner, also became jittery after Erna Breuer's love affair was exposed. People in big cars often turned up at his place, usually between ten and twelve in the morning, business friends, customers, and, as Hubert later explained to her, "Klober may well be involved in all kinds of deals, smuggling maybe, certainly tax fraud, perhaps worse, and an inspection of his visitors and their business is bound to make him jittery."

Between their house and the Klobers' there were only the four garages, and from the bathroom window one had an unobstructed view of eighteen-year-old Friedel Klober doing her "topless thing" on the terrace. She had once caught Erwin in the bathroom staring at the girl through his binoculars, and he didn't even put them down when she suddenly came in, merely confining himself to the remark: "My God, she certainly has two good reasons to sit there like that. . . ."

No, things weren't what they used to be with the neighbors—Helmsfeld complaining, the disaster at the Breuers', and the Klobers pointedly frosty. And weren't the local people already cooler, almost unfriendly, in their manner? Hadn't there been a coolness, if not outright hostility, when she went to fetch the milk with Kit, and wasn't that why she had recently been sending Miss Blum for the milk? Only the Blömers seemed unaffected, or at least to feel unaffected: as soon as the house was ready they wanted to give a big party. Blorr was no longer quiet and idyllic —but maybe it would be so again when she was gone, and maybe she would come back for a visit, for tea at the Helmsfelds' or for coffee at the Blums' or the Beeretzes'—and would find that Blorr was its old self again, and it was time once and for all to put aside the thought of suicide: there was Kit now, and the new baby, there was Hubert, and the desire to live somewhere—where?—without guards. To emigrate, and live somewhere unknown and unrecognized with Kit and the new baby, by the sea, abroad, with an allowance from Erwin and something extra from Father, and perhaps take up some work: translating or knitting, or both. She had always been told how good her French was, and as for knitting, she had really learned that, no one could have taught her better than Käthe, than Mama. Emigrate, knit, translate. Father would see to it that she received commissions, she must get away from Blorr, away from Germany.

Rohner emerged from between garages and front door and quietly, very politely, asked her to leave the terrace, to go into the house if she didn't mind, and to close the terrace door. She nodded and went in, closing the door; dusk was beginning to fall. The certainty that she must leave Blorr today was painful, and she started to cry, letting the tears fall, and drew the curtain. She had loved this village, and the house, which was a little too stylish for her, too open, with too much glass; the trees of Blorr, those old oaks, the beech trees and chestnuts, the walks with Kit, fetching milk and baking bread, the farmhouses—it had been at least some compensation for Eickelhof. Riding in the mornings; taking the horse out of the Hermannses' stable, saddling it, and off across the fields, through the woods.

Erwin had insisted on notifying the press of her pregnancy, now that she had to give up riding for a while and certainly wouldn't be able to train for the championship. Besides, someone would have had to ride with her, some police officer who was used to horses. That wouldn't have been any fun. In the past, too, she had sometimes decided at the last moment to go to a concert in the evening, especially when that young Russian was performing, the one who played Beethoven so magnificently—or to an exhibition, she had seen reproductions of a young painter who was having a show. But ever since she had had to "give advance notice," request security, so to speak, it wasn't fun anymore.

What would the locals think when it got out that she wasn't pregnant by Erwin at all, but by a police officer, the strictest, the youngest of the last-but-one group, by the man none of them cared for that much? He was so serious, and so solemn, "totally devoid of humor," Hermanns had said of him because he had forbidden Hermanns's son to play with old war material, not because it was dangerous but because it was illegal. The boy wandered through the woods, shrubs, and fields, looking for objects left over from World War II, and no one could say that wasn't dangerous either, seeing how many people—farmers and children—had been injured, some of them blown to bits, by old shells; she defended Hubert vehemently—perhaps too vehemently?—over this. Yes, Hubert was serious, as she was, he couldn't just take such things lightly. And Blorr, it was no longer pleasant, going for a walk under guard, fetching the milk under guard, going under guard to the chapel where she used to enjoy taking flowers to the Blessed Virgin, saying the *Ave Maria* under guard, chatting with the locals about God, the world, cattle, children, the weather, Church and state—under guard. The breakup of a neighborhood. Erna Breuer's dire fate, which was quite obviously a consequence of her being guarded; now she was cooped up with that Schubler in his one-and-a-half-room apartment, looking for work, not finding any, Schubler looking for work, not finding any. Breuer's divorce was under way, Breuer had finally gone bankrupt, the house next door was empty, up for sale, and now, because it was empty, under stepped-up surveillance, with even potential buyers being investigated; the disgruntled agent even hinted he might sue for damages, letting it be known that naturally the value of the house had dropped ever since Blorr had become a "police hangout." There was even talk of a citizens' group said to have been formed by those who had suffered loss or damage as a result of the security measures, and that the Klobers were supposed to have joined it; this organization was reputed to have spread to other areas, there being many people who had suffered in this way.

And she longed for Hubert, waited for Käthe, for Mama, who would take her to Tolmshoven, where Hubert was now on duty. She would find an opportunity for sure, would look for one, if necessary talk Käthe into giving a party for all the security personnel and their families: in the conference room downstairs where the Association held its sessions. That was an idea: to show one's gratitude to all these people and their families; one might hire a band, a puppet theater for the children, and then when she had had a chance to talk to Hubert, to meet Helga and Bernhard—then she would look for advice from someone she could trust more than that terrible Kohlschröder. It might be useful, but not helpful, to talk to her brother Rolf: Erwin had never forgiven him for calling his son Holger—"the first Holger, the one he had with Veronica, fair enough, that was seven years ago—but now the second boy, the one he's had with Katharina— to name *another* child Holger after what happened in November 'seventy-four—no, that part of your family is dead, as far as I am concerned, and anyway: setting fire to cars and throwing rocks!" Rolf would be objective, too objective, and although he would understand theoretically that her adultery was weighing on her, he would be too analytical in dealing with the fact that the adultery she had committed against Fischer did not weigh on her at all, while that against Helga weighed heavily. He knew all that, of course, but lacked empathy. Her brother Herbert would no doubt have been amusing but just as unhelpful, he would have laughed, been unreservedly delighted "because of the new life growing inside you, what a joy—a new life, sister!" and would have advised her simply to leave Fischer and to make a new start somewhere—where? where?—with spade and rucksack, so to speak.

Maybe the best thing would be to talk to Katharina. After all, they were almost the same age, close friends too, and had never quarreled—but it all seemed so remote to her when Katharina became political, applied her systems analysis, which sometimes did have a certain appeal, yet this situation wasn't amenable to any systems analysis—or was it? She happened to have remained a Catholic and a churchgoer, and even two hundred lecherous Kohlschröders would never deprive her of that. Hubert was too, and it was serious, not a game, not a "bourgeois escapade," and surely Katharina would understand that, being so dead against porn and promiscuity. Katharina would probably urge her to see a psychotherapist, and he would probably forbid her to use the word "adultery." And there was always the possibility that Erwin, if only to avoid the disgrace and the scandal—the disgrace being worse for him than any scandal—would acknowledge the child, have it come into the world as a Fischer, and suggest that they separate or get a divorce later. She would have no truck with that. She couldn't live another day with Fischer. This longing for Hubert—for his hands, his mouth, his voice, and the serious look in his eyes.

Talk to Father—no, she couldn't confess to him. He wasn't a prude, of course—he had had that affair with Edith, and people in the village still whispered about that business with the young countess, although that was almost fifty years ago. Father might even be "understanding," but he was shy, shy like herself. He had never liked Erwin, of course, and would be glad "we've got rid of him at last," he'd be nice, Father would, he'd suggest she move into the manor with Kit and the new baby; he would do things for Hubert, would be kind, and unable to help her—and then Erwin would fight for Kit, "with bare fists"—he was good at that, fighting with bare fists. It was bound to hurt him—although it would never hurt Father—that it wasn't one of his own crowd but a policeman. And of course he would want to remarry, he needed that for his image, needed it also for the Beehive: an attractive, outdoor type of woman who was also a good housewife—all of which she had been, more or less, and no doubt one of those tit-kittens would be glad to get him. It didn't need much imagination—and she had some, as the nuns had testified and in that respect agreed with Rolf—to picture all the things that would appear in the newspapers, maybe even in her father's paper. She'd be able to cope with that, she'd simply "duck," as Rolf had done. "You know, it's like an old septic tank exploding: the shit flies all over the place, and some of it hits you, but then there's always hot water."

She'd be able to duck, it would pass. But, go on living with Fischer, that she couldn't do, not for a single day. Greet him when he came home, a beaming, expectant father, have dinner with him; leave the door open when she was having her bath, he insisted on that, declaring it to be his conjugal right "because now you really have something to show when you're topless." She could hardly swallow her food, wept secretly when Kit was asleep, sometimes started crying in the middle of the morning, so that kind Miss Blum kept saying: "Why don't you talk to someone? Something's bothering you, and it's not the baby that's on the way and it's not just the security measures either, though they're enough to drive a person crazy." Talk to Miss Blum? To that old-fashioned, warmhearted, unmarried sister of Blum the farmer, who helped her in the house and kitchen, insisted on using soft soap rather than detergent, despised all that "modern cleaning stuff," considered liquid ammonia and vinegar sufficiently hygienic; to stout Miss Blum, who now sometimes also slept at the house; with her bun and her skirts that harked back to 1931, somewhere in her late fifties? Always surprising, shocking, almost obscene, when she lit a cigarette as she worked, her lips holding it at a jaunty angle as she inhaled deeply. "Smoking, Mrs. Fischer my dear, was something we learned in the war during the air raids or an artillery barrage, even here in Blorr—and I like it, I still like it, and in those days I often pinched a liter of milk or a kilo of potatoes from my brother to swap for cigarettes—I can't give it up." That woman who had lost her lover in the war and "was never attracted by anyone else and couldn't marry anyone else, I couldn't, even though I was expecting my Konrad's baby, and there were quite a few who wanted to marry me, when I was pregnant and the news of his death came: Dnepropetrovsk —I don't suppose I'll ever forget the name of that place, I'll take it with me into another life and ask them there what we, what my Konrad, had to do with it—and it was a miscarriage, poor little thing, I would have wanted to keep it, even without a husband."

Did she suspect something, Miss Blum, or did she even know something, when she kept saying "and it's not the baby that's on the way"—but it was the baby. Perhaps they hadn't been careful enough when Miss Blum had gone for the milk with Kit or simply for a walk through the village, escorted by Zurmack, not bothered by the machine pistol he was carrying behind them; perhaps she had noticed something, a look, a gesture, a fleeting touch in passing, maybe picked up something in the summer when she lay by the pool or when Hubert had swiftly—oh that haste, that unavoidable haste—embraced her in the hall, kissed her, or when she gave herself to him completely, "on the wing," as it were? Of course Miss Blum had known for a long time that there was nothing but friction and tension between her and Erwin. Did she know there were not only "other women" behind it, but also another man? Yes, she could have talked to Miss Blum, but when it came to advice or help she could expect as little from her as from Father. Miss Blum had bravely borne the disgrace of the illegitimate child, yet it hadn't been such a disgrace after all since everyone knew that Konrad had wanted to marry her on his next leave: hadn't she been accumulating ration cards for butter and eggs for the wedding cake, and hadn't she arranged with the butcher for an illegal slaughtering, and wouldn't she, when she got to heaven, utter her grievance before the Almighty: Dnepropetrovsk—what business had we being there?

She must get away when Käthe finally arrived, get away with Kit, today, before he came home; no more having to lock the guest-room door where she had been sleeping for many nights, no more having to endure that rattle at the door when he "demanded his rights"—and might not have demanded his rights if he had known she was not three months pregnant but six.

For in Tolmshoven she would be close to Hubert, able to speak to him, perhaps be kissed by him, and perhaps even—in spite of her pregnancy—"on the wing"—they were used to that, after all. Only once had he spent a few hours with her at night,

she had let him in when he was standing outside on the terrace—
the day Kit had fallen asleep at her grandparents' and stayed the
night there. Unable to sleep, she had first stood at the window,
looking through the curtains into the valley where the power
stations flickered on the horizon like circus façades, lighted up but
not shedding light, old Kortschede had once explained it to her:
they had to be lighted up for safety reasons, so that a leak could
be spotted immediately a valve failed, lighted up also for decorative reasons, the "magic of the technical landscape"; but they must
not shed light on anything, "so as not to show up the dirt, the
smoke, the foul air, being released secretly at night."

Through the trees, down in the dip, she could see them, the
circus façades—and her heart beat like—like what? Had it ever
beaten like that? For she knew that at ten o'clock he would relieve
Zurmack, and it was already ten-thirty, the summer sky still
faintly luminous to the west of the power-station lights. He
hadn't yet finished his round, and she didn't even feel like a
strumpet as she unlatched the terrace door, anxious that things
might go wrong since so far they had always done it "on the
wing"—and he did come, purposeful, it seemed to her, determined, a somewhat boyish determination, she found with a smile
—past the little water-lily pond, up the short bank (trampling a
few roses on the way, as it later turned out)—grasped the door
handle and was in the room. He didn't see her at first, the curtain
caught in the door, he pulled it loose, and "I didn't see you," he
said later, "I was dazzled, but I could smell you, oh yes, smell
you, maybe I should say, felt you standing there—waiting"; but
they hadn't said a word, wordlessly and with a naturalness that
alarmed her, he switched on the light, drew the curtains shut,
and looked at her, naked, something he had never been able to
see "on the wing," before switching off the light again and
getting into bed with her, his pistol on the bedside table. The
transceiver on the floor. Only later did they speak, when he had
resumed his post and she had made some coffee, he outside on
the terrace, she inside by the open window, the coffeepot, the

cups, and the transceiver on the windowsill: they had talked for a long time, until it began to get light, never using first names. He didn't mention love, all he said was that he had desired her from the first, from his first day of duty. Told her how he'd been fed up with school, had wanted to do something with his hands, worked in construction, at a conveyor belt "until, believe me, all the romance in that was shot," and had joined the police—yes, because he "loved order"; had been despised by his father, who claimed to be a member of the legal profession and spoke of his son as lowering himself socially. Almost pedantically and in great detail he explained his surname, Hendler, to her, stressing that it was spelled with an *e* rather than an *ä;* that was very important to him, though she wouldn't have cared if it had been an *ä.* He even offered an etymological explanation for his *e:* it probably came from the Bavarian word for young hen, and whether it had been derived from *Händler,* which means dealer, a man who had bought and sold something, or from the poultry keeper of a Bavarian count or bishop who as a result was called Hendler rather than Händler—she didn't find all that dull, really, it was so sweet to stand with him by the open window, drinking their coffee and watching the dawn come up—but she was uneasy about the serious way he lectured her on the etymology of names.

She told him about her childhood and girlhood at Eickelhof. It had been part of the newspaper inheritance, an old-fashioned villa from the 1880's, the kind that an owner of a printing plant and small provincial newspaper who was well off but not exactly rich would have been able to afford in those days. Her father, who had always been pretty hard up, had inherited the villa along with the printing plant and the newspaper—a magnificent house, those huge rooms downstairs, drawing room and dining room, that vast kitchen, even a cloakroom, all the rooms larger than any in the present manor house before they fixed up the conference room downstairs. A tennis court. Everything was a bit decayed, that soft-sweet decay which Käthe had tended so lovingly, the garden they were always arguing about, in fun—whether it shouldn't really be called a park. Fruit trees, meadows, none of those stupid lawns she hated. Outdoor parties, paper lanterns, the dance floor Father had installed for them outdoors, tears, and her agonizing love for that boy called Heinrich Beverloh—"Oh yes, that same Beverloh who's presumably responsible for your standing here and whom maybe we have to thank for standing here together and for having just slept together, for having done it so often on the wing; yes, he's the man who's responsible and whom we can thank for it"—his alarm when she said "thank for it"—and she described to him the boy with the dreamy eyes and the acute intelligence whose lack of `interest in sports and dancing they had all smiled at; well, they had taught him to dance—and how they had whirled around there, outdoors on summer evenings, indoors when it was raining. . . .

All this she told him that summer night, but not a word about Fischer, not a word about Helga, not a word about Kit, not one about Bernhard, nor did she tell him then that she was probably already pregnant by him, and the next day they had nearly gone crazy when he was on night duty again, but Kit was sleeping with her, and Fischer, back from his trip, was sleeping in the next room. She was sad yet relieved when he was transferred the following day to Tolmshoven. She also told him about Bleibl's third wife, Elisabeth, how she had made friends with her, but then she had soon gone off for good to Yugoslavia. "When any of that lot happen to be nice, they soon disappear. She has a hotel down there now and is always inviting me, but I can't very well go there with a swarm of security men." And she also told him about their villa near Málaga, where boredom piled up—she told him a lot, almost everything, more than she had ever told anyone before.

Of course she hadn't given herself to Hubert at once, at first sight; she had liked this young police officer right away, liked him more than the others, he was about her age too, maybe even a year or two younger. She didn't know how old Bernhard was, but nowadays they went to their First Communion very young, and perhaps Hubert was thirty after all, two years older than she. And it was with him that she had done what she would never have thought possible, that with a thousand oaths she would have sworn to be impossible: that she would go to bed with a man other than her husband—someone who would never, never, have asked: "Did you remember to take it?" There had been plenty of opportunities, approaches too, you might even call them propositions, at the Riding Club, the Tennis Club, at parties; and the occasional one, like young Zummerling, was really charming, nice, not too serious, a real tease: "Why so serious, Sabine dear— why always so serious?" No, just Hubert, and she hardly knew how it had happened, whether it had evolved somehow or simply come about, whether it had been avoidable or unavoidable, whether it had been her initiative or his—it had come about, and whether unavoidable or not, let the gods kindly decide that—he had stood there, walked about, for weeks, almost two months, in the daytime, at night, and one thing was certain: with either of his two colleagues, Zurmack and Lühler, it would have been absolutely unthinkable, although they were nice enough fellows too, knew every bush, every tree, every little bump in the ground, every nook and cranny in the house, garden, and neighborhood, had the exact plan in their heads, including the cloakroom, storeroom, ironing room, garages, and tool shed, driveway and kitchen terrace, where Miss Blum sat on fine days shelling peas or peeling potatoes, with Kit beside her, intensely interested in such labors; and of course the hobby room—Fischer had once taken up carpentry but hadn't set foot in the hobby room for a year—the sauna in the basement, the two bathrooms—they knew every nook and cranny in house, garden, and neighborhood, and none of them felt comfortable about all that glass in the picture windows.

Things had become more difficult when she was advised to stop sending Kit to kindergarten, and since she no longer enjoyed shopping. There was simply no way the kindergarten in Blückhoven could be protected with an absolute guarantee of safety.

Children were constantly being dropped off and picked up, food deliveries were made, there were a number of entrances and exits, bungalows scattered throughout the grounds, shrubberies, flower beds, playground equipment—it had been deliberately designed and constructed as an open area with no fences between school and swimming pool; cars were constantly driving up, and it was impossible to search them all, and since the affair of Pliefger's birthday cake the food containers had to be examined too. In the end there was even a minor mutiny among the parents, who felt that *their* children were not threatened (which was not true: "Any child," Hubert had said, "can be kidnapped, including my own"), and that this constant surveillance was causing mental distress leading to psychic damage, and that anyway it was futile, for if they were going to strike at all it would be somewhere quite different.

So she had to keep Kit at home, couldn't take her over to the Groebels' either, where she had always loved playing for hours with Rudi and Monika. The Groebels had made it pretty clear that they regarded it as harmful: always having one or more policemen around. So she had to keep Kit at home, spend time with her, playing, coloring, telling stories, or letting her putter about in the kitchen with Miss Blum. It was easiest in summer, around the pool, with sandbox, swing, slide, and more recently— that had been her own idea, based on a memory of Eickelhof, where Käthe had had something similar installed for them—more recently a mudhole, with clay, sand, and water, where she could spend her time wallowing and building in the mud, where she could get as dirty as she liked, naked when the weather was warm, in briefs when it was cooler, and she had only to be popped into the bathtub or hosed down. And then she had been—again not exactly forbidden but strongly urged not to go to the market in Blückhoven, and she had always enjoyed that so much, and Kit too. With stroller, basket, and head scarf, preferably in the densest crowd, close to people, she enjoyed their contact, even their smell, loved all that milling around, enjoyed milling around with them, hadn't been afraid either—but the graphically described kidnapping threat to Kit had turned her against visiting the market. There were too many half-hidden alleys and gaps between booths and stalls, so many illegally parked vans and trucks delivering mattresses, eggs, chickens, vegetables. A small child like that could be snatched up and gone in a twinkling, before anyone noticed, and the booths and stalls and cars and alleyways and gaps really couldn't be checked and watched, not even as a precaution. So it made more sense to have everything delivered and to leave Kit in the bungalow when she really did have to go into town. But naturally all deliveries had to be examined: every loaf of bread, every head of lettuce, and of course the more intimate items she was forced to order from the drugstore or pharmacy. Well, she happened to be old-fashioned about such things too, and always blushed when the deliveries from the drugstore were examined. This gave rise to tension, friction, intimate knowledge that should never have been allowed to turn into familiarities and yet did. It was difficult to behave all the time as if such things were normal, and always to have two, sometimes three men, but invariably at least one man around the house. One had to be careful when walking half dressed across the corridor or through the hall, into the bathroom, out of the bathroom, into the toilet—and none of them would accept anything while on duty, very occasionally a cup of coffee, and when they went off duty they left in a hurry, in an almost indecent hurry, as if they were leaving a place with a curse on it. And she would have dearly liked to talk to them informally about their wives and children and careers and homes, but there was never anything more than an occasional smile, a proffered cigarette. She wanted so much to know how they lived, what they thought about, whether they felt bored or frustrated, whether their nerves were equal to all this.

Erwin's bonhomie toward these men sometimes came close to

a patronizing heartiness, with something of the manner of an officer of the reserves; he would prattle to them about football, beer, and women who were supposed to have been "laid"— underestimating their sensitivity, not only Hubert's but also Zurmack's and Lühler's, for whose sakes he memorized the football results every Monday—something that didn't interest Zurmack and Lühler at all but, oddly enough, did interest Hubert, although probably not in that form: contrivedly proletarian, in stadium jargon, linking details of football prowess with hints about potency. Erwin would listen to nobody, knew everything better, would blabber away at her in a loud voice, as if at an office party, and in their presence, about "the fuzz," and they disliked that more than anything, that word, they heard it often enough, it was the source of deep resentment, and even when he said it as a joke, as if in quotation marks ("And how's our dear old 'fuzz' today?"), they resented it, even in quotation marks. They were very cool when he offered them cigarettes, and positively winced when he grabbed them by the sleeve or, worse still, slapped them on the back.

It really was difficult to become so intimately acquainted yet avoid familiarity, and what Erwin hinted at she didn't find "dirty" at all, but quite natural: that when lying beside the pool she might arouse their "dirty imaginings." "And even if you were to lie there naked, it would be none of their business, it's up to them to stay neutral." Hubert had confessed that he had desired her from the very first day, that she had aroused him—he spoke not of love but of desire, and the men walked and stood and hung around there as idle as herself, and then came the months, the long months, when the master of the house didn't appear at all, neither at noon nor in the evening, warm evenings, nights when nothing happened, boredom, deathly silence, so that even Zurmack, that nice respectable man who was actually close to forty and certainly settled in his ways, said to her one day: "Why don't you go to a party sometime, see some different people? We'll look after your little girl all right." So she risked going at least to buy shoes at Zwirner's and to look for dresses at Hold-kamp's and Breslitzer's. She left Kit with Zurmack and Miss Blum and drove into town with Lühler; at Breslitzer's he stood around looking like a store detective; and when she went into the cubicle to change or undress, that elegant salon with its frills and velvets and doodads in every shade of pink seemed to exude an atmosphere of sultry eroticism, an odor of physical intimacy, that she brought with her out of the cubicle. There seemed to be —well, something of the air she imagined to prevail in upper-class brothels, something lascivious, inviting, a kind of promise that was not kept—and on the drive home she had been on the point of placing a consoling hand on the arm of that poor Lühler, whom she knew to be a bachelor and lively enough, but she realized just in time that that could be fatal. For the first time she understood what her neighbor, the uninhibited, vulgar Erna Breuer, meant when she would say she wasn't interested in either love or desire, that there were times when she simply wanted to be fucked, and that there were times when men also wanted just that, no more and no less, and Lühler must have also noticed how expensive the two dresses were, almost two thousand eight hundred for the two, and that must seem pretty expensive to him.

And then this spring she had yielded to Hubert, at noon, while Miss Blum was busy in the kitchen and Kit was whooping gleefully in the mudhole because she had finally succeeded in getting the better of Hubert after constantly challenging him on this warm morning, for perhaps the hundredth time, to come closer to the mudhole. He finally did, was pelted with mud, then slipped and fell, and had to go into the house to clean up. Later, long after she had become pregnant by him, even now, she wondered why she had gone into the house with him, since he knew perfectly well where the bathrooms were and would have found the towels without her help. But she had gone with him, led him into the bathroom, even held the door open for him, had brought him towels and washcloths from the shelf, and that was when they came together. She must have brushed his cheek with her bare arm. She hadn't intended to, had never thought of it, yet didn't resist even for a second when he put his arms around her, pushed aside the top part of her bikini, pulled away the lower— and while he was doing this with such apparent expertise she knew he wasn't an expert at all. He entered into her with a sigh, she into him, joyfully she yielded to him, and felt, while he kissed her, that she knew him by heart: his smell, his shaved cheeks, his teeth, his serious, light eyes, his hairline, and not only did she allow it to happen, she nodded her consent, although he held her mouth with his, let it happen "on the wing," and with her left foot closed the door that was still open a crack—Miss Blum on the terrace, where she was cleaning the lettuce, Kit in the garden in the mudhole, this noon hour of a sunny day in May, fifteen minutes before lunch, and she was amazed at how slight her fear was, how great her joy, at the matter-of-fact way she put her bikini back to rights, looked at herself in the hall mirror, adjusting the slight disarray, while in the bathroom he now really did start to clean himself up, to wash the mud off his jacket and pants. Later he let the wet part of his clothes dry outside in the sun, wagged his finger at Kit, retreated to the garage, didn't speak a word to her that day, seldom spoke openly to her, even later on, would sometimes stand behind her garden chair or in the shrubbery at the pool, whispering "Mrs. Fischer, oh, Mrs. Fischer." They always addressed each other formally, although now they came together often, more and more often.

They realized it wasn't a lapse, a one-time indiscretion that had arisen from the situation, simply happened and been forgotten. . . . It lay deep, sank ever deeper, now never to be dislodged, was anchored in countless details that she would formerly have called shameless. The boldness with which they continued to give themselves to each other, in the cloakroom among the hanging coats where he could pretend if necessary to be coming from the toilet and she could hide behind the coats for the two or three seconds that might be needed to save the situation. In the garden, when he came by and stopped as if by chance beside her, he would tell her about his police training, she would tell him about Eickelhof, which had been bulldozed out of existence, tell him more about it than she had ever been able or allowed to tell anyone. Her brothers were fed up with the subject, and Erwin was too, said it was "downright sentimental to grieve over slaughtered cows." Father wouldn't listen at all and, rare for him, would even show annoyance, probably it weighed on his conscience; and Käthe said nothing, it must have been more painful for her than for any of them to give up Eickelhof and Iffenhoven, where she had been born and brought up, to see everything leveled and buried. Gigantic dredges were on the march, mechanical shovels amiably-pitilessly-innocently-inexorably devoured the forest, swallowing the earth, spitting it out again at a great distance, exhumed the dead (reverently, ever so reverently), tearing down churches and villages and castles, and Käthe got "the shudders" when she drove through Neu-Iffenhoven with its new houses and churches.

To shudder was good. To shudder when she thought of Kit, now standing so rosy, so adorable, in the Beeretz dairy, when she thought of how naturally she had given herself to Hubert, had looked for an opportunity in nooks and crannies, in bathroom and cloakroom; to shudder when she thought of Helga, and the strange fact that she felt like an adulteress not toward Fischer or Hubert but only toward Helga; when she thought of how coolly she emerged from a nook, from a cranny, from the bathroom, while Miss Blum was in the house and Kit in her room, how she smiled as she put on her lipstick, tidied her hair, as if nothing had happened; to shudder when she remembered how rapidly—with birdlike swiftness—she had inspected Hubert to make sure there were no telltale traces—and when she wondered where it all came from, how one simply knew such things, that cool way of dismissing something as if nothing had happened, something that was still and always would be called adultery. How did she know that? No one had told her any of this, she had no experience, she, "our dear, good, faithful, reliable Bee—our darling, our treasure," from where had she suddenly drawn this knowledge, displayed the very first time when she came from the bathroom and Miss Blum was cleaning the lettuce on the terrace? God knew this wasn't an everyday occurrence, not for her, yet she had nodded to Miss Blum with a smile and gone into the garden where Kit was innocently playing.

Perhaps Helga would be sympathetic, would let her have him occasionally . . . she would be allowed to love him sometimes, be able to show him the child when she was stuck down there in Italy or Spain. He was a man who pursued his career with such seriousness, such intensity, even love. "Safety and order for all." Maybe a bit too pedantic, and might perhaps have been able to prevent the disaster that struck Erna and Peter, it was strange, she wanted him, wanted to be with him, to sleep with him and yet—live with him?—that probably wouldn't work, just as it didn't seem to be working with Erna and Peter. At first those two had wanted only to sleep together, yet they had become so fond of each other, so terribly fond, Peter more so of Erna than Erna of him—she had quite openly admitted that originally she had just wanted to be fucked by him; yes, that's how she had expressed it, in her vulgar, forthright way. Now he couldn't do without her, or she without him, they didn't care about the scandal or Breuer's rage, weren't bothered by the questionings and interrogations; he wanted his Erna, to have and to hold, maybe even to marry, he was forever pining for her—but for her, for Erna, it was all too shabby, too cheap, in that tiny apartment, whereas Breuer's bungalow and Peter for a lover, that could have gone on forever if it hadn't been for that damn surveillance. And Erna openly swore into the phone, had forgotten about first names, no longer said "My dear Bee," said in a hard, mean voice: "Now listen to me, Mrs. Fischer . . ." and she listened, while her thoughts were elsewhere—she was sick of it all, fed up with Erna, Erwin, Peter, Kübler, Rohner, the Klobers, and always when the sun was shining that topless nymphet up there on the terrace with her raucous music. . . .

Yet she did miss Erna Breuer. She had been such a nice woman, so frank, so spontaneous, even though she spoke too freely about her married life, said quite openly how much she liked doing it, doing it with men. "You know what I mean . . ." And later: "And I let myself get all hot and worked up by that porn stuff my old man brought home, and he wanted me hot, but then he couldn't put out the fire—and so I took the boy who always gave me such burning, yearning looks—well, it turned into love, real love, I forgot all about that porn stuff when I was with that boy—how could I have had any idea? Those damn cops had to mess it all up for me, it could've gone on like that for years, but they had to come snooping around, all because of you, you people, your lousy millions—what's that got to do with me? And if I happen to let Peter into my bed in the morning—what's that got to do with you? Not a thing. And now the fuss with Breuer about the couches and the suitcases, all the knickknacks and the chesterfield set in the living room, he won't even let me have the color TV—don't cry now, don't cry, I wouldn't wish it on you, Bee dear—no, I wouldn't—and anyway it could never happen to you, you're just not the type. . . ."

And it had happened to her, exactly as it had to Erna, and no doubt she had given herself to her Peter just as "quickly and joyously" as she had to her Hubert.

Someday—when?—she would tell him more about Eickelhof, about her years there, and about the time at boarding school with the nuns, maybe also more about *that* Beverloh, who in those days, eleven or twelve years ago now, had been one of those young people "of whom one had had such high hopes," courted by political parties, associations, corporations, showered with bursaries, and they had all thought he would study German literature, or perhaps theater, at any rate amount to something on the cultural scene where he would speak for "our" (whose?) standards. He was considered a conservative (if only someone had ever explained to her what that meant), a reactionary even (if only she had ever been told what *that* meant), looked upon as a Catholic, and devout at that—as she still was, still regarded herself, despite Kohlschröder and Hubert—without knowing exactly what that meant either. But in the end Beverloh had studied banking, here, then in America, together with Rolf, even wrote his thesis on something South American, came back, could dance better than ever—with something cynical, almost mean, about his mouth, was no longer satisfied with just kissing her, wanted more, and she didn't like him anymore, and now, with a dreamy look again, he said, "That's how you get, mean and cynical—or unbelievably stupid, when you've been absorbed for years in nothing but money—and I didn't want to become stupid —in money, working money, in the money you happen to have in your pocket." Then she saw him once more at Rolf and Veronica's wedding, where he made a witty speech, even mentioning the paper without hurting Father; yes, Father, they all liked him, and Käthe, and it wasn't all that long ago. If there was any truth to all the rumors and reports, it was he, Heinrich Beverloh, who was responsible for all this—the protection and surveillance, Erna Breuer's raw deal, the breakup of the neighborhood, the Klobers' rage, the neighbors' coldness, the affair of Pliefger's birthday cake—and the child she was now expecting from Hubert.

Beverloh had now become as unreal as the Eickelhof house, over which the dredges had passed so quickly. "Leveling and digging— that's the answer!" had been Bleibl's motto, and in the end the old Eickelhof place had fetched almost enough for Father to pay for the manor. Rolf had taken into account all the good times and bad times since 1880 and had a computer print out the profit margin—it must have been several tens of thousand percent—in any case, as they all agreed, "a fantastic amount for such a dilapidated old place." And after all it wasn't only the enormous profit, it was also the example Father had to set when, after much palaver and many protests, all of Iffenhoven was leveled and buried.

Sometimes when she drove past there and stopped on the road between Hetzigrath and Hurbelheim to look down into that vast pit, she tried to pinpoint the spot where Eickelhof and Iffenhoven had once stood. For a while the archaeologists had been allowed to have their fun, with Roman and Frankish pottery, shards, burial objects, and, if it was true, even some pre-Frankish, perhaps Celtic—you could see at the museum how much fun the archaeologists had had: the very stuff of dissertations and theses . . . pitchers and bones, stones and shards, shards upon shards, and there was an entire cabinet labeled: "Found at Iffenhoven," and a smaller one that said: "Found on the Eickelhof property, now a brown-coal area."

Of course Father hadn't been able to say no, and of course the Board had urged him: "If you refuse, Mr. Tolm, if you refuse, Fritz, what can we expect from the ordinary folk in the way of understanding economic and energy needs?" And they tore down and tore up, leveled and dug, church and vicarage, village and cemetery, the neglected-looking castle of the counts of Hetzigrath, tore down trees, tore out trees, chestnuts and oaks, hedges and fences, not a shred was left, of course not, for they had to get at the coal. Driven from Iffenhoven and Eickelhof, driven from Blorr, and soon, Erwin occasionally hinted to her, soon it would be Tolmshoven's turn too.

Was it really only eight years since they had been dancing at Rolf and Veronica's wedding, she once again with Beverloh, who began to make a nuisance of himself? No, she had ceased to be in love with him, she had already been afraid of him when, a bit later, after his nice toast to Father, he had been much less nice when discussing the subject of freedom with Father. They had both been a bit drunk, Father weak-willed as ever, Beverloh incisive as he took the imminent vacating of Eickelhof as an example of how little freedom even the freest of the free had in a free economy: for couldn't he see he was breaking his wife's—Käthe's—heart, that his children felt they were being driven out, didn't he love the old place himself? And the money, he certainly didn't need that, did he, with the paper growing and growing? Freedom, force, necessity—what were they but a somewhat more palatable form of expropriation? Only seven years since Father had moved into the manor house with Käthe, after remodeling and modernizing—and that, too, would soon be leveled and buried, and once again the price would be seven to thirty times as high. "Your old man pretends to know nothing about economics, yet he's the smartest of the lot—for him everything pays off, many times over."

It also paid off, of course, when Erwin flew about all over the world, closing deals, installing machinery, setting up production chains, having his fun with the unions—"They play along quite nicely"—increasingly adopted the airs of a playboy although, when he tried to make love to her, he had such a hard time of it— oh well, perhaps it really was her fault, now that her thoughts were only of Hubert, only of him since the night he had spent with her, since those wonderful wordless hours they had spent together when he wanted to see her, she him, since they had shared the coffee across the windowsill in the early dawn, in the distance the circus façade of the power stations that were burning up Iffenhoven and Eickelhof. Naturally, it would never have occurred to Hubert to ask: "Did you remember to take it?" And obviously he hadn't thought even for a second of taking any steps to "get rid of it," didn't dream of suggesting something she would never, ever have done: when she told him she was pregnant his joy equaled the shock. He indicated that, although Helga would no doubt be sad, she would certainly be happy about one thing: the child. In all its seriousness, it hit him right in his own seriousness, during the very days when Erwin, ebullient as never before, returned from—how would she know?—probably from Singapore, with flowers and jewelry and all kinds of exotic gifts for her and Kit and Miss Blum, the very essence of that beaming boyishness that had once so attracted her. He actually carried her in his arms through the cloakroom—where all the coats were hanging among which she had sometimes hidden with Hubert—carried her

across the hall, across the corridor, into the living room and later
onto the bed, and she gave herself to him without surrendering,
and he actually did whisper: "I love you, do you realize that?
And I think our little Kit's been alone long enough, what I mean
is: stop taking it for a while!" Then he had to go on and make
one of his jokes, he couldn't resist saying: "All clear for the
weekend—no speed limits! . . ."

It was already two months then since Kit had ceased to be alone,
and those eternal jokes, those carefully calculated, would-be
impromptu remarks when she performed her duty toward him;
and those parties at his parents', who in some ways were more
vulgar than Erna Breuer could ever have been. The quarrel
between Erna and herself pained her, a quarrel for which neither
was to blame, only those wretched circumstances for which—if
she was to believe Rolf and Father as well as Katharina—Heinrich
Beverloh was to blame, also her former sister-in-law, Veronica
Tolm, née Zelger, a doctor's daughter from Hetzigrath. . . .
Veronica had phoned her twice, the first time the shock had
made her drop the receiver—there it was, that familiar high,
clear voice, that "angel's soprano" as the nuns used to call it, that
had so enriched the choir and sung so many solos from the organ
loft: oh, Veronica's *Kyrie*, Veronica's *Agnus Dei*—those hours
of bliss when there were still special May services, and Veronica
would sing songs to the Blessed Virgin from the organ loft—
wasn't it really Veronica's voice that had made of her such an
ardent worshipper of the Madonna?—and she still was and always
would be, and she must stop by the chapel in Blorr, with some
flowers, say an *Ave*, light candles, and she would probably weep
for herself, for Hubert, for the child in her womb, for Helga and
Bernhard and Kit, and for Veronica, who simply phoned—from
where fromwherefromwhere?—and asked: "How're things? . . ."
and laughed when she picked up the receiver, gasped into the
phone, and replied to the second "How're things, Bee dear?":

"Under constant surveillance, as you must know, and you also know that it's almost like being in prison." And Veronica: "You can't blame me for *that*." And she had asked: "And Heinrich?" "He's figuring, figuring, figuring—tell Rolf that Holger's fine"— and she was gone. Many months later she phoned again, saying only: "Oh my dear, dear Bee—I'm so sorry about all this, so sad —and do you sometimes think of our little nuns—would you like me to sing something?" and she sang "Mary, Queen of May"— and was gone. . . .

She hadn't been able to keep this from Hubert, but he only laughed and nodded: "We know all about that, at least my boss does—you needn't be afraid, everything is monitored, and maybe one day they'll be able to trace the call and we'll nab her, that would be the best thing for her. As you can imagine, all your calls are monitored too—so don't ever phone, Sabine dear, ever, and don't ever write. And of course I can't ever call you, ever write to you . . . ever, and my relief is due any day. . . ."

It was nearly dark after all when Miss Blum returned with Kit from the Beeretzes; she didn't take the so-called security measures that seriously—always said she didn't believe in security anyway. "Least of all from *those* people, they come when they feel like it, out of a clear blue sky in the middle of the night." Kit was proud: for the first time she had carried the four kilos of milk all the way home and had only had to set it down three times, she had been given walnuts and chestnuts that she wanted to roast right away, in the garden over an open fire, "as soon as Papa gets home," and with a pang she realized for the first time that Kit was indeed deeply attached to her father—that she would suffer too, very badly perhaps, and she said: "We'll be leaving soon with Grandma Käthe, and you can roast the chestnuts at Grandpa's in the fireplace—he'll like that."

"Are we staying the night?"

"Yes."

"Then I'll leave some here for Papa, some walnuts and chest-nuts—and what about the milk?"

"We'll put that in the refrigerator, it won't spoil."

"Must I pack my things?"

"Only your dolls, I'll take along some underwear."

"By the way," said Miss Blum after Kit had left, "you needn't be afraid that the neighbors' feelings toward you have changed. After all, who does like having the police in the village for months on end? But they're not blaming you for that, they're blaming those others. . . . I suppose you'll be staying for more than one night, won't you?"

"Yes—what makes you think so . . . what do you know, Maria? Tell me."

"I know nothing, Mrs. Fischer, I don't actually know anything—but I can see, I can feel, that there's more weighing on your mind than the baby you're expecting—something serious . . . would you like tea or coffee now?"

"My mother should be here any moment, there won't be time for tea or coffee—what do you think, should I stay here?"

"No, you'd best go, I think . . . yes. I never had anyone I could go to when I had it up to here with my family—I could only go to my sister in town, but I could never stay for long, just for an afternoon—the apartment's so cramped—when they all come home from work, the children and her husband—I didn't feel like going to the convent, though they might have taken me in—in spite of the baby. . . . Be glad you have somewhere to go to—and go. . . ."

"Would you go with me, if—? Don't cry, Maria, don't cry—I'll be back."

"You won't come back—maybe to Blorr, to visit us, but never again to this house—I'd go with you if—and one thing I do know, and I must tell you, I owe you that, you've always been so good to me: the child is not your husband's, and you can't go to the one whose child it is. . . ."

"Do you know who it is?"

"No."

"Don't you really?"

"No, I swear—but I can count, and five months ago"—and here she laughed a little—"how you could have, I mean, managed it with all this surveillance, without anybody noticing—it's amazing, and I feel scared too—no one would have believed it of you. . . ."

"Scared of me?"

"No—just scared, scared at how artful people can be—there comes your mother now—and don't forget me if you need me, I need you too—sure you won't have some tea?"

"No, thanks, I'd like to be gone when my husband gets home."

From the front door she saw the driver—it wasn't Blurtmehl—get out, hold the door open for Käthe, and then stand beside Kübler—it wasn't Hubert either, which it might have been, it was a stranger, a new man, who looked more like Association than police. Käthe—it was always a pleasure to see her—she must be close to sixty and looked better all the time. She had a manner, hard to define, of always seeming calm while actually being quite tense, and she wasn't always lucky with her hairdressers; this time it had turned out well: the gray, white-streaked chignon suited her, and this time, too, she was obviously upset. She had brought along a little bag of some of her cookies, probably expected some tea, kissed Kit, then her, and said, almost cried out: "Have you heard?"

"What? No."

"They've made him president, Fritz, your father—they actually voted him in, I just heard it on the car radio—so I must hurry home, I can't leave him alone. This is the end for us, we won't have a minute's peace, not a single minute—alone, I mean. Bleibl's had his way after all."

"Oh my God, no one could've expected that—and Father's an old man, and not well."

"But he's just the man for it, you know what I mean—white-haired, kindly, cultured, after Pliefger wouldn't go on—he has such a pleasant manner—and his interview voice, much better than before, I just heard him on the radio. Of course he's pretending to feel honored. Confidence and all that, responsibility and all that—and you, child, we had no idea you were pregnant, and already in your sixth month!"

"Has Grebnitzer been talking?"

"No, Bleibl told us, of all people—he read it in some sports supplement—Grebnitzer then merely told us the month—is that so bad? Why weren't we supposed to know? Don't you want the baby?"

"Oh I do, I do . . ." Crazy to say such a thing about a baby.

"Then what is it, something to do with Erwin?"

A nod—with the front door open, in the hall, a mere nod that said much and nothing, too much and nothing. How could she explain to Käthe how dreadful she always felt after performing her duty, after, not even so much during or before, but after, when he couldn't keep his mouth shut, couldn't lie still and be silent for even a minute—and before, those expert caresses he had learned by heart, of which none, not one, was genuine, that "man of the world" pretense, that "experienced lover" pretense, whereas Hubert—involuntarily her thoughts went to Hubert, and it made her ill, yes, that might be wicked and for all she cared it was—whereas Hubert, when he stroked her eyebrows or pushed her hair back from her forehead or shyly touched the tip of her nose, whereas Hubert was always so nice beforehand, so quiet, so tender, and afterward so serious, so calm—and with Erwin those wretched, miserable jokes, all of which, all, he dreamed up from traffic reports on the radio with hardly even a semblance of variety: "There we've gone again, failing to give right-of-way—ha-ha-ha!"

"This time we really took the curve at seventy"—could she ever explain to Käthe, could she have explained to anyone, say a divorce-court judge, what these stereotype jokes did to her after making the supreme effort of performing that strange duty? He was obviously so fond of those jokes that they had now become a necessity to him. Joke before: "Got off for the weekend—no speed limit, no traffic jams!" Joke after: "Through construction area—traffic jam avoided—ha-ha-ha!"

"Problems with Erwin?" Käthe asked. "And in your sixth month? Isn't that normal, child—I mean, serious enough, but not final, surely?"

"Oh, Mama, I can't go on living with him, I can't stand him anymore. . . . I'm driving back with you right now to Tolmshoven, with Kit of course and"—she gave a bitter laugh—"with my knitting."

"What nonsense—can't go on living with him, can't stand him—that's not unusual with pregnant women—so they go off to their mother for a few weeks!"

"That's exactly what I intend to do, just wait till Kit brings her dolls."

"You mean, no cup of tea, no little chat with your mama?"

"No, no tea, and we can chat on the way, and at home. And, Mama—haven't you learned to count yet—if I'm in my sixth month, when did I—well, let's come right out with it—when did I conceive?"

"Five months ago, I would think."

She looked confused, this dear, elderly lady, who had grown prettier, more dignified with age, and was the only one among all the "boardroom biddies," as Erwin called them—and in this, oddly enough, he agreed with Rolf—the only one who had real style, who had taste and dignity, though not always with regard to her hair, as a girl she must have dreamed of having little curls and would sometimes have her hair done that way. But otherwise, in her dress, gestures, speech, and movements, she had style —yet she was only the daughter of a bankrupt nursery gardener from Iffenhoven who had ruined himself with experiments in tulips and roses because he was no good at figures—and figures were something his daughter Käthe had never mastered either, although she sorely needed to. And she had no idea how to count in this particular category, had never understood why people laughed when a baby arrived five or six months after the wedding, had never understood that they—well, that's to say, before the wedding—although she herself, if Rolf wasn't one of those famous seven-month babies, had obviously, that's to say, before the wedding—and bless her, surely she must know that nine months are nine months, and five are five, and that, if she was now in her sixth, she couldn't possibly be pregnant by Erwin—as Miss Blum had known, of course—yet during the summer Käthe herself had often joked about Erwin being away so frequently and so long.

"No, I've got to leave today, right now, and you can lend me some needles and wool—and don't you remember where Erwin was five months ago?"

Perhaps that was too harsh, too direct, for Käthe—her jaw fell, she turned pale, dropped the bag of cookies—on the very spot where for the last time, when saying goodbye, she had given herself to him, between the cloakroom mirror and the door to the toilet, where the revolting advertisement for the Beehive—the Fischer family business—hung on the wall, showing a naked woman entering the opening of a beehive and emerging fully dressed from the other side. "Beehive Outfits Eve!" and now, facing her mother, it struck her that there was a psychological error in this poster: who would want to enter a beehive, where normally one wouldn't be outfitted but stung? And now Käthe understood, color came back into her face, she took off her glasses, picked up the bag of cookies, and said: "Oh no, child, not you—not you . . ." and fortunately didn't ask the obvious question: "Who was it?"

"Oh yes," she said calmly, "me. Maybe I'll explain it to you sometime—but now let's get going, Mama dear, Kit's brought her dolls . . ." and she longed to throw some of Erna Breuer's words at that innocent, shocked-Mama face; she preferred them to Erwin's sayings or the Fischers' vocabulary, and she knew:

something else urged her on—Hubert was in Tolmshoven, and she simply must talk to him, and of course she would never reveal his name, if only for Helga's and Bernhard's sakes—never!

And also—why not think of that too, it occurred to her—for the sake of his career. He probably wouldn't actually be fired, but he'd be likely to run into trouble if it got out—she supposed they didn't like such things happening while the men were on duty.

"All right then," said Käthe, "let's leave, let's go, I'd also like to get back to Tolm as quickly as possible, he'll be dog-tired, need comforting—and now I suppose we enter inevitably upon Phase One," whispering suddenly: "Has she ever phoned again?"

"No."

"But she phoned me. Got me at Kohlschröder's, and d'you know what she said: 'Don't ever have tea at the Bleibls'.' That's all she said, and when I said to her: 'Come back, child, come back,' she answered: 'I can't, I can't, I wish I could'—and hung up."

Kit was consoled with cookies, with the prospect of walks with Grandfather, of roasting chestnuts over an open fire. Miss Blum actually wept—not sadly, just wept, so that Käthe gave her a searching look, and Miss Blum asked: "What'll I do with the milk?"

"Ask my husband whether he'd like some milk or milk puddings, otherwise take it to Mr. Hermsfeld's or put it out for the cats in the empty Breuer house. Don't cry."

She asked the driver to stop for a moment at the chapel, went in, wiped her eyes, was now calm, almost composed; she would leave Hubert out of it altogether, if he agreed. That would be better for Helga, for Bernhard, for his approaching First Communion; there were enough flowers for the Madonna; the Beeretzes, Miss Blum, and the Hermanns women would look after that, during Rosary month, sometimes they even held a Rosary service without a priest and she had sometimes gone too.

"Fine," she said as she got in the car again. "It'll be lovely with Grandfather. You can feed the ducks again."

And although the driver could listen, a stranger whom she didn't know, Käthe said: "You, child, you of all people!" She shook her head and whispered: "Before marriage, oh well—when you're fond of each other and intend to marry—but while married, with another man!"

III

Blurtmehl had everything ready, had adjusted the temperature of the water and stirred in the bath oil, helped him to undress, in particular to untie his shoelaces; stooping down made him feel panicky, and Grebnitzer had advised him to avoid stooping. Jacket, trousers, underwear, he could still manage all that himself, wouldn't accept any help, only his socks and shoes, Blurtmehl was needed there again, had to help him into the bathtub too, half lifting him as he murmured: "Lost weight, I see, a little lighter again, I don't have to weigh you, I can feel it—six, maybe seven hundred grams." And needless to say, the instant his feet and bottom touched the water he felt the urge to urinate (always those vain attempts to deal with that in advance!) and, wrapped in a bath towel, he had to use the adjoining toilet while Blurtmehl checked the temperature of the water with his left hand, let in a little more hot water, and added another dash of bath oil.

He had had the bathtub positioned in such a way and the window set low enough so that he could at least see the treetops, the sky, which was never completely blue. Today the wind seemed to be blowing from the southwest. The emissions from the power stations, already turned to clouds, moved across the sky, the effect was idyllic, as evocative of nature as in some Dutch paintings, or early Gainsboroughs and Constables—yet twelve kilometers to the west they had still been massive pillars of smoke,

harmless—as Kortschede had sworn to him by all that was holy—
and consisting only of steam, which happened to form clouds,
make weather. Only when the wind blew from the north or
northwest—which it very seldom did—was the sky clear, cloud-
less, it was always gray; only on very rare days—he never counted
them though he had often intended to—blue.

Blurtmehl sat on the stool beside the bathtub, knowing that
he couldn't bear anything or anybody behind him, knowing also
that that sense of panic had its origins in the war, in a few very
sudden retreats that might have been called flight. To be shot at
from behind was worse than being shot at from the front. But
perhaps—this was Blurtmehl's intelligent theory—it was also a
Sparta complex that had been instilled into him at school and
could never be eradicated, a fear of disgrace. If he was right, it
must lie very deep, not quite so deep as the milk soup, confession,
the "alone or with others"; he had never felt disgrace, always felt
fear. They did get him once, and it had been his salvation, taking
him to Dresden, to a military hospital, that was where he had
found Käthe; besides, the wound had been ideal, made to order
so to speak, and right on time; not dangerous, not very painful,
yet not so insignificant that one got stuck in some field hospital.
In Dresden he had merely been afraid that someone might find out
that he, the battery commander, had issued a standing order:
"When they come, as soon as you see them: beat it, scram!" At
least he had stayed, like a captain on his ship, till the last moment
and had taken along only his cigarettes, pistol, and map, staggered
by that overwhelming superiority of tanks and infantry—far
from being "ragged Russians" they were all in clean uniforms.
Apparently no one had denounced him, not even his Lieutenant
Plohn, who always spoke of final victory but obviously no longer
believed in it. Dresden, Käthe.

Today again at breakfast, on the final day of the conference,
before going downstairs "into the labyrinth," as Käthe called it,
"to face the Minotaur"—today he was again struck by the re-
semblance between Käthe's eyes and Rolf's. Hers were a little

lighter, the merest shade lighter, but they also had that quality of poetic sorrow, barely disguised by an optimism masking despair. At the time she had advised him to sell the paper immediately, to keep Eickelhof, and to become a museum director, a minister of culture, or at least the head of a cultural section—he might have had that chance: the British had found him acceptable, and he would have found some political party; his erroneous and harrowing internment had even enhanced his credit, and he really had never been a Nazi—was that mere chance? He wasn't quite clear about that: of course he had found them totally revolting, beyond discussion, and for years, under the countess's patronage, he had managed to make a living as a private tutor and curator, in mansions and archives, cataloguing private art collections and occasionally publishing something in a journal, until the war came and he landed in the artillery.

Fear was already known to him in the years before that, on his occasional sorties from libraries and archives, from improvised schoolrooms, in search of a girl perhaps, or a woman. He recalled the baronial archives, the episcopal librarians, the "dreamers" in clerical institutions who had been the nicest; recalled the compassion shown him by young schoolteachers and waitresses, and by him to them, no doubt; recalled the wistful longing in the eyes of many a baroness that had filled him with fear, though he had engaged in "let's take pity on each other" with a countess; after all, though, Gerlind hadn't been married. He had never been subjected to any direct political pressure, and he still had no idea whether and to what extent he would have succumbed to such pressure, hadn't known even when he took over the paper; he found his political impeccability uncanny, and the British found it incomprehensible, they simply had to accept it. Sometimes—briefly—he speculated on those potential careers as museum director, or minister of state, resident in Eickelhof, and surely they would have had enough to live on that way too, and many things might, might have turned out differently, Rolf might not have gone to prison, Sabine would never have met that fellow Fischer, and Herbert might have become a little more realistic; perhaps even Veronica and Heinrich might—oh well, perhaps they had all gone a bit too far laughing at his "little paper," he, Käthe, the children, and his friends—head of a museum, that would have been the right thing, minister less so, that would have landed him right in all that Party crap.

It suddenly occurred to him that Veronica always phoned Käthe, never him, and that made him laugh: could it be that he was jealous because she never phoned *him*, only Sabine and Käthe, not even Rolf, of whom she was probably afraid? And of course not—even for kicks—that fellow Fischer, he had only phoned him once himself, in dire necessity, begging him somehow, please somehow, to arrange for Rolf to earn a little money at the Beehive, even if only as a packer or a sweeper. No, Fischer had categorically refused because they had named their little boy Holger even *after* it had happened, and Fischer made it very clear that he had no intention of allowing his workers "to be contaminated by a person like that." But, come to think of it, there had been a Holger Danske, there was also a minister-president by that name and, last but not least, Holger Count Tolm, who, somewhere between Málaga and Cádiz, was trying (usually in vain, so he had been told) to seduce female tourists, preferably English and Swedish but in a pinch German too. Well, perhaps it *was* a needless defiance to call another son Holger when one already had a son by that name.

Why did Veronica never phone him? He had never done anything to hurt her, she had always been nice to him, and he to her, although he had never done what Käthe and Herbert probably had: given her money. Käthe was surprisingly openhanded when it came to spending money, was more generous than he, and that could hardly be due to environment. His father had on principle spent half his meager salary on land, on poor soil, in his insatiable greed for acreage. Käthe's father had also been no more than a permanently bankrupt nurseryman, her mother had secretly worked nights cleaning in stores, secretly because the neighbors mustn't be allowed to know what everyone knew: that she worked as a cleaning woman. That had all been very modest, even more modest than their own lives, yet she was quite without inhibitions or complexes, felt neither shame nor triumph when she sometimes spent considerable sums at the dressmaker's or took a taxi to Café Getzloser.

He was sure Sabine hadn't given Veronica any money, Fischer would see to that, he kept her pretty short. He'd only do something, give something, if it improved his image: horses and clothes for pictures of Sabine, sometimes with, sometimes without Kit, that dear little granddaughter of his whom he so seldom saw. Fischer had coolly arranged for her to be voted "most charming child of the month," in May, in a riding habit, barely four years old. The "most charming child of the month" was Fischer's invention: the pictures were published in illustrated weeklies, in Sunday supplements, even his own paper was not exempt, those adorable little creatures popped up on all sides, always displaying Beehive fashions, and Beehive, as almost everyone knew, stood for: Fischer. Sometimes nostalgic, recalling a Renoir or a Rubens, sometimes provocative, as if already in training for striptease, leather-clad and languid, then again exotic, Sicilian, Andalusian— now even Russian in anticipation of the Olympics. The most charming child of the month always wore Beehive, and from among the twelve would be chosen the most charming child of the year; and it had to be Bleibl who had seen it in the paper, told him that Sabine was pregnant again, an item in connection with some equestrian event! Amplanger had sent up the clipping: "Sabine Fischer, one of our greatest hopes, has unfortunately had to withdraw as she is expecting." That was how he discovered that a new baby was on the way, and he could imagine how Rolf, on reading it, would feel like "throwing up" yet grind his teeth with glee at the unmasking of the system, "the inexorably mounting prostitutional elements of the system."

Blurtmehl let out some bath water—added more hot, asked him to exercise his legs: true enough, this was easy in the water, they

became light and would probably have stayed light had his paper
not weighed like lead in his limbs—a light-footed museum director
and a light-footed—no, not minister, but perhaps state secretary.
Those birds against the gray sky with the deceptively white
clouds, those idyllic formations for which they had to thank the
power stations: the clouds moving along as if created by God's
own hand, white, calm, richly varied, yet they came from
Hetzigrath, must have been brought forth by the coal that had
lain below Eickelhof, also created by God's hand that it might
bring forth divine clouds, almost a fine afternoon, already
poetically darkened by the dusk. Even swallows flew into his
field of vision; among all the swifts, the swallows were his
favorites, especially the house martins, nimble, beautiful birds,
skillful and intelligent. But his special favorites were the soarers:
buzzards, falcons, hawks. He loved the falcons that were still nest-
ing in the tower: where would they fly to when Kortschede's
prediction came true? Soaring and sailing through the sky with
scarcely a wingbeat. And over and over again the thought of the
owl taking off from the tower when dusk began to fall and flying
toward the edge of the forest, soundlessly, with a round wingbeat.
Sometimes, too, he saw pigeons from Kommertz's dovecote—how
strange: he didn't like pigeons, didn't like their cooing and cluck-
ing as they nested in wall crannies, didn't like their flight, and
wondered why he preferred the birds of prey: watching them in
the gray, white-streaked square of sky from his bathtub while
Blurtmehl felt his pulse at intervals, and nodded, which meant:
no need to worry.

All he really wanted was to spend the rest of his life observing
birds in flight, drinking tea, watching Käthe knit, listening to her
play Beethoven in her wonderfully amateurish way, "richly" as
she called it; and now he had not only the one enormous, senseless office at his paper but also a second enormous, senselessly
large one, was required to fill both "with his personality," and
hadn't even known that his daughter was expecting a baby, had
to be told by Bleibl of all people, who had seen it in the sports

section of all places; new blood, although it wasn't a young Tolm, only a Fischer.

One thing was certain, anyway: there was a young Tolm called Holger, and he prompted frequent speculations on strange problems of inheritance: if they killed off Rolf as a renegade, and himself as newly elected president, a nice chunk would be left for this seven-year-old boy as Rolf's direct heir, for this grandson whom he hadn't seen for three years, with whom, when the boy was still a toddler, he had fed ducks in the park, as he had with Kit. Had, had, had—not even this was considered advisable now, since that day not long ago when one duck had veered off, in a completely unnatural way, from the flock that was so charmingly patterning the dark water; it swam toward the shore, and out of the bushes rushed Hendler, the young security guard, shouting "Take cover! Down!" and thrusting Kit and himself down onto the grass, flinging himself beside them, while the duck, which later turned out to be made of wood, ended its unnatural course at a projecting piece of turf and began to spin even more unnaturally. Hendler had taken it for a floating bomb, camouflaged as a duck or hidden inside the duck. Fortunately he was mistaken, but the upshot was a detailed investigation leading to a kitchen maid's tearful confession. She had discovered the wooden duck in the basement, cleaned it, and set it adrift, "for fun," as she put it. He had great difficulty in preventing the dismissal of the maid and a report in the press, partly due to the fact of its being an idea, a notion, that someone might pick up. Ever since then he had been suspicious of the ducks, he even began to distrust the birds he had so long enjoyed observing. Presumably it was possible to develop remote-control mechanical birds which, filled with high explosives, would suddenly switch to horizontal flight and fly through an open window bearing havoc in their artificial breasts, in their artificial bellies. With the exception, he supposed, of swallows, sparrows, crows. But pigeons, perhaps, starlings, storks, and wild geese—whole flights, all mechanical, all bearing havoc, and he found himself saying, to Bleibl of all people: "Even the birds of the air aren't to be trusted anymore." Whereupon Bleibl answered: "Nor the cake delivered to your house by the baker." Yes, ever since the affair of Pliefger's birthday cake they had all their baking done at home, if not exactly under supervision, at least with considerable precautions.

That affair of the birthday cake had been a perfect example of the meticulous precision of the planning: someone must have known the baker, must have made exact notes of the delivery van's route, known the moment at which the railway barrier was lowered. The baker's van had been forced by a blue Ford to slow down so that it had to stop just as the barrier was lowered; the blue Ford had repeatedly squeezed in front of the bakery van, at places where the van couldn't pass, and at the barrier the genuine cake had been exchanged for the "hot" one—the genuine one being found subsequently in a garbage can near the barrier. And if somebody hadn't phoned and warned Pliefger—he always hoped it might have been Veronica, who loved to phone: unthinkable. Only Beverloh could have been behind this, he was always said to be "figuring, figuring, figuring." They had copied the cake exactly, TO OUR WONDERFUL BOSS, ON HIS SIXTY-FIFTH BIRTHDAY—and nothing, nothing, the interrogation of the baker, of his family, of the apprentices and staff, of the neighborhood, the examination of the phone lines—nothing had brought any suspect to light. The ladies in Pliefger's office, who had ordered the cake, thought up the text and the decoration (forget-me-nots on white icing), had sobbed hysterically. Everything about the cake had been just right, even the weight; and if Pliefger had cut it, as anticipated, he would have been torn to shreds— Pliefger, his predecessor, "And you can't even trust the bread on your table anymore, nor the packet of cigarettes you tear open. . . ." Since the Plotteti affair.

No doubt they had enough money, perhaps even from Käthe, to hatch such birds, also enough imagination, certainly Veronica did; might have a flock of thirty wild geese (sweeping through the night!) rigged up. Aimed at the manor, they could have the effect of an ultramodern rocket launcher. Why not? With the highly intelligent, minute electronic brains now available, with which, among other things, Bleibl made his money, and of course he hadn't mentioned it to anyone, not even to Käthe, let alone Bleibl, who could have commissioned one of his highly qualified physicists or engineers to take up this idea, if only to produce a new armaments hit, or merely "to enliven the ballistic discussion."

And then, of course, Holzpuke might have been inspired to stretch steel nets across the sky above and around the manor: no more birds, no more clouds, even if they did consist only of Hetzigrath steam. He wanted to go on enjoying his view of the park, the sky, wanted to go on smoking his cigarette with his own hand, blow out the match with his own lips, go on feeding the ducks with Kit, from the terrace—from there one could throw the bread crumbs farther, guide the flocks, produce patterns—at night the owl, the little screech owls, the bats, whose flight habits he didn't know. In his dreams eagles came, vultures, with enormous wingspan, flying straight and hard at him, exploding breast to breast against him, in fire and smoke, with a roar that still sounded in his ears long after he had awoken and grasped Käthe's hand, seeking comfort in her warmth, her pulsebeat. Or he would quietly get up, ring for Blurtmehl, and have him rub his icy feet with ointment. And there had been moments during the day, too, when he flinched at the sight of a pigeon or a swallow flying toward the manor, sometimes just a sparrow, and he had to hold on to himself not to scream the way Kortschede had done.

Blurtmehl cautioned: "Not too long, sir," and he allowed himself to be helped out of the tub, onto the table to be rubbed down with aromatic oils, wrapped in the big bath towel, rubbed and patted dry by Blurtmehl, who discreetly covered his genitals and told him to make treading movements, "treading air," he called that. . . . It wasn't easy, mind you, to find a mechanical solution to the difference between a flying object and a bird, one realistic enough to prevent detection: could the nuances in a bird's movements be imitated to that degree, considering that the explosive hidden in the flying object required its own mechanism that had to be inserted and hidden and still function? Come to think of it, mechanical birds were nothing new, and he recalled a conversation with Veronica on the terrace in Eickelhof, when Veronica had maintained that artificial birds flew "more naturally" than real ones, just as wound-up toy birds "walk more naturally than real ones. . . ."

With his gentle hands, Blurtmehl stopped the "air treading" and began to massage the soles of his feet, asking him to report any pain, even the slightest, soon declared himself satisfied, noting a surprising relaxation, probably due to the disappearance of his fear in exchange for curiosity and fantasy. The oil felt good, as did Blurtmehl's hands; and now, his head slightly raised, he could even look out on the terrace and into the moat, and he wondered: Might it be Blurtmehl after all? Weren't there those mysterious, tiny bolts that could be catapulted into a person's brain? And after all, why shouldn't it come from Blurtmehl himself, perhaps something was hatching in him, at a hidden level, that might suddenly provoke the stranglehold? And without question he was sufficiently versed in anatomy (he was forever taking refresher courses!) to disguise the consequences of a stranglehold as an accident in the tub. Blurtmehl with his long, rather bony hands, with those gentle, sad eyes that masseurs and priests sometimes have in common. How much did "documented data" mean, after all? Born 1940 in Katowice, original name Blutwitzki or something like that; after dropping out of a Catholic boarding school, "disillusioned by postwar developments in Poland," he had renounced his Polish citizenship and taken the strange name of Blurtmehl, the etymology of which no one, not even Blurtmehl himself, had yet been able to explain to him. In the West he had not even tried to graduate from high school, had refused any and all assistance, became a male nurse and, although talented enough in the opinion of all who knew him, never did finish school in

order to study medicine. He stayed with the nuns down south
somewhere in the Allgäu, bought himself a surprisingly powerful
and expensive motorcycle, tore around on it in his free time, at
random through the countryside (whether seemingly or actually
at random could never be established with complete certainty),
from Munich to Hamburg and to Berlin (where no Eastern con-
tacts could be detected), finally becoming manservant, masseur,
and chauffeur to a bishop, whom he served for ten years, until that
same bishop recommended him to Tolm. The bishop virtually
made a present of him: "He's irreplaceable, simply irreplaceable,
but I'll let you have him, provided he's willing—you need him
more than I do, in your position!" (He knew the bishop from his
tutoring days, as well as from his art studies; the bishop had
written his thesis on Hieronymus Bosch and had later crossed his
path somewhere as a sergeant in the artillery—but otherwise it
was always embarrassing when the bishops occasionally turned up
in their organized solidarity, paid social calls, so to speak, because
they wanted to "maintain contact with all social groups"—it was
always a bit embarrassing because it inevitably led to some degree
of servility, a bit of backslapping—those "We're all in the same
boat" gestures—and what did that mean, "in the same boat"?
What boat? Weren't they in the same boat as those poor prosti-
tutes? No, this bishop was really a nice man, had the very
ordinary first name of Hans and an even more common surname,
was still interested in Hieronymus Bosch, and had genuinely
meant to do him a favor.)

Well, Blurtmehl had been willing, had entered his service in
1971, and did turn out to be irreplaceable because of his skills as
chauffeur, manservant, masseur, and because of his character—he
was the very soul of discretion, this slight, pleasant, quiet man
who looked more like a monk manqué than a servant (or was
there no contradiction there?), who looked as if he had no private
life yet did: a mother whom he supported and a sister whom he
visited periodically. They had kept their Polish-sounding name
and lived near Würzburg, and not the slightest suspicion attached

to either of those innocuous people; his brother-in-law was even with the police. Moreover—and this was the real surprise since actually he had always thought of Blurtmehl as a platonic homosexual, or even asexual—Blurtmehl had a girlfriend, thirty-two-year-old Eva Klensch, with whom he openly spent his free days and nights, went to restaurants, movies, the theater; for the last ten years, going back to his time with the bishop, his steady girlfriend.

Eva Klensch, who ran a boutique in Frankfurt: Israeli, Turkish, Arab-Palestinian knickknacks, caftans, and the like, made frequent trips—in the opinion of a number of security experts, according to Holzpuke, a little too frequent—to the Near East, had even set up a whole cottage-industry network in Palestinian refugee camps. Eva Klensch was by no means suspect, but neither could she be classified as "completely above suspicion," and it was solely on her account that Blurtmehl had not been unreservedly accorded that rating. One never knew, did one, what was being whispered, what was being swapped, when she went shopping in the back alleys of Beirut and its surroundings, and near Nablus, not far from Damascus or Amman. And although she could be watched and searched via the customs—for mightn't hashish or heroin be involved, if not politics?—even strict and lawful customs checks had never been able to turn up anything suspicious about Eva Klensch: a pretty, self-confident, businesslike young woman who made skillful and quite legal use of the fluctuating dollar exchange; nor did a perfectly normal and lawful tax audit turn up anything suspicious, apart from a few questionable expense vouchers such as could be found in any tax audit. Her hobby was archery, and here too she was successful, was district or regional champion and always carried bow, target, and arrows with her in the car. Needless to say, her past history had also been investigated: at the age of thirteen, shortly before the Berlin Wall went up, she had come to the West with her father, an electro-welder, her mother, an armature winder, and her ten-year-old brother, by now a professional soldier with the Bundeswehr.

An ambitious and successful student, she had graduated from middle school in Dortmund, had become first a saleswoman, then a buyer, in a department store; at twenty-one she had already opened her own boutique, with what was for her rather bold financing, and had since then even opened a branch, somewhere near Offenbach. Two years ago this attractive Eva Klensch had—a detail that, while not of itself disquieting, had surprised the investigators—converted to Catholicism, quite obviously under the influence of Blurtmehl, who—another surprise—had met her ten years earlier at a Socialist Party function.

These two details—Socialist Party and Catholicism—made him uneasy. Not that he would have had any objection to either one—apart from the Nuppertz traumata—no, he merely felt the lack of a certain consistency, and he was surprised, too, that Blurtmehl hadn't married the girl long ago: there was something there that didn't fit, or maybe *he*—that might be more to the point—didn't fit anymore. Still: bow and arrow were silent weapons.

While Blurtmehl was massaging his neck, moving slowly to the shoulders, where he suspected "extensive rheumatism," Tolm abstained from making an imaginative leap to Blurtmehl's and Eva's potential caresses. No doubt about it: Blurtmehl was known to be an open Socialist Party sympathizer, ever since his days with the bishop, and presumably Eva was too. After he, Tolm, had caught himself itching for months, out of sheer curiosity, to see a photo of this girl Eva (he could hardly expect Holzpuke to show him one!), Blurtmehl had voluntarily produced one, with the gentle remark: "That's her, that's my friend Eva!" and the words "That's her" had confirmed him in his suspicion that Blurtmehl was indeed a mindreader. The picture showed Eva as an extremely attractive, rather small, dark-haired woman with a pleasant bosom, merry eyes, and an intelligent mouth, booted, self-assured. Meanwhile he had learned that she was—something he had long ceased to be—a churchgoer, sometimes with Blurtmehl, usually without, when he would stay home and make breakfast. So this former bishop's masseur, near-graduate of a Catholic boarding school, avid motorcyclist, had brought this young woman from a highly secular background into the bosom of the Church.

Would it be Eva's hands, as slender as they doubtless were firm, from which Blurtmehl would receive "it," transmitted via unfathomably complex Palestinian conspiracies, handed over or whispered in gloomy camps, discreetly passed along in Beirut, transmitted in code, decoded, implanted in Blurtmehl's brain, where it fed and festered? And in the end, in the bathtub or during a massage, a gentle throttling, a pressing of the head under water! After all, Grebnitzer himself was skeptical about all those baths, so an accident in the tub was not unlikely; and the Palestinians had their own secret service, by this time his own grandson might very well be speaking their language. They weren't short of money (money that, as Rolf had once again calmly remarked, "is your own money, energy money that flows dangerously back to you via Libya, Syria, or the Saudis—just so you know what money is capable of").

There remained only one question, to which the answer contained some consolation: what good would it do them to kill him off without at least profiting by the publicity? No bombs, no machine pistols, no "hot" birthday cakes—just an accident in the bathtub —what would they get out of that? What good would it do them to prove their power without being able to demonstrate that power publicly?

Capitalist has accident in the bathtub! So what? What Käthe had sometimes offered him as consolation—his manifest, vouched-for humanity—might be his very undoing. After him it would be Amplanger's turn, one of the "new men": ruthlessly dynamic, jovial, robust—his smile was enough to scare a person, and perhaps they needed him quickly to kill him off spectacularly, and could therefore get himself—Tolm—quietly out of the way. Amplanger stood for stock exchange, Olympic shooting team, tennis, Zummerling, and teeth-grinding ruthlessness. Perhaps they wanted to speed up Amplanger's election—he, Tolm, radiated too many humanistic thoughts, self-doubts, too much capitalist melancholy. And damn it all, why didn't they go for Bleibl, the most ruthless of the ruthless, who never felt a second's pain, never an instant's regret, when a few hundred more people perished somewhere in Bolivia or Rhodesia, while in himself there dwelled this sadness, this elemental sadness, fed by Rolf's "front-line communiqués," by Katharina's analyses and reports; and no doubt it was precisely this authentic sadness whose television value Bleibl had recognized and craftily exploited to catapult him into his present position. Yet surely they knew that he might be bad in his weakness but not the worst, and perhaps that was his grim fate—not to be the worst; and what was the meaning of Veronica's whisper over the telephone: "Don't ever have tea at the Bleibls' "?

"Blurtmehl," he said suddenly, from the depths of his musings, "do you believe in God, in this—in Jesus Christ?"

"Yes, of course, sir—do you?"

In terms of protocol, this riposte was an impertinence, completely at odds with the manservant tradition, it must be a Socialist Party element, and it really did go a little too far; also it was a shock because it was so unprecedented in Blurtmehl, yet he replied: "I do, Blurtmehl, I do too, even if I'm not quite sure who He is and where—but let me ask you one more question, forgive me if I seem too personal—what surprises you most about this strange world?"

"What surprises me most," said Blurtmehl, as if he hadn't had to think about it at all, had kept the reply to such a surprising question always up his sleeve, so to speak, "what surprises me most is the patience of the poor."

That went deep, made him fall silent, was a truly surprising answer that couldn't have anything to do with the Socialist Party after all. The answer was older, went deeper, must have dwelled within Blurtmehl, and it hadn't even been uttered in sadness: "the patience of the poor"—true, penetrating words from the lips of a masseur. And he was tempted to ask, but he refrained, it would have been too crude, too abominably stupid, this question: "Do you count yourself among the poor?" Besides, he was afraid to put the question, because the answer, which surely could only be no, might not be so certain after all. What if Blurtmehl had said yes—what a philosophical debate on poverty would have ensued, and he would have had to haul out his youthful struggle with poverty—which he hated doing, had never done even with his children, nor with Käthe incidentally: the constant hunger in his student days, and when he came home for the weekends no more milk soup, only potatoes, in every shape and form, mostly —because that was cheapest—in the form of potato salad, whereas if they were boiled some sort of sauce was needed and if they were fried at least a few scraps of margarine; because his father was going crazier all the time, diverting more and more of his salary to his wretched land purchases, stinting on heat and light— oh, those fifteen-watt bulbs in kitchen and basement, twenty-five-watt, at most, in the living room.

"Poor," Blurtmehl volunteered, "is what I would call someone who owns no part of this earth, and"—he smiled almost condescendingly—"I do own half the property occupied by my girlfriend's store." He went rapidly through the finishing movements, passed his hands once more over him, then gave a pat to bottom and shoulders, and said, this time genuinely distressed: "I would have continued with the treatment, but I sense some resistance to me, perhaps a lack of trust."

"No, no," he said, while Blurtmehl handed him his underwear and shirt. "No, neither resistance nor distrust. I am merely speculating on who will get me, who and how, so I am going through everyone in my mind—even my sons, my wife, my daughters-in-law—all my friends, my enemies—and you too, of course—maybe you happened to catch me at this thought."

"But who would want to kill you? There's no earthly reason."

"Just because there is no reason—or can you see any reason or motive linked to certain people? Mr. Pliefger is the nicest boss and family man you can imagine—it's not directed at individuals —in their way they are technocrats, separating business from emotions—I'm sure they still have emotions, maybe they are as nice as we are."

The trousers he could manage, but not his socks and shoes, these he let Blurtmehl put on and lace up. Kneeling before him, Blurtmehl glanced up and said: "Yes, there's no such thing as security—and yet there has to be a security system. By the way, this weekend I'll take the liberty of introducing my friend Miss Klensch to you, if you have no objection. Your wife has kindly offered to put her up."

"Oh, I'm glad to hear that, I hope she's staying in the manor?"

"Your wife and Mr. Kulgreve were kind enough to place the guest apartment at her disposal."

After Blurtmehl had brought in the tray with tea, toast, butter, lemon, and caviar, Käthe came into the room, looking tired, pale, a rare thing with her. He had seldom seen her pale, the last time had been at the news of Rolf's arrest, then again when it became certain that Veronica had gone underground. And she had hardly ever looked so tired, almost old; he kissed her, was about to ask: "Anything wrong?" but she caressed his shoulder and said: "Don't take it too hard, I realize you've never been able to say no—and they won't harm you, not you . . . you're so humane, and they know it. . . ."

"That's one very good reason to harm me—just that, believe me."

They had been advised not to use the terrace—it had been found to "jut out too far," to be too "open," too plainly visible from the edge of the forest, the tall trees, "like a rifle range" Holzpuke had said (and Tolm had just recently had heating and automatic windows installed because he loved to sit there, particularly in fall and winter, and wait for the owl)—and Tolm hadn't wanted to close off the forest and the park, free access being an ancient right (not even the stingiest and stupidest of the Tolm counts had ever denied the people that), and of course it was impossible to check up on each individual going for a walk there, there were so many, even from nearby villages, especially at weekends—so they had to stay indoors, to sit side by side over their tea, both looking out onto the park and toward the edge of the forest: "Just like at the movies or the theater!" Käthe had said.

She poured the tea, spread butter and caviar on toast for him. It still tasted good to him, it always did, and he couldn't help looking into her eyes, deep and long, and there he discovered fear. She had seldom known fear, seldom in war or peace; fear of the low-flying planes, yes, and of the "Nazis and Protestants" in Dresden. Anger and rage: yes, over the loss of Eickelhof, sadness at the obliteration of Iffenhoven, where for six generations her ancestors had been buried. Fear rarely, not even when Rolf behaved so stupidly. Some people thought her cool and a bit apathetic, and no doubt that's how she seemed when she had to take part in official functions. She didn't do that very often, and only for his sake, she found it boring and time-consuming—on such occasions she was indeed cool but not apathetic, he would have called it imperturbable; she would say little, was quite the lady, wasn't particularly impressed by ministers, presidents, or heads of staff, found the Shah "so dull as to be almost interesting," and Banzer "more trite than God should ever permit," those bloodhounds. She showed warmth only toward waiters and chefs, sought them out, praised the food, asked for recipes and how to prepare them, laughed with the cloakroom girl, chatted with the washroom attendants; and a shade of contempt came into her expression when she had to listen to dinner speeches or toasts to herself. Of course she was never rude, yet her manner toward dignitaries—and there was plenty of "top brass" around, as she expressed it—was always a trifle patronizing, almost contemptuous, in any case cool and imperturbable.

She had got along quite nicely with a few of the "boardroom biddies," but over the years there had been many divorces and one lost sight of the first, second, and third wives. Käthe always complained about all these divorces: "Hardly have you got to know and like one of them, had a cup of tea and a chat, gone shopping with her—and she takes off as a divorcee to Garmisch or the Côte d'Azur, and a new one pops up, some blonde with a cute bottom and wide eyes, or a brunette with wide eyes and a cute bottom, with bosoms, without—hardly as old as your own daughter. God, how much you men must have missed in your lives in the way of bosoms, bottoms, and wide eyes! Bleibl's Number Four, for instance, is a rather stupid, dangerously stupid, bitch while his Number One was the nicest as well as the prettiest of the bunch—his Number Three, too, was a really good woman, quite charming, that Elisabeth, he seems to have bad luck with the even figures—his Number Two wasn't bad but basically stupid. What's the matter with them all—each time it's going to be the truly deep, irrevocable love, do you believe that? I wonder what Bleibl's Number Five will be like. Will she be another of those dumb sex symbols, like his Number Four—and we're supposed to have tea with her? I'm sure she knocks back her gin and tonic right after breakfast and then looks for a victim she can tantalize with her bosom. I'm convinced Bleibl gives her a good wallop every now and again."

He always blushed a little when she talked like that, usually in the car, openly in front of Blurtmehl, who would then take refuge behind a little cough; on the way home from a party or a reception where he even wore his decorations, the postwar ones, never the others; no, not that, he would have really been too ashamed in front of Käthe—besides, she had threatened him with divorce: "If you do that too"—good God, what else was he supposed to have done?—"if you do that too I'll ask for a divorce!" He felt embarrassed enough wearing the new ones, but he had to—had to?

asked Rolf, isn't this a free country?—had to for the sake of his paper, and also of the Association, despite the fact that decorations, even the new ones, reminded him of the smell of Virginia cigarettes: he had exchanged his own, the one he had managed to sneak through the body search, for twelve cigarettes, but not even Käthe knew about this, no one knew that even on the most cere-monial occasions when heads of state or rulers, generals and Shah turned up, their chests covered with decorations—he would think of the cigarettes they might buy in a desperate situation; had to—just as he had had to sell Eickelhof, and he had never forgotten the incisive analysis of his "alleged freedom" by that miserable Beverloh—just as he would have to sell Tolmshoven in order to feed a new, cloud-forming power station.

Whenever he saw Käthe again, even in the morning when he woke up, and at night when he reached out for her hand, he thought of the evening they had met in Dresden at the military hospital. In the corridor, in that grim gray hubbub, he had been heading for the exit, dressed to go out, hurrying to avoid un-welcome companions who were liable to force themselves upon him at any moment: all that blather in the ward about final victory, that stifling, labored confidence in victory in which his silence aroused suspicion, that scanning of a face to see whether it could be trusted—and how easily one could be fooled. He had asked for an early discharge as "fit for active service" so that he could go on leave and take the train home. His discharge papers in his pocket, he was determined to spend the night outside the hos-pital—and she had passed him in the corridor and stopped, pleasure in her expression, seized his sleeve, blushed, and said: "Excuse me, but—you here? Mr. Tolm?" And he looked down at her, a blond girl with a frank, open face, on the plump side, veiled gray eyes in contrast to the open cheerfulness of her expression, eyes from whose depths he never wanted to, never would, emerge, and he looked at her so intensely that she blushed again. He thought: My God, where do I know her from, am I supposed to know her, know her name? There was certainly something familiar about her. He smiled, having made up his mind to spend the night with her—"somehow." She said: "I'm Käthe Schmitz, from Iffenhoven, my brother Heinrich was a friend of your brother Hans, and our fathers once had a lawsuit, remember?" Yes, that was it, the nursery garden in Iffenhoven that Hans sometimes went off to, and Father had once again acted too hastily in a bankruptcy case, had been less than aboveboard in an attempt to grab yet another piece of land too cheaply. Yes, that lawsuit with Schmitz, and Hans had complained that his friendship with Heinrich had suffered from it.

That's right, Käthe Schmitz from Iffenhoven—somehow, somehow her face had seemed familiar—he must have seen her occasionally, in church (where—at that very time—he sometimes pointedly went in spite of Nuppertz), or in a procession—perhaps at a dance at the vicarage, and there in the corridor in Dresden he asked whether she wouldn't like to go out with him, get away from this vast, stifling hospital, and she had come closer, held his arm again, and said: "Oh, I'd love to, I'm just suffocating here among all these Nazis and Protestants!" Alarmed, she released his arm: "Oh my goodness, perhaps you're one of them!"—and he had merely shaken his head, taken her arm, and said: "If you can get away, it would really give me so much pleasure." He sighed, he knew what was bound to happen, how it would end; he was attracted by more than her eyes. "All right," she said, "I'm prepared to go AWOL if I must—wait for me at Admittance."

Two hours down in the lobby, waiting: typewriters clacking, ambulances being dispatched, sick and wounded arriving, stretchers being carried, screams, pathetic objects—no, certainly not victors—clinging to their mess kits, humbly supplying personal details, showing papers; twice Käthe came to report, she was looking for someone to take her place in the lab where she worked, then at last she arrived, nicely turned out in print blouse and tweed skirt, a fur hat and a soft-blue coat that didn't go at all with the rest of her outfit, and her obvious pleasure was a delight in itself. She wanted so desperately to go out, to go dancing again, without being constantly propositioned, pawed, accosted.

They went to one of those cavernous soldiers' dives that smelled of beer, dancing, and collapse, in those dirty, cynical surroundings that smelled of war's end and disintegration. Later he confessed to having been determined to spend the night with her, and she confessed that she must have wanted the same thing but had lacked the nerve to admit it to herself—a little afraid of him because of that affair with the young countess and the ruckus in the confessional, that Lothario myth that was still making the rounds of the villages. For God's sake, afraid of him! He had to laugh, wanted to go off with her, never mind where, wanted to stay with her, look into her eyes and not only into her eyes, he wanted to have her, keep her, and he told her so when the beer haze, the blare, the smell of collapse became too much for them: the fug from sweaty uniforms, from cavorting hookers; there was even a market for girls who would marry you to get you some leave, if you gave them a few hundred marks and the wedding rations—sugar and margarine for the wedding cake—and later calmly let themselves be divorced as the guilty party. As for Käthe, she was disgusted by all that anyway, she had been a bookbinder, had taken a lab course and held a wartime job as a nurse's aide: blood, urine, V.D. patients; and had landed up here where there was "nothing but Nazis and Protestants"—and roughly a hundred thousand sick and wounded—and no Zwinger Pavilion or River Elbe, no Royal Residence or baroque architecture, could compensate for the misery of whole armies of the maimed. And when they were finally outside, on the street, there remained only one question: "Where shall we go? I want to go with you, I mean it—I don't care what you think of me—I want to!"

Oh, how she hated that kissing and fumbling in corridors, corners, toilets, in prep rooms, even operating theaters, then rather some cheap hotel room, and she agreed, she just wanted to be alone with him, alone, and he with her, in that gray war's-end

turmoil, and of course there were "those rooms" wherever there
were a hundred thousand soldiers, and finding a room was not
nearly as difficult as in his panic he had feared. There were touts
who could earn a few percent, amputees, veterans, consumptives
who, when they saw a likely looking couple, whispered: "Looking for a love nest?" Yes, they were looking for a love nest,
naturally there were differences in price, in category, differences
in time: "For a couple of hours, or all night?" Yes, all night, and
they found one with antlers, a Defregger reproduction, and a
portrait of Katharina von Bora; not bad at all, the room not even
dirty, it actually had a washstand. Oh, love nest—what comforting
words in that lousy turmoil of war! He had expected tears, there
were none, only later when she talked about her brother Heinrich,
who was dead, and he about his brother Hans, who was dead too.
The tears came later, at first there was only her fear of her
"complete inexperience" that made her trust in his "experience,"
though it turned out he wasn't nearly as "experienced" as had
been rumored in the villages. It was lovely to see her naked, to
show himself naked to her, and she turned out to be the more
experienced, while he was made awkward by joy, and there was
reason to laugh about it, and to talk about it, about how men
acquired a reputation for being Lotharios without being any such
thing—there was cause to laugh about the future, to laugh about
her surprise at his actually having a Ph.D.; and he couldn't get
enough of her, had to laugh again and again, look into her eyes—
oh, those cursed twenty-five-watt bulbs!—again and again, under
antlers, Defregger, and Katharina von Bora, and the smell of
autumn leaves drifting in through the open window from the
courtyard. . . .

The following morning, after attending to his ticket of leave, he
simply took her with him, took her home, away from those
"Nazis and Protestants," took her to her father, who had managed
to keep one greenhouse with two small adjoining rooms, briquet

stove and sofa, and the old man laughed because she turned up with "young Tolm of all people," and when she described herself as engaged the old man laughed with his stumps of teeth and his pipe in his mouth, placidly accepted, with a cheerful laugh, the tobacco they had brought him. In such a situation the old countess could be a great help, she had a telephone and knew the right people, she was in urgent need of a woman companion, now that she was on crutches, and the produce of her estate was "war essential"—the timber, the vegetables, and the potatoes growing in her park. The countess had Käthe released from her duties, engaged her, and said: "Fritz, I'd always hoped you would stick to Gerlind—but now you've found someone better: she's good, clever, and beautiful—and so full of fun, she really peps me up." By November they were married at the registry in Blückhoven.

And before the end of the war, when he came home on leave again, she had whispered in his ear that "Something is already on the way."

"Not you, Tolm, they won't harm you," and passed him another piece of toast with caviar. "That really would be a disgrace." "Disgrace," he said, "isn't the right word for them, they know no such thing as disgrace, no such thing as limits. Incidentally, do *we* know such a thing as disgrace? Do I, for instance, have a sense of disgrace now that our paper has swallowed up the *Gerbsdorfer Bote*? We grow and proliferate, swallow up one little newspaper after another—and I'm enjoying my tea, enjoying my caviar, I enjoy the view over the park, enjoy seeing you again, while Blume, who couldn't keep the *Gerbsdorfer Bote* going anymore, may be thinking of suicide. It grows and grows, and you can't stop it—Amplanger warned Blume as long as four years ago: the computer predicted Blume's downfall exactly—and the publishing and printing house had been in the family for a hundred and fifty years; liberal tradition, an important contribution to democratic, even republican, ideas—and now it's being absorbed by our paper, and we know how we feel about that. . . ."

"You're right, we needn't argue about the paper, that champing, trampling dinosaur that isn't even a meat-eater, merely a vegetarian, devouring paper, one newspaper after another, that tiny little *Bevenicher Tagblatt* that was left to you by your uncle in 1945. With all that went with it, and how scared we were—remember? We wanted to sell it, sell it cheap, and keep only the Eickelhof house, and you—"

"I agree, I really should have become a museum director, that would have suited me, but of course I couldn't sell because the license had been issued and was tied to me personally—and we didn't even know that the *Bevenicher Nachrichten* was also included, the paper my uncle had bought from Bert Rosenthal . . . we knew nothing, and then that nice British officer turned up bringing me full rehabilitation, full—and the license, the very first one, and he got hold of some newsprint, even dug up some journalists, those nice émigrés, the nicest was Schröter, the Communist, Katharina's uncle, who left us and disappeared without trace—in the East. He couldn't stand it here for long, and I imagine that over there they locked him up and killed him. He was a follower of Münzenberg and should have known."

"Isn't there anything we can do for Blume now?"

"What do you expect—for me to send him our condolences, invite him for coffee, tell him how much I regret his having implored us to swallow him before anyone else did? Zummerling, for instance? The fact is that Blume prefers to be swallowed by us. He won't be short of money, he can even keep the old family house. Only his work, the liberal tradition—that I can't give back to him, no one can give it back to him. Believe me, we didn't want the *Bote* at all, we didn't want this proliferation, but he wanted us to take him over, at least he prefers our paper to Zummerling and his *mishpokhe*. Disgrace, yes, of course, it's a disgrace, but just ask the two Amplangers whether they feel any disgrace. Young Amplanger will tell you: 'Is it a disgrace for a chicken to pick up a grain thrown to it?' By the way, there's no profit in it at all, that'll only come much later—it simply means occupying a position in the market, buying up ahead of anyone else—it's almost like buying time without any idea of what you want to do with it. Meanwhile we'll use only the *Bote*'s masthead, which actually means a beheaded paper; one more person laying his head voluntarily on the block—of course we must be nice to the Blumes, not only ask them over but go and see them too. He's devoted to me, and I've no idea why—he certainly has no reason, I did nothing to save his head and what's more I couldn't have done anything. That's what is known as inherent law, processes we can neither recognize nor control. One day my head, too, will fall into Zummerling's basket, that's why he can observe my— our—growth quite calmly; meanwhile we look after the adjusting for him so that he can't be blamed for it later, on the contrary: for a while he can afford to be more liberal than the *Bote* was under the rule of our little paper . . . the countess was right: I was and still am a clever boy, I simply wasn't dynamic enough, I was also too lazy to gather dynamic battalions around me . . . or to impose my own law, assuming that I had developed one, on that inherent law."

"I was also just thinking of the countess, I used to sit with her up here sometimes. She'd send for me and open up her little bag of raw coffee beans, roast a handful in the earthenware pot, I had to grind the freshly roasted coffee, then she would pour on the hot water—and we would sit there enjoying the aromas of Arabia, looking out on the park, on the vegetable beds, the potato fields, on the tarred black roofs of the orangery where at my suggestion we were growing mushrooms, and talk about your family. . . . She spoke rather contemptuously of her son, also quite openly about Gerlind, who at that time was traipsing around Holland, and she would say to me so often: 'I suppose you two will live here one day'—how could she know that, have even an inkling, when you were just a raw, impecunious lieutenant in the artillery

—and I, well, I was a mixture of working girl, bookbinder, secretary, maid, housekeeper, friend—yes, she was fond of us, but how could she know . . . ?"

"She wished it, wanted it, may have had a hunch, may have thought that we might lease the place and work it—she couldn't have known what would really happen. She never had much confidence in my own efficiency—quite rightly, too, I have never been efficient—but I was thinking of something quite different, of antlers, Defregger, and Katharina von Bora. . . ."

"Yes," said Käthe, "I often think of that too, and always with pleasure, yes—and not because you got me out of that ghastly chaos there; not only because of that . . . you took away my fear of—well, I was very happy, after all the things one hears in hospitals . . . there's no telling how something like that will end, how it will start. And you had such a bad reputation, you know, in that respect . . . it was quite delectable."

"What was?"

"It was delectable, but let's not have any confessions here . . . don't worry, I don't expect any confessions. The countess was almost totally ignorant about Holger, thought he was stupid, which he never was—he was never stupid, never. But she knew more about Gerlind than I've ever known about Sabine. And yet I was in Sabine's confidence, one would imagine."

"Sabine?" That touched a nerve, the fear in her voice, in her eyes. She hadn't known fear even when Rolf had behaved so stupidly.

"Yes, Sabine," she said, "the child she's expecting is not Fischer's. She's in her sixth month, and five months ago Fischer was away the whole time."

He pushed aside his teacup, put down the piece of toast, reached for the malachite box: "I suppose it's no use my saying 'No, no, not Sabine'—no, surely not Sabine, and when I confess that I have wished for her to have a lover I realize the thoughtlessness of that wish—because it's Sabine, because she was always such a serious, devout child. . . ."

"And yet you know that religious devotion doesn't guarantee a thing. Probably even Kohlschröder is still devout."

"From whom—with whom?"

"I didn't ask her because I know she won't tell me. Let's hope he isn't married. I've brought her here, she's with Kit in the guest apartment. She won't and she can't go on living with Fischer—she's watching TV at the moment, and it's a bad sign, when she watches TV—some stupid program that happens to be on the screen. . . ."

"Does she intend to go to the other man—does she . . . ?"

"I don't know, she doesn't know. Only one thing is certain, and that's serious: she's through with Erwin. By the way, I've had to move Eva Klensch, Sabine simply must have the apartment now. Blurtmehl is too bashful to have her sleep with him. Kulgreve has moved her to the second floor, I believe, into Bleibl's room—by the way, we'll have to warn Bleibl, you know—I must talk to you, not only about Bleibl."

"You don't need to whisper, speak up! Everything is monitored, it has to be. We might have secrets that conceal clues—if they really want to protect us, they have to listen to and analyze every nuance. Remember Kortschede and his young tough, who whispered to him one night: 'I belong to the hard core, I am the hard core, I'm the hardest core you can imagine'—and they had let him slip through because Kortschede vouched for him. It turns out that the boy is actually the head of a gang of criminals, the toughest bunch you can possibly imagine. They've picked up the whole lot—we simply have to endure these things, whether one's a homo or not. Can you imagine all the awkward problems that arise at a closed conference like this: women, for instance? Some of the men used to send out for girls or bring them along, not only hookers and stewardesses but also the kind we call girl-friends—hardly ever their wives. Particularly Bleibl—they say he can't spend the night without a woman—fair enough, he was satisfied with casuals, he'd put them into a taxi, a bit rumpled, and send them home. The male pickup problem that became such a disaster for Kortschede is a new one for us, it may be that they smuggled them in as secretaries, chauffeurs, assistants. I never had any inkling, never knew, not even with Kortschede—but of course he's the very opposite of Bleibl: discreet, suave, reserved, apprehensive, although he ruled over an even greater empire than Bleibl's. But these security measures have, of course, put an end to both, after all you can't take every casual girl or every casual boy and give them a thorough going-over before letting them in: some of them come from East Germany, some of them are intellectual and liberated hookers who are considered particularly dangerous—they hear, see, discover, and analyze too much. And so now we have those 'dry nights,' as Bleibl calls them, evenings that have to be spent sitting together, being bored, watching TV, playing a bit of cards. Music perhaps—or a talk, on tape of course —and then some of them start belting out wartime stuff, Nazi songs, till Bleibl leaves for some 'house'—and the security guards have to go along to the 'house.' I'd like to know what goes on in their heads; at any rate, there are no secrets anymore—everything out in the open, eye and ear—and after all we, that's to say, we of the Association, are no worse skirt-chasers than anybody else."

"And the Fischers, I mean both, senior and junior?"

"Oh no, my dear, no gossip there. I won't tell you a thing about old Fischer, not a thing—read it in his face, his mouth, his hands—and as for Erwin, you can follow his love life in the weeklies, and I'm willing to bet it's not half as riotous as it's made out to be. Even Russian women are said to find his charms irresistible, and he has publicly aired his views on the specific erotic qualities of the women of East Germany, who produce more than half of his Beehive stuff. And he—*he* is the man Sabine insisted on having because, apart from whatever else he might be, he's also a Catholic. Now she has him—and he doesn't have her anymore."

"That sounds as though you were relieved, and the poor child is taking it so hard."

"All the same, I am relieved. He actually wrote to the police suggesting that everyone be automatically listed for investigation who named a child Holger after November 'seventy-four. Even the most rabid bloodhounds there found that a bit extreme—after all, Holger is an ancient, honorable name, Old Swedish or Icelandic, meaning something like: island dweller with spear.''

"I must say, you've done your homework."

"Well, I do have two grandsons by that name. And if Sabine should have a boy—well, Holger's a fine name."

"It's no laughing matter, Fritz—look at your daughter, she's so serious it's destroying her. I'm sure she really loves that man— that—the one whose child it is. . . .''

"Yes, you're right, and I won't joke about it—then there's still the problem of Kit—Fischer will mobilize a whole battalion of lawyers, and Zummerling will supply him with headlines free of charge. One thing is sure, she won't be voted the 'most charming child of the year,' I take it. . . .''

"There we go—Zummerling again—can't you people think of anything else? I find him very nice, I've sat next to him twice at dinner, he was a real charmer—and Bleibl's not so bad either, he has more charm than he thinks, and is concerned about his two sons, though unfortunately we almost never see them."

"I grant you Zummerling is charming, a charming person— and yet without batting an eye he would grab my whole clutch of newspapers for himself with a single stranglehold. It's the era of nice monsters, Käthe, and we must count ourselves among them. They're all nice, Veronica's nice too, Beverloh was nice, he was a regular paragon of niceness. . . .''

"It wouldn't have taken much for Sabine to marry him—I shudder to think of it—just imagine, loyal as she is she would have gone with him."

"Hm, she doesn't appear to be all *that* loyal."

"Of course she's loyal—and Veronica is loyal too! That's the terrible thing about them, that's what's driving them all into this misery. They have to go on, they have to stick with it. And if Sabine Fischer had merely been unfaithful to Fischer she wouldn't be suffering as much, she would regard it as a lapse, confess—and finish; the point is, she is being true to herself . . . she can't be other than she is and transfer her loyalty to someone else. She's the type whose heart is broken by loyalty—if only I knew who it was—she says she wants to work, live and work somewhere anonymously. . . ."

"Anonymously! That'll be a pipe dream for a while. Fischer has seen to that, he's spread pictures of her in every rotten paper, in every Beehive catalogue, in *Sport and Society*, you can even see her in the business supplement. It'll be at least a year, I'd say, before she can think of anonymity."

"Can't you find a spot for her somewhere on the paper? She'll do what your sons never wanted to do, work *on* the paper *for* the paper."

"That's not a bad idea. I might send her to Paris to work without pay for Schneiderplin—her French is so good, she could work her way up, become a correspondent. But with two small children—we would have to pay for a maid. . . ."

"About Fischer she said: never, never, never again. As for the other man, she doesn't mention him at all. I must say I'm curious—but I suppose guessing won't help. . . ."

"I'm curious too, and the only thing I'm sure of is that it's nobody from the Fischer clique, where everything is now synchronized with porn and pop and dope—I imagine she has found a serious, old-fashioned lover with whom she has committed old-fashioned adultery—perhaps she was longing for the good old sins, the way others long for the good old days. . . ."

"For which we have never longed."

"No, never: the good old days, for her that's Eickelhof. For me it was never Eickelhof, never Tolmshoven, it wasn't my childhood home, nor yours. I was too happy with the good new days, which are now over, Käthe. The good new days will be the old days we long for. What's coming now is the very, very new era which nobody will look back on with longing."

"Rolf's era?"

"No, not Rolf's. Perhaps it will come after this very new era —not Herbert's era, not Sabine's or Kortschede's. It is Beverloh's era and Amplanger's era—sometimes I think of Beverloh sitting there, figuring, figuring, figuring—like when the barrier is lowered, when the baker's van starts off, and how it must be held up for how long so that it has to wait at the barrier and the genuine cake can be exchanged for the 'hot' one. Of him sitting there and figuring—and smiling, smiling, casually stroking Holger's hair, giving Veronica a friendly kiss—smiling the way Amplanger smiles. It always turns me ice-cold, as if someone had thrown me out over the Arctic Ocean. No, the good new days have imperceptibly become the old ones, Käthe, and it is their era, also Bleibl's era, who in his own way is timeless. Sabine is in for a hard time, worse if that man is married—that wretched confessional, which she couldn't break away from, still hasn't destroyed her conscience. And of course she had to get pregnant right away, when even the priests know how to do it without having to worry about pregnancy—if they were smart they would found a monastery where adultery can be committed in the truly old-fashioned way, where women find a lover—after all, even illegitimate children are still children. But, Käthe my dear, now I'd like to go out for a bit, get away from here, even if it's under escort. . . ."

"No more meetings, no more appointments today?"

"I don't have to take possession of my big office till the day after tomorrow. Then I'll also have to put in an appearance at the paper, have to be there when they decide what to do with the *Gerbsdorfer Bote*."

"You're afraid of that?"

"Of that, yes. I've lost all proper perspective on all the papers of which I'm supposed to be the lord and master. I'm afraid of those nine hundred square feet of office where nothing happens, where I do a bit of signing, drink a few cups of tea. I'm afraid of Amplanger senior. Not that he's cheating me, he doesn't need to— he's had a whole collection of blown-up mastheads hung on the wall facing my desk, all the ones we've captured since 1945. He calls me the license Napoleon without an army—and tomorrow the masthead of the *Gerbsdorfer Bote* will hang there: one more captured province, county, or city...."

"Amazing what a little English major's actions can lead to— with a piece of paper that is then called a license—have you ever found out what became of him?"

"Two weeks before he was due to retire he was killed on Cyprus—for the sake of his wife's pension he was posthumously promoted to lieutenant colonel; his name was Weller, he was one of those very dry fellows, a Labour man of course. I sometimes think of him when I'm sitting in my huge office—with nothing to do but approve Amplanger's policy, which I do—I can't hold back the growth and proliferation—my function is that of head-hunter. By means of a license, empires are founded that grow on their own, a license, newsprint, a few good people on the staff— all that's lacking is the crown prince, and the head collecting could go on."

"The crown prince chose to throw rocks and set fire to cars— I wonder whether he really intends to stay in that neck of the woods, growing tomatoes and picking apples to the end of time. Bleibl was saying the other day that he would have become one of our most dynamic bankers, if he hadn't . . . was saying that he had experience, organizing ability, an eye for relationships, political, economic. . . . It almost sounded as if he were envious. He praised Rolf's cool, organizational intelligence."

"Well, he might be right—he's fond of his own sons, no question, but he's always spoken enthusiastically about Rolf. He would have appointed Beverloh as his adjutant if there weren't— if there hadn't been that sudden switch, and if he had met him early enough—could have, might have—it just didn't happen. I would be happy if I could find a spot on the paper for Rolf, my own son, as a night watchman or sweeper. Yet of course he should be on the staff of the financial section, as a specialist in real profits —he once showed me some figures to prove that a share in the

Deutsche Bank had yielded fifteen thousand percent profit between 1949 and 1969—fifteen thousand in twenty years—that should interest people with savings accounts."

"But it doesn't—and is it correct?"

"It is correct—and it doesn't interest them—almost everything Rolf calculates is correct. If you were to figure out what the paper was worth when we took it over, and what it is worth, or would be worth, today, you would probably arrive at similar percentages."

"Yes, I can remember Rolf's calculations for Eickelhof. And what about Tolmshoven—how much will we get for that?"

"What makes you think of Tolmshoven?"

"I can see the dredges on the horizon, and I know there's no stopping—you've said yourself that there's no stopping the proliferation. I can hear whispers and jokes, I can hear my son-in-law's insinuations—and I can see Tolmshoven, not the village, just the manor house, like an island in a vast pit—helicopter service to the mainland—conveyor belts, noise, pumps, and dredges all around us, the moat with no natural water supply, stagnant, swampy, the ducks looking sickly—and your grandchildren will be flown in by airlift to feed the last of the ducks. But there's one thing that'll be guaranteed, Fritz, one thing we can really be sure of: security—unless some engineer or miner working down there around us on dredges and pumps and belts gets some silly idea—but how could he reach us, climb up the three or four hundred meters of wall? No, we'll be safe, unless the helicopter crashes just when we're flying out in the evening for a visit—to our sons, our daughter, our grandchildren—we'll be safe all right, and how safe the foundations will be, for the manor I mean, in this wobbly layer of gravel, clay, sand—they'll build us a huge concrete block—and in fifty or a hundred years, when they've excavated everything, Tolmshoven will be standing in the middle of an idyllic lake, and your great-grandchildren will be able to catch fish from the window—is that how it's going to be, Tolm?"

"No, Käthe, that's not how it's going to be. They'll tear it down and bury it, and we'll be living somewhere else—provided we live to see it."

"Will we live to see it? Will energy needs permit us to die here—in security, from security—who knows how? You needn't spare me, Fritz. I'd rather hear it from you than pick it up from whispers and stupid jokes—wouldn't it be better to move out now? Move somewhere else with Sabine, Kit, and the new baby, maybe with Rolf and Katharina, Holger—and Herbert if we can persuade him? Go ahead, have a cigarette—I won't tell any-one. . . ."

She pushed the malachite box toward him, and he lit up. "Sabine," he said, "she's been on my mind all day, and I didn't know why—she'll miss Blorr, Kit won't be able to play here properly, fortunately Fischer is off again tomorrow on one of his long trips—Pottsieker told me at lunch—Tunis, Romania, some Far Eastern refugee camps where they're setting up their knitting machines. At any rate, we'll be rid of him for the next couple of weeks and have time to think things over, perhaps she could even go back to Blorr during that time?"

"She won't do that, I'm sure—I'll bring her over, you have a talk with her while I stay with Kit. . . ."

He went to meet her, waited in the open door, nodded to young Hendler, who was strolling back and forth between their own rooms and the guest apartment. It was very quiet, the only unusual thing being the sound of voices from Blurtmehl's room—Miss Klensch must have already arrived. Käthe's vision of the manor-island in the pit preoccupied him: helicopter shuttle service, the swampy moat—no houses, no church, probably no more trees either, no birds, perhaps just a few crows—cracks in the walls. . . .

Sabine sank onto his chest, not so much a penitent sinner as a confused young woman; she shook her head when he tried to draw her into the room, looked at him, without tears. "Oh,

Father," she said, "I'm so glad to be away from there. It was impossible—I'll move to Rolf's for the time being, don't worry. The garden there has those high walls around it, Kit gets along fine with Holger, and we'll see—I've already spoken to Rolf. . . ."

"It's pretty cramped there, I don't know . . . ?"

"Katharina's finding me a room nearby—in the daytime I'll be with them, I'll give Katharina a hand, I'm good with children. . . ."

"Have you notified Holzpuke? I mean—he has to know. . . ."

"He growled a bit, said everything was running so smoothly in Blorr, and in Hubreichen, well, he knows the circumstances there, the facts—don't be angry with me for not staying, I've spoken to Erwin too, he's off on another trip—we can leave the serious problems till later . . . later. Mr. Hendler will take me to Hubreichen and stay there today—I asked Holzpuke for this, you know he's Kit's favorite. I already feel much better, much easier, I'm not thinking yet of the serious problems ahead of us, for the next three weeks Erwin will be away. . . ."

She resembled Käthe, also his mother—and him—and whom else, someone he didn't know? Had no sadness in her eyes, they just looked serious, and now joyful in a way that made him think almost affectionately of the man whose child she was expecting. He must be very good to her. He thought of Beverloh, with whom she had been so violently in love, of Fischer, who had thrust his way so boyishly into all her "speculative talk" and taken her so to speak by storm; dynamic, Catholic, an entrepreneur—quite witty, too, at times—but not once in all the five years had he seen Sabine's face looking like this: serious and full of joy, the regular features that had given her the reputation of a beauty, moved and mobile—and determined, too. "No more TV, no idiot box—good, very good. . . ."

"No, I was only confused for a while. . . ."

"And the other thing?"

"What other thing?"

"The—I mean, the religious aspect—your whole attitude—I mean, perhaps you feel a sense of guilt—wouldn't you like to talk about it? Perhaps this evening at Rolf's, if we were to go over there?"

"Yes, do come—that would be lovely—come—no, don't worry, Mr. Hendler may hear it all, but—" She turned and looked out into the corridor, smiled. "I see he's withdrawn—discreetly—I do feel a sense of guilt, not toward Fischer and not toward you and Mother, only toward his wife. We'll talk about it. . . . And how about you, what will you be doing now that they've put you right at the top?"

"I shall make speeches and give interviews. I'm not scared anymore, only for you, for the family—we'll be there this evening. . . ."

Kit, that was obvious, and it hurt a little, was looking forward to Hubreichen more than to Tolmshoven. There she would be able to roast her chestnuts in the garden over an open fire and play with Holger, would also be allowed to go for the milk, and help sort the apples that Rolf sold. He had never understood how one could call a child Kit, even if it might be a variation of Käthe—if he remembered rightly it had a different, less flattering meaning. With Käthe's arm in his, he watched them go down the stairs, Kit with her little bag of walnuts and chestnuts, Sabine with her little suitcase, and the young police officer carrying Kit's dolls, two of them, holding them by the legs, bundled together, the doll dresses hanging down over their heads, revealing their underwear. . . .

"She was a different person when I saw her just now," said Käthe, "something must have completely changed her, made her almost happy—anyway she's made up her mind. . . ."

"He must be a very nice man, the father of this child—perhaps she talked to him on the phone—in any case: he is in her. . . ."

"What odd things you say, and you can even laugh. . . ."

"I'm happy for her—but he's married, she told me so. And probably a man like that also has a nice wife. That'll complicate things—and when Fischer gets back there's going to be trouble."

"I don't know, perhaps we should leave her alone today with Rolf and Katharina. I'll try to get hold of Herbert—incidentally, let's hope she didn't phone him, whoever he may be. For then Holzpuke would know what we don't—who it is, perhaps he knows anyway: if anyone knows, surely it must be the security people, considering how closely she's guarded—she must've met him somewhere—and more than once, I'm sure."

"You're right—Holzpuke should know—she must've met him, must've arranged a meeting, and all that. . . ."

"Shall we ask him?"

"No, and anyway he wouldn't tell us—wouldn't be allowed to—he's not allowed to pass on any information picked up in the course of duty that is of an intimate nature: the only thing he must do is to check out that man for security purposes. Let's hope the man knows what kind of circuit he's landed in. If she's really been under watertight surveillance—which I presume she has—only the security people can know who the father of our future grandchild is: if the surveillance is really functioning, the tape will know who the father of our grandchild is."

"Shall I call Herbert now?"

"Ask him whether he couldn't come here—just this once? If we are to drive over to Herbert in his high rise, I'll have to let Holzpuke know in good time. For that place they'll need practically a whole company of guards, which is quite logical: there are all kinds of groups and types hanging out in there, not only students and Communists but Communist students, even anarchists and Maoists—and God knows what; entrances and exits would have to be secured, they'll probably need helicopters—and we'll be sitting there with our son, who won't move out if it kills him because that high rise happens to be part of the Tolm holdings and he wants to keep proving to me what kind of inhuman housing-machine I'm a partner in. They'll be standing there with their machine pistols in front of the doors and on the balconies, occupying the lobby—they have no choice. Visiting Rolf means a much simpler production, only one or two men around the vicarage. But the people in Hubreichen care for that as little as the people in Blorr and the occupants of Herbert's high rise. It bothers them, makes them uneasy and bad-tempered, those highly strung reactions occur not only with Kortschede but also with the police officers, who are under tension for months on end, tension and boredom, tension although or because nothing is happening. And then a few shots may suddenly go off, at random, when a dog runs through the hazel thicket or some boy from the village climbs over the wall and fires his toy pistol. The best we can do is acknowledge the fact that we are prisoners—that we'll perish in security, perhaps from security."

"So that means staying at home—or visiting people who are as closely guarded as we are—the Fischer parents, where I always feel ready to throw up. They're forever conjuring up the Red peril, they're pathological about it and pathologically boring, they see starvation staring them in the face when sales rise by only twenty-nine million instead of thirty-five million, they defend the middle classes, to which they don't even belong, against the Socialist threat while knowing perfectly well that their very concentration represents the greatest threat to the middle classes. I've read myself that the banks are an even greater threat to the middle classes, and Germany is always doomed when even *one* Communist becomes a city councillor someplace. And with luck there'll also be a bishop among the guests, a quiet one who nods and nods and nods to everything—and they all dress and behave and smile like Amplanger, who looks the way I imagine the ones they're trying to protect us from do—and when you think that Rolf almost became a bank manager and that Beverloh certainly would have—with the latest in briefcases, tennis racket, and maybe a little dog under one arm. . . . It's always the same: they happen to have heard twelve and a half words on the radio and five and a half words on TV, and already starvation is staring them in the face and they see the revolution at the door. Oh, Fritz, dear Tolm, why must they all be so boring?"

"Not all—Kortschede and Pottsieker and even Amplanger

senior—there are a few—nor Bleibl, you can't call him boring."

"And yet you're longing to visit your children too and can't,
won't, you've had to hand yourself over to a security in which
you don't believe—which you are really only enduring out of
courtesy. . . ."

"And they'll find some other way through all security
measures—the bomb flying like a bird, a really 'hot' owl, wild
geese sweeping through the night—or they'll send my grandson
Holger to do me in, well drilled, hardened by Alpine and other
training, twelve, fifteen years old, he'll arrive unarmed, pass
through all the checkpoints: grandson visiting grandfather—and
he may well throttle me, won't even need a knife—and if by that
time they've reached the point of tying the hands of unarmed
visitors, even if it be a grandson, his head will be his weapon, like
a ram he'll butt his head against my heart, over and over again
against a heart weakened by several coronaries, jabbing,
jabbing. . . ."

"If Holger is not going to be sent to you as a well-trained
butting ram until he's twelve or fifteen, you still have five or
eight years to go."

He laughed, now did reach again for the cigarette box: "It
won't be long—anyway I'll be president for two years, and I've
long stopped imagining that there is such a thing as security,
internal or external, or within me either, for that matter."

"So I won't be catching you anymore in the morning in front
of the bathroom mirror, whispering to yourself: 'I don't want to
go on.' Do you?"

"Yes, I do, I want to go on with you—yet they're probably
already practicing strangleholds, looking into hypnosis, drugs,
perhaps with drugs they'll persuade a security officer to 'grab me.'
He will be a nice, well-drilled, thoroughly healthy, thoroughly
vetted young policeman who will suddenly throw himself upon
me with an apparently protective gesture that conceals the
murderous grip. There is no security—computers, rockets,

rocketlike artificial birds, psychomanipulations, remote psycho-terrorism—so we might as well resign ourselves to the loneliness of extreme, luxurious imprisonment. Remember my attempt —that went from the absurd to the ridiculous—to take up one of my old pleasures, cycling. Two police cars in front, one behind me, and a helicopter circling overhead—too ridiculous to be endured. And when did we have our last big family dinner where each person was responsible for one course: you took care of the soup and salad, I took care of the meat, Rolf of the potatoes, Katharina the gravy, Herbert and Sabine of the desserts—and I was responsible for the coffee. We all did the dishes together, kitchen and dining room had to be spanking clean before coffee was served, and on those occasions Erwin Fischer was even quite nice, surprising us by producing an additional dessert in the form of fantastic crepe suzettes—until that baby arrived whom they named Holger. Until then he had been able to bring himself to sit at the same table with a 'car arsonist' like Rolf and a Communist like Katharina—but he couldn't stand the idea of a second Holger in the family, and things got so bad that Sabine and Katharina and Rolf could only meet secretly, without Kit of course, who might have talked—not only under complete surveillance but informing on each other too merely because someone had named a child Holger. How about settling for staying here—we could invite Blurtmehl and his girl for dinner if they aren't doing anything and he can forget that he's a servant and allow himself to be waited on for a change. I think we'd better leave Katharina, Sabine, and Rolf to themselves—let's have a quiet evening here."

"We really ought to ask Katharina's parents over some-time."

"Of course, they're Rolf's parents-in-law, in a way, and Luise —I can remember her as a child, fortunately she was never one of my father's pupils, so I'd be spared that topic of conversation. . . . Will you have a word with Blurtmehl? I'm curious to meet this Eva. . . ."

"So am I—I didn't get the impression that they had any

plans. I'll have to leave you now for a while, do some phoning and see what I have in the way of supplies."

Sometimes he had made an unexpected, unannounced visit to Rolf in Hubreichen, asking Holzpuke for a reduced escort and telling Blurtmehl to park the car on the empty school playground. He had walked the hundred paces to the vicarage and gone into the garden where the young people lived in a small separate building known for some mysterious reason as "the annex." He would walk as fast as he could, trying to stay ahead of swift tongues, while his protectors, swifter than he, took up positions by the vicarage wall inside the garden. He would then pause in the hazel thicket, look into the ground floor of the annex, see his son Rolf playing with Holger: building blocks of wood, of stones, wooden vehicles, handmade (he didn't even dare to think the word "hobby"—to them that word was insulting, they insisted on "handmade").

Rolf would be squatting on the ground beside the boy, a happy young father, relaxed, smoking as he sat on his heels, gently guiding the boy's play and, to judge by the movements of his lips and hands, encouraging him too, and he seemed to be singing softly while painting stones, pasting colored paper on wooden blocks. Once too, while Holger was quietly watching him, he hollowed out a turnip into a lantern, giving it eyes, mouth, nose, and moustache, using his knife to cut a holder for the candle. Everything was very quiet, relaxed, and the two were enjoying themselves—and then inevitably had come the memory of Eickelhof, where he had sometimes played truant from the newspaper to play with the children.

One evening, before he had time to walk to the door and knock, he had been surprised by Katharina, just back from shopping. She exclaimed: "Good heavens, Father"—yes, she called him Father!—"why are you standing around here like an outcast? Come on, you won't disturb us, you never do." And he had almost felt tears in his eyes because she was so kind, called him Father, took him by the arm, and led him into the house on that dull, misty November evening. He was surprised at the warmth of Rolf's greeting, and on the bench that he had been unable to see from the outside he discovered a whole gallery of hollowed-out turnips as well as lanternlike torches consisting of black cardboard frames pasted with colored paper, all made by Rolf for the private kindergarten. He also learned that Rolf had been picked to ride through the village as Saint Martin, escorted by torchbearers, Roman legionaries with silver breast-plates and swords, red cloaks. He was offered tea and ginger-bread, allowed to smoke a cigarette, sit by the stove, put on more wood, wood that Rolf had gathered with his own hands in the nearby forest—with permission, of course—and had chopped and cut up, also sacks of fir cones, baskets of shavings. Rolf went around the farms collecting waste lumber, lumber that as a result of rapid modernization (all too rapid, in Rolf's opinion) lay around ready to be thrown away—roof timbers, planks, also discarded furniture that he collected and either cut up for fire-wood or repaired for sale in some student secondhand store. That particular evening Rolf had spared him his analysis of stock-exchange reports, had merely used examples to explain the prin-ciple of throwing away and what has been thrown away. For the first time and with an undertone of regret he had declared Eickelhof to have been thrown away and the energy gained by that throwing away to have also been thrown away.

Did one have to eavesdrop on one's children, take them by surprise, to discover their warmth, to gain insight into their lives? Another day, in turning the street corner on his way to the vicarage, he had seen Katharina, holding Holger by the hand, returning from her shopping, exchanging greetings with passers-by, bending down to Holger, who seemed to be pulling some toy behind him and was holding a lollipop. In her left hand she was carrying what was obviously a very heavy shopping bag; a young woman like all the others, with red kneesocks, loose hair, and when she caught sight of him he had seen that sudden smile light up her face—such a spontaneous smile that once again he felt close to tears. He hastened toward her, relieved her of the shopping bag, was kissed, kissed Holger, and then watched her unpack her groceries in the house, arranging them in cupboards and on homemade shelves, while the boy pulled his wooden dachshund around in circles on the floor. He was given tea and a sandwich, and Katharina shook her head as she removed the packet of cigarettes he was reaching for—then, with a shrug, pushed it toward him again. Quite obviously she was fond of him: that sudden smile on her face out there on the street, the liver-sausage sandwich, the tea, the concern over his smoking: a young woman who might have been beautiful had it not been for that trace of austerity about her. He had no difficulty in imagining her as a nun—yet her good sense, intelligence, and sensitivity were limited to this village. Always, when he saw her, he had to think of her uncle, Hans Schröter, the Münzenberg Communist, whom Major Weller had sent him so long ago for his newspaper, his favorite among all the journalists he had come to know on his paper. He had even suggested to Hans Schröter that they use first names, but Schröter had refused, in a manner that was oddly cool and at the same time courteous, and it hadn't occurred to any of the journalists who had interviewed him this morning to ask: "You were on first-name terms with Communists?"

He had never managed to take Sabine by surprise in this way: at times she was more strictly guarded than he was himself, also because of Kit. So he had simply been driven there by Blurtmehl, the sixteen kilometers to Blorr (which—fortunately no one knew this, not even Käthe—had played a certain role in his doctoral thesis), disgusted by the new bungalows built on the outskirts of the little place that had once been regarded as a paradise of beech and chestnut trees. Each time he had run into the guards there, pursued by his own guards, and invariably he had been disgusted

by the Fischer taste as expressed in copper and marble; Sabine
had always seemed harried and tense. Of course they were happy
to see him, Kit would be delighted, would want to go for a walk
with him, loved to walk hand in hand with him to the farms, to
the farmers who still remembered him as a student when he used
to ride his bicycle around here, researching, sketching, photo-
graphing, noting measurements and construction dates, changes.
Old Hermanns, particularly, enjoyed digging around "in the old
days." But all this acquired a loathsome artificiality due to the
security people constantly trotting behind them, apparently at
random but obviously instructed to keep them surrounded in
swarms. Sometimes Sabine would weep, could give no reason for
it, would simply weep, ask her neighbor over for tea—a dark,
buxom, somewhat vulgar, pretty woman of soothing banality.
That quiet, serious Sabine, his dearest daughter (did she know
that he was so fond of her and couldn't tell her?), would wince
at the mere slamming of a car door outside, or when Kit threw
something against something—perhaps it was better after all to
be like Rolf, not guarded but merely under surveillance? Wasn't
this security, which was no security, being bought at too high a
price?

The days had long since gone when Sabine had been able to
ride off on horseback as she pleased, and since the affair of
Pliefger's birthday cake it probably really was better to have
groceries and other goods that were delivered to the house probed
and checked, for by this time everything had happened, everything, and recently even packages of cigarettes had to be opened
since the day one had exploded in Plotteti's hands in Italy and
severely injured him as he tore it open: mutilated hand, disfigured
face, and there was the constant nuisance with the sherry bottles
and their wrap-around labels that made it impossible to check the
contents from outside: the fancy labels had to be soaked off the
bottles, which, after all, might have been camouflaged Molotov
cocktails. . . .

No, Sabine didn't have the peace of mind still to be found with

Rolf and Katharina; she was, after all, the daughter-in-law of the Beehive, as well as his own daughter. The villa near Málaga didn't help either, nor did she find any peace in skiing: the Sabine who had always found such joy in movement—riding and dancing— was becoming apathetic. Perhaps he added to her tension because his presence required a doubling of the guard, the surveillance around the house.

What he enjoyed least was visiting Herbert, although he would have dearly liked to have a long tête-à-tête with him. He, of course, had an entirely different set of friends, of whom a dozen or more were usually hanging around his place. In some indefinable way, Herbert's friends had more soul than Rolf and Katharina's, or Sabine's friends. They too—Herbert's friends— were vehement opponents of the system: long-haired, almost all of them, the girls with floppy dresses and jute shoulder bags, they baked their own bread, ate quantities of salad and vegetables, yet did from time to time—"out of solidarity," as they called it— go to those "poison places," meaning fast-food shops. They were never embarrassed when he appeared, laughed at the amount of surveillance required in this crazy high rise, laughed not at the guards themselves but at the whole absurd "production," some- times asked one of the guards in for a meal, for a chat, avoided the word "discussion," talked to Tolm about "nonexistent security," about "death, which may occur but is also nonexistent," made music, sang, talked without embarrassment about Jesus Christ, not only were not shy but told him frankly that he wasn't to think he particularly impressed them with his manor house, his newspaper, his huge office that was sometimes shown in magazines along with "the tentacles of that vestibule, the suction cups of materialism," no, they weren't impressed by any of that, they merely found him "nice and broken," broken by the inexorable rise of his paper and the ever-lengthening tentacles, the suction cups into which he himself was now being sucked. Surely that must scare him, not only the system but his paper, which was mainly a waste of paper, wasn't it, especially since the custom had died out that used in some degree to justify the existence of newspapers: tearing or cutting them into handy squares and spiking them on a nail to be used as toilet paper, as had been the practice at almost every social level: *that* had been true recycling!

They told him exactly how many acres of forest, how many trees, had to be sacrificed for both purposes: for toilet paper *and* newspapers, the colossal pressure of the despotism of hygiene. He should think for a moment of how much totally superfluous, absolutely senseless, useless stuff—which nobody ever read—was being printed in leaflets and pamphlets issued by government departments—provincial, regional, parliamentary—as well as radio, TV, and political parties, not to mention all that revoltingly superfluous advertising material, all that junk which moves from the printing press almost straight into the garbage can. How many forests were being "sacrificed" for that, how many American Indians might be living in those forests that are being needlessly wasted every day—yes, every day (and they had no idea how scared he really was for those and other reasons, not the slightest inkling, and eventually he found them a bit too superior and conceited). Yes, and of course they were against nuclear energy, against "murderous" highway construction—not that they were in the least anti-progress or even radicals in the sense of that idiotic government decree banning radicals from jobs. No, they weren't even marginally impressed by him, they didn't even feel sorry for him for having been caught up in the vicious circle of coercive measures—and by that they didn't mean the security measures, which they found absurdly irrelevant (as if someone could postpone the predestined moment of his death—ridiculous!). Absurd—no, they meant growth erosion, that most horrible of all cancers, to which, as he must surely know, his second or third home, his present one, the manor house, would fall victim, so that for the second time—or was it more?—he would become a displaced person. Would he never, ever, grasp that the threat was born of the system, was part of the system?

In one way he found Herbert's friends less to his liking than Rolf's. Without being able to pinpoint it, he found them humorless. When irony did enter into their arguments, it was always unconscious and unintentional. He also found their lack of respect a bit excessive, they refused to concede that his little paper had had its function, and still did, as an important factor in the development or creation of a democratic system and of an order that had proved necessary after the total destruction of all values by Nazism.

Herbert's friends were not as abstractly intellectual as Rolf's friends, whom he occasionally met in Hubreichen. These people were neither hostile nor lacking in respect, they simply regarded him as an utter stranger; they were neither arrogant nor embarrassed, they looked at him as if he came from a totally different star, were probably surprised to find that he actually drank tea and ate bread, while to him they didn't seem so utterly strange at all. He was a fellow citizen, after all, spoke their language, and when he then shyly asked: What do you do for a living? the answer came: Teacher, banned from the profession. Metalworker, blacklisted, even by the union. Social worker, not even particularly leftist (what was that supposed to mean: "not even particularly leftist"?), blacklisted. There were some who said: I was accepted by the civil service (or I got my job) before that lousy decree. They were never against individuals, always against the system, didn't resent a property owner for raising the rent since the system forced him to do so, forced him if need be by terrorism, and they told him how property owners were put under pressure, terrorized—by people throwing rocks, shitting in the corridors, overturning pails of water, because the owners had *not* raised the rent.

They also admitted that they weren't "that badly off" because they too—there could be no doubt about that—profited from the system, that system which existed "somewhere else," very far away, and yielded such immense profits that they could share in them—they were fully aware that they shared in these profits, that they too lived under the pressure of the system, the system that was producing more sick and dependent people every day—over here as well as over there—and by "over there" they meant the Soviet Union. They were neither aggressive nor arrogant, only very reserved and sad, yes, there was a cold sadness in them, and not only although but also precisely *because* they threatened, kidnapped, killed individuals—yes, that's why "they" were criminals, not only in moral or political terms, they were even, if you like, criminals in a philosophical-theoretical-theological sense, for they supplied the system with the very thing that reinforced it, the very thing the system should not be allowed to benefit from: victims, martyrs. They supplied the system with those on a multimedia wave against which, as they sat there smoking cigarettes and drinking cheap red wine, they could not prevail—against this media superiority they could never prevail, ever, were powerless—not quite but almost with their leaflets, their banners. The victims, the martyrs, only served to enhance the power of the media: it was a kind of sorcery, an irrationalism, enough to drive one into total paralysis. On this point they weren't as ruthless as Herbert's friends, didn't even mention his paper, which was, after all, a medium—and what a medium! Naturally they too wanted to live with their wives and children and girlfriends, have parties, dances, picnics, singsongs—but pot and stronger stuff, porn and worse, those were neither for Herbert's friends nor for Rolf's—for pot and stronger stuff, porn and worse, even drunkenness and the like, all those were part of the system that by now they barely hated, merely despised in a way that seemed to him more dangerous than hatred. The system was the Nothing, the "established Nothingness" on whose garbage one could live, had to live. . . .

And he recalled the young people he sometimes met at Sabine's, or rather: had met, for of course the strict security measures kept visitors away too. Among them there had been occasional flirtations with just that: pot and stronger stuff, quite openly with porn; and from time to time, with considerable discretion, particularly at the house of those dreadful Fischer parents, who positively cultivated a kind of porno-Catholicism or Catho-pornicism—at such parties it not infrequently happened that fairly prominent "personalities" had to be dragged, dead drunk, by chauffeurs into their cars—and the magic word one kept hearing was invariably: baroque. "We happen to be baroque people," that was the favorite phrase of old Fischer, who had been quite a modest shopkeeper, the very man to whitewash Bleibl: no, it was a fact that he had never been a Nazi, never, he had even helped persecuted priests, hidden them, these stories were forever being trotted out, stories that could "stand up to the most rigorous investigation"; detailed descriptions of how he had taken soup and bread to the hiding places, had installed stoves against the cold, and "said many a Hail Mary with those in hiding": there were even photos that didn't have to be framed, showing a gaunt nun in a tiny cellar, a pot of soup beside her, beside the pot of soup Fischer, both holding rosaries—there were also photos of Erwin at the age of four or five being blessed by priests hidden in the cellar. There was no gainsaying that: the Bleibl-Fischer connection, which, though never openly consummated, everyone was aware of, was unbeatable, especially since Zummerling had acquired the rights to these photos and could publish them at any time.

And then there was somewhere—where? where? where?—that fourth, additional group: "they"—to call them criminals was to his mind an understatement, quite irrelevant, that satellite world from which Veronica sometimes phoned; and the word "Communists" didn't apply to that world or Rolf's, didn't even apply to Katharina, who was still regarded as one although she denied it in her firm but pleasant way.

"Of course I am communist and will continue to be, but what do I have in common with most Communists?—as much as a Catholic priest who has joined the *guerrilleros* has in common with the Pope or with the Princess of Monaco, who is also a Catholic; besides, it's wrong, misleading, and much too romantic to try and see me in terms of the twenties: I don't belong there, don't belong to the Communists you have known, nor to our Commie Uncle Hans—not to the people you dream about, sometimes enthuse about—just think of the changes in other areas of dogma—I'm not even thirty yet, and less than twelve years ago, when I was almost eighteen, I still believed I would be damned to all eternity if I broke the rule of fasting before Holy Communion. Stop dreaming about the Communists you have known, stop dreaming that I belong to the twenties—and believe me, I understand 'them' as little as you do, perhaps even less—no, maybe we resemble each other in this: we can't understand them, we merely know one thing—they are being coerced like all the rest of us."

Reason enough to reflect on the type of coercion to which he was exposed and to which he was slowly but surely succumbing. A few nostalgic musings were unavoidable, all of them starting with "in the old days." In the old days, when he had already been a pretty important boss, actually less than six years ago, he had still been able simply to escape from his office, stop at a newsstand for a paper, walk over to Café Getzloser, where he had ordered a snack, eaten it unnoticed and unobserved, been waited on with a smile, phoned Käthe from a booth. Or he had simply gone to a florist's, bought some flowers for Käthe, Sabine, Edith, or Veronica, dropped into a jeweler's—now the jewelers with their velvet-lined boxes had to come, under strict guard, to his office, his home, or a hotel. And when had he last been able to browse in antique shops, looking for engravings of the Rhine, its towns, banks, landscapes, not looking for anything in particular, just browsing and coming across engravings and paintings from the era before the Rhine was overrun by tourists—such as his favorite engraving of Bonn, hardly bigger than a cigarette package, engraved with pearly clarity and discreetly tinted by an anonymous artist: the banks of the Rhine, trees, a wing of the palace, on the river a barge and the old customs bastion. And also —impossible today or, if not impossible, so embarrassing that he would never do it—his affair with Edith, who wasn't even a young thing, she'd been all of thirty-five, unmarried, a stock clerk in a department store on whom he was calling to offer his condolences on the death of her brother, his auditor Scheubler. It had almost turned into a scandal—he couldn't understand how other people could actually pursue their amours under surveillance, when surely the very thought of the guard's watchful eye must destroy all spontaneity.

IV

The fear kept returning, growing, fear for him, later fear of him too, that alternated, merged, when he came home "all in, simply all in," made cutting remarks about the house and neatness in the home, often quite grumpy, almost gruff, something he had never, never been before. He complained about the small house being cramped, the garden too tiny; pulled and plucked and grumbled at every scrap of weed and, with a mere, the merest, trace of disapproval, scrutinized her hair—which, naturally, wasn't always as tidy as it should be if she happened to have been working in the garden, the basement, or the kitchen or romping with Bernhard and the dog in the garden. Then there was the occasional bead of moisture on her forehead, or something that looked like perspiration around her nose; there might be garden soil on Bernhard's shoes, blades of grass lying on the driveway or the concrete paths; and he would poke around in his food—which he had never done before—finding the soup too hot or not hot enough, the salad dressing too sour or not sour enough, though she had put in all the ingredients in exactly the usual quantity, knowing that that was how he liked it; or he would find too much gristle in the stew, though he knew the price of meat and that she had to save up for the celebration of Bernhard's First Communion. Besides: they had overextended themselves again, the new car, the payments on the house, the credit that had been much too hastily applied for and so quickly granted and that was turning out to be more expensive than they had been led to believe. And since he had been on this special assignment, always in plain clothes now, never in uniform, his clothing—and he was so fussy!—cost more these days despite the supplement. Without exactly barking at Bernhard, he growled at him, found the boy—strange word—not "graceful" enough, said he was too clumsy the way he rode around the driveway or on the garden paths on his little bike, talked about gym lessons for the boy, shook his head in abject despair when he inspected Bernhard's homework.

He had never been like that—serious, yes, and sometimes strict, too strict she felt, when he tore up the boy's comics, calling them "filthy porn" when really it was comparatively harmless stuff considering what the kids could see at every newsstand. There were worse things than those overblown blondes with their teased hair—at least only their cleavage was visible. What could that possibly mean to an eight-year-old boy who need only go to the public swimming pool to see more—not even the public one, he had only to look through the garden fence to watch their neighbor Ilse Mittelkamp sunbathing or mowing the lawn; he saw more there than at the pool, more than in those dreadful comics with those little blondes with all their "uplift" who might equally well be seven, seventeen, or twenty-seven. Vulgar little bitches, that they most certainly were, a sort of combination of child and prostitute, their vulgar pouting mouths sometimes as naïvely rounded as a little girl's, sometimes as cynical as a tart's. "Consumer hookers," "consumer vampires," that they most certainly were, their heads empty of everything but travel, dancing, champagne, music—"poolside nymphets"—

true, but she couldn't very well let the boy loose in the world with blinkers on, could she? Granted things were pretty dreadful; chaos, disintegration all around, and in the midst of it all the boy was supposed to be undergoing preparation for his first Holy Communion: chastity and all that, while if one were to believe even half of what one heard, the clergy themselves hardly lived like that anymore, and the boy himself probably didn't even know what unchastity meant. For Bernhard was certainly—at least *she* was certain, Hubert had his doubts, and there had been some loathsome arguments about it—not yet sexually arousable. And Hubert had talked to Kiernter, the police psychologist, had obtained some literature on infantile sexuality, and all he had to do was look in the boy's eyes, where he would find only fear and bafflement at the reason for Hubert's anger, not fear about the thing itself, whatever that might be. And needless to say, the monthly payments continued to be too high, they had to economize, and of course the shirts he bought himself were too expensive, simply too expensive, now that Hubert, too, had gone on what Monika called a "cotton kick." Surely it couldn't be the job that made him come home so "all in, all in": standing around outside those fancy villas, or wandering around the manor house, keeping an eye on entrances and exits—ever on the alert. Of course he took it all very seriously—took everything seriously, too much so—and of course the responsibility was great, she could see that, yet she still felt that his irritability and brusqueness toward her were out of all proportion.

He never told her any details about his work, he never had, never any details about his period of training. She knew they all underwent regular psychological examinations and tests, there was a lot of stress, she knew that. Yet his recent preoccupation with cleanliness and neatness seemed to her almost pathological— no longer merely pedantic but almost pathological, the way he sometimes spent almost an hour under the shower, found fault with his freshly pressed trousers, and—this was really an insult— sniffed at his socks before putting them on and, if he discovered the tiniest crease in those expensive cotton shirts, made a face as if seriously offended.

Not so long ago she had looked forward to his coming home, to their evening meal, to having coffee, sitting down with Bernhard and helping him with his homework, drinking a glass of beer on the terrace, chatting over the fence with the neighbors about the housing shortage and keeping up with payments, about bringing up children and the times in general. Sometimes the neighbors had also asked him for a bit of advice, almost always something to do with cars, No Parking and No Stopping zones, or speed limits, and they'd also been asked over by the Hölsters on their right and the Mittelkamps on their left; and they had themselves invited the neighbors, for beer and pickles or coffee and dessert. The whole atmosphere had cooled considerably, not exactly hostile but cooler because Hubert was so touchy about obscenities, which Mrs. Hölster had a way of quietly but rather vulgarly weaving into her conversation. And from time to time the word "fuzz" had been used, when they forgot that he was one of them himself and didn't notice their faux pas, although they would then pretty soon want to know what his duties were, since he was constantly "going off all dressed up in his new car." That was enough to make him clam up completely.

The Mittelkamps were coarser, more outspoken, by no means more agreeable and, when he was briefly attached to the vice squad, wanted details, talked about "hookers and fags" and "this new job of yours—that must really be something—security unit, hm?" To such a question, neither yes nor no was possible, and silence was probably taken for assent. The Mittelkamps were young, in their late—more likely their middle—twenties, he was a warehouse foreman, she a supermarket cashier, with no children, few if any financial worries. The Hölsters were older, getting on for fifty, he worked in the revenue department, while she, when their daughter had finished her training, had "gone back to the office," just for a short time, and was then unemployed, and had once whispered to her at the garden fence, "I simply can't break myself of the habit, that porn stuff, I simply can't—you mustn't mind, Helga, when now and again something slips out." The Hölsters with that daughter of theirs who at first had seemed a bit of a mystery, in her middle twenties, always smartly dressed and driving a smart car, with marvelous hairdos and always a pleasant smile—apparently with no steady or regular occupation. At times she was to be heard typing away for hours, then she would be away again for long periods, sometimes she would sleep late and have a copious breakfast on the balcony; then, at hours when other people were working, she was to be seen sitting in the garden reading, and finally, when asked outright by Mittelkamp, she divulged that she was a convention secretary, taking home taped speeches and letters as well as shorthand minutes of conventions and negotiations and transcribing them at home. Her work was steady, all right, but not regular.

Claudia was a nice girl who didn't seem to like her mother's off-color jokes at all, and she did think Hubert went too far and was unfair in once calling Claudia a "convention hooker." Once he had also called her own sister Monika a hooker, at a time when there was some justification for this description—Monika, who insisted on being called Monka because that name was now "in," had meanwhile really turned over a new leaf, in fact she never had been a hooker, she had merely moved in circles where such suspicions were not entirely unjustified. Monka was now working for, sometimes in, a boutique, sewing, knitting, designing; she lived with Karl, who was still going to the university and earning money wherever he could. Karl spoke and thought pretty freely about many things, but never, as Monka still sometimes did, flippantly. And anyway: this business of living together without being married, Mrs. Hölster and the Mittelkamps—she felt like such an outsider, yet she was only twenty-nine herself, and that apparently (or maybe genuinely) scientific way of discussing sex sometimes revolted her more than Mittelkamp's crudeness— once, when his wife was at work and Bernhard at school, he had had the nerve to ask her over for "fun and games." She had never told Hubert, all hell would have broken loose. She could hardly stand it when a certain occurrence, which she still called fulfillment, was discussed in appropriate scientific terms—or when Hubert once actually speculated on whether their boy, their dear little Bernhard, was already having erections: horrible word!

There had been days when she had been on the point of going off to her mother's, who had at last found her own cottage and garden in Hetzigrath and dreamed of a Silesia that no longer existed, if it ever had: it always sounded as if life there had consisted solely of apples and honey, linen and the Catholic faith, incense and the Blessed Virgin—no tensions, no problems; never war, only peace. And the dreadful experience, of course, of having to flee, leaving behind the apples, honey, incense, and the Blessed Virgin, and needless to say "they" had been to blame, no one else. A fairy tale, and she wouldn't have minded putting up with this Silesian fairy tale for a while if it hadn't been for Bernhard's school. Now at last he had this nice, firm Mr. Plotzkehler for a teacher, a friend of Karl's from the university who was taking such an interest in the boy. No, she couldn't risk changing schools now.

Things were becoming more and more difficult with Hubert, and there was something else of which the mere thought made her blush, and she couldn't talk about it to anybody, anybody at all, not even to Monka, for fear she would laugh at her. She couldn't confess it either, for there was no question of guilt, and the rumors one heard about the clergy increased her doubts about advice from that quarter. Perhaps she could have talked to Karl about it, but he was a man, although undoubtedly discreet and understanding, and would probably have just spouted a lot of scientific words. Fulfillment—not fulfillment of duty—was what she lacked; after all, she did have a sex, female, wasn't ashamed of it, enjoyed it, and had enjoyed Hubert, just as he had enjoyed her, as she well knew. He had always been loving, nice in his quiet, serious way, never crude, had in fact sometimes lost that deep seriousness and been almost merry; never crude, neither before their marriage nor after; gladly had she been fulfilled by him, given him fulfillment, and now she longed for it so much that she was beginning to feel ashamed. She caught herself looking through magazines for appropriate columns and articles, was ashamed of the devices she used, felt like a loose woman when she undressed in front of him, left the bathroom door open after Bernhard had been put to bed and she took a shower, didn't care for such tricks yet used them: scantily dressed and perfumed, with something like an "enticing look," and sometimes he would kiss her on the shoulder, perhaps on her cheek, never on her mouth, her breast, and then sometimes he would start to sob against her shoulder and for a while even give up his grumbling and grousing, didn't even get mad when Bernhard knocked over the can of creosote for the garden fence onto the driveway.

Hubert became even more silent, sat in front of the TV watching the stupidest things for hours on end, stupid junk, "celebrity cackle" he used to call it—that contrived wittiness, that "halfwit-nitwit dingdong." Sports—he watched it all, everything, without seeing it. Sometimes, when she had finished in the kitchen and came to sit by him, she saw him with his head in his hands, his face covered with his hands and not even looking at programs that should have interested him: crime reports, security matters, police deployment, helicopter patrols, brother officers, perhaps even himself on the screen—he didn't even bother to look. And he had stopped going to church choir practice, meeting colleagues for a beer, and she was almost ready to phone Kiernter the psychologist, or Holzpuke, Lühler, or Zurmack, with whom he was now spending most of his time. Yet she preferred this silent phase to the earlier one when he could turn vicious, downright nasty.

Now she was afraid, not of him, but for him. There was something weighing on his mind, and there was only one thing it could never be, never: a woman. Not that, not with him. It had

to be the job, something to do with the job, and she recalled
what Zurmack had spilled the last time they had all met for a
beer—it must have been all of four weeks ago—when he had been
pretty drunk, before Hubert had stopped him: how on one
occasion he had had to go shopping for shoes with that young
Mrs. Bleibl. "It's his Number Four, we could never afford that
many. . . . Just put yourself in their place—they must feel pretty
lonely, sitting around in their huge offices, and on trips too they're
lonely, and the secretaries are the only ones who know where it
hurts, what's hurting them, and then it happens, and she was his
secretary too, and the next will be one too, just put yourself in
their place"—and the way she sat there having forty—no, fifty—
no, sixty pairs of shoes brought to her and trying them on,
smoking and leafing through a magazine, being served coffee,
and Zurmack had had to check every single shoebox before it was
opened; the boxes came from the basement or the warehouse, to
which there were several rear entrances. How easily someone
could have made one of those shoeboxes "hot"—as had happened
with the cake for Pliefger. There were plenty of hidden accesses
and entrances through which they could easily have slipped in
and forced one of the girls, or even taken her place—and so he
had not only had to guard the private fitting room but also to
open and search every box, and he saw "shoes you only get to
see in movies, regular sex sandals of every color and shape, and
they weren't cheap either"—and described in detail how the
salesgirls' faces turned white with anger when, after hours of
strutting and stalking around in front of the mirror—and "gold
slippers and purple slippers and 'Oh's' and 'Ah's' and slippers that
were hardly even slippers"—the "old girl" walked out without
buying a single pair. He also told them about going with her to
Breslitzer Fashions, all that rustling and whispering "and the
lewd giggling in the fitting rooms" and pinning and tucking—
"And she's not that pretty, mind you, certainly not beautiful"—
and then the salesgirls at the shoe store and at Breslitzer's got a
dressing down because they hadn't sold anything, "hadn't palmed

anything off on the old girl." Then Lühler also started in, talking about his experiences at "certain parties," describing women "who are practically topless when they meet you as you come on duty —but just watch out if you behave even remotely like you were a normal man appreciating an offer!" and he was just beginning to tell them about a woman who was always drunk and whom he had had to guard in bars—but at that point Hubert intervened and forbade any further discussion of official secrets.

Good heavens, surely she had enough imagination to know what it must be like, weeks of duty around swimming pools, or at parties where they had to stand at the doors inside and out— watching, listening, being ignored as if they were lampposts or wax figures; always on the alert, unable to relax even for a second, while things were bound to become pretty lively at times, with all that food, liquor, dancing, kissing, and probably worse—and somewhere there must lie the cause of Hubert's changed nature. Some people—including Mother, Monka, and Karl too, she supposed—had always found him a bit too serious, too severe, had always been surprised when he'd suddenly shown his genial side, his wit and his charm. Hadn't he danced delightfully with Monka, not exactly flirting but paying her such nice compliments? Everyone had been so surprised that he could be like that too; never angry, rarely annoyed, only on those occasions when he couldn't avoid being with his parents and his brother Heinz, who had never got over the fact that he had become "only a policeman." Yes, the father was a "member of the legal profession," though it turned out later that he was a bailiff; the brother was a lecturer in philosophy, and they let him feel it, that annoyed him, and he sharply reminded his father of the connections between the courts and the police, and demonstrated to his brother the vagueness of his ideas. And the worst thing was when, at any place at any time, regardless of the context, the word "fuzz" was uttered—once Bernhard had been called a "fuzz brat," and the boy had come home in tears; and on a summer evening one of the guests at a party in the Mittelkamps' garden had called across the fence: "Come on over and join us, Mr. and Mrs. Fuzz!"—he would go white with rage, ready to start a fight; he was touchy, very touchy—and could be so nice, so kind. Now he was so silent, sad, tired, apathetic, stared at the box, not even interested in sports or police reports. Had even stopped grumbling about those who were responsible for it all, were the cause of it all. Gone was the enthusiasm with which he used to go to church—sometimes, it had seemed to her, a bit ostentatiously; that solemn but joyous insistence on liturgical forms which he described as "his right"; that pride in his Church with which he countered the scoffing of brother officers and neighbors. Expressions such as "Bible wielder" had been used, and at the beer table one of his colleagues had once said: "Good God, Hubert—the priests don't have that much clout these days—so why all the fuss?" And he had tried to explain, earnestly but in vain, that it had nothing whatever to do with his career, that it was simply a "deep inner need." And it was true, he had never thought of it in those terms, and the last thing he could be called was an opportunist. After all, he hadn't joined the police for want of something better: he had gone through all that training and the rigorous drill because he prized order, desired it, wanted to defend order. He desired to be a custodian of order, serious but never without mercy: many a time—as she well knew—he had let petty thieves and shoplifters go and as a result had landed himself in a lot of trouble, and he had explained to her that such people were actually the victims of seduction. He hadn't even been very hard on streetwalkers when he was on the beat. No, serious he was, but not hard; he had never been hard on her either, apart from that early phase of his change when he had been constantly finding fault.

Perhaps it would be best after all if she were to give Kiernter a call, or Holzpuke himself, or maybe just Zurmack, who was an older man and very nice. All that watching in shoe stores and dress salons went through her mind, that hanging about the pool where they horsed around, scantily dressed, fancy drinks in their hands —it must be like the movies; and it was unavoidable—in fact it had leaked out—that sometimes, well, sometimes they had to go along and stand around in or outside bordellos. And why not? Needless to say she was against such establishments, was horrified by them, and although during his time on the beat he hadn't given her any details, naturally he had described, "in general terms," what went on there—but if other men went there, why not the ones they had to guard? They always had to be present, to play dead, yet they weren't dead. Presumably money was spent in those places like water, caviar and champagne and all that kind of thing, and if a man happened to be groaning under heavy mortgage payments, had to pay off his new car and those extortionate loans, maybe he did start to do some calculating and have some thoughts about it. He'd always had his thoughts, deep ones, devout too. Yet even before they were married he had insisted on fulfillment, for her, for himself, and hadn't found this contradictory: the Bible said, as he reminded her, "Thou shalt not covet thy neighbor's wife," and he was not coveting his neighbor's wife but his own; that—to covet one's neighbor's wife—he found wicked of course. He was by nature a brooder.

Thank heavens he was now being nice again to Bernhard, no longer radiating that appalling contempt, no longer using that terrible word "graceful," was just sad and quiet, sometimes stroking the boy's hair with such a sad expression that it almost broke her heart—it was almost a gesture of farewell. Did the police psychologist suspect nothing of all this? Perhaps it would be better to ask for transfer to a rural area, where the offenses were more obvious ones—impaired driving, theft, traffic jams, fistfights, failure to obey closing hours—none of that threatening uncertainty that could occur any place any time and yet occurred so rarely, so rarely that it was almost a relief when they happened to catch someone, like that man Schubler she had read about in the paper —they had actually found a pistol in his apartment that he could quite easily have used to kill Mrs. Fischer, from right next door where he was committing adultery with that woman who appeared to be of somewhat easy virtue. He was still under suspicion since no one would believe in his pure love; they found it easier to believe in her naïveté. It was embarrassing for the woman yet represented a success after months of waiting. Not a word about it from him, not a syllable. In his quiet way he had brushed off her diffident attempts to find out something about the affair. Yet she knew quite well that he was on duty in Blorr at the Fischers' and must know the details. In the end Schubler had become muddled during the interrogations, had admitted that he was a leftist, or if he was not, that he had once been one.

Just the same, even though he never mentioned it, she knew: that he was guarding and escorting that young woman and her child, Mrs. Fischer-Tolm. Now *she* really was a beauty, with her warm honey-colored hair like her mother, who was still handsome though she already had quite a bit of silver in her hair—yes, that's where the word "graceful" must come from—a grace that never made her look thin, she was not merely elegant, there was something more than dressmakers could achieve, a quiet, physical beauty; her figure, her mouth, eyes, eyebrows; and there was something high-strung about her, stopping just short of restlessness, that must make her desirable to men—she blushed at these thoughts, found it unnatural of herself, as a woman, to be regarding female beauty as desirable—and a direct reaction at that, not by imagining herself to be a man. That was a woman one could love and fall in love with; not only was she a beauty, she seemed lovable too. She appeared quite often on TV, in magazines—riding, going for a walk, even in church, kneeling with that dear little girl of hers before the Blessed Virgin. Her husband, "Beehive" Fischer, also appeared often enough, certainly a handsome man, no fault to find with him, really, yet he didn't attract her when she saw him or pictures of him: on TV at big receptions, holding a glass of orange juice. Again she blushed, was afraid to look in the mirror; any comparison with Mrs. Fischer was bound to be disastrous. She had nothing to hide, it wasn't that, no reason to feel like a little sparrow, there was nothing wrong with her, not her face, not her hair—though it could have been a bit glossier—

not her breasts or legs or movements, that she knew, could feel it, too, from the way men looked at her, and yet: young Mrs. Fischer-Tolm was in a different class, what might be called a "thorough-bred."

But: where did this "breeding" come from? From the families of an underpaid schoolteacher and an even less prosperous gardener, the magazines knew all about that, also knew about the two sons, the "bad egg" and the "slightly nutty" one, and to her mind the "bad egg" seemed by far the more attractive. And the public was kept fully informed about daughters-in-law and grand-children. About the manor in Tolmshoven, the bungalow in Blorr, everything. It wasn't inconceivable that a person might then find his own little terrace house with its twelve hundred square feet of garden and thousand square feet (including corri-dor) of living area too cramped, his own wife no longer quite so careful about her appearance; not inconceivable that he should have been a bit smitten with her, it was only natural with a woman who had such an aura, yet it was impossible, unthinkable, that he should have "something going" with her. For weeks now, maybe even months—she didn't know for sure—he had been around her, every day, and one kept seeing those rumors in the gossip columns that things weren't going too well between her and Fischer. Too many trips, too many affairs on the trips—there were scads of pic-tures of him in the company of vulgar-looking women, dancing, or beside a swimming pool somewhere in the tropics. And it was constantly being said that she had already moved, or was about to move, back to her parents', although she was expecting another child, and quite soon at that.

Well, that Mr. Fischer wasn't a pleasant character, although he always did his best to look like one, smiling all the time—Karl said of that kind of smile: "People like that have a knife in their face, while a shark has only teeth in its face." Fischer would never be a temptation for her, whereas for Hubert, his wife—that must be it, and she could understand it: he was smitten with her, smitten perhaps too with the luxury, the scents, the materials, the

spacious rooms, and if—the rumor was described as unconfirmed
—she was now moving to her parents', to the manor house, where
Hubert had been on duty for the past several weeks, he would be
close to her again. Mrs. Fischer-Tolm with a policeman—the mind
boggled. Odd—she felt no jealousy, only fear because, if it were
true, it must be so hard on him. He took things too seriously to
get over an infatuation of that kind, it would be a reason to be
afraid, increasingly afraid, for him. Perhaps this was the reason
for his inability—for which there was another of those revolting
scientific terms—to give her and himself fulfillment; and if she
was aware of how this lack of fulfillment made her uneasy, what
must it be like for him, if now he was to see her every day? That
sobbing against her shoulder . . .

Jealousy would not come, fear remained, pity too, and a wish
that greatly surprised her: that the woman, Mrs. Fischer, would
yield to him—though of course he would first have to declare
himself to her, which was unthinkable—and gave him fulfillment.
This idea seemed to her doubly outlandish because it was she—
his wife—who was desiring fulfillment for him by another
woman, and that other woman happened to be a princess. And a
third notion came into her head, and she blushed again: if—then
where, how? He was always on duty, even now at the manor
house. Was she a pervert or something? Had she become part of
the porn wave without being aware of it?

Eventually she did go and see Monka, she could think of no one
else to talk to. Whatever happened, even if Monka laughed at her,
she would keep her mouth shut, she wouldn't even tell Karl. After
all, until Karl had appeared on the scene she had been in Monka's
confidence, Monka had told her everything, intimate things too,
some of which had made her blush, which in their dark bedroom
Monka fortunately hadn't been able to see. She hadn't told anyone

else either, not even Hubert, though it had often weighed on her, the things Monka had told her, about lesbians where she worked, homos at school, stories about boys, stories about men—Monka had, as she herself described it, "flung herself" into the first porn wave, had "at times sunk pretty low," till Karl rescued her—firmly, and with arguments that Monka called "leftist, while the conservative arguments of other would-be rescuers had never made any sense to me." Monka had been—in her own words—"pretty close to stripping," but that was some while ago, four or five years, when Karl had grabbed her by the scruff of the neck. She had developed into a sensible young woman, a bit flighty and flippant: "Let's hope our Silesian nightingale, our dear old ma, never finds out about my past." She was now twenty-seven, designing and making chic blouses, panties, nightgowns, skirts, smoking a bit too much, probably drinking more than was good for her, and at times she looked old for her years, more like thirty-three or -five. She loved her Karl; he looked a bit puny but he wasn't, he had turned out to be a good athlete, a long-distance runner, that little runt with his spectacles and pigeon chest who sometimes looked—as Hubert would say—"as if he had swallowed some ink."

At first it had been difficult, almost impossible, with those two. Hubert simply didn't care for "leftist talk"—"for God's sake, can't you see what it leads to?"—refused to listen to the complex arguments Karl used in trying to explain to him "what the alternative leads to." Eventually they did play badminton together, went off on bike rides, taking turns with Bernhard on the pillion, almost ceased to argue, though the air tended to be a bit thick when Hubert called Karl a "leftist dreamer" and Karl called Hubert a "centrist dreamer." Finally, while discussing a particular person, they found common ground in arguments which she had dreaded: that young Tolm, whom the newspapers called the "car arsonist"—it seemed that Karl had known him before, admitted that he had himself been "very close to setting fire to cars, but had been much younger than Tolm and still too scared." He explained to Hubert that Tolm had deliberately renounced his privileges, had been in jail, and certainly there was one thing he had never been: an opportunist. And in all these conversations that word "fuzz" was never mentioned, and once Hubert told her he was sure Karl didn't even think that word; on the contrary, he was on the side of order too, even of the police, and one had to remember that he had rescued Monka "from the gutter"; Karl agreed that it was right for people to be protected, but banks: never. "D'you really want to get yourself killed maybe, for the sake of those clams, just for the sake of those clams, risk your life for those lousy clams lying around there?"

In some ways they even resembled each other. Not outwardly. Hubert was tall and blond, serious and proud, Karl was puny, swarthy, with thinning black hair. And when she got right down to it she would never—apart from all personal feelings and the fact that he was her husband, in other words looking at the whole thing from the outside, objectively—she would never exchange Hubert for that man Fischer, never; he was quite obviously a cold, ruthless windbag, and she could well understand that things were going wrong in that marriage—and if she assumed that Hubert was really smitten with Mrs. Fischer, then she even knew—painful as it was—why things were going wrong in her own marriage. Karl was a very, very nice fellow one could dance with without getting the creeps, as one did with Mittelkamp and old Hölster. Monka never got them, the creeps, not even with Mittelkamp and old Hölster, she would never stand for anything that might bring on the creeps, always supposing she was capable of getting the creeps; if it came to the worst—and she had witnessed that twice, once at the Hölsters' and later at a studio party in Monka's apartment—she would slap the fellow's face, "to sober him up." Monka was probably used to a lot and had had all kinds of experience, and Karl would laugh and shout: "Let 'em have it, girl, let those fumble-daddies have it!"

Monka wouldn't blab even to Karl, who probably wasn't even curious about such things. Bernhard was always happy when they went to Monka's: he'd be given cake and cocoa, and lemonade, there were dressmaker dummies, and scissors, dress materials, needles, and thread lying around, things weren't "so terribly neat"; in the next room were Karl's models, and he always got a present too: money, or a movie ticket, an invitation to the zoo, there was just one thing he had refused: to let Monka make his Communion suit. She had promised him something extra special. "Mini tails, if you like, or a mini cowboy suit—believe me, the Christ Child would get more of a kick from that than from those stiff blue suits!" But Bernhard insisted on a blue suit, wanted to look like the others, and Monka, who couldn't help feeling a bit hurt, refused to make one.

Monka's obvious delight when they arrived was in itself a comfort, a very great comfort, and it needed only a wink for Karl to grasp that he was to take care of Bernhard; make cocoa, get some ice cream from the kiosk, and some comics, and in his workroom there was plenty for Bernhard to look at, perhaps even to do: drawings and models of buildings, of city blocks, plans, wood, glue, plaster of paris, pots of paints, spatulas, and an enormous table on which Karl built models for architects' offices; there might even be something in all that for school: helping to figure out proportions, the right scale. So she was rid of Bernhard for a while, and she could tell Monka over their coffee—hesitating, faltering, not finding the words, shy of mentioning "fulfillment," talking around it and saying: "You know what I mean," and Monka nodded, smoked, even went on with her work when she had finished her cake. Whenever she couldn't put something into words, Monka would say: "I can imagine," never once laughed, apparently didn't even have to suppress a laugh, ventured only one question: "How long has this been going on?" and seemed relieved to hear it was only five months. Nodded, shook her head, didn't laugh, and finally: "My God, Sis, you must be living in a dream

world, a kind of sexual Silesia—not that I mean the Silesians don't
also have every sexual problem in the book—but you know what
I mean: a sexual dream that reminds me of Mother's dream-
Silesia." Looked very serious, shook her head, and said: "Why
don't you talk to Hubert about it?"

"How can I? I can't say . . ."

"Can't say what? Couldn't you ask him, for instance, whether
after nine years of marriage you're no longer attractive to him?
Forget about those magazine tricks—that's not your style, or his,
that's not for you two, it hurts me just to think of it. . . . Oh,
Helga, forget about all that—it wouldn't even be my style now,
it might have been, once—forget it. You're such a dear, serious
couple—no, that really hurts me."

"Hurts you?"

"Yes, very much—what do you imagine? Do you believe I'm
as hard-boiled as I always pretend—have to pretend? For God's
sake, what kind of a Silesian fantasy are you two living in? What
do you imagine goes on sometimes in a boutique like this, with
lesbians and thespians, with pushy traveling salesmen who pounce
on you without so much as a by-your-leave because they think
of themselves or of you as hot stuff? You simply have to be tough
and, if necessary, hit out, and if things get really tough and I
can't handle them alone, they're amazed when Karl—you know
how they always call him Charlie Boy—suddenly makes a brief
appearance and knows just where to hit. They're all nutty—the
porn wave rolls on, and they roll with it—maybe it's also
rolled over your poor Hubert, or at least he's been swept along
by it—let's say: got a bit wet, and it's no use your pretending
that you're on this wave—with your pathetic little tricks—forget
it, please. I'm afraid Hubert's been hooked, but how and who—
do you really think it's Mrs. Fischer? I can't believe it. . . ."

"Who else? He never meets any other women, and he was
there all summer. . . ."

"And she happens to have just left her mate. I don't believe it,

I can't imagine it, although I can imagine a man—that I can understand—but she's such a quiet, shy person, not all that keen, I'd say, on the circles she happens to move in. . . ."

"You know her?"

"I've read all about her, I've met her too, her mother sometimes buys things here, orders things, for her grandchildren or for herself, her daughter, her daughter-in-law, and I once made some beach outfits for Mrs. Fischer—I must say, she's a goddess when you see her with not much on—but it can't be her, she's a very serious young woman, kindhearted but serious, the no-nonsense kind, wouldn't go for any funny business—I'm sure of that—although . . ."

"What?"

"Well, I'm thinking of her husband. Believe me, there's nothing worse than these men who are publicly committed to beauty and virility—these extroverts, when they laugh it's worse than when others crack nuts between their teeth—that grinding laugh, I remember that from my days at the Hummingbird. They're the kind that throw themselves on your breast and start sobbing. Of course there are some real charmers among them, young Zummerling for instance, really nice, and when he laughed you weren't scared, you had to laugh with him—a gay blade with only one ambition, to have fun, which he does—there's that kind too, but those public smilers, the ones, as Karl says, with a knife in their face—their wives sometimes go nuts, I've seen it myself, I don't want to talk out of turn, after all it was a kind of professional secret, like with the police, an official secret—no, but believe me, their wives sometimes go nuts. . . ."

"D'you know him too, Mr. Fischer I mean?"

"No, only from magazines and TV—and if you only knew the kind of wages he pays, not only in the Orient but also in the Socialist paradise: believe me, they know how to sting in the Beehive—he travels all over the map, stands there beaming beside big-breasted women in every latitude and longitude—and meanwhile your Hubert has to keep an eye on wife and daughter, in summer, by the pool—God, it quite scares me to imagine myself a man and seeing her there wearing less than she did in the shop! Maybe it wasn't Hubert at all, maybe it was her, considering that her guy spends half his time flying all over the map looking for low-wage countries, and then, with those Thai and Hai and Phai girls—oh, Helga, I'm afraid it's a bad scene, certainly a serious one—there's nothing a police psychologist can do . . . there's only one thing left: wait and pray."

"What? Monka dear, you must be joking!"

"I assure you I'm not joking. I mean pray—you wouldn't believe how often that's helped me."

"You? D'you mean because of Karl?"

"Also because of Karl, or do you suppose he's beyond temptation? He isn't, he's faithful all right, but not beyond temptation—he has what he calls a 'strong sense of beauty,' a true aesthete, that guy, can be carried away, as I say: faithful, but not beyond temptation—but at other times, too, I pray to Her, the Queen of Heaven. I do have a sinful past—oh, I haven't told everything even to you, and Karl doesn't know everything either—and sometimes it really gets me, and it makes me cry and pray. But don't get the idea that I suffer terribly because of Karl. He's nice, I love him, I like him, I want to stay with him and he wants to stay with me—but apart from that I do need it. Jesus has never been my cup of tea, I've never really got along with Him, even when I was young, I never really got through to Him—but She, She helps, maybe She'll help you too. But please, please, Helga, no more tricks, don't lower yourself—I couldn't bear that—I can understand, of course, but don't try that. What I mean is, make sure you're always clean and neat, don't let yourself go—but you wouldn't do that anyway. I could have a talk with old Mrs. Tolm, her mother, she'd come if I phoned her. . . ."

"No, Monka, no—it's all just guesswork, and we might start something much worse. Promise me, not a word to a soul. Not a word. Promise."

"I promise, and you know I'll keep my word. But someone

has to do some talking in this business—Hubert with you, you with Hubert, you with Mrs. Fischer, Mrs. Fischer with you—by the way, she's pregnant, it's in all the papers. . . ."

"And she's leaving her husband when she's pregnant?"

"That happens—there are these pregnancy crises—so I've read, anyway. It seems that, in the sixth month . . . you don't suppose . . . ?"

"I can't believe it . . . I can't . . . and I don't believe it—but then: what can it be—have I become so repulsive to him? No, it's not that—I can feel it—please, don't talk about it, not to a soul, please."

"I've already promised. Where is he now, still with her?"

"No, I believe he's at the manor house."

"Where she is too—you know she's moved to her mum and dad? He's off again looking for new low-wage countries—the Beehive borrows from me quite nicely too, believe me, and maybe there's a Chinese woman somewhere who's sewing shirts designed by me—I wouldn't be surprised. . . . I heard on the radio that he'd left. . . ."

There was not much more to say, it almost took her breath away, the mere possibility—not because it might have happened, not because he had somehow wronged her, or Mrs. Fischer—no, it was the consequences, and that the improbable had gained in probability: in her sixth month, that was exactly five months ago. Hubert with Mrs. Tolm-Fischer, pregnancy—surely not even the Blessed Virgin could help here.

Neither the Blessed Virgin nor the porn wave could help, nor sexual liberation, state, or Church: for someone who took things seriously it was a disaster, and now all she could do was wait, maybe talk to him after all, challenge him, ask, release him, stroke his hair and look deep into his eyes again, not be hard, only questioning and perhaps a little sad. . . .

"D'you suppose," she asked Monka, "that you could find out where he—Fischer, I mean—was five months ago? I mean, if she's actually in her sixth month . . ."

"Helga—I can find out. How smart you are! . . ."

Now the tears did come as she took Monka's hand and thanked her, it had done her good, this heart-to-heart, affectionate yet, on the surface at least, light. She was grateful that there had been no laughter and that none had been suppressed and, come to think of it, why despair? Tears were good. So he did have an affair with her, and she was having a child by him, if their guesswork was right; if that's the way it was then the child was surely not a disaster, except that it was bad for him because it must have happened while he was on duty. She felt sure that so far no one had noticed anything. No one knew about it, it was all guesswork. Nothing more. So Hubert was not sick—or whatever the Latin word for it was—he was confused, confused—all she could do now was: dry her tears, take the boy by the hand, and go home on the bus.

On the bus she thought about the woman. For her, too, it must be hard, so serious and quiet as she was said to be, she had a child from that other one, the little girl who looked so sweet in her riding habit. It certainly hadn't been easy, she certainly wasn't easygoing. They had merely lost their heads and got all caught up, sunk deeper than they had imagined, found they couldn't extricate themselves from this business that was always made out to be so trivial, so fleeting ("Here today and gone tomorrow—you know how it is"), and now six people were affected, entangled, and a seventh on the way, a human being, six months along. . . .

V

He had already confessed it, right at the beginning, having driven one Saturday to some suburban church or other where he had actually found someone in the confessional: a youngish priest smelling of lavender soap who jerked upright when, without much preamble, he came to the serious heart of the matter, the matter he felt to be a sin—unfaithfulness, adultery—and he was relieved when the priest seemed to take it seriously. That must have been due to his own confessional voice that permitted no trifling with the matter. He was told to describe the circumstances, did so, spoke about Helga and Sabine, how serious it was or would be for them both. Was later surprised that Fischer never crossed his mind. The advice was unequivocal: to ask for a transfer, immediately. Yes, he repented, but he also knew while he was kneeling there, later sitting, that he would not ask for a transfer. This was long before it turned out that Sabine was pregnant, at a time when he still had to accuse himself of "extreme unkindness toward his wife and son." He could not explain how it was that he had become gentler toward Helga and the boy on learning that Sabine was expecting a child. Often, when he could take an hour or two off on a Saturday, he would drive to the church and go in, but not to the confessional. He didn't like the church, could find no beauty in it: a postwar building knocked together with shoddy material, looking dilapidated, almost shabby, after barely twenty-five years—cheerless, the Perpetual Light barely visible and, if he was lucky, one or at most two lighted candles in front of the Virgin Mary; not a vestige of all that confessional activity which had still existed when he was a teen-ager: lineups at the confessional, the smell of incense from the preceding service, the strange sweetness of the almost palpable repentance as people knelt in the pews murmuring their penances; activity.

Now, a dozen years later, nothing, all he'd ever see would be a lone woman or a small group of giggling children who had obviously been forced to go to confession. Yet he felt attached to this church with its pathetically shined-up Saint Joseph, who stood in a niche and seemed to be the patron saint; felt attached to this shabby church—it was here, after all, that he had found a priest who could still be serious—Monka had told him about some strange experiences in the confessional, about priests to whom the word "sin" was no longer acceptable, and Bernhard's preparations for confession depressed him; Helga did not comment. It pained him to think of her, hurt as much as the thought of Sabine, who had whispered to him that she would never enter a confessional again, never. . . .

Chaos, disintegration, all around—and himself right in the midst of it, and not through anyone else's fault, or—and this was a dangerous notion that Sabine had boldly come up with—it was if anything "their" fault. Her "We have *them* to thank for it" echoed constantly in his mind. One thing was certain, he had to talk to Helga, tell her everything, for Sabine's sake too, for she also was bound by his silence. She, too, would have to talk to someone, her husband, her parents.

The tavern across from the church didn't seem to be thriving: in the last five months the lessee had changed three times. There were a few pensioners sitting around, a few foreign workers, and the meatballs and cold cutlets in the display case looked ancient. But the beer was good, and at least it was a tavern where you weren't constantly inundated with music, the jukebox was out of order, he had never seen any teenagers here, and the landlord was so morosely and pointedly bored that he'd sometimes doze off over his second beer.

A transfer could easily have been obtained at that stage: nerves, fatigue, overfamiliarity with the surroundings; Kiernter would support his transfer, and it would have been possible to transfer the whole team, not split up, they worked smoothly together, had "adjusted to their surroundings," had also been at the Bleibls', at parties and big receptions; he could even have left this assignment and asked for a transfer to another city. There was no lack of sympathy for crises, overtaxed nerves, even personal dislikes, it was openly discussed; they wouldn't be sent to the Bleibls' again anyway, since Zurmack had said: "Never again to that place, never again to that woman—I'd rather be in some godforsaken hole handing out parking and speeding tickets." Kiernter called it "a certain lasciviousness that is bothering you."

After all, they weren't talking about cigarettes but about human lives, about stable nerves. Ticklish matters were discussed, they took the bull by the horns, Lühler kept talking about "those fancy whores who arouse you but won't let you get at them." Yes, it had happened once at a party given by some big shot, where a fellow had felt tense enough anyway in the lamplit grounds because it was so hard to keep an eye on everything. Toward three in the morning, when things started to loosen up, and before their very eyes the big shot, dead drunk, had actually to be dragged to his car, Lühler had become the victim of one of those women who was known not to be averse to a little private stripping too. Lühler, "because she thrust it at me," had made a grab for it, had had his wrist slapped and been stridently insulted: "Get this disgusting fuzz away from me! This instant!" Naturally they had all been on Lühler's side and had discussed the case as well as possible cases of a similar kind that Kiernter and Holzpuke classified as "potential involvements." It had only happened once, and if Lühler had been transferred or disciplined they would have all quit on the spot. The simple solution was never to send him to any more parties where totally drunk big shots had to be dragged like wet sacks to their cars and where some of the women became hysterical; and of course Zurmack would never again be used as an escort on a shoe-buying expedition.

Kiernter asked them to try and understand "the other side too": "You must appreciate that this strict surveillance really does put an end to all private life for those people—they're bound to crack up sometimes: we must not." He was immune to such advances, indifferent to women who offered themselves, he found them worse than hookers, who at least were following a profession, however dubious. Kiernter went on to speak of the "fluid line between promiscuity and prostitution." There was the one eventuality that none of them would regard as likely: that it could become serious—serious, that a woman wouldn't scream for help, rant about the fuzz, slap wrists, yet not be a hooker; a woman for whom it was so serious that she even seemed almost grateful to "them"—those fiendish bastards—for this happiness. And conceived a child, gave no thought to pill or abortion. It was something that simply happened between men and women, happened to millionaires with salesgirls and secretaries and to millionaires' wives with policemen, so it seemed.

And he didn't ask for a transfer, didn't speak to anyone about it, not even Kiernter, who he was sure would have treated it as a sort of secret of the confessional and supplied other reasons for the transfer than the true ones. With a nostalgia that he knew to be founded in self-deception, he thought about a job with the rural police: fistfights at fairs, impaired driving, petty thefts, but also, as he well knew, hash and heroin and that futile poking and sniffing around in whole swarms of commuting school kids who sat around bored in waiting rooms and cafés. Chaos, disintegration, and he didn't want to be sucked in, yet was in the very midst of it, didn't want to make anyone unhappy: neither Helga nor the boy, was glad that Sabine didn't seem to be at all unhappy, only—like himself—when she thought of Helga and Bernhard. And the child she had and the child she was expecting, and her husband? After all, she was married to him, and sometimes the wedding pictures were published again, it wasn't all that long ago: that wickedly expensive "simplicity" with which they were both dressed, radiant and, in that wickedly expensive way, "unpretentious." He didn't ask for a transfer, nor did he go to confession again, he just sat in that shabby church, in that seedy tavern across the street, brooding on the decline of Saturday afternoons, thinking about the seriousness of the priest and the only proper advice: transfer. And he kept remembering Sabine's "We have *them* to thank for it," and that Beverloh, too, with whom she had danced so often. Jealous? Yes, jealous, and again not of Fischer. He couldn't follow the advice, didn't want to leave her, didn't want to leave Helga and Bernhard together, yet he knew: the three of them, or six or seven, together—that wouldn't work, it could never be.

And now he was standing in the manor, walking around the house, unable to write to her, to phone her, and all he could think of was: Doesn't she ever come to visit her parents? She came very seldom, and he tried to imagine what she talked about with her parents: about the child she was expecting; his child. The "my" didn't come naturally to him, he had found the same thing when Helga was expecting Bernhard: my, your, his—that didn't start until Bernhard was born; that was his child. . . .

He didn't dare think what would happen if it "came out" before he had told Helga; even though it might be called a scandal for a policeman and a woman under his protection, was it really that scandalous for a man and a woman—and both married? The world would survive, had already survived many such things, one transitory occurrence piled upon another, graves and grass, it didn't occur to him that Sabine was now "ruined," she wasn't. He only had to think of all that "they" perpetrated, how many thousands of tiny wheels they set in motion, what a fine web they wove: from Zurmack's shoeboxes and the sheer hatred of the salesgirls for that woman, from Lühler's fancy whore to Sabine, and that awful affair of Sabine's neighbor with her lover, who both really did seem to be ruined and, as the public was given to understand, "not without reason"—no, one didn't say "with reason," one said "not without reason"—for they had actually found a pistol at Schubler's place and some obscure pamphlets, though not a single indication of connections let alone plans; the "pamphlets" were out of date, around nine years old, the pistol naïve: an ancient revolver such as kids would hide away as a romantic prop, though there was also some ammunition.

And it distressed him, preoccupied him, nagged at him, that he found the Breuer-Schubler affair disgusting, somehow nasty and vulgar, while he saw what he had been doing with Sabine on a loftier plane; it was "different"—yet there was no difference. While he sat there in the dismal tavern or the still more dismal church, he tried to rid himself of that "It's *not* the same thing," since he was clearly not one jot better but still felt himself to be better. Before, when for a time he had been on the vice squad, he had been disgusted and revolted at the sight of them doing it in doorways and bushes, at street corners and behind trees and God knows where, "on the wing"—and now he was doing the same thing himself, he the fastidious, upright officer, and she, Sabine, who suddenly displayed a cunning in covering their tracks that sometimes frightened him: had she done it in a long-forgotten, long-past life, also on the wing and with that same secrecy ... ?

So now he was standing in the manor, walking around the house, in the corridors, on stair landings, looking for her face in her mother's face, her father's, finding it in both, exchanging remarks with them, brief, courteous, discovering details of re-semblance: corners of the mouth, hairline—and was tormented by the terrible notion that he would have to give her up. He thought more often of Helga than of her, and of the painful fact that he was now forcing Helga into having to seduce him, which only made it all the more difficult for him. Perhaps before talking to Helga he should speak to someone, not Kiernter, perhaps Karl, who really had rescued Monka from the gutter by dint of reason and love, by patience and—it must be admitted—by systems analysis. Chaos, disintegration, all around, and himself sucked in. His parents were the last people he could talk to. They felt their honor to be so impugned by his occupation that they uttered the word "policeman" with more contempt than others who used the word "fuzz." They flatly refused to grasp that there was no reason why he couldn't achieve status equal to that of bailiff, they insisted on the designation "member of the legal profession," which was, after all, a bit of a fraud. They could—if they ever found out about it—jump to the conclusion that Sabine was more suitable for him than Helga, who was actually only the daughter of a refugee from Silesia who, although he claimed to have been a foreman and the owner of a small house, had never been able to produce a picture of that house. Nor could he talk to his brother Heinz, who, in his nasal voice, would always start spouting exact scientific arguments and explain everything in terms of social history; not a spark, not a shred would remain unexplained, though there was so much that was unexplainable. In laborious detail Heinz would immediately have put the blame on society's misguided monogamy-culture—and there might even be something in that—already he was wondering why he wanted to have Sabine and not let go of Helga, and how he could feel tied to Helga in a way he couldn't explain and to Sabine in a different way, which he couldn't explain either, and to both so firmly that it hurt, yet it was all so commonplace: you could read about it in the papers every day, in many variations, and no confessional or scent of lavender could help him, no repentance, not even a transfer: he was looking for her face in the faces of her mother and her father, yet it was a shock when she moved into the manor house.

She arrived with mother, child, and not much luggage, yet it was a permanent move—you could see it, feel it. He was just returning from his round through the park, an inspection of the orangery, and he had stopped in the corner of the inner courtyard so as not to run right into their path, yet stood close enough to permit himself a brief salute: the child raised her arms to wave back—mudhole! And from Sabine's shoulders and arms, in her face, he could read the finality of the move, and he thought of Fischer: what could have happened? It reminded him of those movies with their silent forebodings, not guilt but fate, tragedy, and his fear was not fear for Sabine, or of job complications, not fear of Fischer, only fear for Helga and his son, who wouldn't be able to understand any of it. Fear of the millstone around his neck. Who, who could he explain it to?

VI

In the evenings, after work, the daily ritual Holger insisted upon: walking to the Hermeses' for the milk. Regardless of the weather, he had to set off between seven and seven-thirty, holding Holger's hand with his right and the milk pitcher with his left, while

Katharina prepared supper: usually soup, bread, and a dessert, and later tea beside the stove before the boy was put to bed. On warm evenings they ate outside, in the garden between the vicarage and the wall, and they always lit a fire, the boy insisted on that, maintaining that "the fire tells such nice stories." Sometimes they would be joined by the priest, Father Roickler, young and, in a serious way, tense, restless, unable to sit still, always hinting at problems but never talking about them, smoking his cigar, smiling, never letting on that he found the surveillance a nuisance, sitting there quietly after a glass or two, with such a strange, wistful expression in his eyes when he looked at Katharina or the wives of their friends. Sometimes he brought along his housekeeper, an elderly woman, presumably his aunt, who remained suspicious in a confused kind of way, she didn't know what sort of people they were, was completely bewildered when Father or Mother showed up and the guards with their transceivers stationed themselves around the garden. She "couldn't understand the world these days," and she may have been right; who could understand the world, had ever understood it? So old Mr. Tolm senior would sit there humbly accepting tea and cookies from the hands of the woman who wasn't even really his daughter-in-law. With the woman, the women, one could discuss knitting patterns, or canning and cooking, yet they were—well, what were they? Communists certainly, if not worse, if not "putatively" all kinds of things; vain attempts to explain to the housekeeper the difference between protection and surveillance, no attempts to discuss systems analyses. She was probably surprised, and occasionally implied as much, at the "respectable behavior," by which she must mean no sex orgies, no obscene language. She gave him the hottest tips whenever any "modernization" was going on in the village: people were again dismantling their old windows and doors somewhere, replacing old beams, even ripping out old paneling and closets, and were glad to have the stuff taken away. All it needed was to be hoisted onto the cart, cut up, chopped up; some of it would be carefully stacked in the shed to be reconditioned and sold—at any rate there was no shortage of firewood, so that baking bread was, if not profitable, certainly without financial risk and helped to save money when their friends turned up regularly to buy it, also when the odd customer in the village bought the tasty loaves, while the priest would hardly eat any other kind. The little bake oven that he had dismantled at Klüver's and installed in the shed was beginning to pay off. While the women were discussing canning, he remembered how, years ago—it must be at least ten—at Eickelhof, Heinrich had shown Mother figures to prove that, in spite of advertising to the contrary, home canning was cheaper than commercially canned goods; he had called the craze for canned goods and convenience foods a "pseudo-proletarianiza-tion," all those years ago, and had extolled the virtues of the lower middle class: storing potatoes for the winter, home canning, making jam, preserving fruit, and the best way to buy shoes; besides, not only was baking fun, the bread quite simply tasted better, and Katharina was already beginning to consider sharing in a whole side of beef or pork such as was constantly being offered to them, a sort of "home sausage factory, since it looks as if we'll have to settle in here permanently."

The word "permanently" made him uneasy. The priest's eyes seemed to tell him that there was no guarantee of permanency, and the ritualization of their lives was beginning to lose its soothing effect: in the mornings, work in the garden, work in the shed, pick the crop, store it properly, or clean it or prepare it for sale, while Katharina was out with the children or keeping them occupied in the old vicarage parlor. Here and there he would lend a hand with repairs or the harvest, for which he was generously rewarded in kind; collect wood, chop wood, cut it up —there was plenty to do. He interpreted his desire for the largest possible supply of wood as a desire for security, warmth, and peace—although he had little confidence in that peace, or even in his own peace of mind. No worries about food, rent, clothing, and rarely, very rarely, an allusion to or even a memory of the difficulties, the tensions, of their first year here when there had still been groups that not only were hostile and abusive but had even systematically tried to drive them away. That had been ugly, a nuisance too, and only the fact that Katharina had never whined or complained but instead constantly "put herself in those people's place" and had thus been able to present her intelligent, sympathetic arguments, had saved them and given them this peace.

The day's concluding ritual, going for the milk in the evening, was the strongest and, apart from his casual jobs, the only dependable contact with the farmers. On entering the Hermeses' dairy with Holger and handing over the pitcher, he was usually served by the grandmother, a shrunken old woman with pale eyes and straggly eyebrows, taciturn like himself. For months, each had interpreted the other's taciturnity as hostility: wordless handing over of the pitcher, wordless pouring of the liter and a half of milk, wordless handing over of the exact amount of money, and only on reaching home did he discover that it wasn't a liter and a half but two liters, in fact a bit more, for there was always an extra "titch," as the farmers called it, and over the years he had learned to judge the quantity of milk by the weight of the pitcher. Since the pitcher held only two and a half liters, and at times—for baking or cooking—two and a half liters were needed, leaving no room for that extra, let alone the titch, they had had to acquire a larger pitcher, one that would take three or four liters, for of course that extra—and even the titch, which, as Katharina said, was at least enough for their coffee—meant a considerable saving, and they needed that. Besides, it so happened that Katharina, although not a farmer's daughter, had grown up in the annex to a farmhouse, at her Uncle Kommertz's, and saw no reason why they should let themselves be done out of that extra and the titch. It took a while for him to discover the curiosity in Grandma Hermes's eyes, ironic curiosity which in due course Katharina explained to him: "Don't you realize that you happen to be an oddity to these people? You must see that! Setting fire to cars, prison—plus a father they all know and regard as one of themselves. . . ."

Later the old woman passed a few remarks about the weather, received an answer, and he even began to find amusement in this litany with its prescribed responses. Then she showed Holger and himself the automatic milking machines, the refrigerating plant, gave Holger an apple, told him about her grandsons' schools and their varying scholastic achievements. Much later, after almost a year, she shyly asked for the first time after her daughter, "who lives next door to your sister—Mrs. Breuer," and he had to confess that he had never, not once, been to see his sister and didn't know Mrs. Breuer, adding: "Trouble with my brother-in-law, you know." What never ceased to surprise him was: no gossip, not from the other farmers either; they would make their dry comments, but gossip—never, and Katharina had an explanation for that too: among themselves they would gossip about each other, but to an outsider with no knowledge of the life of the village in all its complexities: never! Odd: that the men were more talkative, more given to gossip, than the women, hinting, whispering even about the priest, "who does make quite a few trips to Cologne, perhaps too many," and again Katharina had to explain this, being familiar with it from Tolmshoven: "a trip to Cologne"—that was an ambiguous, maybe more than ambiguous expression that could mean: confession or bordello, in the case of women, of course, it meant shopping or confession, but since a priest never went shopping, and in his (Roickler's) case a bordello seemed unlikely—mind you, he was still young and "good-looking"—there were only two other possible reasons: a woman or confession, or both; in the old days, the occasional visit to a movie might have been considered possible and accepted, but now with TV the need was less urgent.

For young Hermes, the farmer, he was quite clearly an amusing figure, also a rich source of information. He asked only once after his sister, quizzed him quite openly about his "former activities," wanted to know more about Vietnam, was surprised to hear that the people there were farmers just like himself—scorched earth, burned forests, dying cattle—he could still remember the state of fields and forests after World War II; war is always war against farmers—and he also supplied the extra and the titch; both of these were at their smallest when young Mrs. Hermes poured, she was jittery, probably even nervous, would sometimes even spill the milk, she was evidently afraid of him, sorry for Holger, and she would stroke his hair with a gesture as much as to say: He can't help it, the poor child, and seemed also to regard Katharina as somehow led astray, gave him a little something to take home to her: an egg, or a few nuts. At least he could talk to her about the garden—even though the nervous flicker in her eyes remained; he could ask for tips, also give tips regarding the planting and raising of chard, for instance, or Chinese cabbage, which he had so to speak introduced to the village; but the designation "Chinese"—that already sounded suspect, and he still felt more apprehensive than Katharina on the rare occasions when they went to the tavern in the evening.

Sometimes the peace in their own home became too oppressive for them, too "woolly," Katharina would say. At least Katharina spoke *their* dialect, that made for confidence, and a basis too, and if someone then sat down beside them at the table or the bar they would not react to political questions, even when they weren't meant as a provocation. They would speak only when asked—about money, interest rates, amortization, currency, and would even risk explaining to them that the interest on savings almost always corresponded to the rate of inflation. Amortization, tax savings, investments—they liked hearing about that, knew he was knowledgeable, and he spoke without polemics, quietly, relying on the system to reveal itself, out of itself, to them: how interest rates were lowered to entice them to spend money. They couldn't understand why the politicians tried to dissuade them from saving, and he tried to explain why they were doing it, actually had to do it, tried to explain to them more than the stereotype "We're always being gypped anyway," and into their eyes came fear of losing the security they had laboriously built up for themselves: house and property and the clothes closets filled, the savings accounts they were now trying to make unattractive by reducing the interest rates in such a mean, drastic way. They had no reason to be afraid, not the least, yet they were, and he began to understand them, helped by Katharina, who found it easier because she spoke their dialect and everyone knew she was a Communist. There was nothing "putative" about her, not the least bit, after all they knew her father, had known her uncle, knew her mother, "pious Luise," spoke admiringly of his father, his mother: "You bet we're proud of the Tolms, of Käthe Schmitz!" and they asked him whether it was true that one day Hubreichen, too—and made a sweeping gesture and he shook his head: he knew nothing, yet as soon as they left to go home he was apprehensive again. It was no longer that outright fear, as in the early days: fear that they would smash his windows, set fire to the place, drive them out by force in spite of the priest's intercession—it was fear of the silence, also of the cleanliness, those clean streets where even during harvest time not a wisp of straw, not a handful of hay, not a turnip leaf, was to be found—nowhere even the vestiges of a cow pat.

Not that he objected to cleanliness, of course, that was a good, a pleasant thing, or to the flower beds outside the houses, the attractively painted old wagon wheels, the wheelbarrows planted with flowers—but silence and cleanliness within the farm walls seemed like a silence of the grave. Everything was as well tended as the graves in the little cemetery—that was it, a silence of the grave, and in the midst of this silence the son of farmer Schmergen suddenly strung himself up in the stable, for no discernible reason: nothing was ever discovered, no girl, no woman, no trouble in the army—a nice, quiet boy, well liked and a good dancer—never had any problems, never hinted at any—no motive was ever discovered—and yet on a Sunday afternoon, in the quietest hour, he strung himself up in the stable behind the farmhouse: in the silence of the grave and out of a clear blue sky. And then farmer Halster suddenly killed his wife: a giant of a fellow with a big, well-organized, financially sound farm, and in the interminably long wall a little shrine to the Madonna where there were always fresh flowers and lighted candles—affluent, respected, a taciturn man who treated his employees so well that he had almost become a legend. The Halsters had been on this farm for three hundred years, and the number of priests and lawyers, teachers and civil servants, who had gone out in the world from this family, to Cologne and to Australia, was almost beyond computation. There was no war in which a few Halsters hadn't given their lives, including the Napoleonic and earlier wars—an extended clan, almost a dynasty. And his wife, a handsome creature, almost a beauty, dark-haired, known to be "prudent"—and he shot her dead between his morning pint and dinner. Granted, there were rumors that she had been "depraved," but that was never properly explained, there was merely talk about their childlessness—but to "Why? Why?" there was no answer. Tragedy, sensation, horror —and even before the news got around the village Halster had driven over to Blückhoven and given himself up to the police— from this quiet, clean village where no wisp of straw was to be found on the street, a pretty village with its ordinary churchgoers, the morning pint, the annual rifle competitions and village fair— and in the evening at Hermes's that extra half liter with a titch on top.

A scarifying vision: thinking five or ten years ahead—fear of the loss of permanence, and fear of permanence: gardening, carrots, onions, renewing the wood supply, over and over again: for years, perhaps decades—to reach the age of forty, perhaps fifty, in Hubreichen. . . .

Holger was feeling the cold today, he put first his left, then his right hand into Father's coat pocket: "It looks as if we'll soon have to get our gloves out of the drawer"; and the milk pitcher had to be switched from left to right. He promised the boy they would roast some chestnuts, they were best for warming the hands, and of course there would be baked apples with custard sauce and playing with him in the evening—building houses—why did children love to build houses, why did they love to sit with their parents beside the warm stove, listening to stories, to songs? Today it was young Hermes who poured the milk, he was pleasant, curious, gave an extra-generous titch, almost like his mother—talked about his children, none of whom wanted to take over the farm: Rolf consoled him: "That'll change, things will change, before your children are old enough to decide. The day will come when they'll be fighting each other for the farm." That made young Hermes laugh: "I hope you're right!"

"Just wait and see. . . ."

"If I knew you'd still be here then, I'd make a bet: three months' free milk, if you're right."

"In another five years your Konrad will be eighteen, and probably I won't be here anymore. . . ."

"I wish you'd stay." That was spoken so forthrightly that they were both embarrassed. Holger squeezed his hand, as much as to say: Yes, stay.

"That doesn't depend only on me," said Rolf.

"On us? I mean, on the village?"

"I have a profession," said Rolf, "I'm a qualified banking expert, what's more, with some practical experience—but I don't think they're about to entrust me with the local branch here." They could both laugh again, and Hermes said: "My sister, maybe she'll want to take over the farm—my sister."

Rolf thanked him, picked up the milk, and shook hands with young Hermes before leaving. Damn it, was he turning into a creature of impulse or even an opportunist? Of course the people in the village also had sons and daughters who went to university and sometimes turned up at weekends, smartly dressed, with their little cars, refused to go to church, with leftist airs, sexual freedom and all that; sometimes they had even come to them, grumbling and grousing, talked about Mao and treated him with a certain awe because he had been in the slammer. But he didn't care for

people trying to get chummy with him, he regarded the slammer
as neither a distinction nor fun, and for Katharina's sensitive
Communist heart they spoke too openly, and their comments on
sexual problems were more obscene than enlightened. They had
tried to get chummy, clumsily, and then had stayed away, suddenly,
they must have become scared of associating with them—for the
last couple of years that had no longer been advisable, and only
the one boy remained, Schmergen the farmer's son, whom his
brother's suicide had at first shattered, then made thoughtful. He
came and talked about Cuba, wanted to learn Spanish, and they
found him a Chilean woman—Dolores—who gave him lessons;
he still came sometimes, Heinrich Schmergen, sat quietly beside
the stove, rolling cigarettes, smiling, and didn't leave even when
old friends came, reliable, disillusioned friends, out of work,
banned from their professions, discussing the difference between
guarded and watched, and it pained him to detect from their
faint, very faint undertones that, in the last analysis, in spite of
slammer and surveillance, they regarded him as privileged.

That pained him the most, was worse than if his windows had
been smashed, for it applied not only to his background but also to
Veronica and Beverloh, who somehow, even if they were completely repudiated and loathed, were still regarded as belonging to
the aristocracy. After all, he had been married to one of them,
and the other had been his friend—and he could sometimes sense,
although he couldn't prove it, that they didn't quite accept him.
And he felt something of the same sort with Holzpuke, "in charge
of security," who looked for more in him than he would ever be
able to yield. Shaking his head, Holzpuke kept looking for
motives, found none, questioned him about possible motives, was
still poking around in the psychology that yielded nothing,
nothing: no one had ever "injured" Heinrich Beverloh, no one
had done or wished him harm, he had been sponsored, praised,
given every possible encouragement, that "towering intellect
straight from the people," not exactly a working-class child but
almost, considering that his father had started out as a mailman,

that is, at a working-class level: he had pushed the parcel cart by hand from house to house, had laboriously and diligently worked his way up to the status of clerk, and had retired with a civil servant's pension.

Yet in those days it had still been possible, without bending the truth too much, to sell Heinrich as a child of the working class, highly talented, bordering on genius, even with a sense of humor, likable, with a Christian upbringing, humanistically inclined and educated, and it may have hung only by the merest thread—probably Sabine's childish notion of entering untouched upon the married state—whether they would become brothers-in-law, and instead of Veronica it would have been Sabine who would be living with him somewhere—where?— faithful unto death, including this madness, this murderous, mythical logic that he was constantly trying to explain to Holzpuke, and to himself by discussing it with Holzpuke. When he recalled their time in New York, their conversations there, the frenzy, the horrified frenzy that had seized Heinrich when he discovered the "international continent of money," that ocean no one can cross, those mountains no one can climb—that immensity —it sometimes seemed that Beverloh reached the point of deciding to reverse his intelligence and insight. It wasn't envy, not that, no more so than Saint George or Siegfried killing the dragon out of envy. Indeed, perhaps his motives might be better understood by comparison with the Nibelung saga than by any sort of envy- or hate-philosophy or by something as stupid as resentment. As a banker and stock-exchange operator, Heinrich could have earned more money than he could ever spend, and that was probably his whole motivation: that rampant, rampaging immensity that no one needed, that benefited no one, merely breeding and inbreeding in an obscene incest, that many-headed hydra, he would try to chop off all those heads, not sparing Father either, of course— they had better watch out for him—that was no longer encompassed by the word "capitalism," it was something more, something mythical. They shouldn't count on memories of younger days, gratitude, outings, dances, discussions, games, and carefree parties in lamplit gardens; and next to Father, if he (Holzpuke) wished to know, the person most at risk was his sister, Sabine Fischer. That was the virgin whom he, Beverloh, wanted to snatch away from the dragon. He didn't consider Fischer himself to be at risk at all; in all probability they merely considered him a "conceited young puppy" whom they would not deign to honor with an assassination or kidnapping. But of course they would kidnap the child, Kit, as well, though only in order to spare Sabine suffering.

"Yes, you heard me correctly: in order to spare her suffering. They like her, you see, he does and so does Veronica, my former wife. Of course I can't give you any advice, nor can I guarantee that my advice and my prognoses are accurate—I am trying to get at the motivation, that's all. And I'm reasonably sure that you can save yourself the trouble of keeping my friends under surveillance."

"And how about yourself?"

"In objective terms, since we have a phone and there is a chance of connections being established: keep up the surveillance, of myself at any rate, but not for Katharina, my wife; she will never, never take that route, never."

"And you?"

"In all probability, bordering on certainty: never—but mind you, I said *bordering* on certainty—there might remain the fine line of the border itself—there remains a residue, a minute vestige, that prevents me from guaranteeing for myself."

And at that point Holzpuke sighed and said: "What a pity you wouldn't consider joining the police," laughed and added, "and probably wouldn't be accepted either—or would you?"

"If your 'would you?' refers to my considering joining the police, the answer is: no. Whether or not I'd be accepted, I can't judge. Most likely not, the police protects many things that are worth protecting, but it also protects the dragon that I was trying to describe to you. Keep an eye on me, I'd prefer that, but spare my wife if you can."

"We must keep an eye on your wife too, a protective eye, if you like, she's a potential contact, I'm sure you're aware of that—and we have to protect your little boy, too. How interesting—you say 'money' and not 'capitalism.' "

"I do say capitalism—but those people always say money."

"And your first wife?"

"She's a Socialist—I imagine she'd be happy to get out right now, but she has one terrible trait, the same as my sister, Mrs. Fischer: she's faithful."

"Faithful unto death?"

"Perhaps."

"Unto the death of others?"

He didn't know how to answer this, became embarrassed, and said: "She has a child—and she could be put away for life."

"One more thing: did you *have* to call your second son Holger too?"

"It's a fine old noble Nordic name. My first son is called Holger Tolm, my second Holger Schröter. Is it a crime to call two sons Holger?"

"No, only I find your reference to the origin of that truly fine name—well, not quite up to the standard of our discussion. No, it's not a crime to call two sons Holger if they have different last names. I enjoy talking to you, you always bring me a little closer to this wretched business which I know you yourself condemn. But I'd like to know—I won't pin you down—do you also guarantee for your friends, for their wives, their girlfriends—I mean the people you visit and who sometimes visit you?"

"I guarantee that not a single one of their theoretical or practical utterances puts them even remotely in the proximity of those you are looking for and pursuing; I guarantee that not one of them, even secretly, has ever referred to the police as 'the fuzz.' But guarantee? Whom would you guarantee one hundred percent?

Every single one of your men, that he wouldn't ever crack up, lose his nerve—quite understandably? And don't forget that my friends, their wives and girlfriends, including myself and my wife, would like to work, as teachers, mechanics, and I'm a pretty good authority on banking, I really am—and our friend Clara is one of the best teachers I've ever known. . . ."

"Look, I've nothing to do with the protection of the Constitution or with the Ministry of Education. . . ."

"I know that, and you know I'm not blaming you for anything, but just remember what can happen to people who aren't allowed to practice their profession—we can't go on growing tomatoes forever."

"Is there anything particular I could do for you?"

"My son, the first Holger—do you know anything at all about him?"

"No more than what your former wife sometimes tells your sister over the phone."

"And if you did know anything more . . . ?"

"I wouldn't be allowed to tell you, nor would I—and you know that—for your son's sake as well as for yours, and not only because this is a matter for the police. We're pinning our hopes on the phone—just as you are. Let me ask you one more question, an abstract, theoretical one, maybe also a logistical one: which mode of transport would you use if, as one of those people and theoretically familiar with the logistics, you wanted to approach our area?"

"Plane, car, rail—I'd exclude all those, and there would only be one thing left—and that seems to me obvious, or rather, logical: a bicycle."

"A bit slow—and why not a motorcycle?"

"Motorcycles have a bad reputation—and as for 'slow,' that's of no importance, it's merely a matter of planning, of preparation, of deployment. And now you will say, Why not on foot, then? In my opinion, on foot is too conspicuous—a pedestrian is always taken for a potential hitchhiker, and that's dangerous, while bicycling is fashionable and makes one independent. So my guess would be a bicycle. Let me add one comment: Beverloh learned to calculate when he was a banker, and ballistics when he was in the army—he was with the artillery."

"Like yourself."

"That's right, we were in the army together too—only my brother Herbert refused to serve."

Sometimes he also drove to the Zelgers' to give Veronica's mother a hand in the garden. He would weed, clip the hedges, help pick apples and pears, plums, red currants, and blackberries, dig potatoes, and when they worked together at the far end of the garden, burning potato stalks, she would come close to him and whisper: "Have you had any news of her?" And he would tell her what he had heard from his mother, Sabine, or Herbert: Mary, Queen of Heaven, and all that—and that Holger was fine. Mrs. Zelger, whom he still called Mama, had aged, become quiet and very shy, frail beyond her years. She couldn't be more than in her mid-fifties and had only this one child, Veronica; on several occasions she had been victimized by the media, had talked to newspaper and TV reporters about the criminal nature of banks and the cowardice of the Church; since then she had scarcely allowed anyone into the house. Zelger had given up his practice; at some time or other his enamel doctor's plate had been smashed with rocks, and he had refused to replace it. After all, he had been a doctor here in Hetzigrath for more than thirty years, they should have known him and not smashed his plate and smeared threats all over the walls.

He would come hobbling out into the garden, leaning on his cane, pipe in mouth, mumbling: "Who's supposed to eat all the jam, Paula? Who's supposed to eat all the potatoes? There are no more refugees to give them to. Believe me, Rolf, if she knew where Veronica is she would send her some blackberry jam."

"Yes, I would—and for the boy, too, and even for him, for

Heinrich. Even prisoners get fed, jam too, even murderers are given jam. I would do it, I'd send them all some jam."

Then they would sit down for a cup of coffee and some cake, and if Holger was along he would be given money for ice cream. Old Dr. Zelger would smoke his pipe, muttering to himself, refusing to agree that "the days of hostility are over," that no one in Hetzigrath bore a grudge against him, but no, he said: "Now *I* bear the grudge and will to the end of my days. To hell with their sympathy, their grudges, their confidence, or their suspicion. Night after night I've got out of bed for them, for every little twinge and every confinement, I've never refused my services, for thirty years and not even in those dreadful postwar years when it was dangerous to walk on the streets at night—and then they suddenly throw rocks through your windows, smash up your doctor's plate, smear up your walls—and no one, not a single person, came to us during that time to apologize or just to say a few kind words; not one. And the priest, who's been here just as long as I have, turned aside to avoid the embarrassment of having to greet me on the street—simply turned on his heel and went off in another direction, the yellow bastard. Yes, Paula— don't look at me like that when I call a priest a yellow bastard, that's what he is. No, my dear, no—and why all that? Because you've got a daughter who suddenly veers off and turns to crime —and there they are with all their own criminals in this stinking, dirty, Catholic hole: thieves and murderers, rapists, incest and abortion and fraud—how many of these swine have violated their daughters and their daughters-in-law, and how many times did I have to testify to save fathers from jail and kids from reform school? How many times? Sometimes, Rolf, I get terrorist notions myself, especially toward these yellow-bellied priests: refused to greet me anymore, just imagine, the first who should have come to us."

He would dig out the photo album and show Veronica as a First Communicant, such a sweet little thing in white, a candle in her hand and flowers in her hair; the priest beside her at the tea table, helping himself to some whipped cream. "Look at him, grinning, helping himself to your whipped cream! What kind of people are they? Are we supposed to have the plague? And what if we did? No sir, even if his appendix were hanging out of his navel he wouldn't get so much as a pill from me. And do you realize, Rolf, that we'd be close to starvation if it weren't for your mother? I never saved any money, all I have is the house with its mortgage, that's it, and if I could I'd send her a lot more than blackberry jam. Have we become untouchables because our child has turned to crime? So what? How many of that lot came to me to have their SS tattoos removed? If it weren't for your mother —she's the only one I accept it from. I'd accept it from your father, too. . . ."

And occasionally he would drive on to see old Beverloh, who would let him in suspiciously, without so much as a muttered greeting, and lead him upstairs without a word into the attic of the tiny house to show him Heinrich's old room. They used to call it the cubbyhole, ten feet square with sloping walls and two attic windows, and the old man would point scornfully to the books still on the shelf: Thomas More and Thomas Aquinas and Thomas Mann, "and all those other Thomases," folders, rulers, pens and pencils neatly arranged on the folding table screwed to the foot end of the bed; the blotter was still lying there, and the transparent pencil sharpener still contained the curly shavings; an open package of cigarettes, a butt in the ashtray, on the wall the framed Ph.D. diploma, a crucifix, Raphael's Madonna: an eerie reliquary complete with first lieutenant's shoulder boards. "Heinrich really did well in the artillery—he was their best man on ballistics, they wanted him for the general staff," and the wizened, sour old man even accepted an arm as he hobbled down the stairs, saying at the door: "He always said, The world will hear of me one day—and now it's hearing of him. . . ."

.   .   .

And since it was almost on his way, requiring only a very small detour, he would decide to drive on to Tolmshoven. He and the boy would walk past the security officers to see the grandparents, who were so overcome that they almost burst into tears, and his father would immediately take the boy by the hand, walk with him through the corridors, onto balconies; he loved holding children's hands, his father. Rolf remembered his father's hand holding his own childish hand when they went for walks in the fields around Iffenhoven; he always had two children by the hand, was happy, would switch around, sometimes himself and Herbert, then Herbert and Sabine, later also Veronica—but he couldn't remember whether Heinrich Beverloh had shown up in the family at an age when he could still be taken by the hand. The best thing for Father would probably have been to restrict himself to children's hands and art history, not the paper and certainly not the manor. That was a few sizes too pretentious, too formal—he could no longer simply walk away, a child by the hand, through fields and woods, and forget about the lousy paper. And Käthe couldn't do all her own cooking anymore, her own canning, behave as would have been natural in Eickelhof. The old man had fallen victim to a childhood dream and a childhood trauma.

It was really touching to see his parents' delight when he happened to turn up, to see how Käthe started right away to fuss around in her tiny kitchen, producing one of her incomparable soups, making pancakes for the boy—always in a somewhat strained rivalry with the big kitchen downstairs that they called the conference kitchen. Father there too, happy as a lark, forever taking his package of cigarettes out of his pocket and putting it back again. What a blessing he never talked about the war, never mentioned it, not even in connection with his obvious cigarette trauma; fortunately also never carried on about the "old days," about the poverty of his childhood, the poverty of his student days, merely asking now and again, and somewhat anxiously, whether they couldn't ask Katharina's parents over, since they were living in the village; they were too diffident, Father and Käthe, didn't feel the least bit—as Käthe put it—like "lords of the manor," but nevertheless lived in it. Father had known Luise Kommertz, Katharina's mother, when she was a child, a little girl, when they played "bounce ball" in the Kommertz yard.

Holger loved going to the manor, where there were ancient cellars with old bits of armor lying around, and the tower with its battlements, pagoda-shaped summerhouses on the grounds, and parts of old cannons and stone cannonballs.

Of late there had always been tears, at least moisture in Father's eyes when they said goodbye, yet it was only eighteen kilometers to Hubreichen, twenty to Cologne and Herbert, and seventeen to Blorr and Sabine. Of late Käthe, too, had been inclined to moist eyes.

And of course, once he was in Tolmshoven, he had also to visit Katharina's parents, word got around right away when he was there, "Rolf, who had been such a nice boy, so devout," who, all on his own, without Papa's help, had almost been made a bank executive, if he hadn't—if only he hadn't—set fire to cars and thrown rocks. Old buddies would emerge from farmyards and sheds, men he had played football with, shared altar-boy duties. They would clap him on the shoulder, run their hands over him in imitation of frisking police, and ask in astonishment: "Tell us now, where d'you keep all that dynamite and the hand grenades?" And Holger was admired, sometimes being "a true Schröter," the next time "a true Tolm," and given candles and greetings to his mother by nice, head-shaking young women who used to sing in the church choir with Katharina, and then of course the boy wanted to throw stones into the Hellerbach, the village stream. The dogs chained up in the Kommertz yard were quite vicious, Holger didn't like walking past them. And more hellos and tears even before they left, and more coffee, and tins were brought out and crisp little cookies distributed, and of course Holger had to go with Grandpa to his workroom, where all kinds of outlandish things were welded together. There old Schröter would sit, heaping abuse on the Communists, who had killed his brother, and almost more on Adenauer, who had betrayed everything, every damn thing, sold it all for a mess of pottage. "And just look at that mess, my boy—is it to your liking? I wouldn't think so, otherwise you wouldn't have . . . oh well, it's gone but not forgotten."

He would show Holger everything, couplings and connections, screw threads, fiddle around on a contraption made of old war material, and it really was a bit eerie the way he repeatedly stressed that from his shed he could take "perfect aim, and I mean perfect, at your other grandpa's window, absolutely perfect, especially the bathroom window"—no, he didn't feel at ease at the Schröters', Luise too pious, pietistic you might say, old Schröter forever carrying on about his old dream of the "left Center"—and in the end, when he had fulfilled all his duties, he felt positively homesick for Hubreichen, the high-walled vicarage garden, the red-enamel milk pitcher, their garden, the fruit trees, the stove, and playing with his young son, for Katharina, who, though she could account for the strained atmosphere in her old home, wouldn't deny it. "You must put yourself in their place, understand that bitterness of the leftist Catholics toward the gains the rightist Catholics have made toward their triumphal march. They, the leftist Catholics, have always had to limp behind, footsore, bitter, frustrated, they could never feel happy, had no reason to. And now: just look at that mess."

He was a bit scared by this nostalgia for Hubreichen, for cottage and garden, for being alone with Katharina and the boy, for that sense of security behind the great woodpile that he kept replenishing; and the daily ritual ending with the evening walk to pick up the milk, the generous titch added by old Mrs. Hermes. Yes, he was scared by this nostalgia for a sense of security that might have been understandable when he came out of the slammer and was being hounded by the Zummerling mob, who had even tried to rouse the village people against himself and the priest. But now, four years later, with Holger already three years old, now he should be wanting to get away from Hubreichen—and he didn't. Was he to—did he want to—spend the rest of his life in Hubreichen, restrict his delight in planning and calculating to the garden, to salvaging old lumber, to picking the crops and playing with his son? Possibly become some sort of unpaid, unofficial adviser to the villagers, a person to be rewarded with some fresh-killed meat, a basket of eggs?

He found himself shocked by the routine that had developed from going for the milk: opening the door, placing the milk on the counter, kissing Katharina's cheek, taking off the boy's jacket, warming his hands at the stove, looking into the saucepan that today happened to smell of meat: stew with vegetables and mushrooms, checking to see whether the open bottle of wine would be enough for the evening or whether he should open a new one, closing the shutters, hooking them from the inside, testing the soil in the geranium window boxes. Outside it was damp and foggy, which absolved him from his evening walk. He was relieved to hear that Dolores wouldn't be coming for the Spanish lesson, she was organizing some demonstration or other for Chile or Bolivia, had said over the phone that she was satisfied with their Spanish, on principle spoke only Spanish with them now, ending up with "*Venceremos.*" Where? Who?

They were both startled by a knock on the door and glanced up in alarm, they had been looking forward to an evening of speaking Spanish and listening to music and were surprised when Sabine came in with Kit and the young security officer they were sometimes seeing these days at the manor—in the corridors, the park, the courtyard. Sabine with luggage, that had never happened before: a suitcase, an overnight case, a bag of knitting, Kit carrying two dolls and her ragged old cloth lion from which she never parted. Sabine, her manner appealing, almost embarrassed: "I know it's a bad time to come—but I must see you, talk to you, and—I don't mind sleeping with Kit in the little room. . . ." It was a good opportunity once again to admire Katharina's unfailing openhearted warmth; not for a fraction of a second did her face show surprise or dismay. "Come on in and have supper with us! There's something good tonight, and it'll be very good for Holger to play with Kit for a change, instead of with us. Come on in! But I wonder—your security—and you know I don't mean to be facetious . . ."

"I'm being guarded," said Sabine with a smile. "Mr. Hendler —you've met him, haven't you?—was kind enough to come with me, in Mother's car—I've left my old bus at Erwin's—on Mr. Holzpuke's instructions Mr. Hendler has taken over my security. . . ."

The young officer merely nodded and said: "I'll have to take up my post now, I'll report to my superior on the new situation— most likely he'll send along another man—the responsibility—the vicarage is very large—the garden is enormous."

"It's pretty chilly outside," said Rolf, "looks like rain, anyway fog is dripping. Come along, I'll show you a good spot," then qualifying: "in my opinion good. We must let the priest know too." He took Hendler along the garden path to the cellar over-hang of steel and wired glass. "I think you'll find that from here you can keep an eye on both the garden and the wall, as well as our cottage, and if you—may we bring you something to eat?"

"Thanks," Hendler said, and stood against the wall testing his field of vision. "I think this'll do till the other officer arrives—but, I wonder, would you have an outside light on your cottage?"

"Yes?"

"Would you mind turning it on?"

"Of course not."

"Thanks, and—I hope you understand—nothing to eat, much as I'd like to."

. . .

At that moment light blazed up in the church, falling from the tall windows into the garden, and for some reason that he would never be able to explain, Rolf was frightened. He ran to the vestry door, rattled the handle, then ran back through the garden, out through the little gate, saw Roickler's car outside the door, the trunk open, the back shelf propped up, and a young woman whom he had never seen before coming out of the hallway carrying two suitcases, a bag dangling from each shoulder—she nodded, hurried past him, and he turned around to watch: the pale severity of her face, the long, loose brown hair, her movements. As she put down the suitcases, half turning before placing the bags in the trunk, she smiled. He walked toward her and was about to introduce himself, but she shook her head and said: "I know who you are—I'm Anna Plauck—go in and see him, he won't be coming back, he wanted to leave quietly and write to you—he's only afraid of one thing—that they'll kick you out if he's no longer here. Go in and see him, he's in the church. . . ."

It was a long time since he had been in a church, although he lived so close to one and the priest was, one could say, a good friend of his: yet he was afraid as he walked down the hallway, felt the draft, and entered the chill of the neo-Gothic church nave. Involuntarily he looked for the stoup, dipped in his first and middle fingers: it wasn't really that long, only ten years, ten out of thirty. He even crossed himself and was startled to see Roickler in his surplice standing beside the altar. He was afraid something blasphemous was about to happen, some stupid sacrilege, and was surprised to see Roickler remove the altar cloth, carefully fold it up, take out the chalice from the tabernacle, kneel down, snuff out the candles, and calmly go into the vestry, from which he shortly emerged in street clothes. Rolf was still standing there rooted to the spot when Roickler touched his arm, saying: "I didn't want to go just like that, I wanted to leave everything in order, the chalice in the safe, the vestments and altar cloth in the closet, I'll send the key to the safe to the bishop

—and I'm not leaving because I'm tormented by my sexuality but because I love that woman, I love Anna, I don't want to leave her in loneliness and make myself lonely. I can't go on, my dear Tolm, I can't go on doing secretly what I forbid others to do, what I have to chalk up against them as a sin. It won't affect the people in the village very much, I only hope they'll soon get a new priest. . . . Come, I've something to settle with you."

"What are you going to do?" asked Rolf. "How are you going to manage, what are you going to live on . . . ?"

"For the time being I'll live at Anna's, she'll support me, maybe my brother can give me some sort of a job—he's an electrical contractor. And I can read and write, even do some arithmetic. Don't look at me so sadly: because of you, your wife, and also your parents, also because of the people here, I'm very sorry to leave. Maybe I can come back secretly some evening, sit by the fire and smoke my cigar—are you shocked?"

"Yes," said Rolf, "in spite of my own findings, in spite of my systems analysis, I am shocked—I always thought, we always thought . . . Katharina . . ."

"That I was a good priest—I know, and actually it's true: I wasn't a bad one, only I can't go on like this, and I'd like to take proper leave of my church. . . . Come along—"

They each crossed themselves, almost simultaneously, Roickler smiled as he did so, Rolf did not. Quite obviously Roickler hadn't even taken his books, the shelves were still full, the smell of cigars still hung in the room. "Here's a document I've prepared, but I don't know whether it's valid or whether its validity will be accepted. What it does is extend the lease we signed—you'll have to put in the date—by five years. Today's date, Ferdinand Roickler, priest—I'm still that, I still have that ecclesiastical status—and you sign here: Rolf Tolm. The local church council won't, or I should say: shouldn't raise any objections, the people here like you, and Hermes is reliable. But I don't know what pressure will be exerted from above, and I don't know either how much authority they have up there. Probably it's a matter of interpretation, might mean a court case, but it won't be so easy to throw you out—I wanted to be sure you understood this. . . . Still sad, Rolf? Still sad: we'll meet again, here or in Cologne when you come to see me at Anna's. By the way, I'll give you the vicarage key, and you can use the bishop's room as a guest room in case your parents might like to stay overnight. . . . You know about the record cabinet, the stereo set, and where the wine's kept —and it would please me to think of someone having a bath in the bishop's bathroom, where no one, let alone a bishop, has ever taken a bath. Don't be sad, my friend, and remember me to Katharina and the boy. I took the precaution of sending my aunt off on a holiday, she'll survive. . . ."

Rolf managed to stammer out his thanks for the wonderful time they had had here. "I don't know what would have become of us, where we would have ended up—and without you the people here certainly wouldn't have—come around to accepting us, to being so nice to us—I mean. . . ."

Out in the car Anna Plauck was already sitting at the wheel, smiling, nodding. And then they did embrace, shed a few tears, waved, a car driving off, he turned and went back into the church again and looked at the bare altar, noticing for the first time that the Perpetual Light had gone out too. Fear of this change, fear of the new priest, fear of the fear that seized him at the thought of being driven out; he locked the vicarage door and put the key in his pocket.

Kit was already playing with Holger when he returned, suggesting suitable spots for the accommodation of the lion and Holger's beloved wooden dachshund, a frightful Disney-type creature. Sabine was sitting on the bench beside the stove, smoking a cigarette—he hadn't often seen her smoking lately; was she flushed from the stove or from embarrassment? She had always retained something childlike, not naïve but childlike, and he had never been able to understand why she had to pick Fischer. Not

only were there nicer men in that category but there were really
nice ones—Pliefger's grandson, for instance, whom he had once
met at Father's, and also—like it or not, one must be fair—young
Zummerling, who didn't seem terribly intelligent but was
genuinely thoughtful, considerate, the kind one might call a
"caring" person—and she could certainly have had him: he was
a first-rate horseman, and that, of course, would have been a
fantastic match: the little paper and Zummerling. And why not,
come to think of it? Since it made no difference anyway which
paper one read. And now as he watched Sabine with a smile he
felt a pang and would have wished her more happiness than she
seemed to have had with Fischer. But then Fischer used not to be
as obnoxious as he was now—always a reactionary, of course,
and obsessed with profits, so what, perhaps they were all like that,
had to be like that—but at one time he had been more moderate,
less ruthless; he had used up his charm very quickly—had sometimes even had a wistful look in his eyes. But the nicest of the lot
was certainly Zummerling.

"What are you smiling at?" asked Sabine; she was having
trouble with her cigarette and stubbed it out in the ashtray.

"I'm smiling because I have much better quarters for you than
that little room of ours. I have a genuine bishop's room with a
bishop's bathroom"—and he took the key from his pocket and
toyed with it. "The priest has suddenly gone off on a trip, he had
to leave in a hurry, sends his regards to you, Katharina, and to
Holger too. He's offered me the use of his house—in case we
have guests. . . . Incidentally, I'm delighted to see you, you're
looking extremely well, almost as if you were in love, even your
pregnancy suits you—it's becoming quite obvious. . . ."

She blushed. Perhaps his answer had been too flip. "Don't
mind me. I take it you're staying for a while?"

"For a few days anyway, I've already explained to Katharina
—Erwin is off again on one of his long trips, and I'm sick of
always being alone in that big house. So, if it's all the same to you
two, I'd rather not have either the bishop's room or the bishop's

bath—I'd just be alone in a big house again, surrounded by police. . . . Please, if you don't mind, not the bishop's room."

She smiled, was oddly embarrassed, helped set the table, even remembered where they kept the bowls for the stew, the spoons and the paper napkins. Meanwhile he cored some apples, filled them with jam, and put them in the oven, gave another stir to the bowl in which he had mixed vanilla and eggs, milk and sugar, for the custard sauce.

"This'll remind you of Eickelhof," he said.

"Do you also think so often about Eickelhof? I thought you never wanted to hear of it again. . . ."

"No, not that often, but I know you do, and I want you to feel at home here. Maybe what we have here is a bit of Eickelhof —though only a thirtieth as big. All right, everybody, supper's ready!"

"Yes, it does remind me of it. It must be the wall—and your warm welcome."

She sighed with contentment during the meal—stew, braised vegetables with mushrooms, and salad—put the kettle on for tea without being asked, kept touching Katharina's arm, smiling, almost in tears, at any rate with moist eyes, and although he told her that the officer had declined any food she insisted on taking out "his bowlful." "And later on a baked apple, when they're ready—I know he'll accept that from me, we've known each other for quite a while." By this time it was raining hard, she pulled the hood of Rolf's parka down over her head and carried the bowl of stew under the protection of the dangling garment; she refused an umbrella and closed the door carefully behind her.

Katharina shook her head as he was about to speak. She had never been able to bring herself to send Holger out of the room when they wanted to discuss something. He said softly: "The priest, Roickler, will be away for a long time—a very long time," and he placed the lease, the supplement to the lease, in front of her. They were both equally surprised to see Sabine's blissful smile when she returned, took off the wet parka, shook it out, and sat down again by the stove. Then came the baked apples in Holger's favorite little dishes, brown pottery with red borders, the custard sauce, and it was all so intimate, so gay, as if Saint Barbara and Saint Nicholas were hovering together above the house, the garden, and the village: still fall, yet already wintry, and again he was scared by all that snug security. Sabine shook her head when Katharina held out a little dish of apple and custard for the officer.

"No," she said, "he'd rather not, he's a stickler. I must tell you something—that camper the officers have been living in recently, they're going to move it away from Blorr and park it here—I'm a disturbing element. . . ."

"You can stay with us as long as you want—as long as you like."

"And I won't have to use the bishop's room?"

"No."

Sabine insisted on washing the children and putting them to bed, absolutely insisted. It was lovely to see them together, cuddled up with the scruffy lion and the Disney dog: "really sweet."

"And now," said Sabine, "I can tell you: I've left Fischer for good, left him for good, and the child I'm expecting is not his, not Fischer's—I know, you're staggered, you find it just as hard to believe as Father and Käthe did, but it's true."

It was Katharina's idea to drink a toast to the child. She was always having bright ideas like that, and at the second glass something resembling "defiant happiness" spread over Sabine's face as she said with a laugh: "If it's a boy I'll call him Holger, if only to annoy him: 'all clear for the weekend'!"

"One should never name a child merely to annoy someone. That's not good for the child, and maybe it'll be a girl," said Katharina.

"Then I'll call her Katharina—not Veronica, though that's a

beautiful name too. Father is going to help me, and Käthe already sees me as a great journalist. Is there something special about the priest that you didn't want to tell me in front of the children?"

"Yes, he's left for good—he won't be back, at least not as a priest. He's gone to a woman, his woman. I wanted to spare you that. . . ."

"Spare me? Why? D'you think I don't know what's going on with Kohlschröder—and anyway, it confirms your analyses."

"One isn't always glad to see such analyses confirmed. And by the way, three Holgers in one family—that would simply be too much."

VII

Once again he had to enter the gray area where discretion and security collide and one or the other could explode. If someone had ever predicted that it would one day be part of his security duties to find out in which month and by whom a woman was pregnant, he would have laughed. But, strictly speaking, it could be of the utmost importance to know with whom this woman had taken up that somewhat intimate connection which led to a condition known as pregnancy. And since for obvious reasons the safety of young Mrs. Fischer—and even of her brother, himself a security risk—had been so graphically impressed upon him, it was clearly his duty to pursue the matter. Behind the most charming, socially acceptable mask, the "impregnator"—as he called him for the time being—could be at least as dubious (not morally but security-wise) as that odd young Schubler, who had, if not impregnated (at least as far as was known), intimately associated with Mrs. Fischer's neighbor.

The case of Mrs. Fischer was a rather delicate one. It was not his business to track down or prove adultery, he was merely responsible for her security and, apart from the fact that she happened to be one of the women most at risk, it had now become incontrovertible that she was expecting a child not by her husband. That newspaper fellow who had phoned him at noon had never yet let him down. He had also drawn his attention to the weird contraptions made by old man Schröter, who, after all, did have a clear line of fire on the manor. The fellow had also pointed out old Beverloh's rage and the deep-seated bitterness of Dr. Zelger, all elderly gentlemen whom he had hitherto been keeping only under cursory surveillance as marginal figures, possible contact persons, never as potential activists. However, it was entirely possible that, behind their anger, rage, or bitterness, violence might lurk.

When all was said and done, Mrs. Fischer was a Tolm, was doubly at risk, and all these people stood in some sort of relationship to the Tolms, whom it was hard enough to discipline anyway—the old couple irresponsible, sometimes reckless, especially the old lady, whose kind heart and innocuous nature he would never doubt. Their son Rolf he regarded as completely above suspicion, although he—but that was long ago, and in conversation he had proved himself to be a valuable analyst of the scene. As for their son Herbert, he didn't quite trust him: that AAA (Anti-Auto Action) was something that could turn nastier than the fellow could ever imagine. And now he had reliable reports that Sabine Fischer née Tolm was in her sixth, not her third, month of pregnancy; five months ago, however, her husband Erwin Fischer had been away for almost three months—that in itself had meant plenty of work—he happened to have a taste for shady nightclubs and naïve playboy behavior, liked to show off, and those two things—showing off and security—were difficult to reconcile. It put an unnecessary stress on the frustration of the officers. Well, there was always help from headquarters, and the details were no concern of his. Naturally they had to investigate every love affair or even casual adventure, by now one had to be prepared for anything, and at the same time maintain and guarantee total discretion!

It was the Bleibls who caused him the most trouble, she with her idiotic tit-wiggling and the whole business of titillation that drove his men up the wall—her shopping sprees, trips, parties—and Bleibl with his hookers, whom it was impossible to check up on all that thoroughly, seeing that on this scene, too, there was a kind of "leftist breeze" blowing these days that had to do with women's libbers; in the old days, you had been able to count on almost every hooker being a reactionary, but now the libbers had changed all that, and you had to keep your eyes peeled. He was also having trouble with that nice old Kortschede, who had fallen hopelessly and irrevocably in love with that young fellow—you might call it an old man's last love: though the wretched youth wasn't a putative terrorist, he was still enough of a criminal to be capable of anything—an obnoxiously brutal young punk.

And now Mrs. Fischer, whose pregnancy offended him inasmuch as it cast doubt on the effectiveness of his surveillance. There must be someone around whom they hadn't caught—somewhere, somehow, she must have met him, got in touch with him, yet she had been guarded day and night, for her own protection. Nor could she have made any arrangements with him—with whom?—by phone, since her phone in particular was fully monitored—had to be because of that damn female they called "Mary, Queen of Heaven," who was bound to be caught someday; and Mrs. Fischer knew this and wanted her phone monitored.

Furthermore, of course, he was in a way morally disappointed in her: this nice, serious young woman who was known to be such a devout churchgoer, a shy beauty, almost a Madonna with that cute little kid, but what a cunning minx she must be for her lover to have eluded them. There had been no point in reading and rereading all the statements and reports: visits she had received, visits she had made—it had been totally impossible for a lover to have crept into her room at night. Hardly a house was

as strictly guarded as hers, and damn it all, if she did have someone she loved—which (in his private opinion) was hardly surprising considering what a pompous ass her husband was—surely
she could have had enough confidence in him to tell him all about
it, he talked to her often enough, didn't he? But perhaps the
experience of her neighbor, whom they all called "sex-starved
Erna," had held her back. For the investigations—justified in
terms of security—into Erna's love affair had ended up by wreck-
ing that marriage. It wasn't his business to track down adultery
and destroy marriages—damn it all, he wasn't a detective agency
—but it so happened that there were border zones, risk-filled
conflicts, that one couldn't keep out of. How odd, incidentally,
that her own husband had apparently forgotten the simplest of
arithmetic. Or might she be feeding him that "third month"
myth?

Then, too, there was the strange part played by Dr.
Grebnitzer, her doctor. It had required the pressure of higher
authority—and pretty high at that—to convince him that, in a
case like this, it was necessary for him to break professional silence.
This naïve, exceptionally nice elderly doctor—one of the old
school who would still sit on the edge of the bed, his stethoscope
around his neck, and who had brought young Mrs. Fischer into
the world—was completely stunned when it had been necessary,
and possible, to confront him with figures to show that the human
being growing in her womb (and obviously "thriving, thriving")
could not be her husband's. "Sabine never, Sabine—never!" and
although eventually he confirmed the sixth month and had to
admit to Fischer's lengthy absence during the time in question,
he had still insisted on his "Sabine? Never!" and muttered something about: "You can't always go by figures!"

What can you go by, then, if not figures, when it was a
question of paternity? If the young woman had managed, under
maximum surveillance, to pursue a love affair unobserved, then
Lühler, Zurmack, and Hendler—it was during their time that she
had become pregnant—must have missed something. Perhaps she

had met the "impregnator" when she had gone for the milk, had "given herself" to him—in her case vulgar, popular expressions were out of place, she was the type who would call it "giving herself"—in the Beeretz stable or barn, in which case she must have had accomplices at the Beeretz farm; not very likely, for while she was getting the milk all approaches to the farm were under close observation, and barns and stables were searched in advance. Not even when she was still going horseback riding had she been left unguarded, nor when she went shopping, nor in the dress store, not even when taking a shower at the Tennis Club. Any assignation made over the phone would inevitably be noted, for her phone in particular—she knew this and agreed to it—had to be strictly monitored, since they were still hoping to be able to intercept a call from "Mary, Queen of Heaven."

Yet somewhere she must have performed, unobserved, the act without which no pregnancy can occur. Statements, checklists, read and reread—they yielded nothing: take Breuer, take Klober, Schubler, Helmsfeld, the farmers in Blorr—somewhat unlikely although not impossible—young Beeretz was a thoroughly attractive, articulate, reasonably well-educated young farmer, and she was only human, female, quite often alone and for long periods of time, and in a far from enviable position, God knows. Among the ladies whom she sometimes had to tea there may have been some lesbian goings-on, certainly not on her part or with her, but then, of course, no one ever got pregnant from that. Besides, during the time in question she had hardly gone out, only to one or two cocktail parties, and one thing he felt sure of: she was not the type to do it on the wing, as it were, no, she was a quiet, serious young woman whose devoutness was public knowledge. And even if he was aware that devoutness was no guarantee against a lapse, he was also pretty sure that, if it happened, it would have to be romantic, she certainly wouldn't be interested in a frivolous porn escapade, the kind that sometimes gave his men trouble.

That damnable area between the needs for security and discretion, that jungle of entangled decisions—not only might he stumble but yet another marriage might be broken up, one that would make headlines. That newspaper fellow had hinted as much to him: the Fischer marriage—glorified throughout the press as the ideal, indeed the "most ideal," of marriages, this model marriage between newspaper and Beehive in which, as was constantly being emphasized, "harmony of outlook reigns supreme" —would not disintegrate without a splash. There was still always the possibility that Fischer, in his apparent ignorance and over-weening self-confidence, had never so much as dreamed of counting the months of pregnancy, or that he would pull a secret rendezvous with his wife out of a hat, in the Bahamas or some such place: he would have no trouble refuting such a version at any time.

This affair had to be handled with extreme caution. That newspaper fellow was usually very well informed. He had also been the one to draw his attention to Kortschede's homosexual leanings, and that was how they got onto Peter Schlumm, who was capable of anything (and they had been able to, forced to, listen in on Kortschede tenderly calling him "dearest Petie"). This fellow Schlumm was undeniably a considerable security risk, by no means "putative" but nearly convicted of blackmail and attempted manslaughter, certainly of pimping plus hashish and heroin, barely twenty years old, a devastatingly attractive youth with blond curls and the face of an angel. There were plenty of slip-ups to be expected in that area, slip-ups of a worse nature than in the case of Mrs. Fischer's unexpectedly advanced pregnancy. Maybe he would have another talk with her after all, submit the outcome of his cogitations to her, and ask her outright, for the sake of her own security and that of her child, to let him in on the secret: he would guarantee her full discretion, also advise her of the result of the investigation of the "impregnator," and put no obstacles in the path of her love life; after all, he wasn't a snooper who put spies in beds and closets. If she refused to reveal her secret he would have to talk to Dollmer, and Dollmer possibly to Stabski, before he could instigate strong measures to track down the "impregnator."

He couldn't afford any slip-ups here, and if the marriage broke up it must not be the fault of the police. There was no denying that a Fischer was right in there with Zummerling—and the lapse of a Fischer daughter-in-law would in no time turn into a police fiasco, even though some of the papers were already hinting at a shaky marriage.

It was annoying that the telephone in Blorr was answered only by the housekeeper, who told him that Mrs. Fischer had driven off a few minutes earlier with her mother and little girl; annoying that Kübler didn't report this until five minutes later, adding that "quite a bit of luggage had been taken along" and that it had looked "almost as if they were moving out." Shortly after that, Hendler, in surprisingly similar words, reported from Tolmshoven the arrival of the ladies with the child—"almost as if they were moving in," he had added. Rohner, who had followed the ladies, asked for new instructions: was he to return to Blorr or remain in Tolmshoven? But then Kübler reported from Blorr that Fischer had turned up shortly after his wife's departure, had only picked up some papers and driven off again with a number of suitcases in his car. In his arrogant way Fischer had told him he would be away for a few weeks; and since Miss Blum had also left now, Kübler said, and Miss Blum had merely had instructions to look in on the place now and again—i.e., not regularly—it would no longer be necessary to keep the house under such strict surveillance, and would it be all right for him to go home? At this point Holzpuke showed unexpected irritation and sharply ordered Kübler to be good enough to await instructions. He had reason to be annoyed, up to then Mrs. Fischer had always been most cooperative and understanding, had informed him of any change in her situation and allowed him plenty of time to make new arrangements. All this—the "headlong flight" from Blorr with her mother and the child—indicated tensions, perhaps even panic. Fischer's departure may have been a coincidence, but things became almost chaotic when Rohner reported from Tolmshoven that, after a brief stay, Mrs. Fischer had proceeded with her child to Hubreichen, to her brother, and that he, Rohner, because everything had had to be decided so quickly, had sent along Hendler for her protection; until final arrangements were made, he, Rohner, would take over Hendler's duties in Tolmshoven, things being relatively quiet now that the conference was over— he was just waiting to be relieved by Lühler and would then return for the time being to Blorr.

He confirmed Rohner's arrangements, called Kübler, apologized for his fit of temper, and caught himself feeling disappointed at missing a confidential chat with Sabine Fischer over a cup of tea. From time to time it had been necessary for him to talk to her, explain certain things to her, also to ask for some information, and he had always enjoyed being with the young lady: she had a surprisingly childlike manner of laughing at many things, letting one forget her damnable "station in life," always made the tea herself, sometimes even apologized for the trouble she was causing. He imagined himself to be in her full confidence and had felt capable of broaching even this touchy subject to her, and explaining that the most charming lover might be a front for elements requiring investigation. He had even already prepared some phrases, such as: "My deliberations have led me to the conclusion that the child you are expecting—well, it was security reasons, not moral ones, that pointed to this possibility—well, that it might be the product" (he would have to correct that: "product" wasn't good) "of an intimate relationship other than that with your husband—and since I am responsible for your security, you will forgive me . . ." Probably she would blush, pour some more tea, maybe smile or get angry, indignant, offended, maybe she would throw him out, and it would lead to a reprimand—would have, would have led to a reprimand. For now that she was staying in Hubreichen at her brother's, in that cramped little house, such a confidential chat was no longer possible, let alone on such a subject.

The longer he thought about it, the more improbable did a love affair outside Blorr seem to him. If she had wanted to meet the "impregnator" outside Blorr, she would have had to be away at least a couple of hours, and that would have shown up in the reports, if only with a query, but the query would have been followed up, just as it was when she used to take the child to the Groebels in Hetzigrath, or that time she suddenly changed her hairdresser, stopped going to Szymanski in Blückhoven and switched to Picksehne in Hurbelheim. There were no queries left in the reports; in the end she had stopped going to either hairdresser and had washed and set her own hair, that glorious golden-blond hair he wanted so much to admire over a cup of tea and a confidential chat.

As for the neighbors: his thoughts turned first to the Blömers, that somewhat irresponsible crowd that liked to give free-and-easy parties—a nuisance because some of the shadier guests at these parties had to be checked out at least cursorily—and especially Blömer's brother-in-law Sculcz, obviously a wealthy man (source of wealth still unclarified, he was rumored to be writing popular porn under a pseudonym). Both of them, Blömer and his brother-in-law, were hardly her type, they were too shallow, too irresponsible, certainly not "romantic"—besides he suddenly remembered that he could have saved himself those Blömer ideas: they had only been living there for two and a half months, and she was in her sixth month and was definitely known to have had no previous contact with the Blömers. So there remained young Beeretz, old Hermanns, Klober, Helmsfeld, and, at that time, Breuer; none of them likely, but he had learned not to take probabilities or type-attractions for granted in sexual affairs: Kortschede, that fine, sensitive elderly gentleman who was married, after all, with grown-up children, and played the harpsichord. If one had thought him capable of lapses at all, one would have matched him up with a cultivated, elegant actress or soprano of about thirty-eight as being "his type," yet Kortschede had succumbed to the cheapest type of male prostitute—that thoroughly vulgar, brutal fellow Schlumm. And Bleibl, in whose case one would have guessed at gypsy or at least flamenco types, had taken for his third wife a gentle, smiling Yugoslav cleaning woman: positively an angel of gentleness, yet nevertheless unable to stand living with him for more than two years.

Eventually, after realizing that she obviously had committed what she herself would call adultery, he could exclude no one as a partner, neither the elderly Helmsfeld, who probably lacked the guts if not the desire, nor even bowlegged old Klober; both appeared in the reports as visitors: Helmsfeld probably at tea parties with a literary turn, Klober usually briefly, to deliver "homegrown vegetables"—lettuce, cauliflower, "guaranteed organic, ma'am," couldn't be persuaded not to call her ma'am, was given a cigar, a brandy, but obviously didn't feel at ease, usually left the cigar less than half smoked, and not one of his visits had exceeded seventeen or eighteen minutes; so one was quite justified in regarding Klober as unlikely.

Finally there remained—and every avenue had to be explored to the very end—his own men. Among them Zurmack seemed to him the most suspect, suspect when he looked at it from Zurmack's point of view: he didn't seem to have any inhibitions when it came to affairs of the heart, for all that he was married, had also on occasion—once, anyway, and in a very delicate situation that might have gone wrong—and without denying it for long, started an affair with the mother of a delinquent while actually on duty. He had arrested a young hashish pusher, had then gone back into the apartment to make a thorough search of the place, and had, as he later admitted, "lain down" with the boy's mother.

"Yes, I laid her. She was a nice woman, Elli was her name, I can't even remember her last name, and she wasn't a hooker, and yes, after that I sometimes did go to her while still on duty, I couldn't help myself—and to this day, whenever I pass the house, I feel the urge again because I know her old man and the boy are in the slammer—I'm fond of her, might almost say: I love her—and she simply melts when I arrive, I know it—and Lisbeth, my wife, has never known or noticed a thing. But then I did get cold feet—that it might lead to blackmail—but she never tried anything of the sort, never even hinted at it—Elli, a good woman, a nice woman. . . ."

And yet he did exclude Zurmack, not from Zurmack's point of view but from Sabine Fischer's. He simply couldn't imagine it, almost less than Klober, although Klober was a bowlegged, elderly profiteer and Zurmack was a handsome, fine figure of a policeman, with a bit of the old gendarme look about him, athletic, straightforward, probably—seen through female eyes—not without charm. Lühler—he was taking them in the order of probability—in theory any time, without hesitation, he was game for any adventure, had had plenty of them, was unmarried, but: for him this "Bee" was way out of reach—too risky, but for social, not amorous reasons. She was in any case "media-exposed" —and how! That could mean trouble, and Lühler wasn't keen on that, not Lühler—and anyway, if it did turn out to be one of his men—and damn it, they only human and male—anyway, that would eliminate any security risk, and the only one left was Hubert Hendler.

This was a man he had never quite been able to fathom, he liked him, he was one of the most reliable men he had, was well up on his theory, well informed as to the law, had never committed the slightest indiscretion, even when on the vice squad. Kiernter swore by him, by his stable marriage, his behavior, and ascribed Hendler's occasional edginess, which could sometimes amount almost to irritability, to his financial situation: he had obviously overextended himself in building his house, with his car and other acquisitions, yet there was an "invaluable stabilizing element," as Kiernter put it: Hendler's wife, Helga, sensible, affectionate, quiet—and "almost a beauty." True, in the immediate family there were a few less stable elements, Helga's sister Monika and her friend Karl Zurmeyen, another of those dropout sociologists but about whom nothing, nothing whatever in the least suspicious was known, though he had been in Berlin at times that could have made him suspect. Only one thing pointed to Hendler as the possible "impregnator"—of all the men under consideration he was the only one to be, if not entirely, at least approximately, "her type." A serious boy, devout like herself, not without humor although it sometimes seemed so, and with a quiet virility that must appeal to her; in some aspects a religious fanatic—which she was not—and damnably "righteous," not self-righteous—righteous, had sometimes circumvented regulations and closed his eyes to certain infringements. He was something of an outsider, couldn't stand off-color jokes, was intolerant of obscenities, had often put up with teasing and sometimes worse—nevertheless had earned respect, indeed liking, among even the most cynical of his brother officers. But could Hendler—his mind rebelled against calling him the "impregnator" and he introduced the word "lover" into his thoughts—could Hendler be or have been her lover? The word "lover" reduced the improbability without increasing the probability of the impossible.

One of his own men? He could just see the headlines, it would mean the end of him, and no doubt the best course would be to let the matter rest, not to involve Dollmer or Stabski too soon, explain to that newspaper fellow that Mrs. Fischer's intimate affairs didn't concern him as long as there was no question of a security risk—and there was none: in the final analysis it could only be one of the neighbors or one of his own men, and none of them was a security risk, perhaps merely a moral risk, and moral risks were no concern of his. Hendler? He was no doubt one of the romantic kind. But then there was that splendid Helga, a pretty, levelheaded young woman with whom he had danced on several occasions, and yet: now Sabine Fischer was at her brother's in Hubreichen, and Hendler was there to guard her: the walled vicarage garden, that idyllic little annex, the tall trees, the hazel thickets—if they were having a love affair conditions couldn't be more ideal. Of course her brother Rolf was not one of those free-and-easy, progressive porn types, nor was his capitalistic little sister, in fact he was more of a puritanical socialist type, yet undoubtedly he would neither reproach nor put obstacles in the path of his dear, supercapitalistic little sister if he should happen to surprise her in a tête-à-tête in that splendid garden.

The affair remained sensitive, explosive even, and probably the best thing would be for him to send all three of them— Zurmack, Lühler, and Hendler—off to a refresher course, to Strüderbeken, where there was open heath and forest and a pleasant officers' mess. Jogging, football, a bit of target shooting, some theory—that would do them good, they had earned it, and after the course he would send their names in for promotion; they had earned that too, especially Zurmack, whose nerves had been sorely tried by the Bleibl woman—since then he had categorically refused "to go shopping, or be sent shopping, with any of those broads, or to those spas where I have to look on while they get drunk at the bar and wiggle their tits and a fellow's not allowed to join in the fun. No, thanks. If you don't mind." Refresher course, then some leave, transfer: it would do them all good to resume what he called normal police duties. Granted there would be some personnel problems. Mrs. Bleibl Number Four was planning a trip to one of the North Sea islands, and Bleibl had requested the "necessary measures." This meant he had to consult immediately with Dollmer, perhaps even with Stabski—ask for reinforcements. Not a word about Mrs. Fischer's pregnancy: that was her affair, her husband's affair, her lover's affair, if indeed he knew anything about it. He wouldn't be surprised if she never, never spoke about it; and if the Zummerling bunch should descend upon her she might be in the soup, but he wouldn't. But he must phone that newspaper fellow right away and make it clear to him that the Fischer pregnancy had no "security-risk dimension"; he would convince him that he was under no obligation to supply any further information.

VIII

If it came to the worst, she should be able to prove that Breuer had known of her affair with Peter, that he had tolerated it. All it needed, if he really did go to court, was to produce the trip log, which he had certainly examined and analyzed. It showed quite clearly, once or twice a week, that distance of exactly twenty-three kilometers before a stop lasting one, two, or sometimes three hours. Hadn't he said to Peter with a wink: "Are you seeing someone there?" Hadn't Peter nodded and agreed that those forty-six kilometers there and back were to be booked and charged to his personal account? And didn't Breuer know perfectly well that it was exactly twenty-three kilometers from the office to his home—hadn't they checked that together countless times, if only for tax purposes? There were witnesses who one could only hope wouldn't fail: like Plein the bookkeeper, who might be required to produce the accounts. What possible other conclusion could Breuer have come to? Would he testify in court: twenty-three kilometers for personal use, two hours for a personal visit, and where? Naturally they had never discussed it, yet there was the evidence—bookkeeper, trip log—and it had gone on for eight, almost nine weeks, and could have gone on even longer if it hadn't been for that miserable security business, if Peter's dossier hadn't contained a few awkward things, plus that stupid pistol, too old-fashioned and childish to have been sold to anyone even as a toy: a revolver dating from around 1912, though admittedly with ammunition.

True, her attorney had pointed out that it might easily go through even if Breuer denied his connivance. Breuer, he maintained, might plead, even if he admitted his connivance (which was unlikely), that, though he *had* condoned it, he could no longer do so once it had become a matter of record and thus of public interest—given the press laws that placed Erna, as a neighbor of the Fischers, firmly in the public domain, which was "arguable but not unequivocal." As the husband he could "condone while suffering" (good God, he hadn't suffered all that much, he'd probably got some kinky pleasure out of it!), but he couldn't afford any damage to his reputation, particularly as a businessman, without suing for divorce; besides, it certainly had become public knowledge and—this would have to be argued, it really was arguable—not through her fault or Peter's but through Breuer himself, who could never keep his mouth shut and was trying to blame his bankruptcy on "injury" of some kind. She thought it quite possible that he had phoned some reporter himself: he was certainly kinky enough for that, and if things got rough she wasn't going to pull any punches, the whole dirty business would simply have to come out. And if Breuer really did win this case, she could claim—so the attorney had indicated —to have been "a victim of security." This would create entirely new categories, so her attorney had told her and Breuer's broker had confirmed, categories which might have to be established in a test case. So: if he insisted on the divorce—fine, but no question of guilt, he'd have to cough up, she knew all about his bank accounts.

Klober would certainly be on her side too, the investigation of his callers having led to embarrassing revelations: smuggling, and something about heating oil she didn't understand; but above all, and this had infuriated Klober, many of those types with whom he'd been carrying on, well, not quite legal transactions (Breuer had done the same thing with some mysterious Italian watch dealers!)—those types stayed away because they weren't keen on "stumbling head first into a fuzz trap." The business they

had done with Klober could also be done with others; and Klober
had hinted pretty frankly, without actually spelling it out, that
to face a tax audit would cause him some trepidation. At any
rate, Klober was clearly "a victim of security," and there was
already a group of attorneys collecting "victims of security"
across the country, even in cases where such victimization consisted of no more than the unavoidable annoyance of having the
police on the streets or wherever. There was already a case on
record of a girl who lived with her parents next door to some
big shot, with evidence to show that up to a certain date she had
been doing well in school but had then suffered a nervous break-
down, failed her exams, and committed suicide. A drop in the
value of property due to "security" was also a matter of record.
If it was true, as was claimed, that tax discrepancies and dubious-
seeming transactions, or certain "sexual behavior," were turned
up as the result of security investigations yet did not represent
security risks—if all that was to be handled discreetly or even
kept secret but somehow did leak out through gaps and holes—
who would be responsible for the damage?

On that point her attorney had reassured her. Again and again
he had dinned into her never to indicate by so much as a hint or
a casual phrase that she would probably have run away someday
with Schubler anyway; that could be fatal, might ruin her case,
even in the category of "endangered by security."

Moving from the bungalow in Blorr to Peter's apartment had
naturally been a shock resulting in many sighs, many tears—from
eight rooms and two bathrooms, from garden and swimming pool,
to these four hundred square feet, with only a shower, and she did
so love to lie in the bathtub, go from pool to tub, from tub to
pool, and all that. And she was so short of money, felt so cooped
up—and then there were those single men in the apartment building who didn't hesitate to proposition her, offering her fifty for a
"swinging time"—an odd, not unpleasing expression, and seeing
how short of money she was . . . no, she didn't want to go that
route. In the old days, before marrying Breuer, she had some-

times come pretty close to it, when she was still working as a salesgirl for Breuer and rich foreigners were buying jewelry and one of them would sometimes invite her over for a drink at his hotel. No. She had never done that, never for money—besides, Peter would notice and never stand for it, though he himself sometimes had to put in a tough day for his fifty: heaving and hauling—moonlighting of course—and with jobs so scarce he was in no position to insist on standard wages; it was a hell of a struggle, she knew that. And though he never grumbled she could feel how he resented all this, considering he had almost been "promoted" at Breuer's, not exactly made office manager, say, but maybe something like purchasing agent—after all, he had taken a commerce course. No, no, she had to watch her step, hang on, he really did love her and he made her happy, was never quarrelsome or grouchy, he was just quiet and serious at times, always seemed to have his nose stuck in a book—and he couldn't be persuaded to watch TV; he might go to a movie and for a drink somewhere after, hardly ever took her dancing, considered himself too old for things like discos. Thank God those tiresome interrogations had stopped, and the newspapers left them in peace.

And there was one more thing, maybe the worst: the noise outside, even sleeping pills didn't help anymore. "Those rotten bastards"—who?—had built the freeway right into the city, into the very middle of it, with an access road lying diagonally to it, and that kept grinding, grinding, grinding, day and night, and when it stopped for two or at most three minutes she knew it would come back, swelling, subsiding. She would get up and stand in her housecoat on the absurdly small balcony, smoking and thinking of escape—where to? How wonderful it had been in Blorr, and maybe Breuer would eventually have agreed to some "three-way deal," somehow, if only this rotten security business hadn't ruined things. That grinding that sometimes turned into a roar—it was no use closing the windows, proper soundproof glass was too expensive, and she needed fresh air. If she had to sleep with closed windows, she'd suffocate. There was no solu-

tion, nothing did any good, neither the protests nor the neighborhood initiatives, nor the meetings held at the corner tavern where
they had to listen to the mealymouthed blather of those who were
responsible; the only solution was to move out, move away, run
away.

There were hours during the night when, after many cigarettes and drinks, she would stand shivering on the balcony
and pound her temples with her fists, on the verge of leaving,
simply going away, without any idea where to. Earplugs were no
use, and if it happened to be quiet for a few minutes there was
still that roaring in her ears, on and on, it was still there when she
took the bus to Blorr, looked up old friends who, in spite of their
grins, were still very nice to her—the Beeretz family, for instance,
when she implored them to rent her a room, even if it was just a
poky little cubbyhole where she could get some sleep, sleep, at
last enough sleep. But then came the excuses: oh yes, they could
have cleared out a little room in the attic, fixed it up for her,
would have been only too glad to let her have a quiet corner, "in
spite of everything"—in spite of what?—and would have asked,
if not nothing exactly, at least only very little for it. But what
they couldn't accept was that she might sleep there "with that
man"; that wouldn't do at all—but apart from that . . . And that
wasn't what she wanted: not without Peter, who worked himself
to the bone, took on the filthiest jobs, and anyway was by now
working only with Turks, hardly even Italians—he had reached
the point where a job as a garbage collector seemed to him like a
promotion, a social advancement. And he wasn't to be allowed to
sleep with her? No, in that case forget it.

She didn't like to go to Mrs. Fischer. She was sorry for the
way she had yelled at her over the phone: a nice woman, a
pleasant neighbor, and it wasn't her fault, after all. And she
might have been able to spend a weekend at her place except for
that husband of hers, who had turned out to be a bit of a groper
when she danced with him; no, not that. And as for the Klobers,
they might be useful allies, but in other respects she didn't care

for them, they always got so familiar, wallowing in the details of her divorce and hinting sarcastically at the difference in age between Peter and herself. And it was bitter, too, to see, if only from a distance, the bungalow still standing empty. Obviously Breuer was letting the garden go, the swimming pool stagnate, the lettuce had gone to seed and the broad beans were crawling with aphids. Everything had "gone to pot" there, and going home on the bus she thought with horror of the night ahead, of the grinding, the roar, the hell that in the daytime she felt able to stand; and she reached the point when she would lie weeping beside the sleeping Schubler, get out of bed, go back to the bottle, eventually fall asleep, and wake up in the morning when Peter took his shower. Then she would stagger into the kitchenette and make breakfast, but even the coffee didn't wake her up, and she loved the way he always hugged her as he went off to work, kissed her and whispered: "I'm doing all I can to get us out of here. Don't hold up the divorce, then we can get married. I do love you so."

Those were good words from Peter's somewhat inarticulate lips. But, after all, he wasn't blind, he must see how her skin was suffering, how sometimes in the morning her face was gray and lined, and that with all her washing and massaging and all those oils and creams she could no longer achieve that "milky loveliness" that had once inspired him to such an intense, though brief, poetic paean. She was getting old, older, with every sleepless night perhaps a month or more older, and bouts with the bottle restored nothing; however much she rubbed and oiled, massaged and washed, there remained a faint film of gray, and she didn't want Peter to lose his pleasure in her. He loved her, and those were such lovely words to hear from a tight-lipped student's mouth, and he meant so much to her, and it was quite true, what she had hinted at to the attorney: one day she would have run away with him, but she wouldn't have chosen this apartment or this area, where the noise was slowly driving her up the wall. One more year, maybe six months, and she would have got that much more out of Breuer and opened a store someplace in a quiet area, a little neighborhood store, that'd be just the thing for her, or a boutique. And Peter might have finished his studies after all, and she would have adopted a child. After all, she was a completely normal woman, sexually normal too, wasn't the affair with Peter proof positive of how normal she was? What a shame she didn't have the peace of mind to play games, chess and all that, and other, less complicated ones that he loved to play, even if it was drafts or Chinese checkers: she lacked the necessary peace of mind. During the first few weeks they had almost got into a fight over the TV; she happened to be in the habit of watching the seven o'clock news, then having supper and leafing through the program to find something for the evening. Peter only had that tiny portable black-and-white—and it wasn't even working that well, the box, most of the time it flickered, and sometimes the sound packed up altogether. And at night the roar, the grinding, and not even a phone, though she was alone all day and could have called old friends, like Elisabeth, who was now running a bar, or Hertha, who had actually managed to set herself up in a boutique. As for old boyfriends, she'd better not phone them: it would only lead to embarrassing propositions over the phone, awaken memories of indiscretions best forgotten—and she didn't want to hurt Peter's feelings. Phoning from a booth was no substitute. There was always someone standing outside, sometimes even knocking on the glass. It was quite a different thing to sit by the phone, smoking a cigarette, and chatter away to one's heart's content.

The money was slowly coming to an end too, slowly. Of course she had her own savings account, from the early days, she'd diverted quite a bit of household money—Breuer had never been petty, he'd only become petty now, and these days she had to think twice before taking the bus or streetcar two or three times a day. It was a blessing that she had more to do now than in Blorr, where Breuer had insisted on her doing nothing; now she had the cleaning up, tidying, shopping, cooking—what she enjoyed most was the cooking, because Peter so obviously enjoyed it after all those bachelor years living on fries and hot dogs and, if he was lucky, a warmed-up can or two. She enjoyed cooking, and it took her mind off the grinding and the roar and the thoughts of the coming sleepless night. She enjoyed setting the table quite formally for him—she had been allowed to bring along what was left of the linens in her trousseau—and watching him eat, and his gentle caresses were soothing. He was such a nice boy, not much given to talking, and it was too bad he was so anti-TV, and though he was always asking her to wake him up when she couldn't sleep, she couldn't bring herself to do it when he lay there, quietly breathing away, obviously used to the noise. In sleep his face was less stern, and of course she knew: it wouldn't last forever with him, not forever, and she'd stand in front of the mirror and examine her skin again; it wouldn't last forever, and not much longer either, and then it wasn't likely to occur to anyone to offer her "a swinging time." Perhaps then she would go home, back to Hubreichen, no longer Erna Breuer and not yet Erna Schubler, just Erna Hermes again, still able to run the milking machines, to bring her bedridden father his meals, to wash him, look after him. With Breuer she had never been really welcome there; her family considered him "a slippery customer" or, as her brother claimed, "a bit shady," and with Peter—she wouldn't risk that. But she did have a room there that was always ready: the high-sided walnut bed, washstand with basin, chamber pot. "The room will always be there for you, by yourself, mind you," and: "If you do come, don't try any more of your funny business!"

Who were they talking about? Jupp Halster, who out of a clear blue sky had shot his wife to death one Sunday morning, or young Schmergen, who, also out of a clear blue sky, had hanged himself one Sunday afternoon? True enough, she had "carried on" with a married man, with Hans Polkt, and he hadn't got a divorce after all, and she had moved into town. True enough. But that Tolm boy, Mrs. Fischer's brother, who had a lot more to answer for than her Peter, they allowed him to live there in peace, and he certainly wasn't married to that girl, that Communist, who had a child by him.

That phoning from a booth got on her nerves. When at the third attempt Mrs. Fischer still didn't answer, she phoned Miss Blum, was told that Sabine had gone to Tolmshoven, was told there that she couldn't be given any information, no, not over the phone, but she insisted until she got through to the mother; surely the old lady must remember her from all those afternoon visits, a fine woman, who hesitated nevertheless, then did remember her, and after much digging and hesitation: "I mustn't, I really mustn't, my dear Mrs. Breuer—I'm always being told off as it is" —admitted that her daughter had "moved" to Hubreichen—she said moved, not gone—to her son's, and she even gave her his phone number. But no, she wouldn't phone there, she'd go there herself, by bus, maybe on her bike, maybe she'd even have Peter come along.

She might be able to ask Mrs. Fischer for some money. She certainly had plenty. Three young teenagers, jingling coins, stood outside the booth, whistling pointedly, and one of the boys muttered: "Didn't know call girls were operating from phone booths these days." Did she really look like that—already? Fair game, maybe? It was time to go away, move away. Maybe she could start as a housekeeper on the abandoned Halster farm. She was still capable of a hard day's work, and it wouldn't be bad for her skin, and Peter—he might be able to use his commercial knowledge there, and probably no work was too dirty for him; they would just have to have separate bedrooms, then everything would be all right, though it didn't mean they had to sleep separately. That young Mr. Tolm, he didn't need any separate bedrooms, he was allowed to share his bed with his Communist girlfriend, right there in the shadow of the vicarage, never mind that he was himself practically a "suspect." Much worse, at any rate, than her Peter had ever been or could ever have become. The young punks were still whistling after her.

IX

He couldn't get Sabine out of his mind. It wasn't only the annoyance, the thought of the battle with Fischer and the "kindly
attention" the Zummerling people would once more bestow upon
him, it was the child herself, anxiety over what was to become of
her. If it should occur to Fischer to legitimize the child, un-
contested, she would probably not accept that and thus set in
motion legal problems that were practically insoluble. The
thought of having to leave Tolmshoven became fixed, took root,
grew. Besides, he was tired, very tired, and regretted his suggestion to invite Blurtmehl and his girl Eva for dinner.

His suggestion had been accepted with surprising alacrity,
probably more at the urging of that Miss Klensch, who was
prettier than in her picture, probably curious, too, and not
unsusceptible to big names. More restless, too, than he had
imagined, there was something almost waspish about her, not
exactly pushy but not timid either, or even intimidated. For
Blurtmehl this must all be rather embarrassing, but he mastered
the situation with tact and discretion, was able to switch from
servant to guest with the confidence of a tightrope walker, as it
were, helpful without giving any hint of his dependent position.
He set the table while Käthe laughed with Eva Klensch in the
kitchen, and even setting the table was the helpful gesture of a
thoughtful guest, not the act of an invited servant. This adapt-
ability, these indefinable yet perceptible nuances were also somehow disquieting—it was a game, a performance almost, and he
could well imagine that at private parties Blurtmehl could and
would play every role: the host, the servant, the host/servant, the
helpful guest who made it possible to forget that he was a servant.
Blurtmehl mixed him a cocktail that actually managed to lift him
out of his weariness: allowed him to forget Sabine, conference,

interviews, Bleibl, and the leveling of Tolmshoven. Blurtmehl put on a cassette (low-volume Chopin), sliced onions in the kitchen, cheerful, almost gay, seemed a different person and not the least bit embarrassed when Käthe, now that Sabine had moved to her brother's, offered Eva the guest apartment after all, with the words: "At least you won't be on two different floors then!" He heard them laughing in the kitchen: a gourmet omelet mixture was being prepared, cans of soup were opened and bottles uncorked in honor of the occasion, and Blurtmehl confessed that, although he was very fond of caviar, he had never had the nerve to buy any, and not even this remark, which was an unmistakable allusion to social differences, disturbed the harmony.

It was a bit much, though, when the Schröters turned up too, invited by Käthe—"finally with success." They did live in the village, of course, were relatives, though not officially, and they did have a common grandchild. One problem was the awkward one of how to address each other, something they had never been able to solve even after meeting three or four times at Rolf's. Schröter flatly refused to use first names. The utmost to which he could be induced was to say Tolm rather than Mr. Tolm, and Luise, his wife, went on saying Fritz Tolm, while Käthe positively forbade them to call her Mrs. Tolm or Mrs. Käthe and insisted on Käthe. But since they met so rarely, the forms of address always became confused again and seemed to end up with Mr. and Mrs. Then Käthe would hark back to the old days: "Imagine we had met when I was still living in the teacher's house at my mother-in-law's place and used to walk through the village carrying Rolf or when I was living at the countess's, or even earlier when I was still Käthe Schmitz in Iffenhoven—we would have met, perhaps during carnival or at a church party at the vicarage, and I would have said: Please call me Käthe."

"But that's not the way it was," Schröter would say with his mild yet bitter smile, "that's not the way it was. Tolm without the Mr., I can manage that, but Käthe even with Mrs., I can't manage that—and not to use names at all, I find that too discourteous, ridiculous, and I can't very well call you too just Tolm. All this first-name business is too American for me anyway, it's beyond me."

"I was too young," said Luise Schröter, "to call him Fritz in the days when he went to the village school, and later too, otherwise I might have managed to say Fritz now. Yes please, I like champagne. What are we celebrating? Oh, of course—pardon me, of course! Well then, here's to you and all the best!"

Schröter insisted on beer, smoked his pipe, and when the table was set and Eva Klensch had brought in the soup: "Now I'm going to enjoy this. As long as we don't start talking politics."

"No," said Tolm, "not as far as I'm concerned, I can promise you that."

The seating was Käthe's idea: Miss Klensch beside Schröter, herself beside Blurtmehl, and himself beside Luise Schröter. Plenty to talk about. He could inquire discreetly after Anna Pütz and Bertha Kelz, was told that one was paralyzed, the other dead; was also told that Kohlschröder wouldn't be able to keep his job much longer, seeing how he—well, Luise blushed, she had always been one of the priest's main boosters. Something must have happened that had to do with girls, school kids, and others who had apparently "exposed" themselves or been made to expose themselves to achieve something or other. Luise would say no more than: "This time he really did go too far."

To reinforce Blurtmehl in the feeling of being only a guest here, not a servant, he, Tolm, got up from time to time, poured more wine, opened bottles of mineral water, brought glasses from the buffet. Then he explained the virtues of caviar to Luise Schröter, showed her how she must wait for the toast to cool slightly but not entirely, so that it was still crisp and warm but no longer hot enough to melt the butter, and only then to put the caviar on it, "More, more, Luise, fill the whole spoon"—with half an ear he was listening to the others, was surprised that Schröter was having such a lively conversation with Eva Klensch although Schröter himself had started on politics—socialism,

Catholicism, history of the Christian trade-union movement, imprisonment during the Nazi regime, Adenauer's betrayal, the Christian Democratic Union beyond discussion and the German Socialist Party gone soft—and heard Eva reasonably and vehemently defending her German Socialist Party, and at the same time the Catholic Church too. He was sorry Käthe hadn't placed him beside Eva, he would have loved to have a closer look at this astonishingly pretty person, but then, if he had been seated next to her, it would have meant Luise having to sit next to her husband.

He also helped remove the plates of the first course, poured red wine, was aware of a few momentary mental blanks: it really must have been too much for one day—his election, the interviews, his rambling thoughts on bird flights, the business with Sabine. He apologized to Luise Schröter for his taciturnity, but then told her in detail about Holger Count Tolm, gossip she plainly and unabashedly enjoyed. "Too bad," was all she said, "he's supposed to have been nice enough as a young lad."

He observed Blurtmehl with amazement: he had lost all shyness but not his dignity, kept his distance without distancing himself, was affable with Käthe without a trace of familiarity, yet there remained in his behavior a trace of the professional that would allow him tomorrow to resume in all naturalness his status of servant, prepare his bath, massage him, and not embark on a chat without being asked. Even his polite but uncompromising rejection of any further assistance from Tolm (who in an overly democratic gesture had wanted to help bring in the omelets and the salad plates), the firmness—not authoritarian, merely sensible —with which, without a word, Blurtmehl interrupted Eva's metaphysical conversation with old Schröter and steered her into the kitchen, where she at once started giggling with Käthe again —in all this there was something he could only call personality. It was a resoluteness, an ability to make decisions, that he himself lacked: there was no doubt that Blurtmehl would have made a fantastic president. For the first time something about Blurtmehl's movements struck him, called to his mind a phrase, a description,

applying to those movements for which he had long been searching: the "youth movement" of the twenties that must have per-
sisted longer in Silesia. It may have been that, too, which had—
erroneously—made him think of pederasty.

The evening was clearly turning into what might be called a
successful party: they all enjoyed the food, all were deep in lively
conversations, Blurtmehl even dug up some boarding-school anec-
dotes, spoke kindly of the bishop, and Luise Schröter was so
relaxed that she spoke frankly about their financial worries, how
her brother—"You know what a tough character he always was"
—was increasing the rent, even piling it onto the water rates—
and what a miserable pension Schröter had. He was almost
tempted to offer her money, a loan of course, they would never
accept it as a gift—but his old, his new shyness held him back.
It was always a ticklish business offering money, no matter to
whom: either they accepted it too quickly and wanted too much,
or they froze when he offered it to them; that was something
Käthe would have to look after. Luise even asked point-blank
how much the caviar had cost, and then blushed, and he had to
place a reassuring hand on her shoulder and explain that he didn't
know because—and this might surprise her—he had received it as
a gift, and from whom? From the Russians, of course, although
he had no direct business connections with them—"They'd hardly
want to buy my paper and sell it in the Soviet Union!"—he did
meet them at receptions and conferences. He also told her how
little they cared for associating with their own comrades, how
after a few drinks they sometimes spoke about them as dis-
paragingly, contemptuously you might say, as—well, as bishops,
perhaps, about acolytes or cardinals about lowly prelates. And to
come back to the caviar, it was exactly the same with the cigars
from Castro's empire: he'd been given those, too, by the Russians,
he would never buy them for himself, nor the caviar, and he
confessed to Luise Schröter that he would never, never get over
certain traumas and inhibitions, never: the hungry son of the

penurious teacher of Tolmshoven was still deeply entrenched in him, and he would never, although he had long been able to afford it, pay six or seven marks for a cigar or—"for all I know" —forty for a few spoonfuls of caviar. He was trying to lead her carefully back to the subject of money, and please, she mustn't think he was stingy, no, that he most certainly wasn't, simply that a car, even a manor house, was all right but he would never be able to step across the cigar and caviar threshold. He just wanted her to know the devious routes by which Castro's cigars came into the hands of West German capitalists—like the caviar from the slashed bellies of sturgeons. . . .

For their coffee they moved to the living room, which Käthe also called "our tearoom" ever since they had been advised not to use the balcony. Eva Klensch insisted on making the coffee: "Turkish, if that's all right with you." It was all right, and they even found some little copper pots in Käthe's kitchen cabinet. Turkish? She must have picked that up in Lebanon. Or Turkey or Syria? Did she know he was fully informed about her background? That he knew almost everything there was to know about how often she went to church and what she had for Sunday breakfast, her business transactions and her career, her enthusiasm for archery? A sudden wave of embarrassment made him blush. This nice young woman, who was so obviously enjoying the evening, who was a little cockier than he had judged from her photograph, this efficient, friendly little person: there was a dossier on her, and he had perused it, against regulations, driven by curiosity about Blurtmehl, who, there was no denying, was physically closer to him every day than anyone else. What concern of his were Blurtmehl's motorbikes, his friendship, his love affair? He felt embarrassed, yet had been unable to curb his curiosity.

In the living room they regrouped: Käthe at last next to Luise, Schröter next to Blurtmehl, and himself at last next to Eva

Klensch, who wasn't much older than Sabine. The coffee had turned out well, was probably too strong but he drank it anyway, apologized with a smile for getting up once again to offer cigars and cigarettes, while Käthe placed brandy and liqueurs on the table for them to help themselves. Schröter spoke of the cigar, at which he sniffed voluptuously, as "a fantastic thing, almost too good to smoke." Eva took a cigarette, also a liqueur, inquired after his grandchildren, immediately blushed and bit her lip, but he reassured her. "Yes," he said, "one of them, my oldest grandson, he's off somewhere, probably in North Africa. Why not talk about it? Now the fourth grandchild is on the way—by my daughter Sabine." He swallowed the question of whether she didn't want any children, swallowed what lay on the tip of his tongue and heavily on his mind: Sabine's worries, and the worries he had about Sabine. He asked her about her work, her business, admired her courage, her enterprise, and was afraid to look really deeply into her eyes. She told him about how quickly fashions changed, about the risks—"It's like vegetables that wilt"—about competition and struggle, costings and costs, and he discovered that her apparent cockiness was merely the obverse of shyness, and she spoke of Alois, "who is such a faithful and beloved companion to me," and of her nostalgia for Berlin.

"Now there's a real city for you!"

Käthe and Luise seemed to have had a bit too much to drink, they were not talking now but whispering, village names sounded through the whispering—Kohlschröder again and again—and in the end it was Schröter who said it was time to leave, firmly, simply got to his feet, also not quite steady on his legs, hesitantly holding the half-smoked cigar. No, he couldn't offer old Schröter another cigar to take along, it would have seemed like a handout, a charitable gesture; one, yes, not two, but if he went about it carefully he might be able to send him a box of them; that would be all right, then it was no longer a handout but a gift. Apparently the two ladies had made some progress after all, they were now openly using first names, for as they were leaving Käthe asked: "Isn't there something else we can do for you, Luise?" And Luise said: "I'd just love to have a ride in your car, Käthe."

"Right now?"

"Yes, if that's possible."

It could be arranged, only it wasn't quite far enough to the Kommertz farm, and a detour was decided upon to which Blurtmehl agreed. Eva Klensch insisted on clearing up in the kitchen, wouldn't take no for an answer, and although he would have preferred to go off to bed he felt obliged to go along on the drive, and the security officer had to be informed. Luise un-blushingly observed that the "huge car purrs like a pussycat—you hardly know you're sitting in a car!" She enjoyed the short drive—Blurtmehl made a few detours, calling it a "lap of honor" —and Käthe showed Luise the built-in conveniences: automatic windows, the little bar, and finally the phone, which she asked to be allowed to use. She called up Katharina, first spoke to Rolf, then to her daughter: "Greetings from the flying carpet to all of you, including dear Mrs. Fischer—and don't take it too seriously —right? Politics, I mean." Blurtmehl, who was obviously enjoying Luise's naïve pleasure, turned on the stereo, inserted a Bach cassette, and Luise actually had tears in her eyes: "See Him, Whom? the Bridegroom Christ, See Him, How? a spotless Lamb." Schröter, who found all this somewhat embarrassing, wiped away her tears and murmured gently: "My dear, does it really move you so much?" "Yes," she said, "I've never heard it like that, and I've sung it so often in the choir." She accepted the cassette when they reached the Kommertz farm, and Käthe asked Blurtmehl to rewind the tape. Käthe said: "Believe me, I've never known anyone to enjoy Bach that much—you must accept it. . . ."

"I'd no idea," said Luise, "that there were such things on tape. I'll be only too happy to accept it."

Behind them the security car, from which two officers jumped out; dogs barking, awkwardness, and Luise's parting words:

"Now you'll have to come and see us too, we're relatives, aren't we? They're not married, mind you, but they're our children, and they're living together properly."

He would have preferred to take Käthe's arm and walk the few hundred yards to the manor, but he got back into the car; the trouble caused by such a nocturnal walk would spoil any possible pleasure in it. Tolmshoven was open on four or five sides, clumps of trees, shrubs, the willows beyond the Hellerbach stream: limited visibility, the road poorly lighted. He could feel the anxiety of the officers, the tension in their courtesy, as he hesitated: he helped Käthe into the car, then followed her, supported by Blurtmehl: that seven- or eight-minute nocturnal stroll through the village was not feasible.

Blurtmehl was already undergoing a transformation, not yet quite the servant and chauffeur, no longer quite the guest; in any case the solicitude, one might almost say empathy of his touch and movements went beyond the professional; a man, he thought, whose wealth of nuances I am only now discovering, I always considered him a bit aloof.

It took only two minutes to reach the brightly lit courtyard of the manor: again they got out, again Blurtmehl's hands, his arm, and Käthe pale again, serious too—as he was about to say something in the elevator she shook her head and pointed to the ceiling, where there was no doubt a microphone, her lips hung slackly, she'd probably had a bit too much to drink. Blurtmehl had run up the stairs and was waiting at the top, concerned for them, in a gentle voice offering treatment, a few exercises, a sponging down, and when they refused with a smile, asked them to "ring if you need me."

Eva Klensch had retired for the night: kitchen, living room, dining room, were all neat as a pin. Käthe went into the bathroom, opened the window, looked out: "It struck me," she said, "that from the Schröters' you can look straight up here, almost into here, and down there—look—you can see the light in their house. Now Luise is sitting in Katharina's room, listening to the Bach on a cheap cassette deck, or whatever those things are called. Have you ever been in Katharina's old room?"

"No."

"It's almost like a little museum. On the wall there's her First Communion photo, next to it a reproduction of a Lochner Madonna—Mao, Che Guevara, Marx too, and an Italian whose name I've forgotten—and on the bedside table is her old cassette deck. And she's sitting there now, our good Luise, with tears in her eyes, listening to the Saint Matthew Passion. I'll get her a better set, a nice new one with a full, rich tone. I'm very tired, Fritz, very tired—and you must be half dead after all those goings-on this morning, those interviews—you did very well. . . ."

He came and stood beside her, placed his hand on her shoulder, and looked over to where the light was still burning in the Schröters' house. "You know, during those interviews I had an idea: one could prepare them in advance, for radio and television, as a sort of stockpile: on amalgamation, wages, cultural affairs, on domestic and foreign policy, on security matters. One could even introduce slight variations to provide a semblance of actuality. While chatting away there I was thinking of something quite different and hardly ever gave a direct answer to a direct question, only where it concerned the children. I must talk to Amplanger about it someday, to see whether that couldn't be arranged: spending an afternoon to produce a stockpile of interviews. Of course I would have to change my clothes several times: the clothes are more important than the words, the clothes distinguish the various situations more clearly. The background would also have to vary: that's easily arranged, sometimes a few books in the background, sometimes pictures, sometimes modern furniture, sometimes antiques—that would save a lot of work, a lot of bother —for radio interviews I could change my voice a little, sometimes a bit hoarse, then clear, sometimes alert, sometimes tired. . . . That would make it possible to tape enough interviews for several years in seven or eight hours. I could tape obituaries as well: for Kortschede, for Pottsieker, Pliefger—maybe for Bleibl, too—

for cardinals and presidents—what do you think? Of course, someone from the union would have to agree to a similar manipulation."

"They won't do that, you know how they want everything—what do they call it?—alive."

"Live they call it, but then it's possible that the taped word sounds more alive than the live word—Veronica once tried to explain to me that artificial birds, mechanical ones, can walk more naturally than live birds—I keep thinking about that—in the same way a sound or video tape might sound much more spontaneous than a live interview—what they call live is deader than dead. As dead as the little paper that died under my hands—and proliferates. . . ."

"Afraid again?"

"Afraid of boredom, Käthe, that's the disease Grebnitzer has not yet discovered. Afraid of the growth that's like a prairie fire. The next to throw himself at my feet or on my breast will be Küster. With its inexorable logic the computer has predicted Küster's surrender, up to now Amplanger has always been right in these things. So, after Blume, we'll swallow Küster, then Bobering, and it will all turn into a gray, horrible newspaper mush, with a few tiny dashes of liberalism. I have allowed our little paper to decay, I have allowed it to die. . . ."

"And if you were to retire—completely, once and for all?"

"I was very close to it, but now—Bleibl must have suspected, or he may have even known from Amplanger. And that's why he nabbed me at the very last moment—nailed me, if you like. Why is it that I am never bored at Rolf and Katharina's, not even at Herbert's, there at least I get annoyed—but at the Bleibls', not at Kortschede's, no, or Pottsieker's, not even at Pliefger's, but at the Fischers', and of course never with you. If only we could go for walks together more often. I have a lot of things I'd like to tell you that I wouldn't exactly care to see immortalized on tape."

"So have I—d'you think that here—I don't think so, we're talking half out of the window, aren't we . . . Rolf explained to me that when you hold your head out of the window, speak and hear outside the window . . ."

"He may be right—so let's talk. . . ." Mist obliterated the view, a wind came up, banks of fog drifted past, even the trees became invisible, a foggy dampness that turned into rain. The light in the Schröters' house was no longer to be seen.

"So if you want to confess a few things to your wife, you have to stick your head out in the rain, and she must stick her head out in the rain to hear them: you're still the best remedy against boredom—the children, the grandchildren, and I can't tell you how glad I am Sabine has left Fischer. There have been times when I've been bored at her place, at my own daughter's: I don't like the kind of houses they build for themselves, don't like their taste, let alone Fischer's. Even the finest paintings they have hanging there, paintings I even like, seem like forgeries to me even when they've been proved to be genuine—especially then. There's something about them that kills art, even music—I'm glad our child has left all that behind. Let her stay for a while at Rolf's. . . . Come along, we'll catch cold—d'you hear the screech owls? Don't be afraid."

He closed the window, it was raining harder now, splashing against the panes, and Käthe went over to the corner of the room and turned up the thermostat. "Perhaps you can soon resign—not right now, of course, but in three or four months: illness or something—then they can finally elect Amplanger; why you?"

"I have an invaluable image—and you know that. Moreover, I'm vulnerable and open to attack—Rolf and Veronica and Holger I—and you know that. . . . I've even been successful."

"You? Successful?"

"Now listen. . . . Inherited a little newspaper, obtained a license, newsprint, even the journalists to go with it. And expanded . . . bought a manor house, made president—I'm even efficient, not only successful. . . ."

"You efficient?"

"Now, Käthe . . ."

"You gave Eickelhof away without lifting a finger, you've already given up Tolmshoven—you can't get either of your sons even the smallest job on the paper, your daughter's unhappy. . . ."

"Unhappy? It's years since I've seen her so happy. But I won't claim to be the cause of her happiness."

"You're scared stiff of Bleibl, you're afraid of Zummerling—oh, Tolm, dear Fritz. We should move from here—drive away, move away."

Already in her nightgown, Käthe helped him with his shoes, undid the laces, pulled off his shoes, then his socks—the rest he could manage himself, even hung his jacket, shirt, and trousers on the stand, threw his underwear on the chair, put on his pajamas. . . .

He lay down beside her, took her hand, knew she was praying, was silent, listened to the rain, waited until Käthe crossed herself and sent a sigh after her prayer.

"Sad, old dear?"

"Yes, it's my legs. Because I can't bend down anymore. But it really was a nice evening. I'm glad we finally got together with the Schröters, we must go over there sometime. My children don't make me sad: Sabine is on the right path, at least I'll be able to help her. I'm not worried about Rolf and even less about Katharina. Herbert, there's a lot I don't understand about him, we shouldn't have sent him to that boarding school, although that's what he wanted. Maybe we should move to his place, into that high rise that we own somehow. . . ."

"And is ghastly . . ."

"Horrible—maybe we should take a whole floor there, with a little apartment for Blurtmehl. But then there would be a helicopter circling over the place, day and night, at least half a police detachment permanently on the balconies and stairs and in the elevators—the people would move out, move away. That's not a bad idea, Käthe, move away before we're forced to—why don't you look for a real estate agent, a house that's big enough but not too big . . . ?"

"There are supposed to be some lovely old vicarages around, one could convert them, modernize them. They're all building those new, bungalow-type things. . . . I'm so tired, Tolm, don't forget: Dresden, and the children, and your fourth grandchild is on the way." Her hand dropped out of his as she fell asleep. He listened to the rain, after a while got out of bed, opened the window a bit, set the thermostat lower, stood by the open window and smoked one more cigarette, he would talk to Holzpuke. . . . Move away, that was a good idea. Tolmshoven— he had already taken leave of it, it wasn't all that painful. . . . Perhaps move to a hotel, a suite for themselves, a smaller one for Blurtmehl. But hotels were hard to keep under surveillance. . . .

X

It was still raining, almost harder than the evening before, and when he looked through the window in the dim early-morning light he could see the puddles in the garden that had formed in the usual places; he could also see the officer pacing up and down between vestry and vicarage under the glass overhang, not the same one as last night, a younger man, with transceiver and machine pistol, a loden cape hanging loosely over his shoulders.

While holding the telephone to his ear with his right hand and listening to Holzpuke's elaborate courtesies, he gathered up some kindling as he squatted on his heels, stuffed crumpled paper into the cold stove, piled the kindling on top, and, placing the match-box upright against the cast-iron foot of the stove, tried to strike a match with his left hand. It worked, the paper flared up, the dry wood immediately started to crackle, he put on some more, placed the larger chunks in readiness, stood up, wiggled his feet into his slippers, pulled his bathrobe tighter, cocked an ear to the left where Sabine was sleeping with the children, to the right where Katharina was sleeping. Fortunately he had heard the phone at once, and no one had been roused; it was still early, just past six-thirty, and he kept repeating: "Yes," said: "But of course," said: "By all means—do come over." This mixture of extreme tension, in fact agitation, and courtesy with which Holzpuke tried again and again to explain his early telephone call, asked for an immediate interview, was nothing new. The only thing new was a certain dejection in Holzpuke's voice, as he kept asking whether he hadn't woken the children and the ladies at this early hour, and he seemed barely reassured by Rolf's soothing "No, no, really you didn't."

"I suppose the simplest way would be for me to come to your place, but where can we talk without being disturbed?"

"The vicarage has been empty since yesterday evening, I have a key and I'm authorized to enter," and he couldn't resist adding: "Perhaps in the bishop's room."

"Where?"

"I'll explain when you come."

He added some more wood, lifted off the rings with the poker, put on a kettle of water, carefully opened the door to the bedroom and fished his clothes from the chair, threw them onto the bench by the stove, and groped under the bed for his shoes and socks. Katharina really did seem to be still asleep, and he pulled the cover up over her shoulder, which he had bared in throwing back the quilt as he got up. Then he carefully closed the window.

It was chilly, and he shivered a bit, couldn't resist giving the quilt another tug, pulling it up a shade higher, would have liked to kiss the back of her neck—her long hair exposed a strip of golden-brown skin—but he refrained, afraid he might wake her.

Only now, while dressing, did he discover the second guard at the garden gate: transceiver, machine pistol, a police cape over his civilian clothes, not that young a man. The camper was going to present a problem: there was no wide entrance, only the little gate. He also saw that it was time to harvest the nuts, pick them up off the ground where many had already dropped, the children could do that, they'd enjoy it.

He set the breakfast table, took milk, eggs, and butter out of the refrigerator, bread from the box, coffee from the buffet, searched in the kitchen drawer for the key to the vicarage, found it, and thought about the few people who attended early mass. There were always eight or nine of them, sometimes more, old Mrs. Hermes almost every day: who would be telling them at the locked church door that Roickler had left? Had Roickler at least notified the verger? Would it be the first time in many centuries that the bells didn't ring in Hubreichen at a quarter to seven? Why did he wonder, why did he worry, about things that didn't concern him? He poured boiling water on the coffee, warmed up the milk for the children, sliced some bread, looked at the time: in a few minutes the bells should start ringing.

Last night, while watching Roickler in the church, he had already been seized by an inexplicable sadness, something he had always found ridiculous in his father, who had sometimes expressed a similar feeling: they took something away from people and gave them nothing in return. He also thought of Käthe and Sabine, for whom it would be a bitter blow; then, when the coffee grounds had settled, he poured himself a mug, lit a cigarette, nodded when he saw Holzpuke coming through the gate, and went to meet him, holding his mug, the cigarette in his mouth, put a finger to his lips, went inside again to put more wood on the stove and fill a second mug. He had no trouble carrying them by the two handles in one hand, he'd learned to do this when he sometimes worked as a waiter and had to carry beer mugs.

Holzpuke smiled when he gave him the mug and warned him to walk carefully over the slippery path that was covered with wet leaves. "You're very kind," he said. "It's true I missed my breakfast."

And there she actually was, outside the church door, old Mrs. Hermes with a pale young man who was laughed at in the village for his excessive piety and whose name he didn't know.

"What's going on here, Mr. Tolm—the church locked up, no bells, no mass?"

"Father Roickler left yesterday, it was urgent. I don't know whether the verger . . ."

"The verger is away on holiday, and whenever the verger's on holiday Father Roickler rings the bells himself. . . ."

"I don't know," he said, "I wonder—perhaps you'd better go home, it'll all be explained. . . ." He felt more than sorry for the old woman, it hurt him to see her standing there with her prayer book, in coat and hat, feeling cold and aggrieved.

"I think," he said to Holzpuke, "we'd better go back to our cottage. There'll be all kinds of misunderstandings if you go into the vicarage with me now, people will think the police are involved, rumors will be started that we'll never be able to get rid of; they know you, don't forget."

More people arrived, churchgoers, others from the nearby houses, and he was glad when the gate closed behind them again.

"How's your sister?" Holzpuke asked in a low voice; he was warming his hands at the stove, sipping his coffee.

"Fine, I think, it's getting a little cramped here, pretty cramped—if my parents were to be the next ones to seek refuge here, maybe my brother too, we would all be united on these four hundred and fifty square feet of floor space—in Blorr there will be three thousand square feet standing empty, in Tolmshoven forty-five hundred, in Cologne a thousand—at the vicarage it's only two thousand or twenty-five hundred—a strange state of affairs considering that the circulation of the paper is constantly growing and the sales at the Beehive even more so. . . ."

"You certainly have a nice little place here," Holzpuke whispered. "I can understand anyone seeking refuge here. But now as to why I'm disturbing you so early, had no option. Something very, very strange has happened, something rather worrying, and I don't know anyone except you who might be able to help me. . . ."

He glanced at the two closed bedroom doors, but Rolf shook his head reassuringly, saying: "We have another half hour, I'd say—my wife doesn't get going till around eight, and my sister—I don't know her sleeping habits. . . ."

"Well," Holzpuke said, and sat down, stood up again, picked up the coffee mug. "Your first wife, Veronica, has been phoning again: to your sister, to your mother, to the priest in Tolmshoven, but not one of the three phones was answered. We've no proof, of course, that all these calls came from her—all we have on the tape is the ringing—but then a fourth call, again to your sister, again no answer. And now comes the surprise: since she knows, of course, that everything is monitored, she spoke anyway, three times she said: 'We're coming with the bucket—we're coming with the bucket—we're coming with the bucket'—a coded message, directed unmistakably at us—I just wonder why she never phones you?"

"She knows I wouldn't be very polite to her. And she can't stand rudeness."

"Can't stand rudeness. . . ." Holzpuke laughed softly.

"That's right—I'd bawl her out, I really would, not only because of this lunacy she's involved in—also because of the boy she's been dragging all over the place for the past three years, and it's true: she can't stand rudeness or impoliteness—ask my mother, my sister, my father, or my brother—ask her father. And now you'd like to know what bucket means?"

"The word is used for all kinds of vehicles, it's also used in a metaphorical sense—but here it appears to mean something quite specific."

"We used to call our bicycles buckets of bolts, but never our cars, when we had any . . . so that means . . ."

"That Beverloh is coming on a bicycle—may already be on his way—that would correspond to your theory. . . ."

"It's the result of putting myself in his place. Don't forget, I know him. Whether or not I'd recognize him, I don't know; I don't mean physically—I mean the abstract turbulence of his calculations. . . ."

"Bicycle," said Holzpuke. "I believe there are more than twenty-five million of them by now . . . I must pass that on to Dollmer, maybe even to Stabski; the area around Tolmshoven is almost as ideal for cycling as Holland, and . . ." He broke off. There was a stirring in Sabine's room. Rolf put on some more wood, made a reassuring gesture: "They'll all be going to the bathroom first, to the toilet—it's between the bedrooms, accessible from both." He pointed to the stove, poured more coffee for Holzpuke, who was standing by the door, shifted the saucepan of milk closer to the flames. "Warming room, coffee stall for senior police officers, sanctuary for the desperate wives of prominent, wealthy citizens—will that go into my file too?"

"I'm not worried about what goes into our files but about what *their* files may contain on you. Since you finished serving your sentence, nothing detrimental about you has come to official notice. However, now you're getting a suspicious number of visits from senior members of the fuzz, offering them coffee, and supplying them with information. D'you suppose your friend Heinrich Schmergen is going to like that? And your other friends?"

"Heinrich is learning Spanish, and I am teaching him the basics of political economy, particularly of finance . . . and as to my other friends: don't worry, I'll even tell them this bucket story, they won't object."

"I must ask you to treat that confidentially, not to mention it even to your wife. . . ."

"I can't promise that, I can't have secrets of this kind from my friends or from my wife. . . ." He sighed, and the last vestige of affability faded from his face as he half whispered: "I have something important to tell you about the bucket, something very important, but first let me say this: we are, if not actually persecuted, ostracized—my friends are, at least—we have nothing to hide, not even our thoughts. We don't even *think* of violence in any shape or form, we have even ceased to think of violence toward objects, anyone is free to know whom I meet, whom they meet. We are a large group, we don't even know everyone belonging to it. We are merely determined not to betray the conclusions we have come to, we feel no hatred, not even disgust, only contempt for those who can't stop regurgitating that old garbage—contempt for those who deliver us up to the stupid jabber of our fellow citizens by the use of informers, snoopers, job restrictions—what's dangerous is our pride, our arrogance. And if I help you a bit, my dear, or should I say highly respected Mr. Holzpuke, then it's only because I see a very slight chance of protecting lives, even if it be the life of our distinguished Mr. Bleibl—as well as the intactness—I mean the physical, not the moral intactness—of the far from immaculate breasts of Mrs. Bleibl Number Four, which I would be at liberty to admire in every third magazine if I considered them worthy of admiration —but I suppose I may leave the protection of those breasts to the machine pistols of your officers. It's time to go, my wife is moving about, the children are awake. There is a back entrance to the vicarage, between the vestry and the church. I would prefer not to walk through the excited throng that has been abandoned by its priest. Some more coffee?"

"No, thanks."

"Then I'll take you now to the bishop's room. . . ."

He threw his parka over his shoulders, opened the door, and walked ahead of Holzpuke to the back door of the vicarage, past the guard, who hesitated a moment, seemed about to block his path, but then, presumably at a sign from Holzpuke, stepped aside.

It was cool in the passageways, apparently quiet on the street outside the vicarage, and as they started toward the stairs the telephone rang in the study. Rolf stopped, Holzpuke walked past him into the room, muttering: "It might be . . . ," lifted the receiver, said: "Yes," listened for a minute and then said: "Father

Roickler will be away for some time, I suggest you phone the vicarage in the next village. My name? Never mind that," and replaced the receiver. "Extreme Unction," he said, just before following Rolf upstairs.

The bishop's room was simply and very pleasantly furnished: white furniture, honey-colored carpet, a Chagall print on the wall, a small, valuable Madonna in a niche with a little oil lamp in front of it; a comfortable corner with two rattan armchairs and a round rattan table; a telephone, no ashtray. Holzpuke sat down with a sigh: "You're giving me some long speeches, Mr. Tolm, very long."

"It would be a good idea for you to pass them along, verbatim if possible, to Mr. Dollmer and, if the occasion arises, to Mr. Stabski. I am prepared to repeat them personally to those gentlemen, to explain how many thousands, perhaps hundreds of thousands, are being excluded in this connection, deliberately no doubt, to provide a reserve that can be sacrificed to the Zummerling press—and the banks. But let's take the dynamite first: it comes under the same heading as bucket. I recall that Beverloh, years ago when we were still friends and were planning demonstrations together, and actions too, came up with the idea of the 'hot' bicycle—that's to say, he calculated how much explosive could be inserted into the framework of a bicycle, where the fuses would have to be hidden, and so on and so on. The idea was to place a charge of this kind in fifty, if possible a hundred bicycles—it was all theoretical at the time—and simply park them wherever devastation was to be caused. We were all against it, every single one of us—it remained nothing but a theory. But he might by this time have turned the theory into practice. In other words, the bucket of bolts he's coming on may contain explosives. It might even be—another theory that was considered—easily dismantled and turned into some kind of a firearm, or a catapult. If Veronica was so keen on informing you about the bucket—I don't know"—he looked at the end wall—"whether this place is being monitored. . . ."

"No," said Holzpuke wearily, "the telephone of course, but that's all. . . ."

"You see, I'd like to ask you not to record this information as coming from me."

"That's a promise," said Holzpuke, "an important tip—a valuable, horrifying one—we'll have to check not only the cyclists but also the bicycles, around Tolmshoven, around Horrnauken, around Trollscheid, around Breterheiden. . . ."

"Around Hubreichen, if my sister's going to stay here for a while . . ."

"Is she going to? Has she said anything?"

"Not yet, she likes it here. And of course she can stay as long as she wants—and as long as we can stay here. I have the impression that her life will change considerably. Now that Father Roickler has gone for good, we don't know what the church authorities are going to do about us. Did you know, by the way, that Roickler . . . ?"

"Yes, we know about his—about his relationship with that Mrs. Plauck, we also know—and we also knew that yesterday—he, well, cleared out . . . an honorable man, incidentally."

"So you have informers in the village?"

"Of course. That shouldn't surprise you. And now if I might ask you to get me an ashtray—bishops appear to be nonsmokers."

In the adjoining bathroom Rolf found a china soap dish that could be pried out of its holder; he placed it on the table, accepted a cigarette from Holzpuke, and a light, remained standing.

"The thing's a bit wobbly, but it'll have to do for now. I wouldn't like to go into the other rooms—I only know my way around downstairs. Do you want to speak to my sister too?"

"No, but I have a few more questions for you—about your friends. What you were saying just now—that pride, that stubbornness, that being excluded—or sense of being excluded—those conclusions—those ideas—how big do you suppose it is, the group you have defined in this way?"

"You could figure that out very easily from your own files

and those of other authorities working with you: we are all listed, aren't we—it's not that *we* have a list of ourselves—we don't know how many we are, but you should know, just take a look at this army, this phantom army—review it—let those hundreds of thousands of young women and men and their children parade before you, if only in your mind's eye, and ask yourself whether all their education, their potential intelligence, their strength and glory, exist merely to be kept under surveillance. Casual laborers of the nation, nut gatherers, apple pickers . . . Well, if you have no more questions—I don't feel comfortable here, but at least the bishop's room has for once in its existence been of real service. So now that whole security business is going to be transferred from Blorr to here?"

"Your sister's sudden decision has put me in a quandary: Blorr is surrounded by an outer, an inner, and what you might call an innermost security cordon, that's to say, the officers who are visible—we were not prepared for this move or for impetuous decisions of this kind, they might even be called breakouts. . . . Well, I must confess that at the moment I'm improvising and relying on the walls of the vicarage garden. If your sister . . ."

"May she at least go for the milk?"

"Better not. If you could prevent it—no walks either, or anything like that. Unfortunately the press already knows about it, there are rumors of marital troubles . . . anyway. . . ."

"So I'm supposed to keep my own sister more or less a prisoner."

"If you want to call it that—and the little girl, too, of course. . . . I keep thinking about this bicycle business, although according to your theory he wouldn't harm your sister. . . ."

"Don't be so sure. . . ."

"One more question, if I may: how do you imagine he would be dressed?"

"Neatly, not exactly like a young bank executive, yet not like a hippie—neatly, the way nice ordinary folk dress for a bike ride."

Rolf returned the soap dish to the bathroom, wiped it clean, pressed it into its holder. He straightened the chairs, smoothed the tablecloth, and followed Holzpuke down the stairs. It was still raining, the guard's nod looked more like a grumpy shake of the head. Fruit was lying on the ground, was dropping from the trees, the clock struck eight as they entered the warm living room. An idyllic scene: the warm stove, the children with cocoa rings around their mouths, empty eggshells, the two women with their cigarettes laughing over their coffee cups. "Today we'll have to stay indoors," said Katharina. "Sabine wants to come along and help me, she sings so nicely—and can draw too," she said. "We can make a start on the decorations for Saint Martin's Day."

Sabine, blushing when she saw Holzpuke, nodded to him and said: "I'm sorry, this time I had to act quickly. . . . Are there any objections to my new occupation?"

"Yes," said Holzpuke, "there are. You know I can't forbid you anything, I can only advise you: don't leave the house, certainly not the garden, and naturally I'd like to know, in fact must know for your own sake, how long you intend to remain here. My security measures, I'm sure you understand—after all, we've managed to cooperate with each other very nicely up to now."

"I don't know," said Sabine, "I really don't know"—she sighed—"I'm sure of only one thing: I'm not going back to Blorr, as far as my little girl and I are concerned you needn't bother with any more measures there. My husband is away, for some time I presume. And at my parents' house—for Kit it's better here—for how long?—and you really mean I'm not to go with Katharina to the day center?"

"You may go—only I shall have to remove the two officers from here for the time being and station them over there—I can't spare you that."

"Even if Kit goes there alone?"

"In that case, until reinforcements arrive I would have to leave one here and send one over there."

"Then I'll stay here, look after the stove, get lunch ready, and think of our twelve-room villa in Málaga, which is always empty—where it takes a month to chase away the boredom that's been piling up there, continues to pile up there: can you imagine such a thing?"

Holzpuke gave her an embarrassed look, took out a cigarette, accepted a light from Rolf, nodded his thanks.

"Boredom," said Sabine, "believe me, it piles up, thick, dense, I might almost say palpable, and the only way to get rid of it is to scoop it up laboriously by hand. Handful by handful, handful by handful—room by room—and the Spanish policemen in uniform, the German ones in plain clothes outside the door—the sound of the sea, and the palm trees, well, I presume they wave their fronds. No, I'll stay here, sit by the stove, and roast chestnuts. . . ."

Katharina was dressed and ready to leave, Holger too. "I must go now," she said, "the children are waiting, the mothers have to go work—and there'll be plenty of gossip waiting for me, because of Roickler. They'll blame us for his leaving, just watch, that's how it'll be. Are you coming along, Rolf?"

"Yes, I'll take you there. From there I'll go to the Halster farm—it's being completely renovated, modernized—I get paid double wages for my help and am allowed to take away the stuff they throw out. So long, Sis, we'll all be back for lunch, you know where the books are, where the toys are kept. And here's the phone: call up your mother, your brother too if you like—don't be afraid."

Kit was crying, casting angry looks at Holzpuke, who still hadn't left. Fortunately the child was only crying softly to herself, not bawling, and he cleared his throat and said hoarsely: "There's one more thing I have to talk to you about, alone. . . ."

"I know," she said, still seated, stroking the child's head in her lap. "I know: you're worried about those three months, maybe even anxious."

"Yes," he said, "it might point to a breach in security."

"No, it's not that. I'm not going to name any names, neither to you nor anyone else—but it wasn't a breach in security . . . I mean, it *was* a breach but in my inner security—and that has been closed too. It's a matter between us two, him and myself—and you have nothing to reproach yourself with. Not the least thing, you have done your duty—and you have done it courteously and discreetly, as considerately as possible. . . . I have only one request, my neighbor, Mrs. Breuer . . ."

"Nothing will happen to her—not now . . . not to—her friend, either. She may soon be your neighbor again, here, if you stay on here—you might soon run into her when you go for the milk. She was a Miss Hermes—didn't you know that? She comes from Hubreichen and may well come back here. . . . I was in no position to prevent what happened with Mr. Schubler—we had to investigate him, just as we had to include the priest here in our inquiries."

"Father Roickler too? Why?"

"There are some strange trends in modern theology—and Father Roickler's support of your brother, the vehement way in which he defended your brother here, made him part of the community—that needed to be investigated. But I can assure you, he was and still is completely above suspicion."

He went across to the child, ruffled her hair, and said gently: "Well, Kit, still mad at me?" But Kit wouldn't answer, kicked out at him, and he walked slowly to the door, nodded once more to Sabine, and stepped out into the garden. Buckets of bolts, he thought wearily, how am I supposed to check out millions of bicycles and cyclists? Weigh them, he thought, one could weigh them and the difference in weight would show whether they're loaded. Loaded bicycles.

XI

At times he was on the point of phoning the Tolms just to have a talk with them, to invite them over or go to see them, if necessary to offer them a cup of tea, possibly even to drink one himself. There were prejudices to be cleared away and decisions to be made—prejudices that had been dragging on for thirty-three years, on both sides of course, judgments that would seem harsh but would also have a salutary effect: it was time for Tolm to give up his newspaper, his last illusions must be taken from him. Tolm had really dropped all the reins, including his own, his paper had now become nothing but a jungle to him, he now had only "vague ideas," knew nothing, nothing whatever, had no insight, it was time for him to devote himself to some artistic hobby: Madonnas, perhaps, or Dutch masters; an invaluable, even splendid president who now actually imagined that he was to be destroyed—not the slightest intention of destroying him, on the contrary: they wanted him to live for years, to be guarded and protected, to be finally relieved of the burden of the paper. And if he were to start studying Madonnas, or cathedrals, that would be more than a substitute for his "vague ideas" regarding the paper and the whole economic situation, in fact he would probably enjoy it, and a president who knew something about Madonnas or cathedrals, could even be articulate about them, would really be irreplaceable, invaluable, and naturally he would also have to be relieved of the burdens of the presidency. As a figurehead, yes; making speeches, yes—but that was all, no decisions. And for that Amplanger was not enough, nor was the present advisory staff, at least two new people must be brought in to relieve him, to clear his path. Perhaps, if it wasn't too risky, Kolzheim and Grolzer should be considered; he must think about that.

Unfortunately Tolm's son—there was no getting around it—had gone off on the wrong track, and there was probably no way of getting him off it. The boy had it in him to be another Amplanger, he might even have been a better Amplanger, he was more sensitive and had a better sense of humor, his smile was not so knife-edged (there were some witty sayings about Amplanger's smile going the rounds: "It'll cut anything for you—bread, cheese, sausage, ham. Invite Amplanger, and you can forget about knives"). Nor would young Tolm be as absurdly "with it" as

Amplanger, who knew not only all the newest dances but even newer ones and swung around the still enthusiastic wives of the no longer quite so enthusiastic husbands in whatever was the latest craze. He had an almost uncanny knack of presenting the very latest editorials from the *Frankfurter Allgemeine Zeitung* and *Die Welt* with skillful variations as his own opinions. Oh, he was good, all right, irreplaceable in his way, yet he lacked something that Rolf Tolm had: personality and originality, and that goddamn Something, that odious tiny particle that apparently could be neither learned nor acquired, that detestable almost mystical, elusive quality that his mother possessed in plenty and his father at least to some degree: charm. Moreover, he knew what his father would never grasp: struggle, not reconciliation, was the watchword. Even in the days when he had been setting fire to cars and throwing rocks, he had had this charm—and had never lost it. And of course he had discovered long ago—perhaps just had a "vague idea," like his old man—that there was only one country where there might be a chance for him to do more than pick apples and renovate farmhouses: Cuba. In spite of everything, in spite of everything—that goddamn Cuba, that giant canker in the rose over there. Yes, Holzpuke had whispered that to him: now he's learning Spanish from some Chileans, studying the Cuban economy, getting hold of special reference works, and even has a pupil, that farmer's son in Hubreichen.

Well, one could forget about him, he would never come back, never, and even if theoretically he were to find his way back, he would never come back. Even if nothing came of his plans for Cuba, he would rather go on gathering nuts, growing potatoes, and producing children with his Communist mistress—if only out of pride, out of icy contempt for Zummerling, even though he no longer set fire to his cars, would never again set fire to a car, never again pick up a rock, would stay cooped up in that hole, counting pears and repairing tractors—would, like hundreds and thousands of his kind, observe the law and maintain his cold contempt for the system. Too bad, this crown prince was not in the running, yet he would have been a better Amplanger; would have. A waste of intelligence, of a gift for abstract, highly theoretical planning, a gift that was blended with an equal quantity—not too much—of imagination. Amazing, really, considering his parents, their origins and career. And yet they had something like style: there had never been anything upstart about them, not even in the manor house, never, and that was odd, really, considering that he himself, of comparable origins after all, was marked with it, indelibly: that coarse face of his that seemed to indicate brutality, a trait he had never possessed but which later on, when he was constantly being accused of it, did develop. Who would ever believe that he was a timid person? Lonely, lonely and timid. Hilde had not only believed it, she had known it.

And it was with her that he had split up and since then slithered into a series of unsuccessful marriages. Käthe Tolm was right again: his Number Four, Edelgard, was simply a "stupid bitch"; even her body was in some indefinable way stupid, the few tricks she had learned—where?—or simply picked up had become stale in three weeks. That artificial sensuality, those hoarse whisperings copied from silly movies, it gave him no pleasure, not even her. And her drinking, which now started early in the morning, her pose of melancholy that had absolutely nothing genuine about it—that unhappy-wife mechanism that didn't net her any boyfriends; the vulgarity that happened to be a shade too genuine to seem merely fashionable. A stupid bitch, perhaps a poor bitch who even had stupid hands, warped, had probably slipped into hash and rock as a school kid hanging around bus depots and cheap cafés, had gone to the dogs, part of a generation that apparently couldn't live without music, if it could be called music. From morning till night, and even at night when she couldn't sleep: music, music, music. That would probably provide the true reason for divorce: in every room, even in the toilet, she had her goddamn tape recorders or hi-fi speakers that she switched on automatically almost as soon as she turned the door handle;

in the bathroom, of course, in the bedroom, in all the downstairs rooms, even in the basement when she occasionally played at being a housewife and attended to the laundry and the groceries: music everywhere, cassettes lying around all over the house. Luckily she was going away now for a spell, to Norderney or Kampen, he wasn't sure, and as a result a whole swarm of security officers would be on the move: she enjoyed that, she was jealous of the Tolms because they had still more "security action." That was her latest sport: to check up on the security apparatus and from that to deduce her "rank": was she the second-, third-, or fourth-most-closely-guarded woman?

He'd have to split up with her soon, could only hope she wouldn't be too much of a nuisance. He felt sorry for her parents, they were nice, simple people, the Köhlers, thriftily carrying on with their little store against all economic sense; modest folk who labored eighteen hours a day, which probably worked out at an hourly wage of one mark eighty, at most two marks, and if you added that up, plus the savings in rent in their own building— ignoring, of course, the investment interest of the building—plus the savings through the reduced cost of their personal consump- tion, they might, with each of them working a hundred hours a week as well as having anxiously to watch the shelf dates of milk and other produce, actually arrive at two thousand five hundred, maybe three thousand marks a month, and they would imagine themselves to be earning good money, whereas actually they were toiling away for far, far less than any Turkish immigrant worker was earning, while he himself was earning more than three thousand marks a day. Needless to say, this mustn't be pointed out to them, those nice, modest people mustn't be thrown into confusion. There they sat in their little village, respected, going to church, singing in the choir, even cultured in their own way. There was a certain style about them when they invited you for dinner, the way they set the table, formally, and the way the old man helped in the kitchen, and she would untie her apron and hang it over the chair each time she finished serving a course; it had style. And the wine was excellent, the coffee perfect, the homemade éclairs—probably made by the old man, who had been a baker by trade—were superb. Granted they were a bit reserved, but they were not shy, no trace of shyness with the powerful, the rich, the much-publicized son-in-law who put the whole village in a turmoil with his bodyguard: guards here and guards there, it was almost like a state visit. The milieu reminded him of home: there it had been even more modest, not Catholic but Protestant. More modest—but to make comparisons one would have to know how the Köhlers had lived forty or fifty years ago, before their parents died and they inherited the store. Nice people who didn't quite trust their wayward daughter's career—and they were right. When coffee and liqueurs were served, they would ask her to play the piano, and she did, with a bored sullenness intended to express her contempt for that kind of music: messed up the Schubert, deprived the Chopin of even the last vestige of charm, bitched about "this silly musical dessert." Käthe Tolm was right: simply a "stupid bitch," his Number Four; it was Amplanger who had told him about this, he managed to pick up a lot of interesting things, probably on the phone too.

Let her carry on with her boring tit-games on the isle of Norderney. He would give the Tolms a call, go there for tea or ask them over for tea, if necessary even drink some; there were things to be straightened out. Of course he had "hoisted" Tolm into that position, but not to destroy him, on the contrary: he wanted to lighten his load, wanted him to be released from the paper. It was his paper that was making his bones ache, his legs ache; it was his own fault that it had slipped more and more through his fingers. He wanted him to be released, to recover his health, to be given two more assistants in addition to Amplanger and the experienced advisory staff; he wanted him to get well and live. And then there were those prejudices formed in the internment camp and dragged along for more than thirty years. True: he, Bleibl, hadn't behaved "nicely" there, but then he had never pretended to be nice, had never blazoned "niceness" on his coat of arms; there they had confused toughness with brutality and had spread the myth that he had been born with a silver spoon in his mouth.

That pitiful dry-goods store in Doberach was supposed to have been a silver spoon, where in winter his mother, her fingers stiff with cold, had sold a few cents' worth of this and that: notions and underwear, sometimes as much as a whole roll of elastic to repair bloomers and underpants, where darning needles were bought one (in words and figures *one*) at a time, where a rare sale was a pair of socks, and that bitter struggle behind the scenes as Confirmation Day approached: prices reduced, and reduced yet again, damn it. And of course he had—what else— joined the Brownshirts in the early days, if only for the sake of orders for Papa that later led to something almost like affluence because Papa was given a sort of monopoly, for shirts and blouses, trousers and ties, later even for boots, and all that annoyance with shoemakers and shoe stores, with hatmakers and hat stores, because Papa was also given the monopoly for boots and for caps, and whoever thought in those days of murder? Who? Even nice old Pastor Stermisch, who had confirmed him, had been fooled, used to warble in nationalistic, even anti-Semitic tones, and went so far as to advise Papa expressly not to "overdo your humaneness" in cases involving the takeover of Jewish businesses.

Stermisch enabled him to go to university, and by the time it came to his Ph.D. thesis Papa was able to finance it himself. "Problems Facing the Textile Industry in Periods of Raw-Material Shortage," based on the experiences of World War I, a subject that proved ideal when World War II eventually broke out. Needless to say, he was declared essential to the war effort, was given every opportunity to apply, extend, modify, develop his theory, he never soiled his hands, never accepted a bribe, and found it quite logical for the Americans to lock him up: in fact it was an honor, indicating that they considered him more important than he had ever thought himself to be. The credit for his not taking himself too seriously must go to Hilde, his wife, who by this time was known almost reverently as "Bleibl's Number One"; she had been anything but a "stupid bitch," on any level, including business. Thrifty without being stingy, she had bought real estate, all perfectly legal and normal; she comforted him when he had been upset by the tide of blood-soaked, torn, bullet-riddled textiles—civilian and field gray, with kids' clothes among them too. As the law required, the garments of persons hanged and shot had to be collected from prisons and parade grounds and recycled, not to mention "enemy textiles," which meant not only booty textiles but also children's clothing—and he had children himself: Martin and Robert—oh well, one had to be tough, even brutal if necessary. Hilde had been a good, a clever wife, in business too but also with her music—she was such a good pianist and accompanied her own singing; she had been a good wife to him, a wonderful cook, and in other respects too; in every way.

The trouble was: after the war, when he came out of camp and at Bangors's instigation was reappointed Textile Administrator —they hadn't been able to prove anything against him, not the shedding of a single drop of blood, nothing!—he couldn't go on, couldn't go on sleeping with her, couldn't find his way to her, into her. He had been able to do it with whores when Bangors took him along, even after the affair in the bank, that terrible affair that he had never yet been able to talk about to anyone, anyone, not even to Bangors, who had been a witness, a silent witness: that night in the Reichsbank, when they had been literally shoveling the cash and the contents of the safes into sacks, a young woman had suddenly loomed up, wrapped in blankets, she must have sought shelter there, and he, Bleibl, had snatched up Bangors's machine pistol and shot the woman dead. It was the first time in his life that he had fired a gun, and the last time too, and the dead woman literally turned the pile of money into blood money. They had left the woman and the money lying there on the floor, had thrown the blankets over her, heaped money over the corpse, and fled, into the car, to the camp casino: hit the bottle, tied one on, and not a word to a soul, not a single word! And later he had carefully studied the newspapers for any mention of a corpse or later of a skeleton found in the basement of the Reichsbank: nothing, never a word. Had it been a dream, then, an apparition? He was haunted by the scene, saw it whenever he wanted to embrace Hilde, saw it whenever Martin and Robert kissed him goodnight; tough, harrowing years in which he created his empire: textiles with the politically immaculate Fischer, real estate with Hilde's help, later newsprint with Kortschede and publishing with Zummerling: working fallow land before the old wolves came crawling out of their cages again. No, there had been no silver spoon for him: his father's business had been insignificant, an absurd little store where after the war a few hundred Storm Trooper shirts, which were hard to re-dye, had gradually rotted away.

Eventually he had had to split up with Hilde. He had amply provided for her, she was still his co-regent. Martin was by now a very agreeable, "square" high school teacher, Robert a truly endearing pastor—far away, his sons, as embarrassed as their wives when he occasionally turned up. Those were scenes from another life, scenes from a film that had been made without him— yet they were still his children, his sons, totally unsuited for what Rolf Tolm would have been suited for, and of course he visited Hilde, who was living up there in the mountains, had gone to university late in life and become a chartered accountant: memories that were past bringing to life, fixed forever as if under glass, present yet remote, a ghost of intimacy when he pressed her hands, and still, always her questioning look: why? And he couldn't talk about it, was still haunted by that scene that drove him to drink and whoring, drove him to the dream of possible new marriages, all of which went on the rocks.

No, there would never be a "Bleibl's Number Five." Maybe at sixty-five it was time to give up the idea of marriage. But, goddammit, how come Tolm didn't seem to be haunted by such scenes? Obviously he wasn't, that suave aesthete, that soft old sidestepper, though he'd been in command of a whole battery and had banged away right into the Russians and must have blown many of them to bits, including children, women, when he banged away into those wretched villages and, retreating, had simply ordered his battery to fire at random, anywhere. And those fine military gentlemen who set so much store by their lousy honor: who if not they had the bloodstained, bullet-riddled, torn clothing on their conscience? No, of course, they hadn't "profiteered" from the war. Had he? Who could possibly have benefited from that money lying around there ignored, money that had already been credited to customers' accounts, those pieces of paper in their countless billions that everyone regarded as valueless? Why not use the money to acquire buildings and land, legally, all aboveboard, why not give money to those who desperately needed it, and not at the market, the list price, not at all? What harm had been done? Tolm had been only a very small fish, a lieutenant in the artillery whose alleged crime no one was quite convinced of, so he was promptly released from camp too, after only eight months, and then he was given the newspaper and had done nothing, absolutely nothing with it—wasn't *he* a war profiteer?

Now Bangors had appeared on the scene again, retired, white-haired of course, impressive, had reached the rank of general: Korea, Vietnam, et cetera. He had been obliged to have dinner with him at the Excelsior, with Edelgard unavoidably included—a pleasant evening, as one says, with Bangors's genuinely nice wife who could even risk whispering a few admonitory words to Edelgard. "That's right," said Bangors, "this is Mary, still my Number One": a sporty type, gray-haired, nowhere near as drastically slim as Edelgard always wanted to be—she still didn't realize that drink could make a person fat, and her revolting habit of chewing candy as she wandered from room to room switching on her goddamn music everywhere, all over the house. Nice people, the Bangorses, she seemed nicer than he, and he was the very prototype of a gentleman—yet with his own feet he had scraped money over the body in the vault like scraping dead leaves over a corpse in a forest, had grinned as he sniffed at the muzzle of the machine pistol—and then: clear out, get away. Never so much as a word about it, not even a hint, not even a wink during the dinner at the Excelsior, nor later in the bar over coffee and brandy while the ladies indulged in a Drambuie. And yet, yet— the scene remained, the horror remained, everything stuck in his gullet the time Kortschede asked him: "Think carefully, Bleibl, think hard, they'll go through your life with a fine-tooth comb— are you sure you haven't a skeleton in the closet?" Not meaning it literally, of course, though he might have answered literally enough: "Well, I did leave a body in the vault of the Reichsbank in Doberach." And when he had apparently turned white as a sheet Kortschede had put a hand on his arm and said: "Take it easy—I don't mean anything that's mentioned in your denazifica- tion file—I mean something in your youth, perhaps, some Party connection, that they might sniff out." No, nothing, he had a body in the vault, but there had never been any prosecution, there were no witnesses, or rather the only witness had meanwhile seen or perhaps even been responsible for so many corpses that that particular one had totally vanished from his mind. Coffee and brandy, the ladies with their Drambuie, and even in the bar of the Excelsior that goddamn inescapable music—but at least some people were dancing.

He hadn't been able to talk about it to Margret, either, his Number Two; not exactly a stupid bitch, but still pretty dumb— one of his secretaries, quite nice, but three years had been more than enough. Margret had a cultural hang-up: Florence and Venice, Giotto, Mantegna, and all that, and had even—"What do you expect, in Assisi—what else is one supposed to do there?" —become a Catholic, surrounded herself with witty monks, became co-founder of a magazine, fine, had her heart set on an apartment on the Piazza Navona, fine, better than that music nut, his Number Four, that's for sure, but then she went too far, farther than he could allow, started something with a trendy leftist Italian, an art critic—a real charmer, mind you—something serious, and it got out, became public, and that really wouldn't do, it was all right as long as it remained a rumor, not harmful gossip, but it became intolerable when the pictures appeared showing her naked on a sunny beach with that intellectual crook. Margret had certainly been decorative, and also quite useful as a decorator—what with Florence, Venice, Giotto, Mantegna, and Assisi. But this was going too far, and even his friends were advising him to get a divorce, especially Zummerling, the very one who had been the first to publish the pictures. And though Margret had quite clearly been the guilty party, he had been generous: let her keep the house in Fiesole, for all he cared, and a car and whatever else, let her marry the fellow, well, maybe it really was the love he had never found, could be, she was even married in church, legally, properly, and she even wrote to him occasionally, postcards with strange words such as "I have forgiven you everything, everything." That did make him laugh: by that she could only mean the time he had slapped her when, believe it or not, she had burst into tears at breakfast because some madman had scratched up a Rembrandt someplace. That had really been too much cultural claptrap for him, and he had let her have it. So she'd forgiven him. Fine.

With Number Three he had aimed too high: he was no match for that peasant girl with the Modigliani face; he had succumbed to prejudices that didn't apply—certainly didn't to her, to Elisabeth. Not because she was a cleaning woman—one day, when he was working late, she had actually come into his private office with scrubbing brush, mop, and pail—no, these days many women were earning money by cleaning, although they certainly weren't cleaning women: there were refugees and unemployed women of all categories, no, but this cleaning woman really was one, a peasant girl from Istria: the only way he could have her was to marry her, and that had been a bad time, when he had been a laughingstock, for after all he was nearly sixty and she was around twenty-four. "Bleibl in love, actually in love—good old Bleibl!" There had been plenty of ridicule, and Käthe and Fritz

Tolm were probably the only ones who didn't join in, they may have been a bit surprised that it had really caught him this time. The magazines had had a field day, and he had let them have their field day: standing in front of the humble farmhouse with his parents-in-law and his bride Elisabeth, a peasant wedding with more dancing than he was equal to with the best will in the world, and all those difficulties because he was divorced and Elisabeth was a Catholic, the palaver with the parents, the painful forgoing of a church wedding that was hard for Elisabeth too—and it hadn't lasted long, that third marriage, it had been the shortest, had foundered not only on the scene he couldn't rid himself of but above all on Elisabeth's firm dignity: a cleaning woman! There were only a few among his acquaintances with whom she associated, least of all with the Fischers, with whom he had very close connections through textiles and the Beehive, and it was no use pointing out that they really were Catholics, a matter of proven record, attested to even by serious clerics; nothing helped. Wild horses wouldn't drag her to the Fischers', to the Tolms' yes, but they didn't happen to care for *his* company.

Surprisingly enough she liked Kortschede, and even Pliefger. But everyone else she found "bad company, very bad," and said about many of them: "They stink, you just can't smell it anymore." And just when he had begun to encourage something like friendship between her and Sabine Fischer, the marriage went on the rocks, and she went back to Yugoslavia, had finally even begun to describe senior "government types," if not very senior, as stinking. "They all stink, you people just can't smell it anymore." Eventually she admitted to him that he stank too, "not always, but most of the time," even said so in hours of intimacy when she released him from the mental scene of horror and he could forget about all the whores, but she wouldn't deign to describe the stink. Things became quite awkward when she began to sniff at people and wrinkle her nose, saying laconically: "Stinks" or "Doesn't stink," and it was quite clear that she didn't only mean this morally, toward the end she spoke openly of a "stinking German cleanliness." He had to let her go, back to Istria, gave her money for a smart little hotel where he hoped she wouldn't have to accommodate any other stinking Germans, and he dreamed of her, dreamed of Hilde, of his nice square sons, and thought with apprehension of having to return Bangors's invitation: hadn't there been a flicker in his eyes after all? A connivance, yet he couldn't start anything against him without implicating himself. The body in the vault was not his alone. Probably someone had picked up the "bloodstained money" after them and discreetly removed the corpse.

It was going to be difficult to get rid of Edelgard. She was tough, and she clung in the most tiresome way to the luxury which, for her, included the surveillance; of course the surveillance would be greatly reduced, if not cease entirely. The rest of the luxury meant nothing to her, yet she wanted it, she liked sitting around in the most expensive hotels reading magazines, listening to her goddamn music, making eyes, driving police officers up the wall, and enjoying her "protocol rank," driving men crazy, yet none of them wanted her, none of them really swallowed the bait, and she didn't seem to be all that interested, either. She was worse than a whore, gone rotten early on while hanging around cheap snack bars and bus depots—and she had snared him, had pretended to be panting for him but had then played upon her honor and virginity, had even involved her parents in this crusade of honor, while in fact she had probably been laid at the age of twelve, at the latest thirteen. She had caught him at the right moment, just after Elisabeth had left, when he had had enough of whores and, tired out, was sitting late one evening in his office: a crude approach with freshly made coffee, soft little hand on arm, and a generously granted look at those stupid breasts. Honor, shrieks, virginity, parents, and again a wedding, the fourth. It would be hard to get rid of her, expensive too. There wouldn't be a fifth. What he needed was a life's companion, someone like Käthe

Tolm, in whose follies there was even a certain charm. Holzpuke had indicated to him that she and her inscrutable son Herbert had probably given that Veronica some money. Even her piety was perfectly genuine, she was worth her weight in gold, like her daughter, whose qualities as horsewoman, churchgoer, mother, housewife, and on the dance floor added up to a fantastic image, beyond price; he must really have a serious word with young Fischer to persuade him not to exhaust that young woman, mentally, physically, possibly even in the bedroom, seeing how he was now on a porn kick. She was a jewel, that young woman, more fragile than she looked—she mustn't be handled too roughly, as Fischer was obviously doing with his idiotic playboy pose. There must be no danger of the young Tolm woman flipping, clearing out—never mind where to: she had to stick to her role with her cute little brat. Old Tolm needed support too. That left only Herbert, and no one, not even the police, could fathom him. He was "into" philosophy, and that wasn't without its dangers; one of these days he'd have to discuss all this with Dollmer, maybe even with Stabski—these were problems going far beyond the interests of the Association. They concerned the state.

First of all he had to find out whether by this time Kolzheim and Grolzer had settled down a bit: those two really had flipped, hadn't been able to take all that guff, Amplanger's "knife in the face," they had begun to hit the bottle in a big way and get involved with women who did them no good: greedy bitches out for apartments and furs, wanting to bathe in champagne, so to speak. Out of a sense of surfeit and unrelieved boredom, the two men had then embarked on trendy perversions, three-way, four-way deals, or even by the dozen. As a result, they had dipped into the till, padding their expense accounts. That was inexcusable, they had to be sent back to the front lines, to the harshest, grimmest conditions, and were confronted with the alternative: to be taken to court or to prove themselves in the front line, not at any staff headquarters but right in the trenches. Three or four years behind bars, or demotion: they chose the latter and were sent to one of the supermarkets out in the country, in the sticks anyway, where it was up to them to increase sales, do the dirty work, nag the salesgirls, gyp the customers with wilted lettuce, dream up "special offers," arrive for work on time in their soiled white smocks, bully the cleaning women, and make sure the cash balanced. If they felt like it, they could join outdoor clubs out there in the sticks, have a grand time with the women at fairs and local hops, go hiking over hill and dale dressed up in all the right togs complete with walking stick and red socks, and could prove their impregnable virtue on the thin ice of small-town sex parties. It must be three or four years now since they had been sent to the front. He must inquire as to how far Kolzheim and Grolzer had proven themselves, whether they had managed to work their way up without patronage and pass all the front-line tests. They had been good assistants, university graduates, smart sociologists with a command of the leftist jargon yet capable of arguing from the right. It would be too bad if they went to seed among the lettuce heads and petty affairs with salesgirls and cashiers.

He would have to ask Amplanger for a report, and he must give the Tolms a call, talk to them at long last after they had been lugging prejudices around like heavy lumps for thirty-three years. Perhaps he could phone Hilde too and ask her to be, if not his life's companion, maybe his housekeeper. He'd had enough of this wild-bull image, didn't need it anymore either, was sick and tired of women, including whores. Above all he must convince Tolm that no one in the world was out to destroy him. On the contrary: they wanted to keep him and to keep him well, and at last he was to have time for his Madonnas or cathedrals or cruci-fixes. He was to get well and stay well, for as long as possible, and if Kolzheim and Grolzer had been purified, had been tempered to new hardness, they would be the best assistants for him: stream-lined young whippets, with a sense of humor and, after three or four years in the crucible, a long way from being spoiled. Perhaps Käthe Tolm was the only person he could talk to about his corpse in the vault, about his loneliness.

XII

After breakfast a delegation from the newspaper turned up after all, with flowers and a blown-up front page, mounted on cardboard, of that day's edition, which had been devoted to his election. That was nice of them, it really touched him, especially since they sent only three people—old Thönis, who officially was still editor-in-chief, one of the old émigré bunch originally sent him by Major Weller, newsprint allocation and license alone not being quite enough. From Thönis and the vanished Communist Schröter he had learned at least the rudiments of journalism, again and again they had dinned into him the word "jour, jour, jour," for one day, to last one day. He had understood, but he had never learned it, and in whatever he wrote he had never been able to drop his academic diffuseness and thoroughness. They had also sent along Blörl, one of the old printers, and his secretary Birgit Zatger, not that young either, all of them old-timers, they were fond of him, as he was of them, and they knew that. Thönis had actually dug out Tolm's doctoral thesis: "The Rhenish Farmhouse in the Nineteenth Century"—that pathetic, cold, unfriendly architecture, those little Frankish farmhouses with their tiled walls, their yards, not much more than burrows. He could only hope that no one would read this unflattering dissertation, with its many comparisons with North and South German peasant architecture. Somehow or other those shabby façades had always reminded him of confessionals, and they were something he couldn't stomach.

Pictures of himself: as a boy with his bike outside the manor house, as a student, as a returning soldier, and Käthe hadn't escaped them either—as a young wife carrying Rolf, sitting beside Zummerling at a dinner party. Himself again with his postwar decorations, standing with smiling cabinet ministers. "A full life. A successful life." He actually felt a few tears come to his eyes as he raised his glass with Thönis, Blörl, Miss Zatger, and Käthe; Käthe not quite in tears but moist-eyed. Champagne, cigars, a promise to appear before the staff, who felt they shared in his honor, to accept their congratulations, and on a sudden impulse he suggested to Thönis that they use first names, after thirty-three years, tried desperately to remember Thönis's first name, felt that his suggestion had come too late and at the wrong moment. Thönis was embarrassed, couldn't bring himself to say Fritz, and it occurred to him too late that Thönis was called Heinrich—and all this time he was thinking of Sabine, of her future, thinking of Kortschede's prediction of a new, inescapable expulsion. Where to? Where to?

Already taking mental leave of the manor house, he recalled that the children had never liked coming here, not even Sabine. They had never felt at home here, they clung to Eickelhof as to a lost paradise, which it had never been, that damp, moldering monster of a building that had proven past repair, and all attempts to revive Eickelhof customs had failed. At times he had considered renting a hotel apartment, a suite, in Cologne, where he could meet his children, but Käthe had rejected that as being "really too far out." Still, it would have been easier than dragging the whole surveillance apparatus along for every visit; perhaps one could buy a piece of hotel in Cologne. It wasn't likely they would flatten the city. But presumably it, too, stood on top of that "brown gold," and presumably there were technical means of dismantling the cathedral and rebuilding it somewhere else. . . .

When Käthe called him to the phone, paler even than yesterday, obviously frightened, his thoughts flew to Rolf, then to Zummerling. At the time of Rolf's arrest she had looked just as pale and frightened when holding out the receiver; again when Veronica disappeared with Beverloh and Holger; and both times it had been Zummerling who had not only broken the news to him but also explained, with profuse apologies, that he wouldn't be able to suppress these items of news. It did not surprise him that it was

Zummerling again: his was the best intelligence service, after all, his spies were everywhere, and he suddenly wondered if it might have something to do with Herbert, who not only had crazy ideas in his head but was capable of carrying them out. Before going to the phone, he had the presence of mind to wave back at Thönis, who at that moment was being helped into his coat by Blurtmehl. Käthe picked up the other receiver and nodded to him. "Tolm speaking," he said into the phone. "This time, my friend," said Zummerling in his pleasant, friendly voice, "just so you won't be alarmed—this time your family isn't involved, but it's terrible enough: Kortschede has killed himself, in his car, in the woods near Trollscheid. Are you listening, Tolm?"

"Yes, I'm listening . . . I . . . I just can't take it in yet. . . ."

"Mutilated in the most ghastly way—in his pocket was a letter to you that Holzpuke, probably even Dollmer himself, will hand over to you—an explosive letter, highly explosive, that must never on any account be made public. . . . Are you listening?"

"A letter to me that I haven't read yet, but whose contents you obviously already know—doesn't that strike you as odd . . . ? Kortschede was my friend, a true friend, one of the few I had."

"The envelope in Kortschede's pocket bore no address, so the letter had to be opened. The 'Dear Fritz' and the contents prove that the letter is meant for you. Needless to say, the envelope will be handed over to you too. Besides, the letter had to be opened since it might have contained allusions to perpetrators or accomplices—incidentally, the letter also contains some embarrassing allusions to that boy he called Petie. All in all, a letter showing him to have some kind of millennium obsession. I appeal to you, not only as our newly elected president but also as the owner of the newspaper with all its affiliations. . . . Are you listening, Tolm?"

"Yes, I'm listening. . . . I trust you'll understand that I would like to read the letter before you report to me on it—and, when I have read the letter, for us to consider jointly what is to happen about *my* letter? Nor is it quite clear to me why instead of

Holzpuke or Dollmer notifying me about the letter it's—forgive my saying so—you, since to my knowledge you have no official function whatever."

Zummerling laughed. "But it was Dollmer who asked me to talk to you before talking to you himself and possibly handing over the letter. . . ."

"Possibly? A letter intended for me?"

"This is a matter of such journalistic explosiveness that—there's nothing I can do—Dollmer first called me about it, there's even a chance Stabski will be brought into it. In this situation, my dear Tolm, you shouldn't be so sensitive, considering the family embarrassments you are facing. . . . Are you still there . . . Tolm? Are you . . . ?"

"Yes, I'm still here—have your specialists in pregnancy, that's to say impregnation, opened fire?"

"Look, my dear Tolm . . . I find your daughter's possible lapses more endearing than otherwise, but it so happens that your son-in-law is causing trouble. Not at all on account of some possible lapse, which he's not likely to admit as yet, but because of the environment his daughter now finds herself in. . . ."

"As of yesterday."

"Yes, as of yesterday and no doubt for another few days, if not longer; your daughter seems to feel quite at home there. And apparently your son-in-law is worried that his daughter might also feel at home there, too much so—he seems to be considering legal action, he's still discussing the best procedure. He told our correspondent in Vancouver . . ."

"Where?"

"In Vancouver, Canada—told our correspondent there that he will not accept the situation—those were his words—and will sue for custody, but let's not forget Kortschede . . . the isolation, the quasi-imprisonment, that psychosis, that separation from the boy who was sentenced to five years. It goes without saying that, as his friend and colleague in your new capacity, you will have to give the funeral oration, don't forget who were the real cause of his suicide . . . and as far as your daughter's concerned, we will of course use discretion. Our man in Vancouver . . ."

At this point Käthe interjected, saying quietly: "Kortschede was his friend, his good friend, and he will give the funeral oration, and we will wait patiently for the letter that one day we may perhaps be allowed to read, although it's written to Fritz. As far as our family is concerned, I have no faith in your assurances, I don't expect any consideration, no, I mean it. And anyway, we do have freedom of the press, don't we? So let's not interfere with freedom of the press."

"Don't cry, Tolm," she said quietly, then nodded to Thönis, who was withdrawing in alarm with Blörl and Miss Zatger.

"Come, let's go out on the terrace for a moment."

"But it's raining."

"There's a remedy for that—umbrellas, so I've been told—besides, umbrellas, so Rolf has explained to me, have an additional function: they are a protection against"—she gave a brief laugh—"eavesdropping invasions. Wait." She went into the bedroom, returned with a large yellow umbrella, opened the door to the terrace, and drew him outside. He shivered, hesitated, she took him firmly by the arm and opened the umbrella, which was deeply curved. "The point should be sawn off or broken off, but I don't dare," she whispered, "because then the umbrella would collapse. Rolf told me that, in spite of the metal ribs and tips, it's very difficult to beam in on someone under a curved umbrella like this. Now tell me: did you know about this Petie, or whatever he's called?"

"Yes, I've known for a long time, Kortschede trusted me, he also confided many things to me that I can't speak about—sad things to do with his family. Yes, I knew he was that way, he told me about that boy and how they bugged his conversations with Kortschede's consent because the boy was a criminal. But I suppose it's possible to love criminals too, even criminal sons, isn't it?"

"And criminal daughters-in-law?"

"No, I don't love Veronica, though I was fond of her. But I must say it makes me uneasy that Bleibl should now actually want to have us over for tea—how can they know, how can they have heard . . . he phoned this morning, and his voice was so friendly. . . ."

"Maybe Bleibl's Number Four has been gossiping in bars, someone has heard it—I'm sure they must have ears that listen for them. . . ."

"He seems to have an urge to confess, Bleibl I mean—that's something quite new in him. I don't know whether he has ever drunk a cup of tea—at least I've never seen it, and she hardly looks the tea-drinking type either. . . ."

"She won't be there, he told me. She starts with gin and tonic or straight whiskey early in the morning. Besides, she has a shoe fixation. Do you suppose she once worked in a shoe store . . . ? Are you cold? Shall I get you a blanket?"

"No, thanks, it's quite something to stand under an umbrella on one's own terrace and converse with one's own wife in whispers in the hope that one isn't being monitored—but then why shouldn't they hear us? No, she never worked in a shoe store. . . ."

"Shoes always make me think of Heinrich Beverloh."

"Shoes?"

"Yes, he knew a lot about women's feet."

"What?"

"Knew a lot about women's feet, I say. Why shouldn't a murderer, a criminal, know a lot about women's feet? At Eickelhof he always used to help me pick out shoes. You know how I've remained loyal to Kutschheber, out of sentiment, or gratitude, because in the old days, when I had no money, he always sold me shoes on the installment plan—imagine, once a year, at most twice! Nowadays I buy more shoes and more expensive ones, and pay cash, but I've remained loyal to Kutschheber. When we were still living at Eickelhof I had them send shoes out on approval, the children and all those visitors left me so little time. In those days I had a good adviser—Beverloh. Yes, he knew a lot about women's feet. He knew exactly when you could cross the border line between elegance and comfort, and when not. He always disapproved of my preference for comfortable shoes—by the way, in those days he also used to give Veronica advice, I've no idea whether he still does. In those days you didn't spend much time at home and probably weren't aware of this. He considered my feet too good to stick into 'any old clodhoppers.' From among a dozen pairs he'd unfailingly pick out the pair that did justice to both elements: elegance and comfort. Whenever the conflict between the two elements became too great, he always decided in favor of elegance. Incidentally, he also knew a lot about making jam: his blackberry jam was unbeatable—you've had it often enough. The boy's a criminal, I know that, he's dangerous, but he's also charming and intelligent and extremely sensitive. . . ."

"And nice too, I suppose?"

"Nice too, but that was not the important thing, he happened to be that as well—and corrupt, corrupt to the very marrow of his bones. Yes, you may stare: he was corrupt. He dealt too long, too much, and too exclusively in money—just like Rolf, who went nuts as a result of his banking experiences. Well, Rolf got over it, Beverloh didn't, he's figuring and figuring and figuring, and not in order to figure out his financial advantage—he's figuring, so to speak, for its own sake, and that's enough to make anyone go nuts. You're sure you don't want a blanket, Tolm? We can really have a good talk here. . . ."

He shook his head, smiled, kissed her hand on the umbrella handle, looked out into the park, missed the birds. . . . "Let the headlines scream, Käthe, let Fischer sue. I'm no longer even curious, I'm thinking about the funeral oration, I'll probably talk about love—why not? I'm thinking, too, of the man Sabine, from whom Sabine—perhaps he knows a lot about women's feet. . . ."

"I bet Fischer doesn't know a thing about women's feet. . . ."

"How about me?"

"You would know something, you might. You might even know something about newspapers, but then you've never been interested in newspapers. Old Amplanger, now, he's been very good at exploiting your laziness, your lack of interest, always threatening with Zummerling, although or because he is Zummerling's man. Then you people started buying and threatening, threatening and buying, until you began to be ashamed to look at your own newspaper. You always did prefer to read the *Gerbsdorfer Bote*, didn't you?"

"True, and now that I own it I won't read it anymore. Everything will be drowned in sports and trivia, a bit of local dirt, entertainment. My sons wouldn't touch the paper with a barge pole: too little information, and they're right. I'm also thinking of my daughter—out of a clear blue sky—or is the sky not all that clear and blue?—she gets, shall we say, involved with another man. . . ."

"The child wasn't born to be an adulteress, or made to be one either. I won't even mention upbringing, it doesn't help much, hardly at all—maybe one can only believe in marriage vows if one can break them. Come on now, don't blush, old dear, you weren't made to be one either, you failed as an adulterer . . . forget it, don't feel ashamed, don't go on blushing too long. . . . At any rate you showed good taste and tact, forget it, it's no disgrace. I wasn't made to be one either . . . was never even tempted, not even from boredom; whatever went on at Eickelhof and the paper and all that: I never felt bored. . . . Women's feet, Kutschheber even made the boy an offer to take over the ladies' section. He was gifted in many areas—strange, with that father, not because he was a mailman, but he was boring, like his mother: she couldn't see beyond Blückhoven. Oh well, the old man hates us, as you know, we're to blame for everything, with our easy, affluent life, with the university education you financed for their son, and then his stay in America. He would have preferred to

see him as a letter carrier in Hetzigrath, his career crowned
perhaps by rising to postal inspector in Blückhoven. Perhaps he's
right in a way. He won't even let me into the house, curses at
me if I as much as step onto the threshold, spits at my feet. Well,
at least he wasn't a Nazi, that I know, my father knew him quite
well. . . ."

"You too . . . you've been to see him, you knew him before?"

"Of course, Ludwig Beverloh—his sister Gertrud is an old
school friend of mine, she works at the town hall, she has her
own cross to bear because she's never married and bears the name.
She used to come to Eickelhof fairly often, don't you remember?
But of course you were never there."

"I never liked the place: that mixture of neo-baroque and
neo-Renaissance, decayed, dilapidated, damp, stuffy . . . and I
didn't want to remodel. There's just one thing I'm sure of: your
specialist in women's feet would kill me on the spot, if he
could. . . ."

"But he can't, and I doubt whether he wants to or would like
to—Veronica doesn't want it. . . . Wouldn't you like to go in
now and have another cup of coffee?"

"No, I'd rather shiver a bit in the November rain, under the
umbrella with you, wait for the birds, and accept the fact that
my sons and their friends won't touch my paper with a barge
pole and that they dislike coming to see us here at the manor.
You're right, of course: I've never been interested in newspapers,
only in you, the children, their friends, in Madonnas and architecture, in trees and birds. No, I think I took you too much for
granted for the word 'interest' to have any meaning when applied
to you. I have always had the manor in mind, never liked
Eickelhof, and my paper is, after all, a newspaper which with all
its affiliations has millions of readers or at least subscribers: but
for *them* it doesn't exist, doesn't exist for their friends. The
communication of the system, the information mechanism of the
system, doesn't interest them—probably not even Sabine. Fischer
only when he or his outfit is mentioned. Herbert is even less

interested than Rolf. Every headline in the paper elicits a strangely happy little smile from him, not malicious, not cynical, but happy, like a child laughing at soap bubbles that burst on the instant, and they'll laugh, not at Kortschede's death—they liked him—not at his mangled face and not at the bloodstained car—they will laugh at the pompous, exceedingly pompous funeral, which Dollmer and Stabski will of course attend: a kind of state funeral with pomp and circumstance, with a security force of at least regimental strength, helicopters over the woods of Horrnauken. And I shall make a speech: my first official act in public. You'll be coming too, won't you?"

"Yes, of course I will, but only if by then you have been shown the letter intended for you. Don't you think that might be a reason to resign: keeping a letter from you that is specifically intended for you? Don't worry, I'll come with you, I'll be a dignified figure, pressing Mrs. Kortschede's hand and displaying the distress I genuinely feel. I liked him very much—some of them are really nice, like Pliefger and Pottsieker, perhaps even Bleibl. What do you think—shall we have tea with him, here or at his place? He obviously wants to unburden his heart—if he has one."

"Of course he has a heart, he's been generous to all his wives. I assume that things have come to an end now with his Number Four too, with Edelgard—maybe he chases women because he doesn't have a wife. Have him come here. He might be able to help us if Fischer is really planning to make trouble—the child has been at Rolf's for just one day, and already he's afraid of contamination. Is their system, our system, so lacking in conviction that they have to be afraid of its being exposed to doubt? Why aren't they defending our system, our views, our prospects, against this infiltration? After all, Rolf and his friends have to send their children to capitalist schools whether they like it or not, they've no option, and *they* aren't afraid, they feel strong enough. Remember the big get-together that Kortschede once arranged before his daughter committed suicide? He invited his daughter and her friends, and Rolf and his friends, ourselves, the Fischers and their friends—his aim was the great reconciliation, it distressed him that there were two or three worlds at logger-heads—there was dancing in the garden, paper lanterns, fruit punch and cold buffet, and Communists were dancing with millionaires' daughters and millionaires with anarchists—that was before the days of massive security measures, of course. I can still see them: Sabine with one of Herbert's friends, and Fischer with one of Katharina's. Well, they could dance together all right, but as soon as they started to talk to each other it became acutely distressing: reality versus theory, arguments versus successes—those three kinds of arrogance clashing head on: the arrogance of Herbert's friends, the arrogance of Rolf's friends—and the empty arrogance of Fischer's friends, who had nothing to show but their sales figures. . . ."

"And their efficiency, and even their courage. It was a terrible party, no reconciliation, just confrontation, in the end they almost came to blows. Countries that export raw materials versus those that process them—Cuba versus America. I must agree that our coffee and tea are too cheap and that bananas are almost given away. What astonished me was that Fischer's friends disagreed even more with Herbert's friends than with Rolf's—three worlds."

"A fourth one that we don't know, that of the indifferent, and the fifth, that of the addicts."

"And a further one that's rotting away—like Holger Count Tolm."

"And Eva Klensch—a world of its own. I can't make up my mind where one should place her. We're not qualified to express an opinion, we never were, we weren't prepared, and we still aren't, we're completely out of our depth now—all those young people going off to India, like Kortschede's daughter who was dumped by that student, and she killed herself in that hotel in India, and Kortschede flew there himself to bring back her coffin. That fine old Horrnauken cemetery, deep in the woods, where every second person buried is a Kortschede—in all shapes and sizes: laborers and farmers, businessmen, small shopkeepers—and of course the big-time Kortschedes who made their pile in newsprint, in coal and steel, that huge family of quiet, reticent men and women with fair hair and sad eyes—the priest spoke about 'our Lord, whose rod and whose staff shall comfort us.' So that's where I'll be speaking, surrounded by police officers, mounted police among the trees, armored vehicles on the approaches, helicopters overhead—and no doubt the priest will say once again: 'my rod and my staff . . .'"

"Will you have the courage to read out the letter Kortschede wrote you? I imagine it's some kind of a legacy."

"I won't have the courage, Käthe. I know that without even reading the letter. I've never had any courage, not even that small amount which would have been necessary to prevent the instrument I happened to possess—my newspaper—from sinking to such deplorable standards; not enough courage to put the brakes on Amplanger senior or to keep Amplanger junior at arm's length. I looked on, or failed to notice, as they gradually deactivated my old-timers, and there was always one justification, just one: the public, the readers, who, they claimed, would desert us if we didn't follow the trend. Of course I was attracted by the money, and the successes proved the Amplangers and their cohorts right—I gave way every time. To whom? To myself, till I became exactly like our readers. What did I have to lose? Nothing. There would always be enough for us to live on, for the good life, and maybe it would have been better to allow Zummerling to swallow us long ago, with suitable compensation, instead of us now swallowing other newspapers that consider my paper a shade more liberal and find me a bit more to their liking. Now I'm going to hand it over, remain in the Tolm holding, and Zummerling won't have to swallow me yet because he already has the Amplangers in there. My sons are right: I did not succeed in fooling the system, the system has fooled me."

"You're going to hand over the paper? That's new."

"It no longer makes any sense to lend my name and thus a semblance of liberalness. Let's hope they *have* found a way of monitoring our conversation—then perhaps I really will get the letter meant for me—let's go inside. We'll have some coffee, warm up, and drive to Cologne, there's a new exhibition of Madonnas there that I'd like to see. Shall we ask Miss Klensch if she'd like to come along? Perhaps I can fill in a few gaps in her education, the way I used to with Bleibl's Number Two. We might ask Herbert to join us for lunch, as long as we don't have to go to that horrible high rise of ours. Perhaps Herbert has something to pass on to us under the umbrella." His voice had dropped so low that she had to hold her ear close to his mouth. "Do you have a hand, I mean any money, in that Anti-Auto Action?"

She placed her mouth right against his ear, kissed it quickly, and whispered: "I've managed to talk them out of it. And they gave me back what was left of the money. The plan was simple and terrible: in towns all over the country, some quite widely separated, they rented truck-and-trailer units—fifty-foot monsters, I believe—twenty or thirty of them, I think. According to a precise timetable—which, by the way, your son Herbert figured out—they were going to block all the bridges, all the access roads, all major intersections, placing those huge things somehow across the highway—the idea was to turn the town into a traffic hell within fifteen minutes. They were going to pull out the keys, jump down, and disappear. I explained to them that many people might have fainted, suffered a nervous collapse or a heart attack, or even died—ambulances stuck in traffic and so on and so forth. You can't use the death of others to demonstrate for life, I talked them out of it. Of course they'd had to make down payments or pay compensation to the rental companies—I took back the balance, just to be safe, and yet—when Zummerling called just now . . ."

"You thought they'd done it anyway—and Herbert would be the latest scandal?"

"Yes, after all someone else might have given them the money, they could have got it somehow or other. For a while I trembled each time I listened to the news. It wasn't the scandal I was afraid of—it was the thing itself. It was masterminded by that Wilhelm Pohl, and he really looks like an angel incarnate."

"That's how Kortschede's Petie looks too—like an angel incarnate. He showed me some photos. . . ."

"Yes, I'll remember that, later when you show me your Madonnas. Most of them look like angels too. Well, Tolm, I really made them see all the things that could happen if the center of town were suddenly jammed for any length of time: people would have died, or suffered psychic shocks with long-lasting effects, there would have been fistfights. No, it's not the scandal—the blind involvement in actions with unpredictable results: that's the bad part. And those whom it's supposed to hurt are not hurt: they have their helicopters standing somewhere in a courtyard or on a roof. When all's said and done, Rolf merely set fire to a few cars which he could be certain had no one sitting in them. It's a good idea to have Herbert for lunch and reassure ourselves again. After all, they were fair, wouldn't take a check, only cash. So I'll ask Bleibl over for tea, and for lunch today I'll reserve a table for five, in the private room at Getzloser's, he'll make us a nice lunch. We'll have to invite Blurtmehl too, of course. Those poor Madonnas with their angel faces: I hope they won't wince at the sight of all those machine pistols. Do you really mean to go to the museum today, one day after your election, cause all that commotion?"

"Look, I can't have those hundred and twenty Madonnas sent here, and I intend to see them. Don't forget to let Holzpuke know. By the way, I did enjoy it with you under the umbrella. It was almost like a forbidden secret rendezvous."

"That's what it was."

XIII

Shortly after landing at Frankfurt Airport, a Turkish engineer, traveling on a plane from Istanbul, handed the boy over to the police, who had been alerted by the flight captain. A seven-year-old child who could easily have passed for Turkish, dark-haired, slight, brown-skinned, in jeans, wearing sandal-like shoes, a sort of poncho cape, and a straw hat with a round crown, not quite consistent in style but sufficiently foreign-looking; a quiet boy who even smiled when the Turkish engineer said as he handed him over: "I have the impression this child is dynamite. I was asked to take him with me on my passport, I have an eight-year-old son, but he's stayed behind in Turkey. A woman—I am tempted to say, a lady—handed the boy over to me in Istanbul, flight ticket, five hundred marks, and this letter, which she said was vitally important—for you, the police. Here is the letter, here are the five hundred marks, I don't wish to accept any fee for this slight service. I take the liberty of adding that the lady was in tears. . . ."

"That was my mother," said the boy. It was all he said, even when there was a sudden excitement, amounting to commotion, at the police station, after the Turk had given his address and left. Telephones were picked up, put down again, plainclothes police officers, men in plain clothes not looking at all like police officers. Then a nice woman gave the boy a glass of milk and a piece of cake, although he had sandwiches and a bottle of orange juice in his paper bag. "Tell me, son," the woman whispered urgently, "can you speak Arabic?" He shook his head with a polite smile, keeping his eyes on the door, Veronica had told him: "If photographers turn up you must hide, at least hold the paper bag in front of your face," but none did, there were now more men

in plain clothes around than in uniform. Then one of the uniformed men took him to the phone, and he said: "Hello?"

"Holger, this is Rolf, do you remember me? Do you recognize
my voice, Holger—can you remember Berlin, and Frankfurt?
Holger!"

"Yes, Rolf, and Grandfather—the ducks on the pond, Grandmother Paula—jam—Grandmother Käthe—her cookies—Berlin,
yes . . . how are you . . . ?"

"Fine, fine, just fine. I'm glad you're back. . . . Veronica—you
don't have to say anything. . . ."

"I won't say anything. Are you coming to get me?"

"Yes, no one must know you're back. You know that?"

"Yes."

"You're going to be taken now by helicopter to Grandfather,
you can land in the park, no one will notice, helicopters land
there quite often, I'll pick you up there, in an hour and a half or
so—Holger! I'm so happy—we'll make a big fire, I have a big
garden—and Katharina, do you know Katharina?"

"No . . . but don't I have a brother—a little brother . . . ?"

"Yes, he's also called Holger. We'll have to find a way of
keeping you apart. Well, just come—go along with the police
officers who will be bringing you here. Are you all right? Tell
me!"

"Yes, I'll go with them. I'm all right. Do I have to go to
school right away?"

"No, there's plenty of time for that. Don't worry, just get
here. See you soon."

"Goodbye, Rolf."

Later the officers expressed the opinion that the boy had been not
only calm but cool and collected. Acting on instructions, they
spoke only of harmless matters: from the air they pointed out the
autobahn, the Rhine, the mouths of the Mosel and the Lahn; it
all seemed to interest him: an alert, one might even say a bright

boy who wanted to know the name of every bridge as he sat
there eating his sandwiches—obviously an Oriental type of bread,
incidentally, baked in flat cakes, but with sausage that looked like
a kind of salami—and finding this flight more interesting than
"way up there, because you see more here, almost everything,
you can even see chickens fluttering around down below." No,
there was nothing special about the bottle containing the orange
juice, nothing remarkable, no distinguishing marks. The boy had
even offered the pilot some juice, and the pilot had drunk a bit
from the bottle: no, it hadn't been freshly squeezed orange juice,
just the ordinary stuff one could buy at any supermarket, and no
doubt there were supermarkets in Istanbul too, and orange-juice
multinationals—no, there was nothing remarkable about the juice.
Yet the boy had insisted on taking along bottle and paper bag,
and anyway what more could they have discovered from the
bottle: they already knew who had sent him on his journey, and
they had all read that terse note: "You will bitterly regret it if
you inform the press of Holger's return—and if you try to
question him. Hand him over to his father. Tel. no. below. No
fuss, please! Bev." It hadn't even been typed, but impudently
handwritten on airmail paper, the kind that lay around in
thousands of hotels, these days even in cheap ones.

A nice boy, not a bit aggressive, but not cooperative either;
curious and interested, yes; cooperative, no; alert, asking about
the Niederwald Monument and Ehrenbreitstein Castle, all the
bridges and castles—even minor tributaries like the Wied and the
Ahr—and refusing to reply to the most innocuous questions:
"Must've been pretty hot there, where you came from, mustn't
it?" Gave a kind of significant smile and said only: "Oh, it was
hot all right! But we had snow too, and rain. . . ."

His clothes, superficially observed at any rate, and of course
they had no authority to do more, showed nothing clearly de-
finable: his jeans—well, the kind made by the million; his shirt,
maize yellow, of European cut, but these days they were also
being produced in the Orient; his sandals, nothing specific; his

socks, the most ordinary hand-knitted, homemade kind: the only remarkable items: poncho and hat. The poncho not genuine, certainly not South American, imitation stuff, cotton—they had managed to pull out a few threads. But these things were also available everywhere nowadays: in boutiques, for boutiques, even in department stores. There remained the straw hat, but there had been nothing whatever Arabian about that, it looked quite cheap like that terrible junk sold in tourist centers—could just as easily have been bought in Coblenz as on Crete. And finally the boy himself: more self-possessed than calm, quite obviously on his guard, probably even trained never to give away anything; never anything but polite and, well, unapproachable, actually the only thing he had admitted was that he had felt hot, and as for that you could feel hot anywhere south of Athens or Syracuse. In his pockets apparently nothing more than a few crumpled Kleenexes. He did show some emotion when they saw Cologne Cathedral from above, said: "You can see how big and how small it is"— laughed when they slowly swung toward the manor house, exclaimed: "There they are, the ducks, the ducks!"—and cried when his dad folded him in his arms, that was all. Nothing could be got out of him, but he had actually cried, and his father had too. Following instructions, they had landed as close as possible to the orangery, enabling the boy to get out without being seen and be handed over to his father at the entrance to the orangery; through the orangery into the manor house, from the manor courtyard into Daddy's car, and off. Very sensibly, the old people had not been informed but left to their Madonnas. That was sensible, they would have made a big fuss.

XIV

There were seven photographs in which Veronica Tolm's footwear was visible, altogether four different pairs of shoes with one
thing in common: they were all expensive, as smart as they were
sensible, rather expensive wear for a rebel, brand-name shoes, the
photos taken over a period of five years, and that seemed to indicate that she had remained faithful to that make, and it took only
a single phone call to establish where that make was available in
Istanbul: in five stores and at none of the bazaars, unless—one
never knew what might end up in the bazaars, without the
knowledge of the company—yes, and size 38 was very popular,
and no doubt madam would find what she was looking for in one
of the five stores.

The aircraft carrying the boy had landed at 10:35 a.m., and
the Turkish engineer had been intelligent enough not to rely on
the vagaries of passport control: shortly before landing he had
notified the captain, who in turn had notified the police, thus by
10:50 they already knew about the "delectable cargo" from
Istanbul, about the letter and the warning. The next was routine,
which made him whistle all day long the hit tune he still remembered from the twenties: "Under one umbrella in the evening"—
since he only whistled the tune and wasn't singing the words, he
could mentally supply his own words to the tune: "Under one
umbrella in the morning," and he could laugh too: how naïve she
was, that Käthe Tolm: as if he hadn't known about the preparations for the Anti-Auto Action! As if any group could rent that
many tractor-trailers unobserved! They'd have pounced on them
right away, and there was no way her little Herbert wouldn't
have ended up in jail.

Well, it was a good thing she'd prevented it; he cared just as
little for scandals as she did, but then of course what she hadn't

whispered in the old man's ear was that she had also financed a good number of the Molotov cocktails that had been thrown at and into cars in those earlier days. Not a great deal of money, but still: one had to keep an eye on her, for her own good, she had a somewhat too generous hand—not only for illegal activities, mind you. She supported many people, old Dr. and Mrs. Zelger, for instance, and had tried in vain to get some money into old Beverloh's hands. And he couldn't believe that her son Rolf had tipped her off about the umbrella: surely he knew better. Probably he had said the opposite: never say anything under an umbrella that you don't want anyone to hear—and the old lady had misunderstood him! Good to know, too, that the old man was beginning to rebel: a bit late, but, watch out, he might be capable of spouting some nonsense at the cemetery in Horrnauken, and wait until he saw that letter! They would have to give it to him, he supposed: it was the farewell letter of one of his best friends, but that could wait a few more days. "Under one umbrella in the morning" the two old people had been whispering to each other like lovers. After the phone conversation between Tolm and Zummerling, Dollmer—probably because of Kortschede's letter—had ordered "full alarm." And indeed alarm was appropriate: the old man in rebellion and the boy being sent back meant they were on the march, and it was quite possible that that charming mother of his might need some shoes before starting out. It was fairly certain that they had been lying low for a long time, perhaps for years, in a region where that make was not so easy to come by.

It was just after 11:30 a.m. when he got through to his man in Istanbul; he knew his way around there, must know the city by heart, had been concerned for years with hashish and hippies there, with a whole staff of experienced people, including women who might occasionally go looking for expensive shoes of a certain make and know where to find them. They must know every haunt and hiding place, from the smartest and most expensive hotel to the most miserable hovel; then, too, they had all the pertinent photos and data, for every contingency, although so far Turkey had made no significant entry onto the scene. He had some difficulty in explaining to their man in Istanbul the problem of "knows a lot about women's feet": the latter found it "a bit farfetched," didn't expect anything in the way of results from keeping the five shoe stores under observation. The possibility of catching a big fish, perhaps one of the biggest, seemed in the end to convince the man, but even so he had not only to threaten with Dollmer but to involve him directly and fight his lack of imagination. Dollmer was finally persuaded—and he too only by the mention of the big fish—to reinforce the Istanbul man's motivation and to request official assistance. After all, there wasn't much involved in checking out five shoe stores, later perhaps in Ankara or Iskenderun, where European footwear of that make appeared to be popular too. The returning of the boy was without question an alarming indication. And as to "involvement"—that really made him laugh! After having involved all those men over so many months, all they had caught was that fellow Schubler, Mrs. Breuer's lover, with a pistol of 1912 vintage. Of course official assistance was required: shoe stores were under no obligation to supply information, and he was pretty sure their quarry was no longer in Istanbul, now that the boy had left a trail leading there.

The Turkish engineer hadn't positively identified Veronica Tolm, and the boy's statement: "That was my mother" could have been rehearsed, the tears staged, it was quite possible that they had sent some female accomplice from Lebanon across the border. He didn't want to risk giving the boy a thorough grilling, he really did seem to be a cool and collected little fellow.

There would be no elbow room in Hubreichen, almost impossible to hide the boy, difficult to conceal his origin: he had such a startling resemblance to his father, and the people in the village would begin to wonder, draw their own conclusions, expect to be enlightened, and it wouldn't be long before the press seized upon the cool young customer: the idyll in Hubreichen must be brought to an end, dissolved, particularly since there was trouble with Fischer in the offing—he was afraid of "environmental damage" and was claiming custody.

He had to bring up the massive threat represented by the Zummerling people to persuade Dollmer to make an urgent request for official assistance in the shoe affair. It didn't involve that much: altogether fourteen shoe stores in three cities to be questioned about size-38 women customers, the stores to be kept under observation, photographs to be shown. The Turkish police were always cooperative, Turkish-German relations could stand a minor extra load of that kind, especially as there was glory to be reaped.

On the Madonna front, as he called it to himself, all was quiet, things were running smoothly, quietly, from room to room, and Miss Klensch seemed even to be basking a little in all the attention, while her fiancé sat in the cafeteria reading the newspaper, and good old umbrella-trusting Käthe listened to the explanations of her husband, who for once seemed to have waxed enthusiastic, possibly owing to the rapt attention of Eva Klensch, who seemed to be hanging not only on his lips but on his sleeve, a fact which in turn—as reported in detail by Grobmöhler and his crew, specialists in museums, galleries, concerts, openings, etc.—appeared to amuse nice old Mrs. Tolm. Apparently the swarm of spectators following "in clusters"—as Grobmöhler put it—took pretty Miss Klensch for a daughter or daughter-in-law. At any rate "Cherry Lips"—that was the code name for Miss Klensch—behaved "with deference." All quiet on the Madonna front, and as for the private room at Café Getzloser—that was almost a routine matter, requiring only the usual four men, two in the kitchen, one at the entrance, one in the little courtyard.

In Hubreichen, too: activity but nothing disquieting. Young Papa Tolm, first name Rolf, had talked on the phone with his young son, had thrown down his paintbrush, asked for time off, and unobtrusively collected the little boy in Tolmshoven; surprisingly enough, tears on both sides, tears also from Katharina

Schröter and Sabine Fischer, who questioned the boy about Veronica, evidently to no avail. "But you must know where your mother is, you must know how she is, how she looks. And where does she get her shoes down there? Always walking in desert sand or on sharp rocks—that's terribly hard on them. . . ." The boy—although with more warmth than when replying to the officers—remained cool, saying merely: "She's fine, and she still has shoes. At least I've never seen her with bare feet. Bev is very nice to her."

"Who?"

"Bev." The subject of "Bev" was dropped, the shock must have gone very deep. And of his own accord, unasked, the boy would obviously say nothing. Not even at table. Soup, stew, salad, and bread—when, in answer to questions, he got on the subject of differences in food, he merely said that he had always had enough to eat, and when asked whether he had always liked the food he said no, but added that he hadn't always liked it here either. To questions about games and playmates, as to all other questions, he gave noncommittal answers, until finally his father said firmly, although not angrily: "Don't bother him for a bit, it's quite an adjustment." At table they also discussed and planned for the meeting with the Zelger and Tolm grandparents. He, Holzpuke, didn't want to interfere, that was their private affair. It was first thought that the boy should sleep in the kitchen, since the bishop's room was felt to be rather much for him; but then, after an inspection of the same, the young master graciously consented to take up quarters there, for the time being, "till everything's straightened out," said his father, who around three-thirty calmly went back to his work at the Halster farm. It remained to be seen whether, in the presence of the women and children, the boy wouldn't start talking after all. By five-thirty nothing of the kind was recorded, nor was "Bev" mentioned again; so a call was put through to the grandparents in Hetzigrath and Tolmshoven: great delight on the part of all four old people, somewhat marred by

Schröter and Sabine Fischer, who questioned the boy about Veronica, evidently to no avail. "But you must know where your mother is, you must know how she is, how she looks. And where does she get her shoes down there? Always walking in desert sand or on sharp rocks—that's terribly hard on them. . . ." The boy—although with more warmth than when replying to the officers—remained cool, saying merely: "She's fine, and she still has shoes. At least I've never seen her with bare feet. Bev is very nice to her."

"Who?"

"Bev." The subject of "Bev" was dropped, the shock must have gone very deep. And of his own accord, unasked, the boy would obviously say nothing. Not even at table. Soup, stew, salad, and bread—when, in answer to questions, he got on the subject of differences in food, he merely said that he had always had enough to eat, and when asked whether he had always liked the food he said no, but added that he hadn't always liked it here either. To questions about games and playmates, as to all other questions, he gave noncommittal answers, until finally his father said firmly, although not angrily: "Don't bother him for a bit, it's quite an adjustment." At table they also discussed and planned for the meeting with the Zelger and Tolm grandparents. He, Holzpuke, didn't want to interfere, that was their private affair. It was first thought that the boy should sleep in the kitchen, since the bishop's room was felt to be rather much for him; but then, after an inspection of the same, the young master graciously consented to take up quarters there, for the time being, "till everything's straightened out," said his father, who around three-thirty calmly went back to his work at the Halster farm. It remained to be seen whether, in the presence of the women and children, the boy wouldn't start talking after all. By five-thirty nothing of the kind was recorded, nor was "Bev" mentioned again; so a call was put through to the grandparents in Hetzigrath and Tolmshoven: great delight on the part of all four old people, somewhat marred by the meager news of Veronica. Yes, the ducks on the moat and the blackberry jam from Hetzigrath—and of course the owl—yes, yes, he remembered and was looking forward to seeing them— and yes, they were fine; urgings from both grandmothers not to come today, it would be too much for the boy, and of course they couldn't call old Mr. Beverloh, he didn't have a phone, never had. Silence. The sound of knitting, playing on the floor, chestnuts being roasted, later some singing, or rather humming, the words indistinguishable but it sounded religious.

The lunch at Café Getzloser passed off uneventfully. A discussion of Christianity, Catholic variety, with Miss Klensch and young Herbert Tolm doing most of the talking, controversial, with agreement only on the uniqueness of Jesus, everything else defended by "Cherry Lips," challenged by Herbert: sacraments and divine service, celibacy and the priesthood as such, not a single word of criminalistic relevance, no reference to the canceled Anti-Auto Action. An interesting group indeed: the converted and friendly "Cherry Lips," her fiancé, a quiet one but known to have a fondness for folk dancing, also for songs that he sang to the guitar—folk songs, no pop—and then that Herbert, quite a nice boy actually, a bit too inclined to philosophize, a believer in Jesus but not in Jesus-people, and it was really quite interesting, the way he argued with the Klensch woman, but nothing, nothing, of criminalistic interest.

The analysis of the letter paper had produced nothing new: needless to say, Beverloh's fingerprints were pure cheek, but no surprise since his handwriting was recognizable anyway. The paper itself gave no hints, sold by the thousand, available in every hotel, at every stationer's, in Turkey, in the Near, Middle, and Far East. . . .

.   .   .

His choice for the inner circle around the grave in Horrnauken would have been Grobmöhler and his cultural crew: they were men trained to be discreet, men who had never yet been conspicuous at any opening, and after all it was quite in order to classify a funeral as a cultural scene. The terrain there was difficult: woodland paths, drainage ditches, bicycle paths, camping, playground, and cooking areas, much favored for outings by their Dutch neighbors. Another two or three days, and the "bucket" might already be on its way. Fortunately there was that very comfortable inn in Horrnauken, venison, quiet rooms, and he might even squeeze out a few hours of relaxation, or even half a day, while he was scrutinizing maps, details of which had to be checked on the ground, and arranging for the placing of the various security cordons. Scarcely anyone of rank and reputation would fail to be there; fortunately Kortschede had been a Protestant, so there would be no Catholic dignitaries. But one never knew, perhaps protocol allowed for the presence of cardinals, too. They grasped every opportunity, accepted any risk, at times one was tempted to suspect that they positively lusted after publicity and danger. Too bad he had to do without Zurmack, Lühler, and Hendler. Of course he wouldn't have sent them on a training course if he had known what he would be up against. But surely to recall them now would be senseless. No doubt they were all packed, and after all Horrnauken was in the jurisdiction of a different *Land* of the Federal Republic.

Apparently Mrs. Breuer and her lover were now looking around Hubreichen for a place to stay and for jobs; otherwise quiet reigned there as well. Apparently the runaway priest had returned too, and intended to face his church council, the community as a whole. That was a good thing, that distracted attention from the cool young customer, who seemed to be accepting his restriction to cottage and garden; presumably was used to that.

When he phoned Dollmer to report his move to Horrnauken,

he detected traces of geniality in his voice that should have made him suspicious. Dollmer was really almost nice, said with a laugh: "Turkish honey action is under way," was satisfied with the smooth course of events on the Madonna front, once again strongly advised against grilling the boy, and at the mention of the expected crush in Hubreichen said: "We'll end up having to find a monastery for the whole gang. Then Fischer won't be able to claim environmental damage. So, have a good trip, and rest up a bit, if you can."

All quiet in Blorr. Deathly silence.

XV

As the day wore on, the boy seemed to her more and more weird, as if wound up, embalmed, mummified: at table, walking in the park, on the balcony, in the corridors, in the courtyard. She called him her "frozen grandson"; he told her nothing, allowed nothing to be wormed out of him: Where had he spent those two and a half years? How? Nothing. He had grown handsomer than ever, those eyes, gray-blue, reminded her of the surface of volcanic lakes; cold ("He gets his eyes from you," Tolm claimed). The ducks drew a laugh from him, he said they looked stuffed. But when she asked him whether he had ever eaten stuffed duck, he just laughed and spoke of Grandma Paula's jam and the helicopter flight, reeled off the names of the tributaries of the Rhine, monuments, churches, cathedrals, bridges; a cold, frozen map. And amused himself by ramming his head against Tolm's stomach, over and over again. No, not against his heart, not yet, though he did resemble a vigorous ram. And all the time that wretched telephoning: Dollmer obviously refusing to accept the call, Stabski claiming ignorance, Dollmer's deputy disclaiming any authority, Holzpuke said to have left to organize the security measures for Kortschede's funeral, and both Kulgreve and

Amplanger "regretting" that they couldn't get hold of anyone. Tolm became impatient, then angry, finally shouted at Amplanger: "I want my letter, I want the letter!" She had never seen him so furious, not once in thirty-five years: Tolm in a rage, genuinely furious, that was something new. He skipped his bath, refused to phone Grebnitzer, smoked, suggested to Blurtmehl that he occupy himself with the boy: apparently he too was afraid of his own grandson, whom he had so sorely missed. This child, this stranger, coolly grabbed éclairs, refused tea, insisted on lemonade, dashed about the corridors, and made the officers jittery by aiming at them with imaginary machine pistols, imitating their rat-a-tat with startling realism.

There were now eight of them, three in the corridor, two on the stairs, three in the courtyard: she knew only one—he had been at the museum with them that morning, a quiet fellow who, in the face of Holger I's cold restlessness, had difficulty in remaining quiet and polite. He stood there shaking his head as he watched Miss Klensch take bow, arrows, and target from the trunk of her car and suggest some archery practice with the boy in the orangery. She was a member of an archery club, she said, always kept everything in the car, and made use of every opportunity to practice, even when she was traveling; the boy had turned down all "conventional games" but had jumped at the idea of archery.

Holzpuke's deputy examined the bow, which seemed remarkably powerful, examined the metal-reinforced tips of the arrows, seemed put out that Miss Klensch should have "slipped through" the controls with this equipment, would only permit the game subject to the approval of his superior, took the sheaf of arrows with him when he stepped aside to obtain instructions over his transceiver. Who was he talking to? Was Holzpuke somewhere around after all, was there something going on? What? The officers were all so serious, so close-mouthed, Miss Klensch was embarrassed, almost offended, that gay, enigmatic little person who had been of such help to her in the kitchen, making the éclairs, whipping the cream. Miss Klensch protested that this was a kind of shooting that made no noise at all, she praised the almost soundless whirring of the arrow, the quivering in the target, the "spiritual dimension" of archery, and she had a hard time restraining her impatience when the officer declared that he was sorry but he must "temporarily take charge of the equipment, one never knows what children might get up to—after all, it is a weapon." Miss Klensch insisted with some asperity on its being called "sporting equipment." The officer confirmed her definition but added that some sporting equipment happened also to be a weapon, or capable of being used as a weapon: spear, hammer, hockey stick, even balls of hard material. "This area is regarded as an extremely high security risk—I am sorry. When you leave—of course . . ." There was barely a trace of irony, only extreme tension in her voice when she asked whether they needed to know her date of birth, address, occupation. The officer answered almost gently: "That won't be necessary, that information is all known, to me too." For a fraction of a second it looked as if Miss Klensch were going to fly into a rage—then she burst into tears, threw herself on Käthe's breast, and sobbed: "What kind of life is this? . . . Oh, Mrs. Tolm—I wish we could dissolve into thin air." Throughout all this, Blurtmehl had shown no sign of personal emotion, even now remained calm, smiled, and said: "Then I had better take the young master back to Hubreichen, especially since, if I may remind you, you are expecting a guest."

Oh yes, now she remembered for whom she had made the éclairs, it was Bleibl: she had asked him what his favorite pastries were, and he had answered: "At teatime, éclairs—I'm looking forward to coming."

She held the young woman back when Blurtmehl walked to the car with the boy, and said: "Stay with us, it's a bad day and it's going to get worse."

Tolm stood at the window, probably waiting for his birds,

certainly for the owl, but it wouldn't be flying that early; it wouldn't be deceived by the somber sky and the darkness over the park, it only flew at dusk, and that was still another hour or two away. Maybe a few crows would come, the swallows had already left. He didn't turn to her, sounded so dry, almost morose, as, barely turning his head, he said: "I managed to get hold of him, of Dollmer—they won't give me the letter. Nobody's going to get it, he says it's dynamite."

"So no funeral, no oration, no nostalgia in the glades of Horrnauken?"

"No oration, no, no funeral in Horrnauken, but a different one in Hetzigrath . . . yes, Käthe." And at last he turned, put his arms around her, laid his head on her shoulder, smiled at Miss Klensch, and said: "They got him, buying shoes in Istanbul. He is dead, they say he killed himself. Not Veronica, she's disappeared, gone to earth, she wasn't with him. . . ."

"Shoes," she said, "that means . . . under the umbrella. . . . Tolm, I won't say another word. I can't even cry. Eva, please, make us some tea, a big pot of strong tea."

"In future we'll do what we did in the hotel in Moscow: write notes and flush them down the toilet, but they'll invent baskets to catch the scraps of paper, pick them out of the shit, and stick them together. Just a moment, I have something to tell you. . . ." He pulled away from her, went to the desk, tore a strip off the newspaper, wrote something on it, and brought it to her. She read: "I love you, I've always loved you, the children too, even him, don't say anything. . . ."

She kissed him, tore up the note, went into the bathroom, and flushed it down the toilet.

"He's going to be buried here?"

"Yes, I'm paying for the transportation. I insisted that he be buried here—they've had to put his father away. Dollmer is demanding his price: silence about the letter. Don't speak, Käthe, don't speak, we have to get used to writing again. By the way, the vicarage in Hubreichen is empty, maybe for good. There would be room for us all there, even Herbert and Blurtmehl—it would only need a bit of remodeling, it would be easy to protect and keep under surveillance—lovely trees. . . ."

"Owls in the church tower—little screech owls in the rafters of the barns, I shudder at the thought, Tolm."

"Don't you shudder here?"

"I do, and in Hubreichen I'll shudder too—everywhere. I . . ." She took the ballpoint from his waistcoat pocket, went to the desk, tore off the top of the front page, and wrote along the edge: "Never again will I be able to buy shoes, never again. Luckily Sabine takes my size—but I won't be needing many more shoes, not me."

Bleibl was punctual and turned up carrying a magnificent bouquet: white lilac and red roses veiled in yellow mimosa. He brought the flowers in himself, removed the paper, and she was surprised to see how serious he looked, pensive in a way; changed, like Tolm and the boy. The day of great changes: of the frozen grandson, of a newly determined Tolm, of a pensive Bleibl, who even helped—although it was not quite "done"—to arrange the flowers in a tall vase. How surprising, those hands of his—she had never noticed them before: strong and slender, very different from that quite brutal-looking face, the knobbly, knotty nose, the totally bald head that had not exposed a well-formed cranium. He looked in frank admiration at Eva Klensch as she brought in the tea and the rose-patterned china dish with the freshly made éclairs.

"I'm actually going to have some tea," he said, nodding to them, and, dropping his voice, added: "I've heard the news, I've heard all about it—including the change of cemetery. You know, they'll have your head for this. . . ."

"Yes," said Tolm, "I know, I'll be glad to get rid of it—this head of mine. . . ."

"Stabski has asked me to have one more talk with you. But I know it's no use—is it?"

"It's no use, Bleibl, you can save yourself the trouble."

"It's a funny thing but I was sure you would be adamant, although you're the least adamant person I know. Today, I don't know why, I knew you wouldn't change your mind. I'm glad for your sake—not for ours, no, not for ours—and not because of the brief tenure. President for a day, that's pretty embarrassing, and not even because of that—you were the right man for us, and I never intended to destroy you, never. All I wanted to do was force you to be tenacious, in fact to train you. . . ."

"So now you've succeeded. . . . Don't eat too many éclairs, they're very deceptive—watch it!—won't you change your mind and have a whiskey?"

"No, later, I'd like to be sober when I talk to you both. . . ."

His eyes followed Eva Klensch with unconcealed desire after she had brought in the milk, lemon, and sugar. "My God," he said, "who is that woman?"

"Forget it, she's spoken for, she's Blurtmehl's girlfriend."

"I'd marry her on the spot."

"You've . . ." Käthe poured the tea and blushed.

"Married too often on the spot—that's what you were going to say, wasn't it?"

"More or less—not exactly—but please, not her, Bleibl . . . please. . . ."

"I've never yet taken somebody else's wife away, never—I hope you realize that. Someone took mine—that goddamn leftist aesthete, that Botticelli-worshipper—and that's a fact."

"Do you still hanker after Margret?"

"No, not the least little bit. It's just that: you may laugh but I've always respected commitments, so never fear: your masseur's in no danger of losing that exquisite flower." It was strangely alarming to see him cry, suddenly burst into tears, the brutal-looking face dissolve, under the heavy upper lip, the unexpectedly narrow lower lip, the face twitching with emotion. "Oh, my God, Kortschede," he muttered, "and now that goddamn boy—if you only knew what I have in the vault, I've got something down there in the vault." No, there was nothing humorous about the way he nodded through his tears when Tolm held out the whiskey bottle. "Goddammit, do you know how that terrible boy, that mathematical genius, killed himself—no? They don't tell you that kind of secret, do they? Dollmer has already given the thing a name: the hands-up-spring-gun-machine. You don't understand, do you? That boy built himself a kind of waistcoat that went off when he put his hands up! One half inward, the other—the left—outward: a kind of mini-rocket-launcher to be worn over the chest like a flat life jacket. They're still taking the thing apart. Killed a Turkish policeman, severely wounded a German, and as for himself—well, you can imagine what he looks like—madness—in any event Dollmer is now scared to death of anyone putting his hands up. And now this letter of Kortschede's, which must be terrible. . . ."

"Have you seen it?"

"No, no one has, apart from Dollmer, Stabski, Holzpuke, and the two officers who found Kortschede. Total blackout. Incidentally, Zummerling hasn't seen it either."

"And it was written to me?"

"Yes, I believe it starts with 'My dear Fritz'—and then I'm sure come some grim prophecies—about the environment, nuclear energy and growth and banks and industry—they're bound to be grim—it was written to you, and you have the right to receive it. See to it that you get your rights, and make sure, both of you, that no one—no one, do you hear?—finds out about the funeral in Hetzigrath. I suppose I'll have to give the oration in Horrnauken. You won't object if we say you're ill, seriously ill? I suppose he doesn't have any relatives left? You know they had to actually put his father into a straitjacket."

"He has an aunt still living, she should . . ."

"She should nothing. . . ." He spoke very softly, had tears in had no children from any of them except Hilde, his Number One, who had been the nicest, nicer even than Number Three, whose peasant-girl arrogance had sometimes been too much for her, that austere beauty really had despised everything except herself, and had sold herself at a high enough price.

Tolm remained distrustful, almost cold, Bleibl's tears obviously embarrassed him; he gave an impression that was entirely new: he seemed determined. "All right then," he said quietly, "you can say I am ill—I leave the details to you. And we'll keep his aunt out of it. Just the two of us—and the gravediggers."

"No priest?"

"No, he wouldn't have wanted it, and I'd like to respect that. Besides, the Hetzigrath priest at Beverloh's grave?" He laughed. "No, he'd die on us from fear. No, Käthe can say a prayer, he wouldn't have minded that. Perhaps Veronica will turn up—or phone. I am sure Kortschede would have understood."

Thirty-three years, she thought, and they had never exchanged a sensible word, not one; never anything but that joshing and mild flirting, and finding some common ground: now the dollar was falling again, and gold rising, because somewhere there had been a putsch, she didn't even know by whom against whom, had merely glanced at the financial section of the paper; and the dollar would rise again, and gold would fall because somewhere else someone else had started a putsch, never mind against whom.

"You can stay for supper," she said, "if you like, and of course you can sleep here too, your apartment is free now. Kulgreve has had it all fixed up again."

"No, no," said Bleibl, "thanks, but no. You two have no idea what you have set in motion with this funeral, what utter confusion you have caused, it's going to deprive at least a hundred police officers of their leave or day off, and Stabski and Dollmer their sleep, and Holzpuke will be cursing: he has enough on his hands in Horrnauken. It's madness, Tolm, what you have in mind, sheer madness—I can't talk you out of it—or you, Käthe, or you him?"

his eyes again. "Keep her out of it, don't take anyone with you! Don't say anything to your children either . . . please, please, no crowds, no scenes—I wouldn't put it past Sabine . . ." He poured himself some tea, took another éclair.

"You're right," said Tolm. "I wouldn't put it past Sabine to come along."

"Fischer's coming back because of Kortschede, cutting his trip short. So she's not likely to go to Horrnauken. He's going to make trouble for you, even more after the funeral, and with more valid arguments . . . that uncle, that uncle's girlfriend—and now these grandparents! Oh, it's a shame that Sabine's left Fischer! Good God, what an idiot, a woman like that—and he leaves her, leaves her alone! I would never have left a woman like that alone, I never left Hilde alone either, there was only that vault I couldn't take her into—I was alone down there, lonely, and no one noticed, scared to death, and no one noticed. Funny, when I was talking to Dollmer just now, and later when Stabski phoned me, when I heard all about it, how that terrible boy, surrounded by shoeboxes, set off his hands-up device—and they were all ladies' shoes size thirty-eight which he had had sent up to the hotel to choose from —I don't know, but suddenly I was able to get out of that vault— I had to cry, I cried all morning, and I was glad that the girl—your Veronica—wasn't in the room . . . was glad against my own convictions, I hope she'll turn up alive, hope it against my own convictions, against all my principles. You two are going to be very lonely after this funeral, very lonely—you know that?"

"Yes," she said, "we always have been, really, we just weren't aware of it, didn't want to know it." She poured him some whiskey, but he not only shook his head, he shook himself, and without embarrassment wiped the tears from his eyes with his handkerchief, lifted the teacup, put it down again without drinking, looked toward the door through which Eva had disappeared. My God, how much sadness there must be in him, and what in the world was that vault where he had sat all alone and had come out of? And whyever had he had to marry them all right away—he'd

"No, you can't. Is that why you came, or because you—because you've managed to get out of your vault?"

"I came to see you both, to talk to you, that was all arranged before—you know that. It's simply that Stabski and Dollmer urged me to grasp the opportunity—you can't imagine . . . it's madness, Tolm. Even if the cemetery authorities keep mum, and the gravediggers too—a hundred police officers won't keep mum. . . ."

"You misunderstand me—I'm neither asking for it to be kept secret, nor do I want it to become known. I'm simply going to a funeral. I want that boy Heinrich to be returned to the earth from which he was made—from which I too am made—that's all. I'm not trying to prove anything, one way or another, and I know that Kortschede wrote me that letter so that I would get it, read it, and perhaps make use of it. I am honoring his memory and his intention by *not* going to Horrnauken. After all, we knew Heinrich as a child, as a boy—no, you won't talk me out of it—how about you, Käthe?"

"No, if it were possible I would say: even less so. Even without you I would have gone to this funeral. But of course I'd rather go with you."

"That'll be totally misinterpreted, totally, both consciously and unconsciously—three days after your election. . . . Would you change your mind if you were to get the letter after all?"

"Don't tell me you have it in your pocket?"

"Don't be so unkind! No, I haven't, I haven't even seen it. I'm just thinking of alternatives. You in Horrnauken, Käthe in Hetzigrath—for your own sakes, believe me, for your own sakes. I care no more than you do for these pompous funerals."

"It's too late, Bleibl, too late, the letter is mine anyway, and even if I were to get it—I've made up my mind. . . ."

"You must admit the Horrnauken funeral is one of your official duties. . . ."

"Which I am neglecting, and for which, as you say, I am risking my head. . . . Forget it, Bleibl, stay for supper, have a drink with us—let's celebrate the vault we've emerged from, you and I. I know: they'll say I've become senile. Never mind—I'll make it easy for you to get rid of me, let Amplanger finally have his turn. I'm glad you came, stay awhile, we might have a game of cards? I'd enjoy that."

"No, thanks, I have to leave. I still have to have a word with Hilde—I have a favor to ask. Would you put in a good word for me in that quarter, Käthe?"

"I could, but I won't. It won't help you and it would only offend Hilde. When are you going to grasp the fact that she alone has to make the decision? And you alone. Later, when you've come to an agreement, yes—not now. Will you still come to see us? After the funeral, I mean?"

"How can you doubt that? Do you really doubt it?"

"Not anymore. No. And don't try again to change our minds."

"I was just about to."

She kissed him goodbye, and they both accompanied him down the stairs to the courtyard, where he got into his car. He waved once more. She was amazed at how easily Tolm walked up the stairs, hardly using the banister at all.

"Now give your bishop a call," she said, and when he looked at her inquiringly: "About the vicarage in Hubreichen. We can't stay here."

XVI

One hour after the news of Bev's death, which they heard on the radio, the invasion had begun, the guards were reinforced and the reporters moved in. Now the guards were posted around the wall on all sides, three to a side, and he had immediately called the children into the house from the garden, where they had been picking up nuts and apples off the ground. They were after the boy, of course, believing that Veronica would show up, were waiting; waiting for what?

Shortly before that, Erna Breuer had arrived with her lover. He had recognized her at once from her resemblance to her brother and mother, a distraught woman who complained about the noise, the noise, the noise in town, then withdrew with Sabine and her boyfriend into the bedroom, where he could hear them whispering and complaining. He had advised her not to go out, to wait, if necessary in the vicarage: she would be photographed with her boyfriend the minute she appeared, her case would be recalled, and she would be linked up with a situation where she did not belong and from which she would never escape. After many attempts he had finally reached Roickler by telephone, and the priest had given him permission "to let a few guests stay in the vicarage if necessary. I'd better go there, look after the guests myself—yes, of course I know Erna Hermes, she can stay at my place, with her boyfriend too. I'm coming. Don't worry. They'd better all stay in the house. No, I'll be leaving Anna here."

Katharina had suggested phoning Hermes and asking him to have one of the boys bring over the milk. He said no, he would go himself, even if they were to photograph him to death; he would go if only to feel out the mood of the village, if only perhaps to stick out his tongue at them or raise a clenched fist and shout: "Socialism will win!"—his other hand carrying the four-liter pitcher.

At first Holger I had not grasped the news of Bev's death, then he asked a strange question: "Did he . . . himself?" And when he nodded the boy had burst into tears, asked for his mother, and clung to him: "But Rolf, Rolf, *you're* my father!"

"Yes, I'm your father—you'll stay with me, and I'll stay with you—Veronica is alive—you'll talk to her soon. . . . Bev wanted it like that, the way it happened. Believe me, he wanted it that way. Now you can go into the shed with Mr. Schubler and split some wood, we'll have to keep the stove going all night."

Phoning. Phoning. With Father, Mother, Herbert, all of whom he reassured and asked not to come. "No, please don't, Herbert. You'll run into a barrage of flashbulbs."

Don't worry. That was easily said when, to top it all, Fischer phoned and Katharina happened to bear the brunt. He heard her low voice saying: "Yes, Erwin, she's here, I'll get her for you," and he could tell from her face that Fischer must have made a nasty remark. "Very well, Mr. Fischer, if you don't like using first names with Communists and resent even more their using yours, *Mister* Fischer, I'll get her for you. . . ." But Sabine raised her hand in a gesture of refusal, shook her head, and Katharina said: "Mrs. Fischer does not wish to speak to you. Yes, I'll give her the message—the custody!"

Finally he suggested they make some pancakes and put on some coffee, ordered them all not to leave the house, grabbed the milk pitcher, neither stuck out his tongue nor raised his clenched fist, merely held up the red-enamel pitcher into the blazing fire of the flashbulbs, and set out for the Hermes farm. It was cold, dark, drizzling, he had forgotten to put on his parka and hurried along. He was later than usual, he had to go over to the Hermeses' kitchen to ask for someone to come out, and he stopped in the doorway, gave an awkward laugh, and swung the pitcher. He felt embarrassed at interrupting their supper, they looked so cheerful sitting there in front of their bowls and plates, and he wasn't sure whether what showed in their faces was suspicion, curiosity, or surprise. He was relieved when young Hermes got up, nodded at him, and went across with him into the dairy. "You should warm up a bit," he said as they crossed the yard.

"I have to get back in a hurry, they are all frightened—waiting."

"Tell my sister she's welcome any time. There can't be much room at your place."

"I didn't want her to be photographed under the circumstances. You never get rid of pictures like that. I'd like her to wait till the mob has left—tomorrow, or the day after. The priest is going to help us."

"He's coming back?"

"Yes, he wants to talk to you all—he's coming for our sakes too."

"Was that—was this—was he your friend?"

"Yes, until seven years ago. We were at school together, in the army, both of us in the artillery—at university—yes, I knew him well."

"And his wife?"

"Was my wife, in those days. We separated."

He was glad that Hermes asked him such forthright questions, didn't protest when Hermes refused the money for the milk and said: "Not today—tell my sister it's for her—and her friend. It'll pass, one, maybe two days and they'll be gone. You must know what they're like."

"Yes, I've been through it twice. I'm only afraid they'll get your sister, Mr. Schubler, and the boy. They're standing there as if they wanted to storm the garden gate or tear down the walls— all because of the boy. I'd like to thank you, on behalf of your sister too. She is sick, from the noise, the noise, the noise—that's how she put it. . . ."

"If things get bad, I'll have one of the boys bring you the milk. . . ."

He didn't raise the pitcher when he ran into the flashes again. Dazzled, he stopped for a few seconds, saw only shadows and hands and flashes before unlocking the garden gate.

Schubler and Holger I were stacking wood beside the stove, Erna Breuer was making pancakes—was she really as happy as she looked, or merely flushed from the heat? Sabine and Katharina were knitting, Kit and Holger II were playing with the building blocks and animals, there was coffee on the table; he sat down between the two women, lit a cigarette, and thought about money. It didn't seem to have occurred to anyone that this was likely to become a rather expensive household, first five instead of three, then six people, now eight, and so far he had always refused to accept money from Käthe or Father. He was sure Sabine didn't have any money, she was one of those who live without cash, and he was certain she would get nothing from Fischer, probably no more than the minimum support for the child if he wasn't successful in his custody claim. Probably Sabine was a bit too naïve, too gullible. There were thousands of tricks and dodges to bring her to her knees, in public and in court, and there was no getting around the fact that Holger I was the child of a terrorist. He couldn't make head or tail of the boy, they had thoroughly and ruthlessly silenced him, perhaps with threats, and he was sure Veronica had had to fight hard for his release. Not a sound, not a word, was to be got out of the boy, in a chilly way he was polite, said "thank you" and "please," had proudly demonstrated that he could already write, in German; only once, when he took the boy unawares with a question about Bev, he said: "He was good to me and—" and had clammed up. Now there was really no reason for him not to speak, the shoes having wrecked the whole affair.

He was surprised that Holzpuke didn't show up or call. After all, now it was also the boy's safety that was at stake, and he couldn't guarantee that. No doubt there was still a group of lunatics around Bev and Veronica who hadn't been in favor of sending the boy home. The bucket riders were sure to be already on their way, and Holzpuke was no doubt wrongly assuming that the bucket ride wouldn't take place. Yet Horrnauken cemetery was situated right in the middle of a recreation area that was swarming with cyclists, close to the Dutch border. Even in November and in the rain there would be cyclists arriving since there were huts and covered camping sites, campfire areas, and it had already become quite a fad to go on cycling tours in the rain; he had seen it at the funeral of Verena Kortschede, he had met her in Berlin, had had tea sometimes at her place with Veronica. She had fallen for a trendy leftist and committed suicide when it turned out that he was only after her money—a loathsome character, a lousy sponger, he had left that quiet, sad, pale-blond girl in the lurch in India when it turned out that she wasn't getting much money at all. She had written on the hotel mirror with her lipstick: "Socialism will prevail," and had taken poison.

Sabine had said nothing, had not cried, when she heard about Bev's death; she had merely drawn Holger I close to her and said: "Veronica is alive, she's alive. She'll come back."

Schubler and Holger seemed to be hitting it off, they brought in some more wood, the women sat silently beside him, the children on the floor. Erna called across from the stove: "There's a dozen ready, we can start—one and a half for each—with syrup." The snug atmosphere had returned. He helped Erna divide up the pancakes and put them on the plates, gave her her brother's message and told her about the donated milk and that she would be welcome. "Peter too?" she asked.

"He was included in the milk donation."

"Also in the 'welcome home'? No—am I right? By the way, he knew you in Berlin, in the days when he was throwing rocks and tomatoes. . . ."

"I read about it in the paper, and for that very reason neither he nor you should go outside the house before the photographers have left, and it's not only the reporters who are taking pictures."

"Where can we stay, then?"

"It would be better to spend the night here on a chair than to find yourself in the newspaper tomorrow. Come along, let's sit in there on the bed. We have enough plates, but not enough chairs."

Sabine made room for Schubler in the kitchen and sat down beside Erna Breuer, asking softly: "So it's really true? You're sure?"

"Yes, I waited longer than usual because I wanted to be sure—

I didn't go to the doctor till yesterday, and there's no doubt whatever: I'm already in the fourth month—so Breuer lied to me about that too; it wasn't me, it was him. I'd just like to know where his first wife got her kids from. He probably closed his eyes to a lot of things in her case too—and I suppose that's sufficient grounds for annulling our marriage—and that'll make my parents more reasonable. I want so much to stay here, I never want to go back to that apartment. I simply can't stand it anymore!"

"You'll find a place, I'm sure, and a job too, and I—I believe I really will go to Paris. I'm so very sorry, it really grieves me to think of all that's happened to you."

"I think about it differently now, I suppose it had to happen that way. It was unpleasant, especially for Peter. But a lot of things have been resolved for him too, and he's as happy about it as I am. It's funny, I daren't say it aloud but, you know, we can thank those maniacs for it, those crazy criminals. It makes me quite dizzy to think that, yet I do think it: those people and the police—it's really a joke. Oh, if only this siege were over!"

Suddenly the bells started ringing, the church was brightly lit, lights were being switched on in every room in the vicarage, even the garden was bathed in light. They all set aside their plates, put down their cups, went to the door. Schubler opened it; now they could not only hear the rain but see it, and the guards standing between vestry and vicarage.

"Don't go out, no one is to go out!" Rolf said sharply. He yanked Schubler back from the threshold: "They're sitting right on the wall, just waiting for someone to show his face—if anyone has to go out it'll be me, they have me anyway. Roickler's back, he'll give his speech or his sermon. And you will be sleeping in a nice wide bed," he said to Erna, "don't worry. And it'll be quiet, there won't be a sound."

·   ·   ·

When Erna asked if they had a game that several could play, he suggested Monopoly; she looked at him in amazement, then felt embarrassed, asked: "You—Monopoly? In your home?"

Katharina, who was already pulling the game out from the shelf and opening it out onto the table, said with a smile: "We're the very people who must know Monopoly and play it, it has to be played ruthlessly, that makes it the best introduction for children to learn about the cruelties of capitalism. The cruelties of socialism, of course, are something they learn in school."

Solemn Peter Schubler smiled, said he would look on or cut up some more wood, and Holger I said: "But then you'll have to go alone, I want to play with the others, we often played it in . . . ," broke off, blushed, and when everyone looked at him expectantly said: "I mean—in the place where I was, we played it. . . ."

Sabine, insisting she must have "a breath of air," went outside in spite of his warning headshake, and when he pulled back the curtain and opened the shutters they could see the flashbulbs above the top of the wall. Sabine hesitated, walked on toward the vestry, then closer to the wall and stuck out her tongue at them. A good thing she's not clenching her fist, he thought, even so there would be a few misinterpretations, but not too many. Anyway she would—one way or another—get into the headlines, and the garden, the brightly lit church in the background, the guard standing in front of it, would all make a fine picture. Katharina had picked up the dice. "Come along, everybody, let's throw for who starts."

XVII

Not content with merely pinpointing the guards' positions on the map, he had taken them personally to the various locations, where they had discussed the positions in detail, tested visibilities, and paced out the intersections of the cycling paths, the rest areas, and the camping sites. The rain would keep off many cyclists but not all, some of them were already on their way. He issued orders for checkpoints. His suggestion of cordoning off the entire recreation area until after the funeral had been rejected, Dollmer had laughed at his bucket theory and, after talking to Stabski, had said there would be trouble with Holland if they cordoned off the area: bad press, crazy Germans, and all that. He also decided where the two armored vehicles were to be stationed: one among the trees behind the cemetery chapel, the other at the point where several cycling paths crossed the road. Grobmöhler wasn't coming till tomorrow, the day of the funeral, when he and his men would secure the chapel from the inside as well as the route to the grave and the grave itself. Furthermore someone had, as Dollmer put it, "contrived some ecumenical crap again," a Catholic was coming after all, a bishop probably, who wasn't likely to let himself be done out of saying a few words, TV coverage being guaranteed, of course. No doubt—it wouldn't be the first time either—the bishop would speak about the "fellowship of sufferers," totally oblivious as always. Certainly no one would have told him anything about Petie, about the mutilated face, let alone about that terrible letter which by this time had become a sort of top Federal secret. Anyone who knew about Petie, about the mutilated face, about the existence of the letter, even if not the contents—and he felt sure the two officers had leaked them, certainly to some of their colleagues—anyone who knew anything would feel a sense of embarrassment. Sacrificial life, sacrificial death. Things like that did nothing to raise the morale of his men, it was all so distasteful and made them cynical.

He cursed with rage on hearing, from the landlady of all people, that they had actually caught Beverloh in Istanbul, and that he was to phone Dollmer immediately—Dollmer having of course stolen a march on him by holding the press conference without him. The landlady had heard the press conference on the radio and said something about "thanks to some clues pointing to certain purchases, the result of our own deductions."

Damn it all, there were such things as transceivers, as helicopters, but apparently Dollmer hadn't wanted to share these juicy spoils with anybody, yet he had laughed at his suggestion about possible shoe purchases. He cursed openly and copiously when Dollmer went on to tell him about the old Tolms' crazy idea: that meant at least fifty men for that godforsaken hole. The entire scene might blow wide open, there would be crowds of people, and if to top it all the old couple should turn up, there would be—would be a scandal, and those two nice old characters would be ruined. "That has to be stopped, Mr. Dollmer," he said, "if necessary by force—with roadblocks, by arranging a minor accident—somehow or other that *must* be stopped. If you can't get anywhere by reasoning."

"Are you suggesting I arrest him?" Dollmer shouted.

"No, I told you—roadblocks, arrange for a few accidents, bashed cars making the road impassable."

"Then he'll simply walk there. . . ."

"But he'll get there too late, the funeral will be over. As it is, I have to cancel all the training courses, call back many of the men from leave, and I'm not even thinking of the problems for the police, we're used to those, I'm thinking of the political consequences. . . ."

"Mind you, they've known Beverloh from infancy, he was almost like a son to them, at least for many years. You're forgetting something again, my dear Holzpuke . . . are you listening? You're forgetting that letter! What would be worse politically: for him to receive the letter and publish it, or for him to get a bee in his bonnet and go to the wrong funeral? The letter, if he publishes it—and he wouldn't hesitate—will affect us all, everyone involved: the wrong funeral will only affect him. Stabski completely agrees with me, we've discussed it from every possible angle, and once it becomes known that the letter exists it won't take long for its contents to become public. Well, what do you say?"

"Even so I would see to it that a few wrecks get hopelessly entangled on all the access roads. Of course they'll have to be supplied with license plates. In any event I'll cancel all the training courses. Well, what do you say to shoe size thirty-eight?"

"Terrific, practically a stroke of genius. It won't pass without leaving its mark on your career. But there's one thing, I believe, we can forget about now: there'll be no bucket trip."

"I'm not so sure about that. After all, she did get away, and there are still the sympathizers."

He started several times to call the manor house, kept sighing, picking up the receiver, replacing it, had to force himself to dial, and was startled when he heard her voice saying: "Yes?" He was silent for a few seconds, until she said: "Who is it, please—who's there?" He diffidently gave his name, adding: "Don't be alarmed —you can imagine what I'm calling about. . . ."

"Yes, I can—but we won't succumb to your blandishments either. No, my dear Mr. Holzpuke, you have become a good companion to us—I'm only interested in one thing: am I now going to get my reward? You know, because of the shoes, which, you must admit—yes, it's odd, I mourn his death but I'm not sad about it—can you understand that? And the shoes, the reward— am I going to get it?"

Oh damn, he thought, I mustn't cry. He was close to it, he had heard it all, all the things the old couple had whispered to each other like lovers, about adultery and no adultery, about Madonnas and children. And every single argument, even those one called or might have called human, was on his side. He too would never forget shoe size 38, and the plain fact was that he was fond of these two old people, more so of him than of her, and if he discounted all the political and police angles he found himself thinking that it was downright fantastic for them to be going to that funeral. He already regretted having given Dollmer the tip about the roadblocks. He wouldn't put it past Dollmer to use that trick anyway and later—in front of Stabski and elsewhere—claim the credit for it. Yet they knew it wouldn't be effective, for then the old man would insist on the letter, and that would mean partial if not total disaster: all that stuff in it about nuclear power stations, lobbying, corruption, forecasts for the future, growth. And the old man did still own his newspaper. That meant a score of publications that might, for once, print something inopportune— might.

"Are you still there? Or are you too ashamed?"

"I am very much ashamed, dear Mrs. Tolm—and I'd rather not mention at this point something that I might mention: necessity—no, I'd rather not. I'm only ashamed about the reward —rewards are only for voluntary information, not for involuntary. . . ."

"Are we going to see you here tomorrow?"

"No, I won't be able to get away. But we'll meet the day after. I won't duck out, forgive me. . . ."

"Will you do me a favor?"

"Yes, of course."

"Give them a call in Hubreichen. Tell them no one must leave the house, no one, not even any of the guests. Zummerling is lying in wait."

XVIII

In the café, as he was helping her off with her coat, Helga grasped his hand and said: "It's a good thing we're going to be separated for the next three weeks. The training course in Strüderbeken will do you good, me too. I've packed all your things."

"You'll have to unpack them again, Helga dear, there's not going to be any training course. Haven't you been listening to the news?"

He ordered tea and coffee, asked for the menu, took the lighter from Helga and lit her cigarette, took a cigarette himself from the package. "You must be in a bad way if you're starting to smoke—yes, of course I've heard the news. They caught that fellow Beverloh, he's dead, and the woman has gone underground. Where d'you think the boy can be?"

"They sent the boy back, the woman will soon turn up again. That all indicates some imminent action, and it wasn't only those two, you know—it's a far-reaching network, Helga, a burrow with all kinds of side passages, secret passages. I only hope they cancel Strüderbeken early enough and don't get us up in the middle of the night again."

He broke off, waited until the waitress had served the coffee and tea. "Yes, a bit of jogging, a bit of football, target practice, and some theory—maybe that would have done me good, maybe. But at this time of year the heath around Strüderbeken isn't all that attractive, the woods are damp and chilly, and bare. I'd rather have some proper leave, not go away, just stay home. Get some sleep, have a heart-to-heart with Bernhard, maybe go to the movies, argue with Karl—talk to you. What did you mean when you said my training course would do you good too?"

"To be really separated from you for once, not the way it's been lately: with you here yet farther away, much farther away, than if you were in Africa. Not to have to talk, talk. You're kidding yourself: she's in you, and you're in her, and when I say that I don't mean the child she's expecting, and if it weren't for our son, for Bernhard, wouldn't you have taken off with her long ago? Then I would cease to count, and very quickly too. No, I'd rather leave your things packed—maybe you'll need them if you change your mind and go away with her." She smiled when he stubbed out the half-smoked cigarette. He handed her the menu.

"Would you like something to eat?"

"No thanks, would you?"

"No." He took back the menu and laid it beside his glass of tea. "Separate, did you say?"

"Yes. Perhaps you should live with her for a while to find out that you can't live with her. You're dreaming all the time, aren't you, of being with her?"

"Yes," he said—yes, and thought of Sabine's wet hair when she had brought him some food that night and kissed him and kissed him again, over and over again, and he had put the empty bowl down on the windowsill before the relief officer had arrived. "Yes, and you may well laugh—it will break my heart when I think of you, not only when I think of Bernhard—and when I have to quit the service. . . ."

"I won't laugh, I do know you a little bit—and I know that you'll go away with her or follow her."

"And do you know if I'll come back?"

"No, I don't know that, but of course I'm hoping you will. Yes, that's what I'm hoping. I suppose you're scared of actually doing it?"

"Yes, I am, but I'll do it. I'm worried, though—I'm worried about our debts, and what am I to do when I have to quit the service, when I have to get out of the police?"

"Well, one thing's certain, and you mustn't mind my saying it: you probably won't have to support us. It's funny, but I can't be angry with her, she has such a pleasant voice and she's so happy with her little girl. I'll get a job, stay at Monka's for a while, there's plenty of work there, and Bernhard will be happy there. And you—don't you dare leave the police! I'll go to Holzpuke, to Dollmer, I'll even go to Stabski if I have to—after all, that standing around beside swimming pools, at parties, and in shoe stores—you're not the only one to blame, if you're to blame at all. No. The point is, I married a policeman, and if this policeman comes back to me, *if*, I want him to remain a policeman. Ask them to put you in the shark department, if there is such a thing—I mean, to kill those money sharks who are skinning us alive. Oh, Hubert, if you're going, go soon."

"Yes," he said, "I'll go today. I'll drive over there right now and take her away, after all I'm still her protector. I'll leave the car in Hubreichen, you can pick it up there."

He left the car in the driveway, helped Helga with her grocery bags. Bernhard came running toward him, holding out a slip of paper: "You're to call this number, Dad." He drew the boy with him toward the phone, put an arm around him as he dialed the number.

It was Lühler's number; he had recognized it although he didn't have, or want, much private contact with Lühler.

"You've probably heard already," said Lühler.

"I can imagine," he said. "The training course is off."

"Right. Cemetery, and not Horrnauken but Hetzigrath. They want us to close off the whole place. Everything strictly hush-hush—top-secret funeral with top-secret participants, including the corpse. Special orders: uniform. Seven-thirty a.m. outside the village on the road to Tolmshoven. Holzpuke sends his regards. Dollmer himself will personally conduct the deployment in Hetzigrath, invisibly of course, probably from inside the town hall or from a helicopter. Quite a famous corpse—infamous too—not as a corpse but when he was alive. See you tomorrow. Training course not canceled, merely postponed."

"I won't be there—I'll be far away . . . I . . . ."

"What? Are you sick?"

"No . . . I'm just going away. . . ."

"With Helga and your boy?"

"No."

"Alone?"

"No . . . tell Holzpuke to look for a replacement. . . ."

.   .   .

Helga had already carried the suitcase and the bag to the car and opened the trunk. "Your uniform is in there too," she said, "I didn't want to unpack it again"—she smiled—"maybe it'll come in handy, you never know. And now I suppose you'd rather stay here, wouldn't you?"

"Yes, I would—but I'm leaving."

"Don't make too much of it with Bernhard, don't be too solemn about it. I'll tell him some story about special duty, make it sound all mysterious."

"Till the papers find out and the nature of this special duty becomes known. No, please don't use that expression."

He looked at her, her voice so unfamiliar, part bitter, part wistful with a hint of cynicism. "Don't forget," said Helga, "that it isn't that simple, that easy, nor for her, either."

He gave a wave to the boy, who was just coming out of the house, quickly got into the car, turned the ignition key, and drove off.

XIX

The tears wouldn't come when she discovered the picture in the newspaper. The first thing she noticed was the shoeboxes lying around in tumbled heaps, some of them bullet-riddled, and on one of them she could still make out the printed 38; an official, obviously German, was bending down behind the shoeboxes over something that must have been Bev. Originally she had been determined to carry out all his instructions, except the very last one, to the letter, and she wondered whether it would be fair to give up now, so close to the target, whether she shouldn't accord Bev a final honor, a final act of loyalty by proving to him—to the very grave, as it were—that his plan could be precisely carried out, and that all their security fuss was useless—would have been useless if she hadn't been determined from the very outset *not* to carry out his final instruction. She would not place the bomb, the loaded bicycle, under their noses: instead, she would sound the All Clear.

Rain was falling onto the plastic roof of the snack stand in the eastern outskirts of Enschede; she ordered another portion of croquettes, and some bread, helped herself to mustard, ordered another Coke. Only ten kilometers to Horrnauken, and she started to have some strange thoughts: was she to favor a German police officer or a Dutch one with the glory of nabbing her or of her surrender? She had read of cases where such triumphs had not turned out too well for the officers. In some cases the glory had gone to their heads and they had run amok in their private lives: excesses, porn, divorce. Besides, she wasn't sure whether she would be able to explain the dangerous nature of the bicycle to a Dutch officer. They might think she was nuts and handle the bike carelessly, while a German security officer might have received the bucket warning and would know what it was all about.

So far everything had gone according to plan: the bicycle, identi-fied by a blue ribbon tied to the saddle, had been standing as arranged in front of the main post office in Enschede, and it sent a little shiver down her spine to imagine how many secret helpers he must have had and that he had been in contact with all of them. Bev had specifically told her that it was Germans, not Dutch, who had booby-trapped the bike. "In case they catch you and make you talk. So don't forget: Germans. So they can't unload their jitters."

Her passport had attracted no attention whatever, and in her light-blue woolly cap, her round glasses and yellow waterproof jacket, she must really look like a Dutch teacher or student. The game appealed to her, as well as the loyalty to the precision of his plan, although he hadn't allowed enough time for the shoeboxes to be picked up. In Horrnauken she was to ride straight to the cemetery and demand admittance. She could produce a passport in the name of Cordula Kortschede, a relative from the Dutch branch, and she had come over here to visit her grandmother's grave. It remained to be seen whether they were really callous enough to refuse a grieving granddaughter permission to visit her grandmother's grave, and if they did she was not to hesitate to make a scene and have herself removed by force. The important thing was to push the bike into the hedge between entrance gate and chapel and leave it there; the crucial thing was first to push aside the two safety catches on the handles, then to twist the handles inward, the left one to the right, the right one to the left. He had assured her that nothing, absolutely nothing, could happen before the safety catches were released and the handles twisted inward, and even then there would be a further interval of forty-five minutes.

The important thing was that, whether she was allowed in or not, no one would notice the bike in the anticipated hubbub. She had made sure of the safety catches on the handles, and of course she would never release them, never. But the idea of actually riding to the cemetery and asking for the officer in charge of security there was tempting; tempting, too, was the thought of actually going to Verena Kortschede's grave, but then she would never bring that off, Verena was buried in the family plot where her father was going to be buried today. She remembered the funeral they had all attended, the whole lot of them, including Bev and Rolf and Katharina: a summer's day on the heath, and it must have been from that occasion that he remembered the cemetery so vividly that he had been able to tell her the location of the grave of her alleged grandmother Henriette Kortschede: "In the right-hand corner, toward the edge of the forest, the last row but one, so that you can walk there purposefully and then disappear into the trees."

. . .

Even more tempting was the phone booth next to the snack stand: she had to speak to Rolf or Katharina, right now, explain that the boy, Holger I, was the time bomb; he had become a stranger to her, even more of a stranger than she could ever be to her parents and parents-in-law—in him, with him, the word "alienation" acquired an entirely new meaning. "They"—who, who?—probably Bev too, had fed something into Holger that was more dangerous than the stuff used to make bombs; Holger was in urgent need of—treatment. How? by whom?—Rolf should think about that, discuss it with Katharina. The expression "bomb in the brain" had been used—that made dynamite or detonator superfluous—and obviously the boy had the bomb in his brain; it had—how? how? how?—to be defused. How to handle him—hands, not words, might be able to heal him.

But at this distance it would be easy to trace the call, and she didn't want to be caught, she wanted to give herself up, to prove to them how easy it was to get this far with the bucket, and how easy it would have been to make her way into the cemetery. Probably it was better not even to begin the last set of the game, to forgo the final serve—that might mean hours, maybe days of delay. The best thing would probably be to give herself up immediately after crossing the border onto the German side. Yet she would have so much liked to visit Verena Kortschede's grave again. It had been really heartbreaking the way that miserable pseudo-leftist had bagged her for himself and then dropped her as soon as it turned out she didn't have that much money. And that weak tea at Verena's in Berlin! It had always been weak, though her father was supposed to be one of the big tea merchants; the mild chatter about socialism; she was kept quite short by her parents, they were thrifty not from avarice but on principle, you could see it just by looking at her pale-faced father who was going to be buried over there today. Tolm would be sure to give a wonderful speech. No, she would call off the game before the last set.

. . .

She attached herself to a group of four cyclists riding toward the border. They seemed to be really enjoying the rain, singing as they rode along. On the Dutch side she was waved through with the group, on the German side there was a thorough inspection: identification, baggage, even the bicycles. There were not only border officials but police, motorcycles, transceivers. Detaching herself from the group, she walked over to one of the police officers who was holding his crash helmet and watching the inspection. She pushed back her hood, took off glasses and woolly cap, and said: "I'm the person you're looking for. It's urgent, serious, call your boss and tell him: the bucket has arrived, Veronica Tolm has brought it as far as the border."

"Don't try and be funny," he said.

"I'm not being funny," she said, "and watch how you handle my bike, it's loaded with explosives. Please, call him. . . ."

He still hesitated, she said softly: "Go on, you won't make a fool of yourself. I promise. It's really me."

At that he raised his transceiver and said: "Victor eight urgent call for Oscar one." By this time the Dutch group had ridden on, the officers were crowding around her. She heard him say: "There's a young woman here who claims to be Veronica Tolm, and I'm to tell you: the bucket has arrived, she's brought it as far as the border." She couldn't hear the reply, but the policeman held the instrument out to her and said: "Go ahead, speak."

"Hello," a voice said, "my name is Holzpuke, you'll be seeing a lot of me. What's this about the bicycle?"

"It's booby-trapped, I don't know how, I only know how to release the safety catches. Have it put in a safe place, and don't let anyone twist anything on it."

"I'll be there in a few minutes, I imagine you'd like to make a phone call. I recognized you by your voice."

"Yes, I'd like to make a call—if you'd permit it."

"Of course. Let me speak to the officer again." She handed

back the instrument, heard the voice indistinctly, then the officer placed his hand on her shoulder and said: "Come along, I'll take you to the phone. . . . After that . . .''

XX

As she turned the key, took it out, and dropped it into her purse, she was struck by the silence. The guards were gone, the photographers and the reporters seemed to have disappeared too, and there was no sign or sound of Holger the older, of Sabine and Kit, of Erna Breuer and her friend: nothing. Rolf had left with Holger the younger to go to the doctor's and do a few errands and wouldn't be back before one o'clock. It was still raining, not quite as hard, and she stopped for a few moments to listen: nothing, not even an apple falling from a tree, not a nut onto the concrete paths; in the distance, infinitely far away it seemed, she could hear the Polkt twins, who had been picked up by their mother and were noisily making their way home. Although there was no need, she made doubly sure that the big room was locked and realized she was nervous about having to walk the hundred and twenty steps diagonally across the garden. As she stepped out onto the path, hesitantly as if walking on thin ice, a logical train of thought passed mechanically through her mind: if the guards are gone, Sabine is gone too, and if the photographers are gone, Holger the older is gone too, and if . . . She was startled to see Roickler coming out of the annex toward her, and the expression "bearer of bad news" came to her mind. And indeed his smile was somewhat forced as they drew near each other and he took her arm; he looked very tired and smelled of cigar.

"Yes," he said, "don't be alarmed—a lot of things have happened," and started by telling her how he had gone with Erna Breuer to her parents' and that "prodigal daughters have a

worse time of it than prodigal sons"; told her—and dropped his
voice so that she could hardly hear him—that Veronica had
turned herself in and had phoned and urged them to keep an eye
on Holger the older; too late, he had managed to slip away, early
in the morning just after Rolf had left, he had persuaded one of
the photographers—well, it was all so crazy—to take him to
Tolmshoven and there he had—well—started a fire while Mr.
and Mrs. Tolm had been burying Beverloh in Hetzigrath. "A lot
has happened," Roickler said, "and no one's been hurt," and
finally her sister-in-law had been picked up with her little girl by
a police officer in uniform whom the guards had cheerfully greeted
as one of their colleagues without even bothering to question his
orders, and it had turned out to be not exactly an abduction yet
an action that, if not exactly criminal, "was certainly dubious,
with disciplinary repercussions still to be investigated." Roickler
smiled and repeated: "A lot has happened, and no one's been
hurt—yet someone is sitting in there waiting for you who has
nothing whatever to do with what has happened but to whom
something has happened: your friend Heinrich Schmergen. The
main thing is: your sister-in-law Sabine would naturally have
liked to thank you and say goodbye, but circumstances didn't
permit it. Everything had to be done very quickly. She"—he
smiled again—"asked me to wait for you and explain it all and
tell you how very much she is looking forward to seeing you
again. By the way—in case it wasn't quite clear—the police
officer is her lover, the father of the child she is expecting. I
suppose it's all a bit much."

"Yes," she said, "it is rather much."

He held her arm as they walked toward the cottage and told
her about his long conversation with a senior police officer who
had described "that Mr. Hendler" to him as a particularly reliable
colleague, teased but also respected for his piety. Roickler then
pondered for a while on the fact that the only four people "in
this strange ensemble who were actually or apparently fully
integrated, your parents, your sister-in-law, and that young police

officer," had cleared out. "But now I must go, to my Anna, and you must go and look after that young fellow who's waiting in there for you."

Heinrich Schmergen was sitting beside the full ashtray and the coffee cup and told her haltingly that he had been on the bus from Cologne to Hubreichen reading a book called *Castro's Path*, minding his own business and not noticing how the people around him were reading newspapers with reports of Beverloh's death, and suddenly, just before Hurbelheim, he had been startled by the deathly silence in the bus—he had looked up and seen them all staring at him, at the book, silent and hostile, icy and grim, "as if they were ready to strangle me any minute," and he had been scared, properly scared, so much so that he'd almost done it in his pants, and he had got out in Hurbelheim and walked the rest of the way, and now he wanted to get away, just get away, never mind where to. "Any place where a person can read books, even on the bus, without being scared like that. I don't mind arguing. I don't mind even having a row with someone—I don't mind, well, maybe even a debate—but those silent, murderous looks . . . oh God," he said, "Katharina, I believe you're kidding yourself, we're all kidding ourselves—I'm getting out of here, I just wanted to say goodbye to you, to thank you and ask you if you could let me have some money, perhaps—I'll look for a country where I can sit on the bus and read whatever I like in peace."

"Cuba?" she asked, and bit her lips, she felt her question had been cruel.

"No," he said, "but Spain perhaps—right away, I want to leave right away. Today, right now—I won't even say goodbye at home. Say hello for me to Dolores and Rolf, and let me have some money, just for the first few days, I'll go to Holland first—I'm prepared to do any filthy job till the end of my days, carry shit if I have to—I'll send you back the money. . . ."

.   .   .

She took her purse out of her handbag, placed it beside his coffee cup, opened it, and said: "Take half," and when he hesitated in embarrassment she said firmly: "Go on, don't be squeamish, come on," then took out the bills herself, tipped the small change onto the table, sorted it with her fingertips to left and right into bills and coins of the same denomination, divided a fifty-mark bill by pushing it to the left and maneuvering twenty-five marks from left to right, counted "sixty-eight for each of us," and finally pushed the ten-pfennig pieces toward him, thirteen of them, saying: "Take those too, it might be a cup of coffee, a loaf of bread, maybe ten cigarettes, I don't know how much they cost in Holland—and matches, lots of matches . . . take it." And as he was still hesitating, she stuffed it all into his jacket pocket, saying: "Those who ask for money should accept it. You'll have to learn that . . . and more than that. It's too bad, we've been very fond of you. Maybe you'll come back someday."

She started to cry as she watched him cross the garden toward the gate, through the rain, with his shapeless peaked cap, his jacket collar turned up. He had forgotten the book *Castro's Path*, it lay on the table beside the coffee cup.

She found that Sabine had taken the time to wash the vegetables and peel the potatoes, she needed only to put them on to boil and take the sausages out of the refrigerator. She was still crying when Rolf and the little boy came toward the house.

XXI

Hetzigrath looked as if the population had been evacuated and the emptied village placed under the strictest guard: at every street corner, uniformed police officers, plainclothesmen, near the cemetery some mounted police, the school playground between church and cemetery—also empty. They might even have given the schoolchildren the day off. Not a sign behind the window-panes, not a sound; on the market square, at some corners, police-men with megaphones. Silence. Apparently an invasion had been expected that had not arrived: men with long hair, women in ankle-length coats, the so-called sympathizers, but apparently the invasion had not taken place. He was quite calm, Käthe tense, holding the wreath on her lap. Blurtmehl was not himself either: at every intersection he looked uneasily to right and left as if expecting something that hadn't arrived. Behind the plate-glass window of Breilig the butcher he could see Breilig, one of his schoolmates; next to Breilig, a woman customer.

"You should have worn your coat after all," said Käthe. "It's chilly and damp."

"I can't wear my decorations on my coat, and I felt this was an occasion to wear them."

Blurtmehl, who was well versed in matters of protocol, had said that of course decorations could be worn at funerals, but whether at *this* funeral he really couldn't say. Certainly no sashes, Blurtmehl had said, and Käthe had also advised against the sashes but approved of his decision to wear his decorations. "I'm sur-prised at how many good ideas you've come up with in two days, Tolm," she had said, "and fortunately the distance from the mortuary to the Beverloh grave isn't far—thirty yards, fifty at most; not far from there are the graves of my grandparents, and their parents too, and there are as many Beverlohs buried there as Schmitzes, it's one of the oldest families in the place; peasant stock."

A helicopter circled above, then hovered almost directly overhead as Blurtmehl helped them out of the car. The decorations were fairly large, gold with some red in them, one of them quite garish, foreign, almost as big as a saucer. Instead of attaching the bars, as regulations required, he had removed the medals from their

sashes, and Blurtmehl had attached them to his jacket with safety
pins.

She insisted on carrying the wreath herself: yellow roses and
lilac, no ribbon, but she allowed one of the gravediggers to hang
it on the plain bier. It all went so fast that she could hardly get
into step, and in no time the gravediggers had lifted the coffin
onto the ropes placed in readiness and lowered it into the ground.
The helicopter was hovering directly above them. Tolm whispered
to her: "Say a prayer, Käthe," and she murmured a *Paternoster*,
then an *Ave*, threw some earth into the grave with a little shovel,
handed the shovel to Tolm, looked at the gravestone. Most of the
names were obscured by the freshly dug earth, she could read
only the top line: "Ulrich Beverloh, Farmer in Eickelhof, 1801–
1869."

"Come," she said, but Tolm did not move. He looked into
the grave, up to the sky, back to Blurtmehl, who was talking in
low tones to a police officer beside the chapel.

"Käthe," he said, "there's something I have to tell you."

"Yes?"

"You know I have always loved you. And there's something
else you must know."

"Yes, what is it?"

"That some form of socialism must come, must prevail. . . ."

The helicopter veered off as they walked back to the gate.
Blurtmehl turned away from the officer; until that moment he
had not recognized him as the young Lühler whom Holzpuke had
introduced to him. He knew him only in plain clothes, in uniform
he looked younger.

"You forgot," said Käthe, "to give the gravediggers their tip."

He walked back again, took out his wallet, and gave one of
the men a hundred-mark bill. "That's for the two of you," he
said. His attention was caught by the helicopter landing on the
school playground. As he turned around, that young puppy of a

photographer emerged from the chapel. He must have hidden there with Holzpuke's consent, or even Dollmer's—the same one who had caught him the other day after the election smoking a cigarette—and now he caught him full face: top hat in hand, medals on his chest, and behind him the gravediggers and the grave, on which the name Beverloh could be discerned. The boy didn't grin, didn't smile, showed no emotion as he took his shots, snapped him once more with Käthe as they were about to get into the car; snapped, snapped again. "He'll do well," he said to Käthe and Blurtmehl, "he'll go a long way."

He felt no apprehension until he saw Dollmer standing by the car, beside Blurtmehl, whose hand was on the door handle. Dollmer looked drained, utterly drained. He hesitated a moment as to whether he should approach Tolm or Käthe, then walked toward Käthe and said: "A day of bad news, dear lady—not only has your daughter, shall we say, run away with one of our officers—your grandson—the manor house is on fire—he must have somehow slipped past the guard in Hubreichen."

"Is anyone hurt or in danger?" asked Käthe.

"No."

"Then I could think of worse news," she said before getting into the car. "Even the news about our daughter doesn't strike me as bad."

But she was surprised to hear Tolm laugh.